One Arranged Marriage Murder

CRIME SCENE DO NOT CROSS LINE

Get in touch with Chetan Bhagat and access content created by him here:

Instagram

X

Facebook

YouTube

Threads

LinkedIn

Spotify

Moj

Website

CHETAN BHAGAT

One Arranged Marriage Murder

NE DO NOT CROSS LINE CRIME SCENE DO NOT CROSS LINE CRIME SCENE DO N

HarperCollins *Publishers* India

First published in 2020

This edition published in India by HarperCollins *Publishers* 2022
HarperCollins *Publishers* India, Cyber City,
Building 10-A, Gurugram, Haryana – 122002, India
www.harpercollins.co.in

2 4 6 8 10 9 7 5 3 1

P-ISBN: 978-93-5629-145-4
E-ISBN: 978-93-5629-149-2

Printed and bound at
Nutech Print Services Pvt. Ltd.

This book is printed on FSC® certified paper
which ensures responsible forest management.

*

HarperCollins *Publishers*, Macken House, 39/40 Mayor Street Upper, Dublin 1,
D01 C9W8, Ireland

To those who loved and supported me
through my toughest

Acknowledgements, and a Note for My Readers

Hi all,

Congratulations—you picked up a book! You left YouTube, Instagram, Facebook or whatever exciting stuff we have on our phones and picked up a book.

And you picked up my book—so thank you for that.

It is never just my book, though. It belongs to a lot of people who helped me through the process of writing it.

My readers, who support me despite the digital invasion. I am fortunate to have so many readers who shower me with love and encourage me to do better.

Shinie Antony, my editor, friend and first reader—thanks for your invaluable help, not only for this book, but over a seventeen-year association.

The group of early readers who gave wonderful feedback on the manuscript (alphabetically): Anjali Khurana, Anusha Bhagat, Ayesha Raval, Bhakti Bhat, Mahua Roy, Prateek Dhawan, Ranodeb Roy, Shameeli Sinha, Virali Panchamia and Zitin Dhawan—thank you all for your help and suggestions.

The editors at HarperCollins India. The entire marketing, sales and production teams at HarperCollins India. The online delivery boys and girls who put the book in my readers' hands. Thank you for your hard work.

My social media followers. Those who love me. Those who don't. Everyone contributes in their own way.

My family—a pillar of support in my life. My mother Rekha Bhagat, my wife Anusha Bhagat, and children Shyam and Ishaan. Thank you for being there.

Life never goes as planned. Neither do arranged marriages.

With that, you are invited to one arranged murder.

Chapter 1

'Where did the milk go?' I said, empty Amul carton in one hand and fridge door in the other.

'Back in the cow,' Saurabh said. He sat on the sofa, tying the laces of his new, sparkling white sports sneakers. His fiancée Prerna had given them to him four months ago. Of course, Saurabh is more likely to enter a ladies' toilet by mistake than a gym.

'It's not a joke, Saurabh. It was a full carton. Now I can't even make a cup of tea.'

'I had biscuits in the afternoon,' Saurabh said, attention still on his shoelaces.

'And?'

'I don't like my biscuits dry.'

'You dipped them in a litre of milk?'

'I used what was there.'

I shut the fridge in disgust, threw the empty carton in the dustbin and sat on one of the dining table chairs, staring at him.

'I'll get another packet later. And as we discussed, let's avoid talking. Message me if there's something important,' Saurabh said.

Like a twelve-year-old, Saurabh had stopped talking to me. Even though we lived together, we communicated mostly through messages.

I WhatsApped Saurabh even though he sat seven feet away from me.

'I want milk now. To make tea.'

Saurabh looked up from his shoes to check his phone screen. He saw my message but ignored it. He pulled up his socks, stood up, picked up his wallet from the dining table and put it in his kurta pocket. The olive green Fabindia kurta made him look like a baby elephant, especially with his thick black woollen sweater over it.

I typed another message on my phone.

'Please respond.'

He typed a response.

'In a rush. Will sort this out later.'

He opened the Uber app on the phone.

'Damn, no cabs. Uber or Ola,' he said out loud, after swiping away on his phone for five minutes.

'What happened?' I said, looking up from the dining table.

'I didn't speak to you,' he said.

'Nobody else in this room. Did you speak to the wall?'

'Let me be,' Saurabh said, fumbling with his phone again.

'Do you want me to book a cab for you?' I said.

'No. And please don't talk to me.'

'Saurabh, time you stopped sulking.'

He ignored me and kept staring at the phone screen.

'I can book—' I said, but he interrupted me.

'Keshav, we have two months before the lease ends here. Until then, can you please stay out of my way?'

'I said sorry enough times.'

Saurabh shook his head, eyes still on the phone.

'I will take an auto. Damn it, I will freeze in this cold,' Saurabh mumbled to himself and stormed out of the house.

❖

I continued to sit in my house, staring into space, aware of the silence left behind by Saurabh.

Hi, I am Keshav Rajpurohit and I'm not a particularly nice guy. Not emotional either. I don't believe in love. I use Tinder to meet girls for the sole reason of having sex with them. Oh, and I am quite good at it. I slept with ten girls last year.

As you just witnessed, even my flatmate doesn't want to talk to me. Saurabh and I used to be best friends. Now he hates my guts and is waiting for our flat's lease to end. It is harder to break up with a best friend than with a girlfriend.

Why did it become this way? Well, I'm a dick. I don't blame him for wanting to move out.

Saurabh and I both work at CyberSafe, a cybersecurity company. Working together complicates things further when you've had a fight. Anyway, like any other corporate job, CyberSafe sucks. My real passion is the little detective agency Saurabh and I own as a side gig, Z Detectives. We started it after we solved a murder case last year.

Z Detectives is located in the Malviya Nagar market, next to kirana shops. We don't get exciting cases. We aren't James Bond. RAW and IB don't approach us for help with international terrorists. We don't even get any hardcore criminal cases. Most of our inquiries are from aunties in the area, suspecting their maids of stealing their gold necklace or their husbands of having an affair. Apart from the occasional robbery, where someone's laptop or cell phone is stolen, Z Detectives is a tame affair. Hell, the one thing I want is for us to get a real juicy murder case. Turns out Delhi isn't quite the crime capital it is made out to be.

My phone pinged. Message from an unknown number.

'Need urgent help on a case.'

'Who's this? What is this about?' I replied.

'Myself Pramod Gupta. I suspect my driver has not been filling petrol for the money he takes from me.'

I threw my phone down in disgust. I would deal with this nonsense later. I thought about Saurabh. Why was this fatso so oversensitive? Prerna had made him that way. But no, nobody can say a word against his fat bride-to-be. Yeah, I called her fat. Fat just like Saurabh. Am I body-shaming? I told you, I'm not so likeable. Anyway, what's wrong in calling a fat person fat? And why the hell do I still care so much about fatso? And why can't I make a decent cup of tea? And can someone please kill someone in this city? I really need a good case.

Okay, so let me tell you what happened between us. Of course, this is my take.

Six months ago, Saurabh went into an overdrive to get married. Now, I have nothing against arranged marriages. It was I who took Saurabh's profile picture from his thinnest angle, or his least fat angle, for the matrimonial websites. I wrote his bio as well.

'I am Saurabh. I am a well-placed IITian with an easy-going, fun-loving personality. I work in a multinational software company and live in south Delhi. I like food and lots of food and even more food. I also enjoy alcohol and my idea of a good weekend is sleeping for two days straight.'

Of course, Saurabh had kicked my butt and deleted the last two lines. He replaced it with 'decent family from Nagpur, no dowry, prefer a well-educated and ambitious career woman'.

I ran my hand over the dining table. Saurabh had first video-called Prerna from here. After several failed attempts, Saurabh had finally met someone he felt excited about. He had planned to give her a quick two-minute call but they ended up speaking for two hours.

'I'm so sorry I delayed lunch. This went on longer than expected,' Saurabh had said when he finally ended the call.

'She's the one,' I said.

'Really? How do you know?'

'You gave up food for her. For two hours. If that's not true love, what is?'

Turns out I was right. Saurabh fell head over heels for Prerna Malhotra, the only daughter of Ramesh and Neelam Malhotra. She lived in a Punjabi joint family in New Friends Colony. She was what Saurabh wanted: ambitious and career-minded. She had her own internet startup, and it was doing really well.

'It's called Eato. Curated food delivery,' Saurabh told me. 'Like a hand-picked Zomato. They test the dishes and tell you the tastiest ones to order.'

'I can see why you like her,' I said. It had to be about food.

'Yeah, told you I like career women,' Saurabh said.

'Of course,' I said.

Over the next few months, Saurabh and Prerna dated, if you can call it that in an arranged marriage situation. Maybe arranged dating or arranged courtship, if there is such a term. Soon the two were more in love than any love-marriage couple I knew.

It's like meeting Prerna rewired Saurabh's entire DNA. One night I heard him talk in a singsong voice mothers use for six-month-old infants.

'Ole my Prernu bebu. You became tai-ll-ed. Why you wol-k so hard my sona bebu,' he said.

I almost puked. You also had to see the transformation in the way he dressed. Gone were the T-shirt and pyjamas, Saurabh's official costume. In came full-sleeved, collared shirts. He even wore Calvin Klein nightsuits to bed.

The entire room smelled of aftershave as we sat down for dinner one evening.

'Is that cologne?' I said.

'Yes,' Saurabh said.

'Were they distributing it for free?'

'It's always nice to smell good.'

'And you realised it just now? After twenty-eight years of living your life cologne-free?'

'Prerna suggested it,' Saurabh said in a voice as soft as the phulka in his hand.

This domestication didn't bother me. I felt happy for my friend. Prerna was not just his bride-to-be. She was his only crush, love, girlfriend and, in fact, his only female acquaintance.

Okay, let me come to the point, however shallow it might be. Prerna is actually a nice person—affectionate, smart and loving. But … she is—how do I put it?—big, large, overweight. I won't beat around the bush—I've already said it before, haven't I? She is fat. Yes, I called a perfect girl in a perfect relationship with my best friend fat. So judge me. But then, let me judge people's weight too.

Food connected them. Almost all their dates were at popular eateries. Even their terms of endearment for each other were related to food.

'You are my laddoo,' she would message him.

'My jalebi,' Saurabh would answer.

'I find you as sweet as rasgulla syrup.'

'I love you my little gujia,' Saurabh would reply.

Seriously, they were as into each other as they were into food. Soon they ran out of sweets to describe each other. When you are down to gujia, you know you have exhausted the mithai list. I shuddered to think what their future kitchen would look like. It would be a mithai bunker large enough to sustain humans forced to hide underground in the event of a nuclear holocaust.

Of course, every now and then one of them would see a post on Instagram about fitness and they would make plans to exercise.

'My little boondi, we are going to get fit together, no?' Saurabh told her on a call. Firstly, if you are planning a fitness routine, stop referring to each other as desserts. So they made plans to get fit post-marriage. Right now, they decided, they would have fun as 'this time wasn't going to come back'. Well, this time may not come back, a heart attack might.

I must add, I might be the fitter one, but she has the fitter career. She, along with her business partner, had managed three rounds of funding for Eato. A private equity firm had just invested thirteen million dollars, or ninety crore rupees, into her company for a thirty-five per cent stake.

'You're so lucky for me, my kaju katli,' Prerna had told Saurabh after the funding round closed. 'This is huge for me.'

Honestly, I didn't resent her for this. I was happy for Saurabh. Fat and rich is good with me, and so long as she keeps my best friend happy, I'm happy.

Well, Saurabh was insanely happy. The only problem—he just wasn't my best friend anymore. Something changed. He never had time in the evening. I understood that, newly in love and all. However, he started neglecting work at CyberSafe.

'I'm going to Amritsar for a few days. Can you make the pitch presentation Jacob's asked for?' Saurabh said.

'Why are you going to Amritsar?'

'Prerna really wants me to try the Amritsari kulchas there.'

'What?'

'It's her hometown. Her father has his factory there too.'

'The project deadline is next Friday.'

'Handle it, no,' Saurabh said and mock-punched me in the chest.

'Only this time,' I said.

Except it wasn't only that one time. Saurabh was ready to drop everything for her. He was so in love that he was once debugging the Eato app for Prerna for like two weeks. It was around the time we had to finish a crucial piece of code for a CyberSafe client. I couldn't complete it on time alone. Our client at CyberSafe complained to Jacob, who then vented on me.

'Sorry, bhai, I didn't realise the Eato debugging would take so long,' Saurabh said.

'Jacob gave me a warning,' I said.

'Wait, Prerna's calling me. I'll talk to you later,' Saurabh said and disconnected my call.

I put up with everything. I even went to meet Prerna's entire family—her parents, brother, maasi, chacha and daadi. All of them stay in the same three-storey house. I helped plan the engagement, picked out Saurabh's clothes and danced more than any other guest at the party. Of course, he forgets all that. All he remembers is the one time I lashed out. I'd had a bad day. Fine, I could have chosen my words better.

But now the dude doesn't want to talk to me. He wants to move out of the house, change departments within CyberSafe and close Z Detectives. And I am the bad guy? Seriously?

Chapter 2

Hello, this is Saurabh Maheshwari speaking, taking over from his lordship Keshav for only a short while.

I am on my way to meet my fiancée Prerna on Karva Chauth.

I took an auto rickshaw to New Friends Colony, a roughly half-hour ride from Malviya Nagar, and rubbed my hands to keep them warm.

'Left?' Prerna's message brought a smile to my face.

'Yes, in an auto,' I replied.

'Come soon. I'm hungry.'

'Yes,' I replied.

'Drive fast, bhaiya,' I told the auto driver.

I looked at my phone and smiled. Could there be a luckier man? My fiancée decided to keep a Karva Chauth fast for me, even though we aren't technically married. Isn't she sweet?

'Haven't eaten anything all day. No water even ☹,' Prerna messaged.

'Have something, my chikki.'

'No, the moon rises in less than thirty minutes. You'll be here by then. That's when I break the fast.'

'I love you,' I texted.

'I love you too.'

Another message came immediately after. 'I have something special to share with you.'

'What?'

'Come and I'll tell you.'

'What is it?'

'Something unbelievable but special. I just found out.'

I called her on video call. She picked up. She was in her room. I saw her super cute face. She shook her head.

'What?' I said.

'Don't look at me like that. I want you to see me in my Karva Chauth clothes for real. When I am fully ready.'

'Wait, what did you want to tell me?'

'I'll tell you—come quickly, no? I'm hungryyyy.'

'I am cominggggg ...' I replied. She cut the call.

As the auto rickshaw waded through the Delhi traffic, I thought of Keshav.

So Mr Keshav Rajpurohit has allowed me a tiny space here to tell my side of the story. This is *after* he has given you *his* version. He's already brainwashed you, I'm sure. He has perhaps told you that I am just an oversensitive sissy on his way to becoming a henpecked husband. That it is me who overreacted. Mr Oh-so-cool Keshav was just making some sarcastic comments and I should just get over it. Oh, and I'm sure he told you I slacked off on work at CyberSafe and ignored Z Detectives completely? Good, believe him.

I fell in love, that's what happened. For the first time in my life. Just looking at Prerna smile makes me melt inside like a chocolate lava cake. When Prerna calls, every word she speaks is a happiness injection right into my veins. Call me a romantic fool.

Unlike Keshav, I have never had a long-term girlfriend or any short-term hook-ups. Did he tell you about his Tinder addiction? Yes, it is an addiction. He's slept with ten girls since last year. He doesn't even know their last names. In some cases, not even the first. You can call him a stud or whatever. To me, it is a sickness. He can do whatever the hell he wants. But he has to understand I'm different. I have one, and only one, Prerna. That's who it is going to be for the rest of my life. To make her happy, I skipped work a few times. I took a trip with her. I helped her in her work. Of course, Mr Keshav, upset that I wasn't giving him a hundred per cent attention, sulked like a baby. He has forgotten how I used to cover for him at Chandan Classes, our previous job, when he would skip work to meet his girlfriend. I would not only make good excuses for him, but also finish his assignments. Even at CyberSafe, he once had a Tinder match who could only meet in the afternoon. He dashed out of the office and I covered for him and told Jacob he had a family emergency. Of course, when time comes to return the favour, Mr Six Pack bitches and whines about my relationship.

And then he crossed all limits one day when Prerna was at home. You want to know what happened?

'Why have you stopped?' I said to the driver when I realised we hadn't moved for five minutes.

'IIT signal. Takes a long while here,' he said.

I checked the time. It was 7.24 p.m. According to Google, the moon would be visible at 7.46 p.m. I had some time. I didn't want Prerna to wait in hunger a minute more than she needed to. I just had to get there before the moon did. Of course, the moon didn't have to deal with Delhi traffic.

'Where have you reached?' Prerna sent a message.

'Twenty minutes away. IIT signal is a pain.'

'Cool. Take your time. I will try not to faint.'

'Hungry, my gulab jamun?'

'On the roof, all decked up, waiting for you.'

'Moon there?'

'Don't see it yet.'

'I will reach soon,' I said.

'Take the stairs. The back door is open.'

The signal turned green for the third time and my auto finally got a chance to cross. I checked my pocket for the gold necklace I had bought for her.

Fifteen minutes later, the auto entered the quieter lanes of New Friends Colony, passing the metro station, and then into A Block. Prerna lives in a four-hundred-square-yards kothi, or bungalow, located in a lane of posh bungalows. A narrow lane passes behind these kothis, allowing access to the back entrances. Entering from the front door would mean meeting the entire Malhotra clan. Neither Prerna nor I wanted to be ridiculed for being this lovey-dovey couple that keeps a Karva Chauth fast before marriage. We had decided she would keep the creaky metal back door open for me instead.

'Right here,' I said to the driver when we reached the back lane.

'Main entrance is in the front,' he said as he fumbled for change.

'It's fine,' I said and stepped out.

The grey evening, cold breeze and dim light made the alley seem darker than usual. I looked up at the sky. No moon yet, or at least I couldn't see it from where I was. I gently opened the back door and shut it from inside. I climbed up the steps from the ground floor, where the Malhotras had their main living room. I passed the mezzanine level, which had the kitchen for the entire house. I heard the whistle of a pressure cooker and could smell rajma being made. This is a gift—I can tell what is being cooked in a kitchen far away by just breathing. I guess the Malhotras were readying themselves for a post-Karva Chauth feast. I paused to catch my breath on the first level. Maaji, Prerna's grandmother, stayed here with Anjali, Prerna's cousin from America, and Prerna's aunt Bindu, who taught in a school and looked a bit like a scary headmistress with her spectacles, stocky frame and curly hair. After a few seconds of rest, I climbed up to the second level. Prerna lived here with her parents, Ramesh and Neelam, along with her fourteen-year-old brother Ajay. I panted as I climbed up to the third floor. Aditya, Prerna's father's younger brother, occupied this entire floor. He lived alone, but also had his music studio here. I could hear music being played inside. I reached the final few steps that took me to the terrace. I checked that my sweater and kurta were in place. The climb had made me sweaty but I had carried my cologne with me. After a few liberal sprays, I pushed at the already open terrace door.

'*Mehndi lagake rakhna, doli sajake rakhna,*' I sang the song from *Dilwale Dulhaniya Le Jayenge*, the movie which had a classic rooftop Karva Chauth scene.

The sky had become pitch black. The slight fog made the shimmering lights of the New Friends Colony houses twinkle in the background. As I sang the song, I looked at the sky. There it was—the fourth day of the moon, which all the married ladies in Delhi would be flocking to see along with their husbands tonight. In this case, husband-to-be in three months.

'*Lene tujhe, o gori ...*' I continued to sing. I looked around for a Prerna dressed in traditional wear, metal sieve in hand, smiling shyly. She does that—goes shy on me when I least expect it.

'Prerna, bebu, I'm here. You can eat now,' I said and laughed.

No response. Near the terrace door I found a switch for the light. I flicked it on. A yellow bulb lit up brightly. The entire terrace became visible. Still no Prerna.

'Jalebi, where are you?' I said a bit louder.

In one corner of the terrace, a red and gold dupatta lay on the floor. I went over and picked it up. It lifted in the wind and the mesh-like fabric hit my face. I removed the dupatta from my face and looked at the floor again. Three feet from me I saw a metal sieve. I lifted it up and turned it around in my hand a few times. I looked at the moon through it, as Prerna was supposed to see it. Had she gone down to use the restroom? I took out my phone and dialled her number. There was no response.

I heard horns blaring from down below on the main road outside the house. There seemed to be a traffic jam. I looked over the ledge of the terrace. Traffic had stopped on both sides. A crowd had gathered below, right in front of Prerna's house. I tried to see what had happened. I couldn't figure out much in the darkness.

I dialled Prerna's number again. I couldn't reach her. I typed a message.

'Where are you, bebu? Waiting for you on the terrace.'

She didn't read it—only one tick on WhatsApp. The message didn't even get delivered.

'Aren't you hungry? Come, eat,' I sent another one.

Even this message went undelivered. The noise below rose in volume. I still couldn't figure out what was going on. Maybe something had happened and Prerna had gone down to join the crowd as well, I thought. I turned towards the terrace door to take the stairs down.

Before I could reach the door, Prerna's father Ramesh and two other men came running upstairs to the terrace. I recognised Gupta and Arora, neighbours of the Malhotras.

'Hello, Uncle—' I said before Ramesh interrupted me.

'Saurabh? You were here with her?'

'With Prerna? I came to meet her. Where's she?'

He didn't respond. He touched the dupatta in my hand.

'I found this here, Uncle, when I came.'

Gupta took the metal sieve from my other hand. He showed it to Ramesh and Arora.

'Malhotra ji,' he said, 'you better not let this boy go.'

'Go where?' I said, perplexed.

'Uncle, what's happening? I just spoke to Prerna,' I said to Ramesh. He remained silent as we walked down the stairs. Gupta held my elbow tight.

'Uncle, why are you holding my arm so hard?' I said to Gupta as we reached the ground floor.

On the ground floor, we crossed the living room, the front patio and the main gate to come out of the house. There was still a crowd on the road. Traffic remained choked. A few cars were trying to take U-turns, away from the jam. Many of Prerna's family members stood there as well.

'Saurabh?' Neelam aunty, Prerna's mother, saw me first. She wore a shocked expression. She looked at me as if she knew my name but could not place me.

The crowd had formed a circle on the road.

That was when I saw Prerna. Face down on the road. In a red and gold lehenga that matched the dupatta I'd had in my hand a few minutes ago. Her shoulder-length hair covered the back of her head and the side of her face. Even in the darkness I could make out the pool of blood around her head. The people around her stood in absolute silence.

'Prerna,' I said as I ran towards her.

'Stop,' Ramesh said and grabbed my wrist.

'Uncle that's ... is she hurt?'

He shook his head.

'What?' I said.

'She's gone,' Ramesh said, fighting back tears.

My heartbeat paused for a second. I looked at the others, stunned.

Aditya and Prerna's brother Ajay stood with frozen expressions. Next to them, Neelam sobbed as she held Bindu, who herself was visibly trembling.

'I just spoke to her,' I screamed loud enough to startle everyone.

Aditya came and placed his muscular arm around my shoulder. He patted my back unsteadily.

'Aditya chachu, what happened?' I said.

'She fell down,' Aditya said, pointing to the roof of the house.

I extricated myself from Aditya's grip. I ran up to Prerna. I went down on my knees and touched her hair.

'Prerna, I am here. Let's eat,' I whispered.

Gupta and Ramesh came up to me and tapped my shoulder.

'The police are coming,' Gupta said. 'Better we don't disturb the body.'

'Police? Body? What?' I said. 'She needs to be taken to a hospital.'

'Come back, Saurabh,' Ramesh said, his voice soft yet firm.

Both of them held me and helped me to stand up. They pulled me back a few steps. Gupta had self-assumed the role of guarding me. He gently held my right hand with his, sort of like a light leash I could not get out of.

Neelam and Bindu were crying loudly by now. Some elderly ladies came around to console them. I saw Ramesh bite his lip to fight back tears. Ajay hid his face in Aditya's chest. With the family in shock and sorrow, the neighbours tried to determine what to do next.

'Let's move her to the side,' Arora said.

'No, we should wait for the police,' Gupta said.

I felt numb. This had not just happened. Maybe I took a nap at home in the afternoon. This was a horrible dream. I will just wake up and rush out to meet Prerna. We will feed each other sweets on the terrace looking at the moon.

Blood from her body was travelling to my feet. I stared at its slow progress in the darkness. I looked at Prerna again. Properly. Her hands had henna on them. She had specially applied it for Karva Chauth. I told myself to wake up. Nothing is wrong with Prerna. My mind went into a blur as it disconnected from reality. I could see the scenes around me but could not make sense of them. I heard the siren of a Gypsy; the police were here. I saw cops speak to Prerna's father. One of them took pictures of the body from the top, sides and several close-ups. He also took a picture of the house and the terrace.

'Shall we move the body aside?' Arora said. As colony president, he was keen to disperse the crowd and get the road functional again.

'Come, let's lift her,' I heard someone say. Almost like a robot, I joined six other people who lifted Prerna's heavy body.

'Not the side of the road. Let's take it inside,' a constable said. She was an 'it' now?

They took the body into the house, without any clue where to keep it. First they kept it on the patio. After some intense discussions, they told us to lift her up again and take her to the living room. We had no idea where to place her there either. After all, a living room is for living people, who can sit anywhere, on the sofa, easy chairs or even the dining chairs. Where do you place a dead person in a living room? Someone suggested the carpet. Blood still dripped from the body, leaving an eerie trail wherever we carried her. Bad, bad dream, I told myself, even as my eyes followed the bloody track.

'Place newspapers,' one of the neighbours had an ingenious idea. Old papers were spread on the rug in multiple layers. On pages of *Delhi Times*, which had an interview with Varun Dhawan and Alia Bhatt, we placed Prerna on her back. I could see her face now. Covered in blood, her nose, cheeks and one of her eyes were badly wounded. They would take a long time to heal—if she was alive, I added to myself. A cop told us to move aside.

'What happened to her?' I said to the cop.

'She fell down, what else? Head must have burst,' the cop said.

He placed her arms and legs in a respectable, straight position. Dead bodies don't just lie down gracefully. They have to be put in place.

The cop went about his work as if he were arranging clothes on a shelf.

'I spoke to her twenty minutes ago,' I said.

The constable looked at me, surprised.

'When life ends, it doesn't even take a minute,' he said.

I looked at Prerna's face again. With the blood, dirt and injuries, she looked almost unrecognisable. I put my hand on her closed fist.

'Don't touch her, please. We have to collect evidence,' the constable said.

'She's my fiancée,' I said, my voice breaking for the first time.

'I am sorry,' the constable said. He covered her face with a sheet of paper; a Swachh Bharat ad stared at us.

'Get something better,' Gupta said. A few minutes later, someone brought a white cotton sheet. They used it to cover her entire body, including her face. I couldn't see her anymore.

It was then that it hit me—Prerna is gone. She would never come back. She fell from the terrace. She went there because of me. Odd sounds escaped me as I began to whimper. Some neighbours tried to calm me down, but I got steadily more hysterical. A senior cop walked up to me.

'Were you on the terrace?' he said in a firm, cold voice, unaffected by the tragedy around him.

His abrupt question startled me. I stopped crying but did not respond. Three other cops had also come into the room. The neighbours started to leave. The few that remained spoke to Prerna's family members, offering them their support and condolences.

'I am talking to you,' the cop said, his voice louder.

'Yes,' I said.

'Why did you go to the terrace?' he said. I noticed his nametag, Vijender Singh. The epaulettes on his shoulder told me he was an inspector.

'To meet her,' I said.

'You met her?'

'No, I didn't find her there.'

'Did you meet anyone else in the house?'

I felt uneasy. I didn't like his line of questioning. I had my own detective agency. I knew where he was going. I also knew that when it came to cops, it was best to speak as little as possible.

'No,' I said.

'Why?'

'I came in from the back entrance. And took the stairs up.'

'Why terrace?'

I took a deep breath and looked around me. Everyone seemed busy, either crying or consoling.

'We had a plan to meet upstairs, sir, for Karva Chauth. She would see me and the moon, and break her fast.'

The inspector narrowed his eyes.

'Karva Chauth?'

'Yes, sir. It's today. The fourth day of the moon. When married women fast for their husbands.'

'I know Karva Chauth. You aren't her husband. Victim is not married.'

Victim is called Prerna, and she is the love of my life, I wanted to tell him.

'We were getting married in three months. She decided to keep the fast as a gesture,' I said.

'Hmmm,' he said in an unconvinced tone.

I repeated the sequence of events. I told him how I took an auto rickshaw, spoke to her and came up to the terrace only to find it empty.

'And then Uncle came and brought me down. That's it,' I said.

'That's your version then,' Singh said.

'That is what happened,' I said.

He went 'hmmm', again. He turned to Ramesh and started asking him a few questions. I felt alone in that room, surrounded by people, many of whom were my would-be relatives. A car honked outside. Aditya went up to the front door and walked to the patio. He saw the occupant of the car and opened the gate. A white cab came in. Anjali stepped out. She had her backpack with her, which seemed heavy and huge compared to her skinny frame.

'Hi, Adi mamu, what's up?' she said in a cheerful voice, with the hint of an American accent.

Aditya nodded with a serious expression.

'What happened?' Anjali said. She looked around—something was clearly amiss. Aditya didn't respond. Both of them walked into the living room. She noticed the body on the floor, covered in a white shroud. Someone had died.

'What happened?' Anjali repeated. 'Is it Maaji?'

'We lost everything. Prerna's no more,' Ramesh said, swallowing a lump in his throat.

Anjali walked up to the body, bent and lifted the sheet from the face. She saw her cousin lying there, dead.

'Prerna didi?' Anjali said in a shaky voice.

Aditya pulled her aside.

'She … she was fine,' Anjali said, now in tears herself.

Ajay, somewhat lost until this point, went up to Anjali. They both hugged and cried. The room felt like it was under water, drowning and sinking and going down, down.

'When things are calmer, we would like to speak to each member of the family,' Singh said to Ramesh.

Ramesh did not respond.

'And him too,' Singh said, pointing at me.

Ramesh looked at me with blank eyes and half-nodded.

'We will wait outside for a bit. Let's talk once more before we leave,' Singh said to Ramesh. The cops left the room.

I leaned against the wall, staring at her body. I didn't know what to do next. Should I leave? Am I allowed to leave? But am I even supposed to stay? I needed someone. The one and only person in the world who could help me think through this situation. I took out my phone.

Chapter 3

I couldn't hear my phone in the noisy Malviya Nagar market. When I checked it after grocery shopping at Mahavir General Stores, near the Z Detectives office, I saw that I had four missed calls. Saurabh had called me multiple times.

Why would he call me, I wondered. He had not initiated conversation with me for a month. Maybe he had sat on his phone and butt-dialled me by accident. I didn't want to call back and hear more insults.

I kept my phone back in the pocket of my shirt. I lifted the two heavy bags full of groceries and started to walk back home. My shirt lit up as the phone flashed again.

Irritated, I kept the bags on the ground. I took out my phone again. The call was from Saurabh. Had he come back home already? Maybe he'd forgotten to carry his keys? And wanted to use the bathroom real bad? He could go to hell. I shook my head in disgust. The ringing wouldn't stop. I finally picked up.

'Yes, Saurabh?' I said in a frosty tone.

'Keshav, where are you?'

'Bought milk. And other household stuff. That you keep finishing. Carrying twenty kilos in my hands right now. You have a problem with that?'

'Bhai, can you come here?'

'What?' I said. His voice sounded urgent and disturbed at the same time.

'Like right now, bhai?'

He had called me bhai after two months. Was he drunk?

'Where?'

'Prerna's house. You have come here before, right? A–956,' he said, voice still tense.

I checked the time. It was 8.30 p.m. Why was he calling me there? What about the 'let's not get in each other's way' fight we had an hour ago? And why the hell should I do what he wanted me to?

'Why?' I said.

'Just come, bhai, please. Will tell you everything. Start right now.'

'I have to keep the daal and atta at home first.'

'No, bhai, I beg you. Now.'

I wondered what had happened. Did Prerna dump his romantic ass?

'Fine, I will come with the bags. You better help me carry them back.'

❖

I reached Prerna's house in under twenty-five minutes. Meanwhile, Saurabh had called me three more times to check my location. He was standing outside when I arrived. I saw a Delhi Police Gypsy parked outside Prerna's house. Cops sat inside the vehicle eating samosas.

The vibe said something was wrong.

'What's going on?' I said to Saurabh.

'Bhai,' Saurabh said and gave me a tight hug. He continued to hold me, and then he began to cry.

'What happened, Golu?' I said, addressing him as I used to before our recent differences. It is funny how you forget fights and automatically switch back to caring mode when your best friend really needs you.

'Prerna,' he said, still in tears. 'Bhai, Prerna.'

'What about Prerna? What happened?'

He didn't say anything. He continued to sob and pointed at the house. I walked in. I saw a body covered in a white sheet. Aditya and Ramesh stood there.

'Uncle, what happened?' I said. Ramesh gave me a blank look. Saurabh came in after me.

'Bhai, Prerna is gone,' he said and held my arm again, his tears uncontrollable.

My eyes opened wide in shock. Saurabh went up to remove the sheet from Prerna's face. Aditya gently stopped him.

'The police said not to disturb her,' he said.

I really wanted to know what had happened. However, I had to console Saurabh first.

'She was my life,' Saurabh said, clutching my collar.

'I know, Saurabh. I am so sorry.' I patted his back. Even though I hadn't known Prerna well, I choked up to see my friend cry like this.

'What happened? You came to see her, right?'

Between sobs, in broken sentences, he narrated the events of the evening.

'Oh my God,' I said as I heard the entire story.

A few minutes later, a senior cop came up to us. Three other constables followed him.

'Who's he?' the senior cop said, eyeing me.

'He's Keshav. Saurabh's friend,' Ramesh said. 'Keshav, this is Inspector Singh.'

I offered my hand to the inspector to shake. He ignored me. Singh looked to be in his thirties; he stood straight-backed, had a light complexion and sharp features.

'You were at the terrace with your friend too?' Singh said.

I shook my head.

'Inspector sahib, you don't have to stay here so late. We will be fine. Thank you for your support,' Ramesh said.

'The kind of case this is, we have to,' Singh said.

'Case? What kind of case?' Ramesh said. 'She fell down, right?'

'We don't know,' Singh said, staring at Saurabh. 'We need to talk to everyone here. Where did the ladies of the house go?'

'They went upstairs. They need to be with my mother. She still doesn't know,' Ramesh said.

'Who was the young lady? She came with a big backpack a little while ago.'

'My niece, Anjali. She returned from a trekking trip,' Ramesh said.

The inspector took out a notebook.

'Okay. And who are the other women in the house?'

'My wife Neelam, sister Bindu and my mother.'

'Who else in the house?' Singh said, taking notes.

'My son Ajay. Maid Gopika. But why are you asking me all this?' Ramesh said.

'We have to figure out what happened.'

'An accident. She fell down from the terrace,' Ramesh said.

'We don't know that, do we? What do you say, Mr Saurabh?' Singh said.

Saurabh looked at the inspector, surprised at the cop's accusatory tone.

'Singh sir, it is better you come and talk to us later. Everyone is too disturbed,' Aditya said.

'Later is no good. People get time to make up their stories.'

Aditya walked up to the inspector and folded his hands.

'I am sorry, Inspector sir, nobody needs to make up stories. Please leave my brother alone. We haven't even had time to absorb this. We haven't even told my mother,' Aditya said softly. 'The body is right here. We haven't even thought about the funeral.'

I don't know about the inspector, but the three constables seemed to sympathise with Aditya. Or maybe they were just tired and wanted to go home.

'Okay,' Singh said after a pause. 'Can I just speak to him?' He pointed to Saurabh.

Aditya looked at Saurabh and me. Saurabh nodded.

'Let's go outside,' the police inspector said, snapping his fingers at Saurabh. 'Let the family be for now.'

Chapter 4

'Been in a police Gypsy before?' Singh said.

Saurabh and I sat squashed in the backseat with two other cops in the overcrowded vehicle. I had taken my grocery bags with me. One of the constables drove the Gypsy. Inspector Singh sat in the front.

Saurabh didn't answer. He still seemed to be in a daze.

'Yes, sir,' I said.

'When?' Singh said.

'We helped the police solve a case last year.'

'Really? Which case?'

'Zara Lone's case. Hauz Khas Police Station handled it. Inspector Rana.'

'Rana sir? You know him? He's ACP Rana now, by the way. Thanks to that case.'

'Inspector Singh, we helped him with it ... Where are we going?' I said as I noticed him take a left on the main road.

'My station is just around the corner. The tea isn't bad there.'

I looked at Saurabh. He was sitting with his hands covering his face. He seemed to be in distress.

'We can talk here, sir,' I said.

'Why? You have a problem going to the police station?'

'No, whatever,' I said and became quiet.

Inspector Singh sensed my displeasure and gestured for the constable to stop the car. It was an empty and dark lane.

'Fine,' Singh said. 'Let's talk here.'

He signalled for his constables to exit the vehicle and looked at me, waiting for me to leave as well.

'What?' I said.

'I want to talk to your friend.'

'Please go ahead. I can be here. Saurabh you want me here, right?' I said. I looked at Saurabh. He took a few seconds to nod in response.

'Okay,' Singh said. 'Let me ask this straight off. Why should I believe you didn't push her over?'

'What?' Saurabh said. Within a second, his sadness turned to shock.

'You expect me to believe she just fell down?' Singh said, scratching his stubble.

'I don't know, sir,' Saurabh said.

'People don't just fall off terraces. When we left the family, I inspected the terrace. The ledge is four feet high. No way did she just trip over,' Singh said.

'It seems unlikely to me too,' Saurabh said. 'But when I reached the terrace, she wasn't there.'

'You believe him?' Singh said to me.

'Of course,' I said. 'If he's saying she wasn't there it means she wasn't there.'

The inspector heaved a huge sigh.

'Either that,' Singh said, 'or when you reached the terrace, she didn't notice you. You found her looking at the sky, trying to find the moon. And you gave her a little push, and, well, that's it. Dhum.'

As Singh said this, he made a pushing gesture in the air.

'I pushed Prerna? I killed her?' Saurabh said. 'Are you serious, Inspector? I killed the love of my life?'

'You would be surprised how often that happens,' Singh said and smiled. Everyone became silent. We could hear the sound of crickets in the night. The inspector spoke again.

'What do you do, Saurabh?'

'I work in CyberSafe, a software company.'

'Engineer?' Singh said.

'Yes.'

'How about your friend?'

'I work in CyberSafe too. We also have a small detective agency on the side,' I said.

'What?' Singh said, surprised.

I told him about Z Detectives, and our tiny scale of operations.

'Oh, so I am dealing with professionals here,' Singh said and laughed. 'You are not going to tell me the true story, isn't it?'

'Sir, we are telling you the truth,' I said.

'How do you know? You weren't even there,' Singh said. 'Or were you also with him?'

'No, sir. I wasn't there.'

'So? How can you say? How well do you know your friend?'

I know him too well, I wanted to say, but didn't. Annoying the police is never a good idea. Saurabh finally spoke up.

'Ask me whatever you want, sir. I am disturbed, but I will tell you everything. You can see my chats with Prerna minutes before I reached the terrace. We had so much love between us,' Saurabh said. His eyes welled up again.

'Control yourself,' Singh said.

Saurabh nodded and composed himself. The inspector spoke again.

'You don't understand. This is a high-profile case. New Friends Colony, posh area. Business family. Young girl. Karva Chauth. The family may kick us out now, but soon everyone will be all over it. Cross-examinations, post-mortems, media nonsense, it is all going to happen. Just because we are in a quiet vehicle right now doesn't mean it is going to stay this way.'

'I know, sir,' I said.

'I can take you to the police station right now. File an FIR against your friend. It will really help my case tomorrow morning when the media arrives at the police station.'

'FIR? Sir, what are you saying?' Saurabh said.

I thought about what to do next. Only one name came to mind.

'You can speak to ACP Rana. Ask him about Saurabh and me. If anything, we can help you find the real culprit, sir,' I said.

'Rana sir knows you well? He will vouch for you?' Singh said.

'Yes, sir. I told you, we helped him solve a case,' I said.

Inspector Singh stared at me. He didn't like me dropping a senior police officer's name. He spoke after a pause.

'Fine, call Rana sir.'

Chapter 5

Inspector Singh, Saurabh and I sat in ACP Rana's office in the Hauz Khas Police Station. Saurabh repeated what had happened.

'A Karva Chauth murder,' Rana said, taking a sip of tea. 'Delhi never ceases to amaze me. This chai is boring. Singh, you want a real drink?'

'On duty, sir,' he said.

'You are also boring,' Rana said and smiled. 'Anyway, my gut feel … actually leave it. Singh, this is your case. You handle it.'

'No, sir, please give me your thoughts,' Singh said.

Rana finished his tea and kept the empty glass aside. 'Complicated. Could be anything—accident, suicide or murder.'

'I will explore all angles, sir,' Singh said.

'It's not suicide,' Saurabh said.

'Huh?' Rana said. 'Why?'

'She was looking forward to seeing me. I have the chats.'

'So accident or murder,' Rana said. 'To save everyone a headache, let's just hope it was an accident.'

'People don't just fall off like that, sir,' Singh said.

'Good luck then. Media will be all over this. They will hang you for not finding out who did it in two hours. What about the post-mortem?'

'We will do it, sir,' Singh said.

'Good,' Rana said. 'Do a full forensic as well. Lot of people in the house?'

'Joint family. A maid. And him too,' Singh said, pointing at Saurabh.

Saurabh was about to speak when ACP Rana stopped him.

'Singh, these boys are fine. They may look stupid, but they can actually be useful. I hate to admit it, but they did help in that Zara Lone case. And now I finally have this ACP office.'

'But, sir …'

'Well, Singh, solving a high-profile case will help your career like nothing else. Take all the help you can get for this one.'

'He was on the terrace, sir,' Singh said. 'He's a suspect.'

'But don't do an FIR yet. Talk to the family first. Can you do that for me? I take responsibility. He won't run away.'

'Why would I run away, sir?' Saurabh said.

'Can you keep quiet when I'm talking on your behalf?' Rana said in a stern voice.

Saurabh nodded, looking downcast.

'That's doable, sir,' Singh said.

'Good,' said Rana. 'Now let them go home. Take family testimonies and we will discuss again.'

Singh nodded. Saurabh and I stood up to leave. Rana walked us out of his office.

'Thank you, sir,' I said to Rana as we came outside the police station.

'Welcome. But even if you have done the damn murder, don't run away,' Rana said and laughed.

'Of course not, sir,' Saurabh said. 'I mean I haven't done anything.'

'Good. Now cry less and think more. If the media sticks the blame on you, it won't be easy to shake it off. Arranged match, right?'

'Well, technically yes, sir. But ...'

'But what? Then why cry so much?'

'I loved her.'

Rana laughed and shook his head.

'Love screws you,' Rana said.

He hailed an auto rickshaw for us. The driver saw the police officer and screeched to an immediate halt.

'What's in the bags, Keshav?' Rana said.

'Milk, atta and daal. Want some, sir?' I said as the rickshaw sped off.

Chapter 6

'It's in the papers,' I said, passing the newspaper to Saurabh. The article was on one of the inner-city news pages.

Fasting woman falls off terrace on Karva Chauth

Internet entrepreneur Prerna Malhotra, 26, succumbed to her death Thursday night after she fell off the terrace of her three-storey house in New Friends Colony. More details are awaited at the time of filing this report. Neighbours say she was on the terrace to break her Karva Chauth fast when she had the fall. Inspector Vijender Singh of the New Friends Colony Police Station said they reached the site of the incident after receiving a call from one of the neighbours. He added, 'It is impossible to reach any conclusions at this point,' and refused to comment further. Investigations are on.

One of the neighbours said the girl was engaged to be married, and had been observing the fast for her future husband. The neighbour said that perhaps the victim was dizzy after staying hungry all day, and hence could not keep her balance. The victim was the co-founder of startup Eato, a food delivery app.

Saurabh tossed the newspaper aside. He sat on the sofa and stared at the wall in front.

'Skip work today. I will inform Jacob,' I said.

Saurabh nodded. I stood up to go take a shower.

'She wanted to do the fast thing. I told her no need,' Saurabh said from behind me.

I sat on the sofa in front of him.

He continued to speak.

'Really, I should have been more firm. Told her not to fast.'

'It's not your fault.'

'Then whose fault is it? Look at this bullshit newspaper article. She fell down because she was dizzy? She was talking to me, all cheerful, minutes before.'

'It's a hurriedly written piece. Some neighbour spoke some nonsense.'

'They are making her out to be this stupid girl who felt dizzy and tripped over a four-foot ledge. Seriously?'

'Ignore it. Did you inform your parents?'

'Not yet. I think they know. They called. I didn't answer.'

'Ramesh uncle must have told them.'

'Who knows?' Saurabh said and shrugged. 'Is it on TV?' He picked up the remote and flipped between news channels. One of them was reporting on the incident. A female news anchor spoke in an enthusiastic voice.

'We are just hearing reports that Prerna Malhotra, a young lady living in New Friends Colony, had the most tragic Karva Chauth last night. She fell from the terrace. Police are awaiting post-mortem results. Your channel will keep you updated on what could be either a tragic accident or yet another high-profile crime in one of the poshest areas of Delhi.'

'There you go,' Saurabh said. 'Welcome to entertainment from death. It's already content for them.'

I snatched the remote from Saurabh's hand and switched off the TV.

'This will not help. Trust me,' I said.

'Then what will? Nothing, right? Nothing can get her back.'

'I can be here today if you want.'

'No need. Go, do your work. The media is doing its job and getting TRPs. The police are trying to save their ass. You go sell software. The rest of the world has to go on. Only my world has collapsed.'

Saurabh broke down. I patted his back as he continued to cry.

I typed a quick message to Jacob explaining the situation. I added that Saurabh and I would not be coming to work for a few days.

'Let me make some breakfast,' I said.

'I don't want to eat,' Saurabh said, something I had never heard him say. Ever.

Chapter 7

Almost a hundred people, most of them dressed in white, occupied the front room of Malhotra House. They had come to offer their condolences. The family was waiting for the cops to bring back the body from the morgue, so that they could take it to the electric crematorium.

'The police is here,' Aditya said. The police mortuary van drove up to the front entrance of the house. Inspector Singh and a constable accompanied the body. They too had come in plain white clothes, in keeping with the situation.

The women in the room reacted first. Neelam, Bindu, Maaji and Anjali huddled together and cried loudly when they saw Prerna's pale and still face. Ramesh and Aditya stood quietly by. Ajay hid in one corner of the room. He seemed unable to process his emotions and looked intimidated by the crowd in the house. Prerna was wrapped in a white shroud and was in a glass case. The police had cleaned up her face. There was no blood, only calm.

Saurabh began to cry again, his hand tight in mine. Saurabh's parents arrived soon after and stood next to their son with folded hands. Saurabh's mother too tried to comfort him.

A priest chanted a few mantras, after which the body was taken back to the mortuary van. The family had decided not to do a procession. Family members and other visitors sat in their respective cars and followed the van to the crematorium.

The crematorium staff, too used to doing this, mechanically moved the body to the tray that went inside the electric furnace. Within minutes, Prerna was in the opaque combustion chamber. Smoke flew up the chimney, high above the crematorium building. Prerna rose up to the sky, leaving us forever.

Inspector Singh came and stood next to me.

I nodded in greeting.

'What are you thinking?' Singh said.

'Feeling bad for my friend,' I said.

'And?'

'Thinking of someone in my past who died as well.'

'You know what I am thinking?'

I shook my head.

'That if Prerna was murdered, the murderer is right here at the funeral.'

I looked at the inspector. I didn't know how to respond.

'True, isn't it?' Singh said.

I turned my gaze to Saurabh, who stood sobbing between his parents. 'In that case, Inspector, for the sake of my best friend, let's find out who did it.'

Chapter 8

'Thank you for letting us come,' I said. Four days after the funeral, Saurabh and I had accompanied Inspector Singh to the Malhotra residence. Singh rang the doorbell.

'I didn't have a choice. You made Rana sir call me,' Singh said.

'We are only here to help you, sir,' I said.

'I've managed to do my job all these years without your help,' Singh said.

A maid in her early twenties opened the door. She recognised Saurabh and let us in.

'What's your name?' Singh said.

'Gopika,' the maid said.

'How long have you worked here, Gopika?' Singh said.

'Three years,' she said, somewhat surprised.

'You like it here?' Singh said.

'Let me send sahib,' Gopika said and scurried out of sight.

'So sorry for your loss again, Ramesh ji,' Singh said as Prerna's father entered the living room.

'Thank you,' Ramesh said. 'Hello, Saurabh. When did you come?'

'They came with me,' Singh said.

'Oh,' Ramesh said.

'I just had some routine questions,' Singh said in an extra-gentle, fake voice.

'Sure, tell me,' Ramesh said.

'The media is saying she fell. Like in an accident,' Singh said.

'I read the news,' Ramesh said.

'Do you think that is what happened?' Singh said.

Ramesh took a deep breath. His eyes darted across the room as he looked at Saurabh and me in quick succession. Fifty-year-old Ramesh Malhotra, with his henna-tinted white hair and stubble, looked older than his age. His wrinkles looked more pronounced on his fair skin. He slouched on the sofa and adjusted his loose shirt.

'No idea, Inspector sahib. All I know is I lost my daughter,' Ramesh said. He turned his eyes to the floor.

Gopika came in with a tray carrying several cups of tea.

'Thanks for allowing the post-mortem,' Singh said.

Ramesh nodded.

'Did the post-mortem reveal anything?' Saurabh said.

Inspector Singh looked at Saurabh, surprised and slightly upset. Who was Saurabh to ask all this?

'We're still awaiting a full forensic report. However, the cause of death is injury to the head. There isn't much else at the moment. Some minor scratches on arms and neck upon an early examination, but that's it.'

'Scratches could mean struggle, right?' I said. The inspector glared at me.

'Minor scratches, I said. Could be due to the pebbles on the road as well.'

'Okay,' Ramesh said.

'I told you. The forensic report is awaited. It will tell us if there was someone else with her. Fingerprints, DNA, we are checking everything,' Singh said.

'That's good,' Saurabh said.

'Oh, so now you will tell me what is good or not?' Singh said.

'No, sir, I was just appreciating the thoroughness,' Saurabh said.

'These two have a detective agency as well, Inspector sahib.'

Saurabh nodded.

'This is a serious case, Mr Malhotra. Investigating if the maid stole a cell phone is different from a potential murder,' Singh said.

'Murder?' Ramesh said, surprised.

'What else if it is not an accident?' Singh said.

'But murder? Who will kill my little girl?' Ramesh said.

'Investigation will find out,' Singh said. 'My investigation, that is.'

The inspector glared at us. We weren't welcome, clearly.

'Saurabh knew Prerna. He can help you, sir,' I said.

'And you? What's so great about you?' Singh said to me.

I became silent. Singh turned to Ramesh.

'They went to my senior. Inserted themselves in the investigation. ACP Rana said they can be useful, but I don't really see how,' Singh said.

'It's okay. Let them be involved. Saurabh is like our own,' Ramesh said.

Saurabh nodded. I was not one of their own, but I half-nodded as well.

'I need to talk to everyone in the house. Take their statements,' Singh said.

'Sure,' Ramesh said.

'Can we join you?' Saurabh said.

'No,' Singh said.

'But Rana sir told you—' I said and Singh interrupted me.

'Tell Rana sir I said no. You can read the statements later. If you want to work with me, it will be *for* me. You don't dictate terms. I tell you what to do,' Singh said, his voice loud.

Saurabh and I nodded.

'Don't be upset, Inspector sahib. Have your tea,' Ramesh said.

'Ramesh ji, what exactly is the living arrangement in this house?' Singh said as he took out his notepad.

'Myself, my wife Neelam, son Ajay on the second floor.'

The inspector scribbled as he spoke.

'Prerna too?'

'Of course ... My brother, Aditya, on the third floor by himself. My mother, sister Bindu and niece Anjali on the first floor. That's it.'

'Any staff?'

'One full-time domestic help, Gopika. My driver Anwar. He doesn't stay here though.'

The inspector wrote everyone's name in his little book.

'And who were the important people in your daughter's life?' Singh said.

'Saurabh can tell you that better. But I would say Saurabh and her business partner Namrata.'

'Business partner?' Singh said.

'In Eato. Her startup company,' Saurabh said. 'She co-founded it with Namrata.'

'Namrata who?'

'Namrata Taneja, my own partner's daughter, actually,' Ramesh said.

The inspector jotted down her name as well.

'Good. Let's start the family testimonies tomorrow?' Singh said.

Ramesh hesitated a little. 'You know we are in mourning, but you do what you have to.'

'I am sorry, sir. Only doing my job,' Singh said.

'I understand. I won't be the most cheerful company right now, but may I offer you a drink?'

Singh looked at Saurabh and me.

'I can stay for one. But we don't need these two for that.'

❖

'Ass,' I said as we stepped out of Prerna's house.

'Insecure,' Saurabh said.

We walked along the main road outside Prerna's house as we searched for an auto rickshaw.

'Why can't we sit in during his interviews? We could ask some questions he might miss,' I said.

'Shall we talk to Rana?' Saurabh said.

'We can't keep going to him like cry-babies,' I said.

'She fell here.' Saurabh pointed to a spot on the road.

'Did they find her phone?' I said.

'Someone found it on the other side of the road. Smashed. Nothing can be retrieved from it.'

'Other side? That's weird,' I said.

We went past a few houses and reached the end of the road. A woman from the last house called out to Saurabh.

'Hello, how are you? Remember me, Mrs Goel?'

She wore thick spectacles and looked over seventy.

'Son-in-law of the Malhotras, no?' she said.

'Hello, yes, Mrs Goel,' Saurabh said, placing her at last. 'You came for the roka and engagement.'

Saurabh and I greeted her with a namaste.

'So unfortunate what happened,' Mrs Goel said.

Saurabh nodded.

'Newspapers are saying she slipped,' Mrs Goel said.

'The police is investigating,' Saurabh said.

'Good.' She paused and then said, 'I don't want any trouble with the police.'

'What do you mean?' I said, one eyebrow up.

'This is Keshav, my friend,' Saurabh said quickly.

'I don't like talking to the police. But ... I heard her that evening.'

'Heard her?' Saurabh said, surprised.

'I was on my terrace to take the dry clothes down. I heard screams and yelling. The Malhotras are three houses away. Considering what has happened, I'm now sure they came from the Malhotras' house.'

We looked down the road. The three houses between the Goels and the Malhotras were at a lower height than theirs.

'What did you hear?' I said.

'Just yelling. I couldn't hear the words.'

Saurabh and I looked at each other.

'Please don't get me involved with the police. I shouldn't have said anything,' she said in an anxious voice.

'There will be no trouble, Aunty,' Saurabh said. 'Thank you. This helps.'

'Actually,' I said, 'may we see your terrace?'

We climbed up the stairs to reach her terrace. The evening light gave me a good view of the neighbourhood.

'I can see the Malhotra terrace from here. You didn't see anything?' I said.

'It was much darker that day. And after my cataract, it's hard ...' Her voice trailed off.

'You heard her?' Saurabh said.

'I heard yelling. And a scream. Definitely a scream.'

'What time?'

'Between 7.30 and 8. My TV serial starts at 8, so it was definitely before that.'

'Male or female voices, Aunty?' I said.

'I couldn't tell. Sometimes you just hear a noise.'

Chapter 9

I served Maggi noodles cooked with paneer and peas as dinner. Saurabh ate like his usual self for the first time in weeks.

'Sorry, I didn't leave much for you,' Saurabh said, taking eighty per cent of the noodles from the serving bowl.

'I am happy you are eating,' I said.

'First time you approve of me eating.'

'Take another week off. I will handle office.' I smiled.

Saurabh twirled his fork in the noodles.

'When I was in the auto, Prerna said she wanted to share something with me. She said she would tell me when I reached,' he said, slurping up the noodles.

'Really? What?' I said.

'I have no idea,' Saurabh said and took out his phone. He scrolled through old chats and read them out. She said, "want to share something special I just found out".'

'Seems like good news. Something work-related you think?'

'No idea,' Saurabh said.

'Tell me about this Namrata Taneja,' I said.

'You met her at the engagement briefly. In the back garden, remember?'

'Yes, but tell me more.'

'Namrata didi is co-CEO in Eato. Older than Prerna. Thirty-five, I'd say. The Tanejas are the Malhotras' old family friends from Amritsar.'

'Unmarried?'

'Yes.'

'Prerna got along with her?'

'I think so. I met her a few times. Seems like a stylish lady. Lived and worked abroad before.'

'What about her family?'

'Taneja uncle lives in Amritsar. He also has a car dealership like Ramesh uncle. They are partners in some other business venture as well.'

I added some more noodles to Saurabh's plate.

'How was Prerna's relationship with her family?' I said.

'Her dad was proud of her. She was the only one in the family who became an entrepreneur like him.'

'Did he ever scold her? Did they have arguments?'

'Nothing major. She worked hard, came home late. He would tick her off sometimes. That's it. Prerna was the star of the family. Nobody really scolded her.'

'Okay, tell me about her mother.'

'Neelam aunty? Oh, well, you have seen her. She is a typical docile Punjabi bahu. Mostly in the kitchen. Never speaks a word against her husband. Dealing with diabetes, otherwise quite a foodie.'

I could see that, given her large frame.

'Anything odd? How was she with Prerna?'

'Frankly, I think they were not so close.'

'Mother and daughter not close?'

'Yeah. Prerna used to say her mother likes Ajay more. Typical, you know. Beta and all.'

'And Ajay?'

'Studious kid. Studying for his boards. Prerna loved him a lot. Never mentioned any issue with him.'

I nodded.

'Who could have an issue with Prerna? She was so sweet, remember?' Saurabh said.

I smiled. My mind went to the first time I met Prerna.

Chapter 10

Six months ago

'Tuck in your shirt,' Saurabh said to me while buttoning up his own. We had come to Lodi—the Garden Restaurant in Lodi Gardens. Saurabh had already met Prerna twice and now wanted my approval. Of course, he had already fallen in love.

'This is a romantic date kind of place. Why here? I'll be the odd one out,' I said. We sat at our table, under one of the canopies. Lanterns lit up the place as sunlight waned.

'She is coming with her cousin, Anjali,' Saurabh said. He picked up the menu and scanned it like a radiologist checks an X-ray.

'Do you think we should order before they arrive?'

'Saurabh, let's talk about how you want to proceed with this important life decision rather than choosing appetisers.'

'You meet her first. Your view is important to me, bhai. Okay, how about a mezze platter?'

'Looks like you have already made up your mind.'

'Well, the French fries look good too.'

'I meant made up your mind about Prerna, Golu.'

'Oh. I'm still trying to impress her. That is why I chose this fancy place. I would rather go out for chaat, or some good Punjabi food.'

'Golu, focus.'

'Shh ... Here they are.'

I turned around. Two girls entered the restaurant. They were the same height and had the same fair complexion. One of them was overweight and the other one was stick thin. From the pictures and video calls, I could recognise Prerna. She wore a maroon salwar kameez with a mustard print, had silver jhumkas in her ears and a tiny black bindi on her forehead. A large black leather handbag filled with documents was slung over her shoulder.

The girl with Prerna, her cousin I presumed, wore jeans torn at the knees and a white T-shirt with several tiny holes, which, I understood, was an intentional distressed look. She had short hair, and with her thin frame and backpack, she resembled a boy in middle school. Prerna waved at Saurabh as they walked to our table.

He stood up to give Prerna a restrained hug.

'Hello,' Saurabh said, his voice formal, eyes fixed on Prerna. He couldn't move or say anything else.

'You must be Keshav,' Prerna said and laughed. 'Your friend isn't introducing us.'

'Huh,' Saurabh said, coming to his senses. 'No, I mean, yeah, Keshav this is Prerna, my ...'

He stopped mid-sentence, figuring out the right label for their current relationship status.

'Friend?' Prerna smiled. 'Or, to be more accurate, potential marriage candidate. For Keshav to evaluate?'

'C'mon, Prerna. That is not true,' Saurabh said.

I shook hands with Prerna.

'This is the first time he has brought me to meet any girl. I am guessing you are special,' I said.

'She sure is. I'm Anjali, by the way, since it's self-introduction day,' Prerna's cousin said.

She had an American accent. It did not sound fake like that of those posh Delhi kids who got an accent by watching *The Big Bang Theory* or *Friends* on TV.

'Oh, sorry, sorry. Anju, meet Saurabh and Keshav. Anjali is Geetu bua's daughter from Seattle.'

'No more Seattle. I am from here, National Capital Region, now,' Anjali said and laughed. Maybe it was her lean frame or her unusual couldn't-care-less casual way of dressing or her strange accent, but I couldn't take my eyes off her.

I noticed two tattoos. An eagle poised for flight on the side of her neck, and 'Maa' inked in Devanagari on her left arm. Chrome bangles and a nose ring, three tiny silver earrings in each ear. How did she ever walk through a metal detector without it going crazy?

The two girls sat in front of us. Saurabh continued to look at Prerna with a permanent grin on his face. Several moments passed. Saurabh didn't say a word. I looked at Anjali, who seemed equally amused watching the two lovebirds.

'Order something?' Prerna finally broke the silence. She picked up a menu.

'Yes, yes,' Saurabh said, trying to sound coherent. 'That's what I was telling Keshav.'

'Okay, how about the mezze platter, along with some French fries?' Prerna said.

Saurabh looked at Prerna with his mouth open.

'What?' said Prerna.

'That's exactly what I was going to order.'

'Whatever,' Anjali said. 'I have not come here to eat. I have come to meet, if I may say, my future jiju.'

'Shh.' Prerna elbowed Anjali.

Anjali laughed hard. Her thin frame shook as she covered her mouth with her hand.

Why couldn't I stop looking at her?

After the waiter took our order, I said, 'So, what do you do, Anjali?'

'Oh, me?' Anjali said. 'I am a badly paid, lowly journalist at *The Ink*.'

'Don't be modest. *The Ink* is one of the hottest news portals right now. You head the social and environmental issues desk. True or not?' Prerna said.

'Oh, Prerna didi, you do make me feel better,' Anjali said and laughed.

'It's really inspiring, guys. What they are doing there,' Prerna said.

Anjali shrugged.

'Environment? Great, Delhi needs it. Look at the pollution,' Saurabh said.

'I agree,' Anjali said. 'So, doing my bit.'

'You moved here from Seattle?' I said, my eyes on her nose ring.

'Yeah. I studied journalism, focusing on environmental issues. Graduated when Trump came to power. Couldn't stand the political atmosphere there. Came to India. To work and reconnect with family. Hoping to make people in India care about pollution and climate change.'

'These are important issues—' I began, but Prerna interrupted me.

'Guys,' Prerna said, flipping through the menu again. 'This place is fancy, but you know what I would love?'

'Clearly climate change not as important an issue as food,' Anjali said in an aside to me.

'With this guy? Definitely not,' I said, pointing at Saurabh.

'What, bhai?' Saurabh said, attention on his girl. 'Sorry, what would you like, Prerna?'

'Maybe I sound middle class, but I would love a chaat and then some tasty north Indian food,' Prerna said.

Saurabh locked eyes with Prerna. Imaginary fireworks burst in the sky. He had found her. The girl of his dreams. Forget planets matching in horoscopes. If the choice of dishes matched, this had to be a match made in heaven.

'Can I say something? Two things, actually,' Saurabh said, continuing to look into Prerna's eyes.

'What?'

'One, let's leave this place and just go to UPSC Lane to have chaat.'

'Sure,' Prerna said and smiled. 'What else?'

'I think I am absolutely clear now,' Saurabh said, standing up from his seat to go down on a knee. 'Prerna Malhotra, will you marry me?'

Chapter 11

'Too much, Aunty, really,' I said. But Neelam anyway added three more laddoos to my already crowded plate of snacks.

Technically, Saurabh and Prerna's roka was supposed to be a small affair. People were only meeting for tea. Of course, a single tea session in a Punjabi household often has more calories than the daily recommended calorie intake for a normal-sized adult. On my plate were chole bhature, pav bhaji, hakka noodles, dahi bhalla, gulab jamun, samosa and now three laddoos.

Saurabh's parents had arrived in the morning. They loved food too. They fell in love with the Malhotras the moment they were served kaju katli even before they entered the house. The well-rounded parents sat with their well-rounded son as they awaited their well-rounded bahu. Okay, I'm being a bit mean here, but at least well-rounded sounds better than obese or fat.

It was the first time I had gone to Prerna's house, the impressive three-storey bungalow in New Friends Colony. The ground floor had been emptied out to make seating arrangements on the floor. Over sixty guests filled the hall. Little Punjabi kids criss-crossed the living room, spilling cold drinks along the way.

Prerna wore a green lehenga with elaborate gold embroidery on it. Saurabh wore a cream-coloured shervani and turban. With his smooth clean-shaven face, he looked like those overgrown kids in a children's traditional wear commercial. The roka ceremony started with a small prayer conducted by a priest. After that, Saurabh's parents gave Prerna a pair of gold bangles as sagan, or an auspicious gift. Both sides exchanged insane amounts of mithai, some in baskets so huge, you could carry an adult in it.

'Ramesh ji, you have won our hearts with the khatirdaari and hospitality,' said Pyare Lal Maheshwari, Saurabh's father.

Ramesh folded his hands. He stood in the adequately timid posture expected from the girl's father.

'Now she is yours,' he said.

'Arrey, not yet, Ramesh ji. But let us fix a date fast. What do you say, Saurabh beta?' said Roshni, Saurabh's mother.

Saurabh and Prerna looked at each other. Saurabh was ready to get married in the next one hour, but Prerna wanted a bit more time. Her startup still needed attention. She said she wanted to enjoy planning her wedding as well.

'Why not do both? Run the company and plan the wedding at the same time?' Saurabh said.

'Let's fix the engagement at least,' Ramesh said.

Before Prerna could respond, a tall, fit man in his late thirties entered the room carrying a guitar. He held the hand of an elderly lady.

'Aditya chachu. Finally. Where were you?' Prerna said, looking up at her handsome six-foot uncle, who looked younger than his age.

'Had to bring Maaji down. Anyway, I have a special song for you,' Aditya said.

Prerna's grandmother, silver-haired Nirmala Malhotra, or Maaji, slowly walked across the room. She wore a white silk salwar kameez and two heavy gold necklaces. She sat on a chair right behind the couple of the moment. Prerna and Saurabh touched her feet.

'Munda sona hai, sehat hai,' Maaji said—the boy is good-looking and healthy. For Punjabis, fat is sehat, or health.

'Thank you, Maaji,' said Saurabh, beaming.

'Where's Anjali?' Prerna said.

'I told her to change. She wanted to come down in shirt and jeans. Is this the way a girl dresses at a function like this?' Maaji said.

At that moment, Anjali entered the room in a yellow kurti with gold embroidery and a pair of black tights. She was still underdressed compared to the rest of the guests. Saurabh saw me staring at Anjali and frowned.

Maaji was handed a plate with her share of thousand calories on it.

'I will feed her,' Bindu said, pulling up a chair next to her mother. She had dressed in a red and gold saree, her hair obviously styled in a parlour, a departure from her otherwise stiff curls. She had also given up her spectacles for the evening.

As Maaji ate her second samosa, she began to cry.

She spoke loudly in Punjabi, addressing everyone.

'If Ramesh's daddy was here, he would be so happy, kinne khush honde si,' she said between sobs.

Ramesh, Bindu and Neelam nodded solemnly.

'Ramesh's daddy had seen such tough times. He never stayed around to see any of this,' Maaji said. She spread her hands, to indicate the expanse of the living room and the array of gifts on the floor.

Maaji should have stopped her speech right here, while on a high note. She didn't.

'I was one year old when my parents had to move from Lahore to Amritsar. They hid me in a basket of apples. Like this one.'

She pointed to one of the fruit baskets. She continued, 'I was only eighteen when I married Ramesh's daddy. He was just a simple scooter mechanic.'

Every guest at the party had tuned in to Maaji.

'Look at my Ramesh. When Ramesh's daddy passed away, he raised this entire family. He used to work in the garage. Borrowed money to open a small scooter dealership.'

Ramesh reached behind Maaji and pressed her shoulder. She grabbed his wrist.

'Beta, God should give a child like you to everyone. And a bahu like Neelam. She raised Aditya, Geetu and Bindu better than I could. Never raised eyebrows like those evil TV serial bahus when Ramesh did things for his family.'

Neelam seemed happily surprised at the unexpected praise from her mother-in-law.

'Scooter dealership to Maruti dealership to Pocha dealership. It's no joke.'

'Not pocha, Maaji. Porsche cars. Por-shay,' Ramesh said.

Maaji ignored her elder son and went on.

'From an eighty-yard-plot house in Amritsar to this palace in Delhi. Mrs Goel was telling me she checked on MagicBricks. A kothi like this would cost thirty crores.'

'Maaji, please,' Ramesh whispered, hoping his mother would curb her enthusiasm a little. She ignored him.

'By God's grace, my son has achieved so much. And today, such a beautiful day. Thank you, Waheguru.'

All of Prerna's family members teared up a little. I think Saurabh did too.

The guests clapped, not only out of genuine appreciation for Maaji's speech, but perhaps also to tell her to end it.

The evening continued with everyone taking turns to bless the couple and stuffing their mouths with something sweet.

Finally, the mithai-feeding became too much even for Saurabh.

'Enough, Bindu bua,' Saurabh said, mouth full of besan laddoo.

'Nothing is enough today. You are our son from today,' Bindu said. I think Saurabh's parents shifted a little in their seats at this appropriation.

Aditya strummed his guitar to get everyone's attention.

'Hello, everyone,' Aditya said in his husky voice. 'I am Adi, Prerna's chachu. I am the other brother. The one who didn't do much for his family like his amazing brother, Ramesh.'

Prerna, Anjali and Ajay broke into 'awws' to negate his comment. Aditya smiled and flung back his curly hair as he took position to play his guitar.

'To my little niece,' he said, 'who makes us so proud.'

He sang a Hindi song, originally about brothers and sisters, but replaced 'sister' with 'niece' in the lyrics.

Phoolon ka taaron ka, sab ka kehna hai
Ek hazaron mein, meri bhatiji hai ...

The rest of the evening involved alcohol, a local Punjabi DJ, more food and even more food. Saurabh went mental on the dance floor. His frantic moves probably caused his would-be in-laws to have second thoughts about their damaad. I had to accompany him on the dance floor, of course. Along with a dozen other Punjabi uncles and aunts, we did an intense bhangra.

Later, I saw Anjali leaning against the wall and went up to her.

'You're not dancing?' I said.

'I would, but my ankle is sprained.'

'Oh. What happened?'

'Come on, don't fuss over me. I'm not used to it.'

'No, seriously, what happened?'

'Trekking trip. Twisted it while descending.'

'You trek?'

'I'm not just a boring desk-job journalist. I love nature. Trekking is my passion.'

'Cool. Where did you trek?'

'Just came back from Manali. Later this year I might do the Everest Base Camp.'

'You will climb Everest?' I said, eyes wide.

'Just the base camp,' Anjali said and laughed. 'It's where Everest trekkers start their journey.'

'It's still impressive,' I said.

'I've climbed since I was little. My stepdad used to take me, in his better moods. I continued even in boarding school.'

'Oh,' I said. 'Are your parents here?'

'No, they couldn't come for this from Seattle. They will come for the wedding.'

Saurabh had told me Anjali's mother, Geetu, had married a cab driver, Jogi, in the US. She had moved there several decades ago. They split up, and Geetu married Greg Davis, an American schoolteacher in Seattle.

'Anyway, why all this boring talk? You go to the dance floor. Give your friend company,' Anjali said.

I smiled and walked back to the makeshift dance floor made of plastic with bright multicoloured lights beneath it. The song *Baby Doll* started. Saurabh moved his hips like Sunny Leone did in the original. Okay, stop Golu, I wanted to tell him. They could see this and still back out.

'Bhai, I am so happy,' he said in the middle of the song. 'Now I understand what you meant when you told me about love. It really is an amazing feeling.'

I shrugged and smiled.

'What, bhai? You are not happy?' Saurabh said, moving his hands as he spoke to me.

'I am happy for you.'

'You should also find someone, fall in love and get married. It's beautiful.'

'Never going to happen, Golu.'

'Why? How long will you keep making me meet these meaningless Tinder bhabhis?'

I laughed and looked at Anjali again.

'Not her, bhai. Please promise me you will not search for hook-ups in Prerna's family.'

'What?' I said. 'Of course not.'

'I saw you talk to her.'

'I called her to dance. She's twisted her ankle. That's all we spoke about.'

'You sure?' Saurabh said, and began to move again to the Sunny Leone song.

'Yes. And that's not the step. You have to move like a serpent. Let me show you,' I said.

Chapter 12

Prerna and Saurabh's engagement ceremony resembled the coronation of a prince in a small kingdom. Held in New Friends Club, it had a budget of fifty lakh rupees.

'No, no, absolutely no,' Saurabh said. Ramesh had presented him with a set of keys. Were they really offering him a Volkswagen Jetta? And was he really saying no?

'You explain to him,' Ramesh said to Saurabh's parents. They just smiled, as if touched by their only son's generosity. Deep inside, they wondered what the hell Saurabh was doing. Sometimes it is not dowry, it is love, isn't it? Especially when it involves a Volkswagen.

'She is all I need,' Saurabh said, pointing to his new fiancée. Prerna wore an orange lehenga, which had cost two lakh rupees. She'd got her make-up and hair done by a professional, which had a separate bill of fifty thousand bucks.

The couple sat on two thrones in a hall in the club. Guests took turns to bless them, one at a time.

I stood near the couple, wondering how strong the stage was to take the weight of so many overweight Punjabi relatives.

My parents had come to attend the engagement from Alwar as well. After blessing the couple, my father and mother made for the dinner buffet. My mother came up to me.

'You should also consider settling down,' she said, plate in hand.

'Not for me,' I said.

'What do you mean?'

'Nothing. And sit and eat properly, Ma. Why are you standing? Go, Saurabh's parents are sitting there,' I said.

After my mother left, Aditya tapped my shoulder.

'Bored?' he said.

'Huh? No, I'm fine.'

'Come, let's hang in the back garden,' he said, and signalled for me to follow him.

❖

Anjali sat on a bench under a tree in the backyard. She had a glass of whiskey in one hand and a cigarette in the other.

'Ah, the best man arrives,' she said when she saw me with Aditya.

'He was looking lost,' Aditya said.

Both of them laughed. Aditya took out a bottle of Black Label whiskey and two glasses from under the bench. He poured the golden liquid into the glasses.

'Cheers,' I said as I accepted one.

'Did you see? Your friend rejected a nice car,' Anjali said.

'That's who he is,' I said.

'I'm impressed,' Anjali said. 'Not what I expect Indian men to do.'

'I could use that car. If only Bhaiya would give it to me.' Aditya laughed.

'Shut up, Aditya. Sorry, I meant don't say that, Aditya mamu,' Anjali corrected herself. 'Sorry, mamu. Didn't mean to talk like that.'

'It's okay,' Aditya said. 'If you can drink and smoke up with me, you can address me by my first name and talk to me like a friend too. Keshav?'

He offered me the cigarette. It didn't smell like tobacco.

'Just some Manali hash, don't worry,' Anjali said. 'Brought it back from my trek.'

I took a puff. The smoke touched my insides and made me feel calmer.

I handed the joint to Anjali. She took a drag.

'Ah, this is good,' she said.

I noticed Anjali was wearing the same torn jeans she had on when I'd first met her and Prerna. She also wore a long white kurti with silver embellishments though, perhaps to pacify all the aunts.

'I don't understand, Anjali. On the one hand, Bhaiya says business is not good when I ask for money, on the other, look at this lavish engagement,' Aditya said.

'Indian dads lose all rationality when it comes to their daughters' weddings. Also, Prerna didi is partly paying for this function.'

'And what about the car? A freaking Jetta? As an engagement gift for their damaad?'

'Inside story is, Uncle knew Saurabh would say no. He had strictly said no even to tiny gifts. Ramesh uncle thought, why not do the grand gesture anyway? The car is never going to leave the showroom.'

'Really?' I said.

Anjali winked at me and laughed. Aditya laughed hard too, causing his curly hair to shake a little.

'He should have taken it. I would have loved to see Bhaiya's face,' Aditya said between peals of laughter.

Anjali drank her whiskey bottoms up. She held out her glass for more.

'I've had a shit week at work. I need this.'

Aditya poured her another drink.

'At least you have work,' Aditya said and laughed. 'Look at me. Sitting around in my house all day.'

'It's not just a house. It's your studio too,' Anjali said.

'Yeah, but, what am I even doing there? Last song I put up on YouTube got three thousand views. That's it.'

'It's a good song. I love it.'

'Who cares? Nobody,' Aditya said.

'And that gig at Taj? In the bar?'

'Bhaiya said no. He said how can the brother of the owner of Malhotra Motors work in a bar? I might take another one at the Leela though. Bhaiya never goes there. He won't find out.'

'Ramesh uncle is so regressive sometimes, eesh,' Anjali said.

'I'm sure I will be selling cars soon.' Aditya smirked.

'No. Please don't. You are too cool for that. My rockstar mamu.'

Aditya's phone rang. It was one of his relatives to say that they needed him inside. He excused himself and left. Anjali and I sat on the bench, next to each other.

'What happened at work?' I said, more to make conversation than anything else.

'People getting fired. Media sucks right now,' Anjali said, dangling her feet.

'Yes, Facebook and Google are taking all the ads. Is your job safe though?'

'For now, yes. Lucky my boyfriend founded *The Ink,* right?' Anjali took a puff of the joint.

'Oh,' I said. A tinge of pain and disappointment ran through me. I refilled my glass.

'Oh what?' she said.

'Didn't realise you had a boyfriend.'

'Why? I seem that unlovable?' Anjali burst out laughing.

'No. Sorry, just didn't know.'

'I moved to India for this idiot, Parag. Damn, I must be high. I never admit this,' she said and held up her glass.

'Parag is your ...'

'Boyfriend slash boss. Yes,' she said and laughed. 'Maybe fiancé and husband one day.' She pointed to the festivities inside. 'Of course, I'm not going to do all this wasteful Punjabi drama.'

'Everyone has a right to celebrate the way they want,' I said.

'How non-judgemental of you. Anyway, *The Ink* had layoffs. Sucks. We are a left-wing publication. Nobody in this country wants to hear left-wing views anymore.'

'That's not true,' I said.

'They don't want to read about how Hindus and Muslims are being divided. Or that pollution is a huge issue. Or there are still caste-based atrocities. Nobody clicks on those articles. They want, I don't know, free food deliveries, I guess.'

'These articles do sound a bit depressing,' I said.

'They are relevant,' Anjali said, her voice firm.

'Of course.'

'That's why we write them. That's what makes me stick around. A sense of fairness and justice. Well, that and Parag.'

'I'm sure you guys will find your audience. Politics always has two sides. There will always be takers for both.'

'Hope it happens soon. Anyway, my job should be safe. I sleep with the boss,' Anjali said and laughed.

I kept a poker face, unsure of how I should respond. Damn, the one girl I liked in years was taken. That sucked way more than layoffs.

'You want to go inside?' I said.

'Honestly, no. I hate it there. All these people decked up in their jewellery like Russian czars. Pretending to love and care, but essentially showing off how rich they are.'

'You really are a left-wing crusader, aren't you?' I said.

'I don't know who I am,' Anjali said, her voice slurring as the whiskey and marijuana took effect. 'My head is spinning.'

She turned sideways and placed her head on my lap. Lifting her legs, she straightened them on the bench.

'Ah, nice,' she said. 'Look at the trees and the stars above. Nothing flashy, Punjabi or capitalist about them. Yet so grand and magnificent.'

She took another drag of the joint and passed it to me. I bent forward towards her to take it. Our eyes met. I didn't notice Saurabh enter the back garden.

'Keshav, you are here? Been looking for you all over,' Saurabh shouted.

I took my eyes off Anjali's face and turned towards Saurabh. There was a lady with him.

'Oh, hi,' I said.

Anjali lifted her head from my lap.

'Hi, Saurabh,' she said, 'and hello Namrata didi, you look amazing.'

'What are you doing here, Keshav?' Saurabh said, ignoring Anjali's greeting. From a distance and in the darkness, he had probably thought we were sharing more than a cigarette.

'Just came for some air,' I said.

Saurabh seemed upset. However, he remained silent.

'Hi, I'm Namrata. Prerna's partner at Eato,' the lady introduced herself. She wore a magenta raw silk saree with a red border. In her early thirties, she had waist-length hair, which complemented her sharp features.

'Saurabh told me about you,' I said. 'Congrats on all the success.'

'Long way to go. Lots of pressure when you have so many investors riding on you.'

'Lovely saree, didi,' Anjali said. 'Would you like a drink?'

Namrata shook her head. 'You know I don't drink.'

'Saurabh?' Anjali said. Saurabh shook his head as well.

'People are dancing inside. I don't get engaged every day. Would you like to continue your moonlight bar here or dance at your best friend's engagement?' Saurabh said. Clearly, the groom was angry.

'Of course,' Anjali said. 'It's Prerna didi's engagement. We have to dance. And I don't have any broken ankles today.'

Anjali and Namrata walked ahead of us as we went back in. Saurabh spoke to me when they were out of hearing distance.

'What the hell were you doing?'

'Sorry, Golu. Just came out for some air. Aditya chachu and Anjali offered a drink and ...'

'Where's chachu?' Saurabh interrupted me.

I looked around.

'He just went in.'

'She's my wife's relative, Keshav.'

'What?' I said, surprised. When Saurabh calls me by my name instead of 'bhai', he's definitely upset.

'She's Prerna's first cousin. Not one of your Tinder hook-ups.'

'What are you talking about?' I said.

'I saw her in your lap. Your mouths were—'

'We were smoking up. She lay down. I did nothing,' I said, interrupting him.

'Exactly. When do you ever do anything? Your charm pulls girls to you, isn't it?'

'Golu, nothing was happening. She has a serious boyfriend.'

'Just show some respect, okay? Parents are here.'

'I swear—'

He cut me off mid-sentence.

'You found no better place to smoke weed than my engagement? Namrata didi saw it. Now she will tell Prerna. What will she think of me?'

We walked in silence. I put an arm around Saurabh's shoulder.

'Golu, chill. Listen, before we go in and dance ...'

Saurabh stopped mid-step.

'What?' he said.

'There's Black Label under the bench,' I said.

'My parents won't like it,' Saurabh said.

'One sip.'

We ran back. He took a few quick chugs from the bottle.

'Don't fuck around in Prerna's family,' Saurabh said.

'I won't,' I said. 'I swear, I didn't even think of it. Now come, let's go in and show the Malhotras our famous cockroach dance.'

Chapter 13

'The family seems normal,' I said, coming back from the memories of our embarrassing cockroach dance. 'Like any other Punjabi family.'

'We need to see the family testimonies,' Saurabh said.

It was midnight. Saurabh was sipping on a cup of hot chocolate.

'We should meet other people in Prerna's life too. Like Namrata,' I said. 'Anyone else?'

'There's the ex-boyfriend.'

'Ex-boyfriend?'

'Long before me. During her first job. I never told you.'

'What do you know about him?'

'She used to work at Kotak Mahindra Bank before starting Eato. She dated this guy Neeraj there. They broke up. It's part of the reason why she quit.'

'What happened?'

'Prerna never told me much. He broke up with her for stupid reasons. She was heartbroken. Later he wanted to get back. But Prerna quit the bank and moved on.'

'They were still in touch?'

'No idea,' Saurabh said. 'Such a loser to leave someone like Prerna.'

❖

'No, you can't make copies,' Singh said.

We sat facing him in his ramshackle office on creaky wooden chairs. A brown folder with a bunch of loose white sheets lay in front of us.

'Can we take pictures on our phones?' Saurabh said.

'You think I'm an idiot?' Singh said.

'In what sense, sir?' Saurabh said.

'What?' Singh said.

'No, sir. He means, "No, sir, you are not an idiot",' I hastily said.

'What's the difference in taking photos and making copies?' Singh said.

'Pictures are easy to take. Saves paper too,' Saurabh said.

'You think I am not letting you take copies to save paper? What do you think I am? An environmental activist like that Great Thunder girl?' Singh said, now visibly agitated.

'No, sir. You are a police inspector. Not Greta Thunberg,' I said.

'Exactly. I don't want these testimonies leaking out to the media. They are part of an ongoing investigation.'

'We won't share with anyone, sir,' I said.

'Read it here, in that room,' he said, snapping his fingers and pointing to an empty cabin next to his office. 'And now that you mention it, surrender your phones.'

I looked at Saurabh. If he hadn't said it, maybe we could have taken a few clicks.

'Sure, sir,' I said. We kept our phones on the table.

I picked up the brown folder.

Saurabh looked at Singh.

'Yes? Anything else, sir?' Singh said to Saurabh in a sarcastic tone.

'If we could get some chai and biscuits,' Saurabh said even as I pulled him away by his sleeve.

Chapter 14

Preliminary investigation into the death of Ms Prerna Malhotra

Transcribed testimonies of residents of Malhotra House, A–956, New Friends Colony

Testimony 1: Maid Gopika (Translated from Hindi)
Interview by Constable Shyam Gehlot

What's your full name, age and where are you from?
I am Gopika Paswan. I am twenty-two years old and I am from Gaya in Bihar.
Your relationship with the deceased?
I have worked in Prerna didi's house for the past three years as house help.
How did you get this job? And what are your duties?
I was hired from a domestic servant agency in New Friends Colony. I live in the Malhotras' home. I clean the house, wash clothes and help Neelam madam and Bindu madam in the kitchen. I also do the shopping from the nearby grocery stores.
What is your relationship like with the family, in particular the deceased? Were there any disputes or conflicts?
I always do a good job. People in the family are nice and they like me. They buy me gifts. They gave me a saree each for the roka and engagement ceremony of Prerna didi.
Prerna didi never spoke to me much. She used to be very busy. Sometimes she would come back from work at midnight and I would give her dinner. At other times she would leave for work at seven in the morning and I made breakfast for her. She was very particular about her food and always wanted it to be tasty. She loved my gobi paranthas.

The only time she scolded me was when she found Anwar in my room. Anwar is like my brother. Sometimes I make tea for him after he brings back Ramesh sir in the evening. She told me it is not good for drivers to come upstairs to my room. I said sorry to her. Matter was finished.

Where were you on the night of 17 October?

In the house itself. I finished making evening tea for everyone, cleared and washed the plates. Neelam madam came to the kitchen to prepare dinner. She has diabetes so she can't fast for Karva Chauth. I offered to help her with the cooking. She told me to go rest in my room as I had also prepared lunch, served tea and set the table for dinner. I went to my room and lay down for a while. Later I heard a lot of noise. Everyone in the house ran outside. I saw that a crowd had gathered on the road, where Prerna didi had died.

Was there anyone else with you in your room?

I have told you everything already.

Answer the question—was there anyone else with you in your room?

Anwar was there. I had kept some tea and snacks for him. Please don't do anything to him. He may be Muslim, but he is a very nice man.

How long was Anwar there in your room?

Ten minutes. Maybe a little more ... (after a pause) maybe half an hour. He left before all the noise downstairs. I swear (after a long pause) ... Please don't tell anyone, Havaldar ji.

Does anyone in the house know about your relationship with Anwar?

No, Havaldar ji. Please don't tell them. They will fire Anwar from his job. Even that last time, Prerna didi scolded him a lot.

What did Prerna tell Anwar?

Anwar is forty-five years old and married with children. Prerna didi was right. She asked him why he came to my room. We said it is only to have tea. We swore that we are like brother and sister to each other ... (pauses) Okay, I know what we are doing is wrong, but his wife is very far away in Aligarh. And he told me if I become a Muslim, I can also be his wife. It is allowed in their religion, Havaldar ji. Please don't give any trouble to Anwar. He is a very nice man.

Did Anwar get upset with Prerna?

He is human only, Havaldar ji. Of course, at that moment he did, but he did not say anything to Prerna didi ever.

What did he say to you?

(stays quiet)

We are the police. You better tell the truth. What exactly did Anwar say about Prerna after she scolded him?

He said, 'Who does this woman think she is? She was a child when I first came to work in this house. And now she is yelling at me even though Ramesh sir has never shouted at me. I'd like to slap her.'

Did he talk about hurting her?

No, Havaldar ji. Nothing after that. I told you, Anwar is a very nice man. Nothing will happen to him, right, Havaldar ji?

Chapter 15

Saurabh and I kept the folder aside. One of the peons in the police station brought us two cups of tea.

Saurabh took a big sip.

'What do you think?' I said.

'It's good chai by police station standards. Biscuits would make it perfect.'

'Saurabh, I am talking about the transcripts.'

'Oh,' Saurabh said and put the cup aside. 'Anwar and Gopika. Wow. Nobody had any idea.'

'Maybe Prerna discovered the affair. Yelled at Anwar and humiliated him. He saw her go to the terrace. Pushed her in anger.'

'You think so?'

'He could have. Gopika couldn't have. She's too tiny,' I said.

'Too early to make judgements. Let's keep reading.'

Testimony 2: Ramesh Malhotra (father of deceased)
Interview by Inspector Vijender Singh

Full name, age and where are you from?
My name is Ramesh Malhotra. I am fifty years old. We are originally from Amritsar but I now live in New Friends Colony in New Delhi.
Where were you on the night of 17 October?
I was in the New Friends Colony market. I had gone to purchase paan. While in the market, I received a call from my wife, Neelam. She told me to come home immediately as my daughter Prerna has had an accident. I rushed home to find her dead on the road.
Anything different you noticed about your daughter in the past few months?
Prerna was about to get married. By nature a workaholic, she was very excited planning for her wedding. She spoke to Saurabh a lot.
Was she stressed or upset about anything?
Not to my knowledge. She would sometimes feel work pressure to meet investor targets.

Did she have any enemies, or disputes with people?
(Pause) She had a break up with her ex-boyfriend Neeraj Arora, over two years ago. Before the break up they had fights. After the break up she was in depression for six months.
You mean like depression where she needed treatment?
No, nothing like that. But she was sad for a long time.
Why did they break up?
I'm not sure. Children don't tell everything to their parents these days.
How were her relations with people in the family?
Prerna was the star of the family. She was not only an achiever, she was a good person and helped everyone. She had no dispute with anyone in this house. We are a deeply connected family.
What work do you do?
I have a car dealership in Delhi, and I am a partner in another one in Amritsar. The Delhi one is for Porsche and the one in Amritsar is for Volkswagen. We also have an auto parts factory in Amritsar.
How is the financial position of the family?
Well, as you can see around you, we are quite comfortable. By God's grace we have everything.
How is business right now?
As you may have read in the papers, the auto sector is going through a downturn. Car sales are down all over. But it is cyclical, ups and downs keep happening. I am sorry but how is this relevant to my daughter's case, Inspector?
Just curious. Anyway, how are your relations with the rest of the family? Your brother, sister, mother and wife?
My mother blesses and thanks me every day for bringing our family to this level. My brother Aditya and I are not great friends.
Why?
The main issue is work. I want him to lend a hand in the dealership. He refuses to join the family business. He wants to be a rock singer. Tell me something, in the land of Mohammed Rafi and Kishore Kumar, how can a rock singer make a living? He's built a fancy studio on his floor where he keeps making noise. I am nice to him. I tell him to join the business anytime he wants. He just won't.

What about your sister?

I have two sisters. Geetu lives in Seattle, US, with her American husband. Bindu is unmarried and stays with us. Geetu's daughter, Anjali, stays in my house free of cost. I mean, of course—I can't take rent from my sister or her daughter, obviously. In Punjabi families, brothers look after sisters.

Bindu, my other sister, is a primary school teacher. With her salary, she can't afford a decent place either. But I told her, your brother is around, stay with us.

What do you think happened to Prerna that day?

Isn't that what you are trying to find out?

But still, give me your best guess of what happened?

I don't know, Inspector. It is all a shock to me. God only knows.

'Well, for now God only knows,' Saurabh said as we finished reading Ramesh's testimony.

'God, and the killer,' I said.

'Good point. Keep going?' Saurabh said.

I nodded.

Testimony 3: Neelam Malhotra (mother of deceased)
Interview by Inspector Vijender Singh

Your full name, age and where are you from?

My name is Neelam Malhotra. I am forty-seven years old. My family is originally from Ludhiana. After marriage, I moved to my husband's place in Amritsar. Ten years ago we came to Delhi.

Where were you on the evening of 17 October when the incident occurred?

I was in the kitchen. It was Karva Chauth, but due to my diabetes I can no longer keep a fast. I was cooking dinner for the entire family when I heard Adi shouting and Bindu running down the stairs. I followed them outside the house to find Prerna ... on the road.

Was there anyone else with you in the kitchen?

Not at that time. Bindu, who normally helps me with dinner, was in her apartment. I had told Gopika to set the plates for dinner and then go rest in her room as well.

Why did you send your maid to rest in her room?
She had worked a lot all day and seemed exhausted. We can't be inhuman.
Do you know of anyone with whom your daughter had enmity?
Prerna was beloved to all.
Do you suspect anyone of foul play, in the family or outside?
In the family? What are you talking about? We are a very respected and close-knit family. All of us have grown up together. Everyone loved Prerna. Outside, I don't know. She never spoke to me much about her work or her life outside.
What do you think happened?
I told her not to keep the Karva Chauth fast, it will cause weakness. She is not used to it. If I don't eat food for several hours, I feel dizzy. I think the same thing happened to her. She didn't eat anything all day, so she must have been feeling giddy. She stood on the terrace holding the thali, the sieve and the phone. Not paid attention while checking her phone, slipped, and due to light-headedness, tipped over.
You think it was an accident?
What else could it be, Inspector sir?

Testimony 4: Aditya Malhotra (uncle of deceased)
Interview by Inspector Vijender Singh

What's your full name, age and where are you from?
My name is Aditya Malhotra. I am thirty-seven years old. Born in Amritsar but moved to Delhi ten years ago. In between, I also lived in Goa and Manali for a year.
Where were you on the night of 17 October?
I was in my apartment, on the third floor of our kothi. I was making music.
What do you mean making music?
I'm a musician by profession. I sing as well as compose songs. I have my own studio in my apartment. I work on several projects at the same time. Anyway, I stepped out of the studio to smoke and came to the balcony. A crowd had gathered downstairs. I ran down and

saw Prerna lying there. I came back inside and shouted, asking everyone to come out.

Do you always work from home?

Yes, I do, unless I have a gig outside.

What is a gig?

A job to sing somewhere. I sometimes do gigs at The Leela Palace.

Did you notice anything strange in Prerna's behaviour in the past few months?

I think she was stressed at work. The wedding preparation was extra work. Also ... (pause)

Also what?

She wanted to lose weight before the wedding. She was trying really hard. She even took fitness tips from me. I gave her some advice about diet and exercise. She couldn't do it. Added to her stress levels. I think she kept Karva Chauth because she wanted to fast.

Did you know of anyone who may have had a grudge against her? As in people who had an issue with her, to the point that they could be motivated to harm her?

She was under a lot of pressure to grow Eato. She was tough and a strict boss. So one of her employees may have held a grudge against her.

You think an employee could kill her?

Dude—I am sorry, I mean, Inspector sir, I have not worked in an office for even one day. How would I know?

What do you think happened?

I have no idea.

How is your family?

What do you mean how is my family? They are like any other family. We are normal.

It's a joint family?

Yes, but there are other joint families too. And we all have our own space. There is a lot of love and respect.

Do you think anyone in the family could be involved in the death of your niece?

Impossible. Prerna was the baby of the family.

How is your relationship with your brother?

Why is that important?

You just said there is a lot of love and respect in the family. But we understand the relationship between you and your brother is not good?

(Pause) Bhaiya doesn't understand passion and following your heart. He thinks unless I sit in the showroom, I am not good enough. Bhaiya won't support me in my career like he helps everyone else ... (pause) ... Anyway, how is that relevant?

We are just chatting, Mr Aditya. Please, don't get agitated. So can one say that you have a grudge against your brother?

What kind of grudge?

Your brother is doing well. Your niece was also doing well. Star of the family, the apple of your brother's eye. You think you could ...

I could what? Have you lost your mind, Inspector? You told me this was just a chat. And now you are insulting me.

I am not doing anything.

Please, do I have the right to stop this testimony? I do not wish to speak any further.

Testimony 5: Bindiya Malhotra (aunt of deceased)
Interview by Inspector Vijender Singh

What's your full name, age and where are you from?

My name is Bindiya Malhotra. I am forty-two years old. I live in Delhi. From Amritsar originally. Everyone calls me Bindu.

What were you doing on 17 October?

I was correcting unit test papers of my students. I'm a primary school teacher in the New Delhi Municipal Corporation School in Maharani Bagh. I heard Adi shouting in the house, telling us to go outside. I ran out and saw ... my little girl ... the little girl of our family.

Bindiya madam, if you need time to calm yourself, we can ask the questions later.

No, no, how much will I cry? What's the point? She is gone now. Anyway, ask what you have to.

Most of all, we are trying to figure out if Prerna had some rivalry, dispute or conflict with someone.

I really can't think of anyone. She was always working. I told her to slow down, take care of herself. She wouldn't listen. Plus, all that dieting before the wedding. She must not have been feeling okay that day.

You think this was an accident?

What else could it be? Who would want to harm a little girl?

Bindiya madam, you never married?

No.

If I may ask, why is that?

I just never found anyone. When I was in school, I had a relationship with someone. My heart was broken. So, for many years I refused to see any boys for a match. I couldn't trust anyone. Then it became too late.

Do you regret not getting married?

Sometimes, but not really. People get married to get a good family. I already have a great family. Why are you asking me all this?

Prerna was getting married soon.

Yes, she was. What is the connection?

All the celebrations in the house. The happiness she felt. Did you ever feel envious of her?

What?

Envy or jealousy. She had what you never did. Is it difficult for you on Karva Chauth? To see other women dressed up like brides and fasting for their husbands?

Yes, I do feel a tinge of emptiness on Karva Chauth. But I was so happy for Prerna. She was like my daughter. No envy there at all.

Are you sure?

What do you mean?

Nothing. Anything else you want to say to us?

While doing your work, please don't be insensitive to our grief.

Testimony 6: Anjali Davis (cousin of deceased)
Interview by Inspector Vijender Singh

What's your full name, age and where are you from?
My name is Anjali Davis. I am from Seattle in the US. I currently live in my uncle's house in Delhi. I am twenty-six.
Your surname sounds unusual.
My father, I mean stepfather, is American. I have his surname.
What happened to your real father?
My parents divorced when I was three years old. My mother married Greg Davis and I consider him my father. He's real enough to me.
Where were you and what were you doing on the night of 17 October?
I had just landed back in Delhi after a trekking trip to the Everest Base Camp. I took a flight from Kathmandu to Kolkata and then another one to Delhi. I took an Uber from the Delhi airport. When I arrived home, I saw a crowd in the house. Prerna didi's body was on the carpet, covered with a white sheet.
What time did you take the Uber ride, and what time did you reach home?
Here, you can check my phone. (The phone was handed over to the investigating officer)
Note from Inspector Singh:
The phone of Ms Anjali Davis was examined. The Uber app history had details of the ride. A Maruti Swift Dzire cab was booked. It was driven by Kartar Singh who had a 4.6 stars driver rating. The ride started at 6.51 p.m. from the Indira Gandhi International Airport Terminal 1. The Uber taxi took the Ring Road and reached A–956, New Friends Colony at 8.07 p.m. The fare paid was Rs 458. The distance travelled was 21.3 kilometres. The phone was returned to the person giving the testimony.
Anjali madam, according to her fiancé, Mr Saurabh, he reached the terrace at 7.50 p.m. and she was not there. Is that correct?
How can I answer that question? I was on my way home.

Are you saying Mr Saurabh could not be telling the truth?
I am only saying I can't confirm it. If this is what he said, then I have no reason to disbelieve him.
Do you have any reason to suspect Mr Saurabh Maheshwari?
No. He seemed to be deeply in love with Prerna. He was very excited about the wedding.
What about other family members?
What about them?
How would you describe the relations of the family members, particularly with Prerna?
If you ask them, they will say they are a loving joint family with a lot of regard for each other.
Is that true?
No. Not in my opinion. They are as dysfunctional as any other family, if not more.
Why do you say that?
The two brothers, my uncles, hate each other. My grandmother is losing it. She may have dementia setting in but no one acknowledges it. Ramesh uncle's business is not doing well. Aditya mamu doesn't have a job or any source of income. Neelam aunty and Prerna were constantly arguing. In Neelam aunty's eyes, from dressing to work, Prerna could do nothing right. My own mother is abroad, largely ignored by the family. Even my stepfather doesn't want to be with her or me anymore. In fact, I forcibly inserted myself into this house to find some semblance of a family.
That's quite different from what the others have been saying.
I told you. In the eyes of the world they behave like a perfect Punjabi khandaan. But it is a mess. But then, which family isn't?
You didn't mention anything about Ms Bindiya?
Well, she is nice. But, of course, she has major issues of her own. Things she needs to face up to. But I'd rather not say.
What kind of issues?
I told you, I'd rather not say. Family matters. Nothing to do with Prerna's death. Why are you so curious to get into our domestic issues?

Nothing like that. I am just trying to figure out what happened. People are saying it is an accident.

It isn't. It so clearly isn't.

Why do you say that?

Because Prerna is not stupid to fall off a terrace just like that. She was absolutely fine. Also, the neighbour, Mrs Goel, told me she heard screams and arguments from the terrace.

Really? Who is Mrs Goel?

A–959. Her house is the same height as ours, and all the houses in between are lower. She told me when I took a walk to the market yesterday.

We will definitely talk to her.

Thank you. Have you spoken to everyone else in the family?

Yes, almost. Only your grandmother is left.

Oh, good luck with that.

Testimony 7: Nirmala Malhotra (grandmother of deceased)
Interview by Inspector Vijender Singh

Pranam, madam, are you okay if I ask you a few questions?

No, I am not. But you are going to ask anyway, right?

It is just a request. We can't force you. After all, this is for your granddaughter. Just a few questions?

What can you do for my granddaughter now? She is gone now. Hun ki (now what)?

We are trying to find out who did this to her.

Who can do anything? When it is time to go, it is time to go. It's her kismat.

That's true, but we have to find out who did it.

O aaya si (he was there).

Who was there, Nirmala ji?

The one who did it was there. In my home.

Your home? Who was in your home?

How do I know? It was dark. I had just woken up from a nap. I wasn't wearing my spectacles. But he was there, I know.

This is serious. Are you saying the person who killed Prerna Malhotra was in your home?

I told you already. Are you deaf that you can't hear the first time?

Did you talk to him or her? Do you know if it was a he or a she?

Seemed like a man only. O aaya si. He didn't answer when I shouted at him. Just flew out of the room.

Flew out? Nirmala ji, I am being serious.

I am doing comedy?

You are saying the killer flew out.

So?

Nothing. Can I ask some general questions? What is your name, age and where do you come from?

You keep calling me Nirmala ji, so you know my name, isn't it? What will you do with my age? I don't know it myself. My father said I was born a little before Independence, in Lahore. We moved to Amritsar after Partition. And then here. Why? Why do you want my biodata?

Nothing like that, Nirmala ji, just doing routine queries. How is the relationship between everyone in your family?

What do I know? Nobody tells me anything. Everyone does his or her own thing. This Prerna used to come home at midnight. She said she came from work. What kind of work do girls do at midnight? And look at this Geetu's daughter. She stays in the next room. Roaming around in shorts that resemble underwear. Neither Ramesh nor Aditya is hard on these girls. Neelam is another one. Feeding her daughter more and more until she became a buffalo. I tell you, Bindu is the only one who cares about me in this house. Otherwise, I would be dead too.

Why would you be dead?

Everyone in the neighbourhood is jealous of us. Ours is the tallest kothi on the street. Everyone who knew us in Amritsar is also jealous of us. Who is happy to see other people successful? They all want to hurt me.

'All' meaning who? And what about people in the family?

I told you, everyone we know. Even in the family, I don't trust Neelam. You never know with bahus. I eat whatever she has cooked only after she has tasted it first.

Your daughter-in-law wants to hurt you?

Every daughter-in-law wants to hurt her mother-in-law. What sort of stupid question is this?

I am sorry, but do you have any specific reason to believe Neelam Malhotra wants to hurt you?

She comes every night.

Where?

In my dreams. One day she will tell me not to breathe in my sleep. What will I do then?

Note: *Given her mental state, the police officer decided to end the testimony. This completes all the testimonies taken at this stage.*

❖

'That's all,' I said, placing the sheets back in the file.

'Let's discuss over dinner?' Saurabh looked at his watch. 'It is eight o'clock. Eating late doesn't suit me. Haldiram's?'

I looked at Saurabh and shook my head.

'What? I get acidity. Oh, that reminds me, I have to get stomach medicine. Let's stop at a chemist later as well.'

Chapter 16

'Two chole bhature please, and one plain lassi,' Saurabh said at the cashier's counter.

'I told you I don't want anything,' I said.

'Yeah, I know,' Saurabh said. 'This is only for me.'

We had come to the Haldiram's in C Block Old Market in Malviya Nagar. The place does extraordinarily well because of its delicious comfort food. Haldiram's understands Indians like McDonald's understands Americans. However, being in a popular place meant noisy kids and even noisier parents. We had to shout to have a conversation.

'Nice place, no?' Saurabh said. He tore off a piece of the puffy bread, releasing the steam trapped inside.

'You get food, you are happy,' I said.

'Happy? Are you kidding me? I am just trying not to feel awful after my life has ended.'

'Your life hasn't ended, Golu. You are here, with me. Please don't say things like that.'

'Prerna loved this place,' Saurabh said, and I could see his eyes become moist again. I wasn't sure if it was due to the grief or the green chillies in the chole.

I changed the topic.

'The police have only taken statements from those in the house. They haven't spoken to others.'

'Like?' Saurabh said, covering his mouth with one hand to hide a small burp.

'The business partner, Namrata. And that ex, Neeraj, from the bank. We should talk to them ourselves.'

'Sure,' Saurabh said. 'The list of suspects is so long, isn't it?'

'Seven family members in the house—Ramesh, Neelam, Ajay, Aditya, Bindu, Maaji and Anjali.'

'Apart from that, the maid Gopika and driver Anwar. Add Namrata and Neeraj too.'

'Eleven people so far. Too many. We have to narrow it down,' I said.

An extended sardar family two tables away from us started singing happy birthday. The group sang in unison.

'Happy birthday to you, happy birthday dear Google …'

I wondered if the global search engine had so many fans that people had actually come out on a Wednesday night to celebrate its anniversary. Then I saw a cute sardar kid blow at five candles on a cake. I figured Google was his name or nickname. 'We can't discuss anything here,' I said. 'Too loud.'

'Fine, let's go home,' Saurabh said, and stood up. 'Just one stop at the chemist to buy Kayam Churna, Pudin Hara and Eno. For my stomach.'

'You have three stomachs? Why do you need three medicines?'

'Each has its own function. I'll explain on the way. Let's go.'

❖

My phone showed the time: 2 a.m. We recalled whatever we could from each testimony and made notes while we had it all fresh in our memory. We sat on the living room floor, sheets of paper and our laptops around us. I turned on the convection heater.

Saurabh scratched his head and pulled at his hair before he spoke again.

'We have to rule out some people. Let's exclude the parents. They couldn't have done it, right? Parents don't kill their kids.'

'It's extremely rare. Unless it's an honour killing or something.'

'What honour killing? They were honoured to have me as their son-in-law. Offered me a Jetta at the engagement.'

'Which you refused. I'm proud of you,' I said.

'Whatever. So no honour killing. Let's strike out Ramesh and Neelam Malhotra.'

'For now,' I said.

Saurabh looked up at me and sighed. He had eleven names written on a sheet of paper. He struck out Ramesh's and Neelam's names.

'Gopika is unlikely to have done it. Saw her size? Four feet nothing, forty kilos max. Tiny, like a kid. No way could she have pushed Prerna over,' I said.

'Are you again saying Prerna was too fat, bhai?' Saurabh said.

'Can you drop that? I am serious.'

Saurabh struck off Gopika's name.

'The driver could have done it,' Saurabh said. 'I am keeping Anwar's name.'

'Namrata?' I said.

'She is such a refined lady. But we haven't spoken to her yet, let's keep her for now,' Saurabh said.

'And what about the ex, Neeraj?' I said.

'Definitely keeping him. And meeting him soon too. Neeraj Arora, bastard.'

'Easy, Golu. Focus on the list.'

'Rule Maaji out?' I said.

'Yes,' Saurabh said and exhaled noisily. 'Though she seems the most psycho.'

'Couldn't have grappled with anyone though,' I said.

I crossed out Nirmala Malhotra's name from the list.

'Anjali,' Saurabh said. 'She was not in the house. The police have confirmed and checked her phone too.'

'Okay, strike her out too. Bindu?'

'She loved Prerna a lot, bhai. In fact, in that house, Bindiya bua loved her the most.'

'What makes you say that?'

'She would pack her tiffin for work every day. She would check on her twice a day, if she had eaten or not. Many times she would defend Prerna when Maaji or Neelam aunty made a nasty comment. No way, bhai, Bindu bua is not possible.'

'Hmm,' I said.

'Bindu bua is thin. She is weak too,' Saurabh said.

I did not respond.

Saurabh crossed out Bindu's name from the list.

'We are eliminating too many too soon,' I said.

'Let's focus,' Saurabh said, 'on the key ones. If proved otherwise, we can come back.'

'Fine, the last name here is Aditya,' I said. 'Keeping him for now.'

I checked the time. It was close to 3 a.m.

'How many do we have left finally?' I said.

'From eleven to four in this round. Anwar, Namrata, Neeraj and Aditya chachu.'

'Fine, let's talk to all of them,' I said.

My eyes began to close.

'Sorry, bhai, keeping you up. For my work,' Saurabh said, collecting the sheets.

'Not your work, our work,' I said.

Saurabh smiled.

'Speaking of our work, we have a pitch tomorrow morning in office.'

'Screw office,' I said as I dozed off on the rug.

Chapter 17

'And that, ladies and gentlemen, is CyberSafe's patented triple-layered safety protocol system that we plan to implement in your bank. The most secure safety solution in the market today,' I said, concluding my presentation. The group of eight men and women continued to sit motionless in front of me. Forget applause, I would have settled for a small grunt of approval or a one-word comment like 'interesting' or even 'okay'. No such luck. People who work in corporates have every bit of lifeblood sucked out of them. They don't react with enthusiasm. They simply exist and breathe, as if waiting for their eventual funeral.

'I finished my presentation, guys,' I said, in an attempt to bring the eight frozen faces in front of me back to life.

The oldest person in the client group, a gentleman with a French beard called Mr Nandy, finally broke the silence.

'That is all very good, but what would this package cost us?'

'My colleague, who has been budgeting this, will answer that,' I said.

I turned to Saurabh. He was engrossed in his phone.

'Saurabh?' I said. He continued to type a message with both hands.

'Saurabh?' Jacob, our boss, who was sitting next to Saurabh, spoke up.

'Present, sir,' Saurabh said in reflex, as if in class. He looked up from his phone.

'The client wants to know the annual maintenance budget on this,' Jacob said, and then hissed, 'The client, Saurabh.'

'Yes, yes, sir,' Saurabh said. 'One second.' He opened his laptop.

'Sorry, what was the question again, sir?'

❖

'What the hell were you doing?' I said to Saurabh.

We were in a shared Uber taxi. We had just left our office in Cyberhub Gurgaon for the Porsche showroom in South Extension. No other rider was in the car with us yet.

'Fixing a meeting with Namrata. And trying to locate Neeraj Arora.'

'In the middle of a client presentation?'

'I don't care. I am obsessed with the case. I have to find out who did this to Prerna. Anyway, we are meeting Namrata this Friday.'

'What did you tell her? Why are we coming?'

'I told her I'm quite disturbed. Want to talk to people who knew Prerna well, etc.'

I looked at Saurabh with disapproval.

'What?' he said.

'Did she buy it? Sounds a bit strange.'

'What else could I have said? I can't say we are investigating. I can't say I want to hang out.'

'Did you try the "we want to pitch CyberSafe" thing?'

'That's even more unbelievable. My fiancée and her co-founder died two weeks ago and I want to pitch business to her? Had to be an emotional reason.'

The driver pulled up on the side of the road. A girl in her early twenties got into the taxi. She sat in the front, but her three big shopping bags full of clothes wouldn't fit there.

'I'm sorry, can I put them in the back?' she said.

'Sure,' I said and smiled.

'Thanks. I'm Ruchi, by the way,' she said, brushing back a lock of hair from her forehead.

'I know,' I said, pointing to the Uber app on the driver's phone, which showed the names of the riders.

'Oh,' she said and laughed. 'Good to meet you.'

'Keshav,' I said, and extended my hand. 'Big shopping day?'

Over the last year, I had perfected a method of talking to women. Play it cool, show some interest but don't be too keen, and pitch a date fast.

'Yes,' she said. 'Going on a holiday with friends to Goa soon. And I had no clothes.'

'Or rather, you needed an excuse to buy new clothes.' I grinned.

'True. But a girl doesn't need an excuse to buy clothes,' she said with a laugh. I noticed she had the cutest nose.

Saurabh gave me a dirty look. Sure, I had deviated from our discussion. But a) he had booked the share cab as he is cheap and wanted to save money and b) why should I leave an easy score?

Our cab reached Ramesh's Porsche showroom and stopped outside.

'You here to shop too?' Ruchi said, surprised by the stop at the luxury car showroom.

'A man doesn't need an excuse to buy cars,' I said and winked. I think she believed it for a second. I guess it hadn't struck her yet that a supposed Porsche buyer had arrived in a shared Wagon R taxi. We exchanged smiles. I pointed at my phone, to check if she wanted to exchange numbers.

The driver seemed to be in a hurry to leave and began to move the car as soon as Saurabh stepped out.

'RuchiWanderer on Insta,' she shouted as the driver sped off.

'Wrong. So wrong,' Saurabh said. We walked towards the showroom.

'What's so wrong?' I said.

'Bhai, she is young. Seems to be in college.'

'Don't discriminate on age. As long as they are adults.'

'And I know you are not serious. This would be another of your flings.'

'Hook-ups, yes. She isn't looking for anything serious either, Golu. Just timepass.'

'What has happened to you, bhai? You used to be all about everlasting true love.'

'I was stupid. I don't believe in all that anymore.'

'What?'

'True love doesn't exist. The world is selfish. Nobody really cares about anyone.'

'Really? What about Prerna and me? Why are you giving so much time to this case? You do care.'

'I like solving riddles.'

'That's not true, bhai. There's more ...'

'Shh. Now where in this parking can we can find Anwar? And why do they have so many security guards all around the showroom?'

Chapter 18

'It's okay, sahib, I just had tea,' Anwar said. We were in the teashop across the showroom, and he was sitting on a stool with his back straight. His thick muscular frame and strong forearms made him look younger than his forty-five years of age. He wore a dark blue uniform, which had the logo of Malhotra Motors on the shirt pocket. The early evening light fell on his tanned face, making his beard even more prominent.

'Why did you want to talk to me?' Anwar said.

'Nothing to worry about,' Saurabh said.

'Worry?' Anwar said. A boy came and placed three cups of tea and four samosas in front of us. Saurabh lost focus for a few seconds as the aroma of fried dough hit him.

'We are not the police, so relax. We just want to know the truth,' I said.

'Truth?' Anwar said.

'About what happened to Prerna,' Saurabh said, mouth filled with samosa.

'I don't know, sahib. Prerna madam was absolutely fine. I myself took her for her wedding shopping several times. She seemed so excited and happy.'

'You had an argument with her,' I said.

Anwar was taken aback by my firm voice.

'Sahib, police already troubled Gopika about it. We had no quarrel.'

'Gopika's already confirmed in her testimony that you had an argument with Prerna. About you being in Gopika's room,' I said.

Anwar looked at Saurabh, surprised.

'It's okay, Anwar. Just answer him,' Saurabh said.

Anwar wiped the sweat on his forehead with a handkerchief.

'Madam used to work too much. She had a bad mood one day. She shouted at me. Only because I came up to have a cup of tea in the maid's room,' Anwar said.

'You were in Gopika's room when Prerna fell from the terrace?'

'Yes, sir, but …' Anwar fell silent.

'Go on, we are listening,' I said.

'Prerna madam was like my child. She was five when I started working for the Malhotras. I took her to school every day. In Amritsar and then in Delhi. Please don't suspect me.'

'Show me your phone,' I said.

'What?' Anwar said.

'If you have done nothing wrong, show me your phone. Right now.'

'What, sahib? I better go. Ramesh sir will call me,' Anwar said and stood up.

'You want me to tell the police that you refused to show your phone?' I said.

Anwar sat back down. He looked around the teashop. He took out his phone from his trouser pocket and handed it to me. The home screen had a picture of four kids, ranging in age from thirteen to two years old.

I opened the photo application on his phone. I found a few pictures of him and Gopika. In one of the selfies, she rested her head on his shoulder and he had his arm around her. In another, Anwar grinned while Gopika kissed his cheek.

'This is you having tea?' I said, displaying the photo to him.

Anwar turned to Saurabh and folded his hands.

'I don't have a bad niyat, sir. Please tell your friend not to talk to me like that. I am going to make Gopika my begum.'

'You are already married. The kids on your home screen are yours, no?' Saurabh said.

'My abba also has two wives. I love Gopika, sahib.'

'She is how old? Twenty-two? And you are forty-five?'

'I know, sahib. But she loves me too. In fact, that night I video-called my home in Aligarh. I wanted her to talk to Ammi and Abba.'

'What about your wife?'

'I introduced her to my wife too.'

Saurabh looked at me in shock. I shook my head and smiled. Some people manage quite well without Tinder, I guess.

'Prerna madam saw us in each other's arms. She yelled at me a lot. After Prerna madam found out, I thought I would make Gopika my wife first. That's why I went to her room. To introduce her to my family.'

'How long was the call?' I said.

'Maybe thirty minutes.'

'How did you do the video call?'

'On WhatsApp. In Gopika's room, I get good wi-fi. That's why I went there, sahib, I swear. Not for anything else.'

I went to Anwar's call history on his WhatsApp. On the day Prerna died, he had made a video call to a contact called 'Abba mobile'. The call lasted from 7.29 p.m. to 8.02 p.m.

'You made that call?' I said.

'Yes, sahib. My eldest son likes to take screenshots during video calls. He sent them to me. You can check in the photos section.'

I checked the photos on his phone again. It had four screenshots of a video call, with Anwar and Gopika in the frame. The time stamp on the screen matched the time of the call.

I returned Anwar's phone to him.

'He's clean. He has an alibi,' I said.

Saurabh nodded.

'Can I go, sahib?' Anwar said.

'Any other questions you have for him?' I said to Saurabh.

'Only one. How can you love two women at the same time?'

Chapter 19

Saurabh and I entered the Cherry Bar in The Leela Palace Hotel in Chanakyapuri. The elegant bar had views of the garden, fountains and water bodies outside. In a corner, a three-member band played music.

Aditya played the guitar and sang as well. A drummer and a keyboard player sat behind him. Aditya wore a black sleeveless T-shirt with a skull motif, along with ripped blue jeans. He had a bandana on his head and metal chains around his wrist.

He sang an old Guns N' Roses song, *November Rain.*

When I look into your eyes
I can see a love restrained
But darlin' when I hold you
Don't you know I feel the same?

A waiter handed us the menu. Saurabh went over the cocktails list in the dim light.

'Damn, eight hundred rupees for a mojito?' Saurabh said.

'That's before GST,' I said.

'Of course. The government has to take a few sips of every drink we have.'

We ordered two small bottles of Bira, the cheapest drink on the menu.

Aditya hit perfect notes even as he raised his volume and pitch.

Nothin' lasts forever
And we both know hearts can change
And it's hard to hold the candle
In the cold November rain.

The band took a break after the song ended. A young girl came up to meet Aditya. They spoke for a few moments and exchanged numbers. She gave him a tight hug, whispered something in his ear and kissed him on the neck before she left. Aditya moved to sit alone at one of the tables near the stage.

'Let's go,' I said.

Saurabh took a deep breath and stood up. We exchanged nods, reminding each other to be smooth.

'Hey, Aditya chachu,' Saurabh said.

'Saurabh?' Aditya said, looking up from his cup of green tea.

'Yes, wow, you sing here. We had a client meeting in the lobby. So cool to see you,' Saurabh said. 'You've met Keshav?'

Aditya rose and shook hands with me.

'Of course. Can I get you guys a drink?' Aditya said.

'We have our beers. We're good,' I said and pointed to our table.

'Come sit with me. I have ten minutes until my next set.'

We brought our drinks to his table.

'No drink?' I said.

'Not at work,' Aditya said and pointed to his Adam's apple. 'Affects my voice. Anyway, alcohol is not my high.'

I nodded. I noticed he had love bites and lipstick marks on his neck. He caught me staring at them and rubbed his hand on his neck.

'Sorry.' Aditya grinned. 'Perks of the job. Don't tell Ramesh bhaiya I work here, by the way.'

'No way,' Saurabh said.

'He sort of knows, though. He's extra disturbed these days, that's all,' Aditya said.

'Yes, so shocking. The whole thing,' Saurabh said.

'Yeah, man,' Aditya said and sipped his tea.

'Chachu, why would anyone do this to Prerna?'

Aditya placed his cup on the saucer and shook his head.

'Yeah, man, why? So fucked up,' he said.

'You have no idea, like, really? Your floor is right below the terrace. You didn't hear anything?' Saurabh said.

'What do you mean, man? I told you I was making music.'

'What music?' I said.

Aditya turned to me.

'You know about music? How can I tell you what music?'

'You sing covers, I'm guessing, going by the Guns N' Roses number. So what original music are you *making*, actually? Just curious,' I said.

'I got my own stuff, man. Working on various things ...' Aditya's words trailed off.

Saurabh spoke after a pause.

'Are things okay between you and Ramesh uncle now?'

Aditya shrugged.

'You know him, man. Rigid as fuck. He lost his daughter, so I don't say anything. But, yeah, he needs to calm down.'

'I agree,' Saurabh said, 'but you think ...'

'I better go. Need to warm up for the next set,' Aditya said, interrupting Saurabh. 'Mention my name to the waiter. You will get a discount.'

Chapter 20

'How can we find out anything if I can't interrogate them? Chit-chat won't get us anywhere,' I said.

'What to do? Aditya chachu is family. They see me as their son-in-law. I can't make them feel uncomfortable by asking too many questions,' Saurabh said.

We were in the reception of Kotak Mahindra Bank's New Delhi main branch on Barakhamba Road.

'Neeraj Arora,' I said to the receptionist for the third time. She had told us to wait for a moment twenty minutes ago.

I turned back to Saurabh.

'At some point the questions need to get a bit tough.'

'With this Neeraj creep, please be tough. I hate him,' Saurabh said.

'Why?'

'He was with Prerna.'

'But well before you.'

'Doesn't matter.'

A tall and milky white man emerged from behind the reception.

'You are here to see me?' He smiled in an over-friendly way as he walked up to us.

Saurabh grunted.

'Are you ... ?' Neeraj stopped smiling as he tried to place Saurabh. 'Are you ... sorry, I am confused.'

'Yes, I'm Saurabh. We never met but you must have seen my pictures.'

'You were Prerna's fiancé,' Neeraj said.

'Can we talk?' I said.

'About?' Neeraj said.

'Let's step out,' I said.

We headed to the Starbucks right outside the bank. Neeraj sat opposite me on an enormous sofa. His staff identity card hung around his neck from a lanyard. His gaze swung from Saurabh, who was ordering coffee for us, to me.

'Sorry, why did you want to meet me?' Neeraj said.

'To have a chat about Prerna,' I said.

Neeraj stiffened. His grey eyes now almost black, he spoke with long pauses between his words.

'What about Prerna? What happened to her ... it was terrible. Terrible.'

Saurabh returned from the counter with three cups of coffee and a plate loaded with muffins, cinnamon rolls and croissants. Did we really need to do a semi-buffet every time we investigated someone?

Saurabh took a seat next to me.

'Saurabh, I wanted to express my condolences. Totally unexpected,' Neeraj said.

Saurabh had a muffin in his hand. He paused from taking a bite and stared at Neeraj.

'Someone killed her,' he said, 'plain and simple'.

Neeraj swallowed at the word 'killed'.

'The papers said she fell down. An accident.'

Saurabh and I didn't respond.

'Why are you guys looking at me like that?' Neeraj said.

'When did you last speak to her?' Saurabh said.

Neeraj glanced at his wristwatch and stood up to leave.

'I don't have time for this. I'm expecting some customers.'

'Do you want the police to come to your office and do the interrogation instead?' I said.

Neeraj took a deep breath.

'I broke off with Prerna two years ago. What would I know?'

'You treated her so badly,' Saurabh said.

'I didn't mean to,' Neeraj said, and tilted his head to avoid eye contact. 'We were both too young. Anyway, how does it matter?'

'Why did you guys break up?' I said.

'I was young. She wanted commitment. I couldn't give it.'

'Is that it?' Saurabh said. 'Don't lie, you selfish asshole.'

'Saurabh,' I said.

'Fine. I felt I could do better. All my friends said I look far better than her. I told her to lose weight.'

'You dumped her because you thought she was not hot enough!' Saurabh said.

Neeraj kept his cup down, eyes darting here and there.

Saurabh continued, 'Do you know she went into depression? She quit her job. She lost her confidence.'

'Yes, but did she tell you how many times I apologised for it? I told you, we were young. I got carried away. My friends were all bringing their super-skinny girlfriends in short skirts to clubs. I felt I also wanted that. I was wrong.'

'Sick you are.'

'I told you I was wrong. I told Prerna I was wrong. I wanted to get back. Get married. I still did.'

'What do you mean "still did"?' I said.

'Nothing,' Neeraj said.

'I have some questions, answer truthfully,' I said.

'Sure.'

Saurabh chomped hard on his second muffin like it was an apple, taking out his frustration on the helpless food.

'How often did you speak to Prerna in the last year?' I said.

'Not much. I would send a message on chat every week. Mostly, she ignored me.'

'You sent messages after you knew she was with me?' Saurabh said, his big cheeks now pink like a baby's bottom.

'Yes,' Neeraj said.

'You ass ...' Saurabh stood up to strike him.

'You said be truthful,' Neeraj said, cowering in his seat. I pulled Saurabh back.

'Calm down, Golu. Focus on what we came for.'

'I came for this too. I always wanted to beat the shit out of this guy,' Saurabh said. He lifted a fork and pointed it at Neeraj.

'Cutlery down, Golu,' I said.

Neeraj continued.

'I wanted to get back with her. Saurabh came into the picture. But it was an arranged marriage.'

'So people in arranged marriages don't have feelings?' Saurabh said.

'Shh, Saurabh. Neeraj, did you guys actually speak? Did you meet her?'

'We spoke on the phone the few times she picked up. I met her twice this year.'

'This year? You fucking met her *this* year?' Saurabh said. When Saurabh uses the F word, you know all bets could be off soon. I knew how to calm him down. I slid the cinnamon roll towards him. When stressed, offer sugar.

'Try this. Really good,' I said. Saurabh looked at me in surprise, but took the plate anyway.

'When did you last meet her, Neeraj?' I said.

'I waited outside her Eato office in Noida. I begged her to talk to me when she left work. I told her to forgive me. I had been shallow and insensitive. Prerna had rare qualities. Smart, hard-working, caring, kind and fun. She was a dream partner.'

'You fucking realised she is going to be rich with Eato. That's the only reason you wanted her back. Isn't it? You light-eyed, extra-thin asshole,' Saurabh said.

'No. I missed her. I loved her.'

Something snapped in Saurabh at these words. Completely out of character, he leaned forward and grabbed Neeraj's throat. Neeraj's eyes popped wide as Saurabh choked him.

'I am going to kill this bastard.'

'Please, please, leave me,' Neeraj said. Customers and Starbucks staff turned to look at us. Of course, in Delhi nobody gives a damn about such small fights. Until blood is spilled, people remain cool and sip their lattes.

'Stop, Golu,' I said and yanked Saurabh's hand away from Neeraj's delicate neck.

We are here to get information. Remove jealous fiancé cap, wear the detective hat, I wanted to tell him.

'Neeraj, when was the last time you had any contact with her?'

'We chatted the day she died,' Neeraj said.

Saurabh and I sat up.

'About what exactly?' I said.

'I told her, it's Karva Chauth and the only person I can imagine as my wife is you. Saurabh don't hit me, please.'

'He won't,' I said, clasping Saurabh's hand tight. 'Saurabh, did Prerna ever mention this? Neeraj trying to get back with her?'

'No. She did say he keeps apologising. Nothing more.'

'What time did you chat with her?' I said.

Neeraj took out his phone from his pocket. He scrolled through his chats.

'Around six in the evening.'

'Can I see the chats?' I said.

'I wanted to formally propose marriage to her. Karva Chauth seemed like an auspicious day,' Neeraj said, handing me his phone.

Saurabh looked at the screen in my hand from the corner of his eye.

I scrolled up to the chats on 17 October, at 6.05 p.m.

Neeraj: Please P, meet me for five minutes.

Prerna: No N. I can't. Family at home. It's Karva Chauth.

Neeraj: But you are not married yet. Why are you celebrating it?

Prerna: I can't meet.

Neeraj: There's still time. We actually loved each other.

Prerna: Past tense. Am sure you have plenty of those mini-skirt girls now.

Neeraj: I don't want that. Please. Five minutes.

Prerna: Can't. And sorry, am busy. Have to go.

Neeraj: I just want to give you something. I am outside.

Prerna: Outside?

Neeraj: I mean in the A Block park of New Friends Colony. Right outside your house. I can see your bungalow.

Prerna: Are you stalking me??

Neeraj: No, I came here so it is easy for you. I am sitting on the corner bench.

Prerna: You are wasting your time. Go home.

Neeraj: Please P.

Ten minutes later, at 6.20 p.m.

Neeraj: Are you there?

Twenty minutes later, at 6.40 p.m.

Neeraj: I tried calling thrice. Please pick up. I saw the blue ticks. You have seen the messages.

One hour later, at 7.47 p.m.

Neeraj: I am leaving. All I wanted was five minutes.

The last message remained unread. I returned the phone to Neeraj.

'So you were there? Near her house when she died,' I said.

'Yeah. But I never met her. May I leave now? I have shown you everything.'

I nodded. Neeraj stood up to leave.

'Do you know what your being next to her house at that time means?' Saurabh said.

'What?' Neeraj said.

Saurabh grabbed his collar with both hands.

'That you are a fucking suspect. And I am on to you,' Saurabh said, his pink cheeks now an apple red.

Chapter 21

Namrata Taneja, co-founder of Eato, met us at the entrance of her office.

'Welcome, Saurabh,' Namrata said. 'So nice of you to come by. You are Keshav, right? We met at the engagement.'

'Yes,' I said, as she shook my hand firmly.

Eato had its office on the tenth floor of a building in Noida Sector 16. The two thousand square foot space had a long white desk with ten white chairs arranged on either side. Staff, all of them in their twenties, sat in front of computers typing code or preparing spreadsheets. Floor-to-ceiling windows filled the office with sunlight. There were three giant TV screens on the walls. They displayed statistics, like the number of users currently on the app, the current server load and the fulfilment rate. Namrata's cabin, which she used to share with Prerna, was at the other end of the white desk.

'Please, have a seat. Would you like peppermint tea?' Namrata said. She wore a sky blue raw silk saree. She had accessorised it with a thin silver necklace, along with matching earrings and bracelets.

Outside Namrata's window, I could see the DND flyway, the road that connected Noida with Delhi. She lowered the blinds halfway to cut the sunlight. We sat facing each other with the desk between us. The minimalist design made the room look straight out of a spaceship.

'Beautiful place,' I said.

'Thank you,' Namrata said. 'Prerna had a lot to do with the interior design.'

Her gaze shifted to Prerna's desk and chair, starkly empty on the opposite side of the cabin.

Saurabh stood up and walked up to the desk. On it were framed pictures of Prerna's family, and her computer. There was also a photograph with Saurabh from their engagement. Both of them clasping each other's hands, the new engagement rings clearly visible on their fingers.

'You have come here before, Saurabh?' Namrata said.

'Yes, a couple of times,' he said, wiping a tear from the corner of his eye. Namrata stood up. Her high heels click-clacked as she walked up to Saurabh.

'I am so sorry,' she said, and gave Saurabh a hug. I remained at Namrata's desk. I noticed the two trophies on it.

'Hot startups award', said one.

'Woman entrepreneur of the year award—Namrata Taneja', said the other.

A bunch of printed A4 sheets were next to the trophies. The keys of her Volkswagen acted as a paperweight. I leaned forward a little to see better.

'Eato Financial Reports for the latest quarter' was all I could read from the top of one of the sheets.

'You fine?' Namrata said to Saurabh. He nodded. They returned to her desk and took their respective seats. A staff member came in with a leather and wood tray, which had three cups of peppermint tea on it.

Along with the tea was a plate of walnuts and brick-red raisins.

'Goji berries. Superfood, lots of antioxidants,' Namrata said. When you have super eaters like Saurabh, how super the food is and how good it is for you doesn't matter. Saurabh took a fistful of nuts and goji berries in his hand, hoping to drown his sorrows in calories.

'You wanted to meet for a particular reason?' Namrata said, as she took a tiny sip of her tea.

'No, Namrata didi. It's just that I can't figure this out. What happened is so strange. One moment we are planning to spend our life together. The next she is gone, like forever.'

'I can relate to your pain,' Namrata said and sighed. 'She

and I built this company. Brought Eato till here. And now she's just gone.'

'I wanted to meet people close to her. To help understand the whole thing better,' Saurabh said.

Namrata took the corner of her saree and wiped her eyes.

'Sorry, I didn't mean to get emotional,' Namrata said and smiled. 'I am the founder CEO. What will the staff think? I have to stay strong.'

'It's busy here?' I said.

'Yes. We are growing. Three rounds of funding mean three sets of investors. They want to see performance, growth and profits. Raising money isn't all fun. You have to earn back much more.'

I squashed a goji berry in my fingers as I wondered how to probe further without raising her antennae.

'Did the staff here like Prerna?' I said.

'Like? Everyone loved her. I loved her. She was like a little sister to me,' Namrata said.

'Did the staff outside see her as strict? Anyone she had upset?' I said.

'Not at all. Ask Saurabh, he knows how considerate and kind she was.'

Saurabh nodded.

'How did you even start this business together?' I said. 'Just curious.'

'My dad and Ramesh uncle are old friends and business partners. When Prerna decided to develop this startup, Ramesh uncle sent her to me. I used to work as a software consultant. I loved her spirit and business plan. Both of us had some money saved, which we invested. The rest is history.'

'What happens to Prerna's stake now?' I said. Namrata looked startled.

'We have to figure out the paperwork. It would be her nominees, mostly Ramesh uncle. Really, Keshav? You think that's what we should be talking about?'

'I'm sorry,' I said. 'I'm considering a startup of my own, so had some questions.'

'One should still be sensitive, isn't it?' Namrata said, looking steadily at me. 'Anyway, I have an investor call now.'

Chapter 22

'You think your plan will work?' Saurabh said. He had put on enough cologne to be an air freshener for the entire planet. We were on our way to Malhotra House. I rolled down the window on my side to let in some air.

'Depends on your performance,' I said.

'Fine, I will try,' Saurabh said as our cab pulled into the driveway of the house.

❖

'It feels nice to have you here. Otherwise this house is full of sadness these days,' Bindu said, serving two scoops of daal in Saurabh's bowl.

'Thanks for having me over,' Saurabh said, 'even though I invited myself.'

'And for letting me tag along,' I said.

'What tag along? You are like family too,' Bindu said.

We were sitting at the twelve-seater table in the dining room on the ground floor of the house. Saurabh and I were to the right of Ramesh, who sat at the head. Neelam, Bindu, Ajay, Anjali and Maaji were also with us. Gopika kept coming from the kitchen with batches of hot phulkas. We had them with yellow daal, baingan ka bharta, bhindi masala and palak paneer.

'Where's Adi?' Ramesh said, tearing his phulka.

'He said he will be working late,' Neelam said.

'Singing at a bar while people get drunk. Some work,' Ramesh said.

'Why are you after him?' Maaji said. She only had yellow daal and rice on her plate. She mixed them with a shaky hand and ate slowly.

'Who is after him?' Ramesh said.

'Leave it, Ramesh ji,' Neelam said. 'How are you, Saurabh? Your parents came to see us last week. So nice of them.'

'They send their regards. I am good, aunty. Happy to be here tonight,' Saurabh said. 'You treat me like a son.'

'Of course, you are our beta,' Bindu said.

Good, Saurabh had laid the groundwork for our plan well.

'So, are you still helping the police?' Anjali said. I saw her properly for the first time that day. She looked pretty in her pink Donald Duck T-shirt.

Saurabh caught me staring at Anjali and coughed.

'Not really,' I said, composing myself. 'The police don't seem too keen to take our help. You heard from them, Ramesh uncle?'

'They said something about forensic reports being ready soon. They also wanted the mobile details of everyone in the house, God knows for what. She had an unlucky fall. Now close the matter.'

'What are you saying, Veerji? We must at least find out if someone did it,' Bindu said.

'You want neighbours to see a police Gypsy outside our house every day?' Ramesh said.

'O aaya si,' Maaji said, eyes still on her plate as she mumbled to herself. 'O aaya si. O aaya si.'

'Maaji, please be quiet,' Ramesh said. Anjali patted Maaji's back and gave her a glass of water.

'Sorry about that. Maaji is not keeping well,' Ramesh said. 'Anjali, take her to her room, please.'

Anjali held Maaji's hand as she stood up. Slowly, they walked out of the room to go up the stairs.

'I heard you met Namrata,' Ramesh said after they left.

Saurabh had just picked up another bite, and his hand froze on the way to his mouth.

'Yes, last week,' he said in a small voice.

'How come?' Ramesh said.

'I missed Prerna. Eato meant so much to her. I wanted to see her office again.'

Bindu patted Saurabh's wrist in support.

'Namrata called me. She was happy to meet you. But she seemed surprised at your friend's questions,' Ramesh said. 'Something about Prerna's stake. Why, Keshav?'

'Oh,' I said. 'Sorry, Uncle. Got curious.'

'Keshav beta, Namrata is like family to us. We have known her parents a long time.'

'I apologise on his behalf too,' Saurabh said.

'It's okay, beta. We trust Namrata. Prerna's share will be sorted out in due course. She shouldn't feel I sent you to put pressure on her.'

'We will be more careful,' Saurabh said as Anjali came back to the table.

Neelam topped up our katoris with more subzi. Punjabis assume you need a refill unless you do a near-violent protest.

'Enough, Neelam aunty. I'm full,' I said, waving my hands vigorously.

'You hardly eat,' she said, continuing to add more paneer.

'No, no. Really, I've had enough,' I shouted and covered the katori with my hand.

Anjali smiled at my attempts to ward off Neelam.

'Enjoy Neelam aunty's hospitality and love, Keshav. It's rare to have this,' Anjali said.

'Why? Geetu didn't feed you well or what?' Neelam said.

'She did, if you count pointing to a can of baked beans and bread in the kitchen as feeding well,' Anjali said and laughed.

'What? Geetu didn't cook?' Neelam said.

'No, both my parents hate cooking. Also, in America, meals are never so lavish. Nobody can beat you, Neelam aunty,' Anjali said.

Neelam gave a shy smile at the unexpected praise. She moved over to fill Saurabh's plate, and he didn't resist at all.

'Ramesh uncle, I had one little issue,' Saurabh said. 'I need your advice.'

Saurabh had finally come to our plan. Ramesh looked up from his plate.

'Advice? Yes, yes, sure. Tell me,' he said.

'Our lease expired in the Malviya Nagar flat. Work kept us busy. We couldn't finalise a new place. If you could suggest a guesthouse for a few weeks, we could move there,' Saurabh said.

'Ah,' Ramesh said. 'Let's see. There might be some places near the showroom.'

He tapped his forehead as he thought of options. This was not the outcome we wanted. We had to make this more emotional. I signalled to Saurabh to try harder.

'For food we can just eat bread and butter and manage. Ironic, I thought Prerna and I would take a new place together, now I have to figure out something.'

'Yes, life can be so cruel,' Ramesh said.

Damn, he was still not getting it.

Fortunately, Neelam saved us.

'Bread and butter? You need proper home food. Ramesh ji?' Neelam said and glared at her husband.

This time it worked.

'Oh. Why a guesthouse? What is this big house for? Stay here. Only for a few weeks, you said?'

Saurabh looked at me. It was my turn to play the part.

'No, Uncle, we can't. We can't impose …' I said.

'What impose? There's nothing like impose for family. Just the two of you, right? How much space do you need?'

'One room is enough,' I said. 'Wherever in this house is convenient for you.'

'Aditya has an entire floor,' Bindu said.

'No, don't ask him. He will complain. They are my guests. If it is okay with you boys, Prerna's room is there. Will that work for you?'

'I would have asked you for the same,' Saurabh said, as he high-fived me under the table.

Chapter 23

'Sorry, I'm late,' Anjali said.

In a maroon turtleneck and black slacks, with her huge laptop bag on her shoulder, she looked sleek and elegant.

'Coming from work?' I said.

'Sort of. I freelance now. I work out of a Starbucks near my old office.'

We were at Dunkin' Donuts in Cyberhub. Saurabh ordered hot tea with ginger for all of us and a selection of a dozen donuts that came in a massive pink box.

'Who is going to have so many?' I said.

'Chill, this is a takeaway box. We will take home whatever's left,' Saurabh said, picking up a sugar-glazed donut.

'Thanks for meeting me, guys,' said Anjali. She looked cuter than ever in her turtleneck. I wondered if Saurabh would be okay with me dating her now. After all, the family taboo didn't apply anymore.

'Donut?' Saurabh offered. She declined.

'I wanted to share a few things with you about Prerna didi's case,' Anjali said.

'What?' I said.

'About the family. It's not as perfect as they make it out to be. They are as dysfunctional as any other family.'

'Okay ...' I said, not knowing what to expect next.

'You guys still investigating the case?'

Saurabh and I looked at each other.

'We can't. I mean, we aren't able to,' Saurabh said. 'You heard Ramesh uncle. He didn't approve of Keshav asking Namrata didi questions. How will we ever investigate the family?'

'What about the police?' Anjali said.

'They don't seem that interested. Just doing some routine reports. To show they did work before closing the case,' I said.

'Yeah. Ramesh uncle wants to close the case. But Bindu masi and I, we both want to find out what happened. Even Maaji says she saw someone. Mrs Goel heard someone. How can we accept it as an accident?' She took a sip of her tea.

'We are not accepting that,' I said. 'You said you wanted to share something?'

Anjali leaned forward.

'Well, I'm sure you will find out more as you will be staying in the same house soon. But this family is expert at keeping a façade.'

'As in?' I said.

'Ramesh uncle's stressed.'

'Car sales overall are in a downturn.' Saurabh nodded.

'It's more than that. Uncle drinks alone in his house. Every night,' Anjali said.

'How do you know?' I said.

'I have seen and heard him. Fighting with Neelam aunty. Arguing with Prerna. Shouting at her. Walking up and down the stairs of the house at night. Smoking late at night, outside the house or on the terrace.'

'Wait, did you say terrace?' Saurabh said.

'Yeah, sometimes,' Anjali said. 'Why?'

'You think Uncle could be involved?' I said.

'I don't know. I'm just saying, why does he want the case closed so bad? Why does this entire family have a tendency to cover up things?' Anjali said.

'What other things have they covered up?' I said.

She pursed her lips.

'What, Anjali? Is there anything else they have hidden?' Saurabh said.

Anjali stared at the table, still silent. She seemed to be choosing her words carefully.

'Take your time,' I said, picking up my cup.

She sighed.

'I found out something I wasn't supposed to. Personal.'

'What?' I said.

'They made me swear not to tell anyone. It can bring shame to the whole family. Frankly, it is not connected to the case. I would rather not share it. Sorry, it has to come from the family first.'

'What is it, Anjali?' Saurabh said, keeping his third donut down.

'Nothing connected to the case, trust me on that. All I am saying is this family avoids the truth. They may want to give up on the case. You don't.'

'We are not going to,' I said.

'Yeah, thank you for that. Anything I can help you with, I'm there,' Anjali said.

'How well do you know Namrata?' I said.

'Her partner?'

'Anything about her? That you would be concerned about?' I said.

'Oh,' Anjali said after a pause. 'She's a suspect?'

I looked back without blinking.

'Are you serious?' she said and looked at Saurabh.

'She's not the only one. There's Neeraj too.'

'Didi's ex?'

'Yes, do you know him?'

Anjali shook her head.

'They broke up before I came to India. I do remember her being devastated though,' she said.

Saurabh and I looked at each other. More than anything, we wanted to know the shameful family secret now. However, pushing her wouldn't work. We'd have to be patient and not come across as too keen.

'There's six donuts left,' Saurabh said to Anjali. 'You want to take three back with you?'

Chapter 24

'This is Prerna's room, as you already know,' Ramesh said.

'Yes, Uncle,' I said, as Saurabh struggled to speak. 'Thank you so much.'

We entered the room on Ramesh's floor with two suitcases each.

'I can't tell you what a help you have been,' I said.

'Don't be formal. And join us for meals whenever you want. Or, Gopika can bring the food to you.'

'Oh, Uncle, we will order …' I said.

'This is home. Nobody needs to order from outside here,' Ramesh said as he left the room.

I opened my suitcases to arrange my clothes in the closet.

'Don't hit on Anjali,' Saurabh whispered.

'What?'

'Nothing. I have been meaning to say that. We are in this house now. Please don't use it as an opportunity.'

'Of course not,' I said, even as my heart sank a little. I guess she was still a no-no. I kept my empty suitcases along the wall.

Prerna's closets still had her clothes. Saurabh saw a maroon and mustard salwar kameez.

'I remember this. She wore it to Lodi Gardens, when you met her for the first time,' Saurabh said. He caressed the fabric, breaking down.

I placed my arm around his shoulder. 'Are you sure you can stay in this room?'

He nodded, collecting himself.

'This is the only way we will find out what happened to Prerna.'

❖

ACP Rana had an air-conditioned office three times the size of an inspector's cabin and ten times as clean. Inspector Singh had called me in the afternoon, asking Saurabh and me to come over. In his new role, ACP Rana worked on managing police deployment for VIP security and rallies. He saved the spreadsheet open on his computer and turned to us.

'I miss crime,' ACP Rana said. 'Murder, rape, robbery. Much better than these stupid reports and paperwork.'

'Prerna Malhotra's case may not even involve a crime, sir,' Singh said.

'Hundred per cent there is a crime. She wasn't a petticoat left to dry to just fall off the roof,' ACP Rana said. He looked at Saurabh.

'If nothing else this hero must have pushed her.'

'What are you saying, sir?' Saurabh said, his face white. ACP Rana guffawed. Nobody else even smiled.

'Joke, guys.'

I fake-smiled.

'Anyway, what's the progress? Singh wanted to meet here. Are you troubling him?'

'No, sir,' I said.

'These boys are not telling me anything,' Singh said. 'They read testimonies, which I gave them access to. After that they questioned people. They even moved into Malhotra's house.'

I looked at Inspector Singh, surprised.

'You thought I wouldn't find out? Ramesh Malhotra told me you guys are staying with him,' Singh said.

'Well done, ghar jamai.' ACP Rana looked at Saurabh and chuckled.

'Sir, please.' Saurabh squirmed.

'If I don't joke, what is my life? Sit in front of this stupid computer in the office, listen to my stupid wife at night,' ACP Rana said.

'You don't seem keen to work with us either, Inspector,' I said to Singh.

'Why should I work with you? I'm police. Who are you?'

'Don't fight like my mother and my wife do,' ACP Rana said. 'Use them, Singh. They are in the house. They can help you.'

Singh let out a huge sigh.

'The family is not keen to pursue the case. There are no leads. Maybe we should close it.'

'Testimonies revealed anything?' ACP Rana said.

'Nothing, sir. Just normal family disputes,' Singh said.

ACP Rana leaned back in his swivel chair. He turned to Saurabh and me.

'What do you guys think?'

'No way can we close the case,' I said. 'We have even shortlisted some suspects.'

'Suspects?' Singh squinted at me.

'See, they are overconfident idiots. But sometimes they do come up with good things. Listen to what they have to say. Don't get ego into it, Singh,' ACP Rana said.

Singh let out a huge breath and turned towards us.

'Fine, tell me. Who are the suspects?'

'Aditya, Namrata and Neeraj right now.'

'How did you reach that conclusion?' Singh said with exaggerated patience.

We told him about our meetings and how we arrived at our shortlist.

'Just theories,' Singh said.

'Next step is collecting evidence. That's why we moved into the house,' Saurabh said.

Singh did not respond.

'You see their value? Work together, you will solve this. They need your backing. You need their intelligence,' ACP Rana said.

'Do you mean I'm not intelligent, sir?' Singh said.

'Don't get touchy now, Singh. My wife does this. I will tell her the maid has cooked well, and she will say, "Do you mean I don't cook well?" Annoying, it is. Just use them. They are already in the house.'

Singh remained silent.

'Deal? Friends?' ACP Rana said. 'Shake hands now.'

Singh, Saurabh and I obediently shook hands.

'Good. All the best,' ACP Rana said and stood up. 'I have to go. Meeting my wife and mother-in-law at Ambience Mall. She wants to see *Housefull 4* in gold class. See the ticket prices? That's a crime right there.'

Singh shook hands with ACP Rana and left. Saurabh and I remained in Rana's office.

'Listen you two, don't reveal everything to Singh.'

Saurabh and I looked at him, surprised.

'You made us shake hands,' I said.

'This Ramesh could try and cut a deal with Singh. To close the case.'

'Ramesh uncle won't want to find out who killed his own daughter, sir? To get her justice?' Saurabh said.

'Some people just prefer peace of mind over justice. Anyway, I better go. My wife hates missing even a second of Akshay Kumar.'

Chapter 25

'Sit in the car,' Saurabh said, pointing Neeraj to the Ola cab we had hired for his second round of interrogation.

'I have a meeting,' Neeraj said, swallowing hard. 'My performance review with my boss.'

Saurabh grabbed Neeraj's collar.

'I'm your boss,' Saurabh said. 'Sit in the damn car.'

The Ola driver turned around to look at the commotion going on in the backseat. Saurabh released his grip on Neeraj's shirt.

'Keep driving. We will give you five stars,' Saurabh said to the driver.

'Actually, there is even a six-star rating now. Please give me that along with a compliment.'

I had put the destination as Ridge Road, a forested area in Delhi. At least in the newspapers, all kidnappers in Delhi take their victims there.

'What do you want?' Neeraj said when the vehicle started to move.

'You are one of our prime suspects,' I said.

'Suspect?' Neeraj said.

'Forget suspect. I am pretty sure you did it,' Saurabh said, jabbing Neeraj in the ribs.

'What?' Neeraj said, shocked.

'Have you ever sat in the park outside her house before?' Saurabh said.

'No,' Neeraj said.

'And the day you do she falls from the terrace and dies,' I said.

'Well, I was shocked too,' Neeraj said.

Saurabh took the lanyard of the bank ID around Neeraj's neck and tightened it like a noose. Neeraj began to scream.

'Help, help,' he said.

The driver turned around again.

'Sir, what is this? I thought you were decent people.'

Saurabh let go of the lanyard. Neeraj gulped some air.

'Don't be over-dramatic, okay? I barely tugged at it,' Saurabh said.

'I could report you to the police for what you just did,' Neeraj said.

'The police are working with us. So, go fuck yourself,' Saurabh said.

'What?' Neeraj said.

I flashed my Z Detectives business card.

'We stopped the police from coming to the bank,' I said. 'They were coming. With a warrant to arrest you.'

'What? Why?' Neeraj said.

The driver turned around again.

'Is he a criminal, sir?' he said to Saurabh. Saurabh nodded and gave a business card to the driver as well.

'Are you police?' the driver said, eyes back on the road.

'Detectives,' I said.

'Then it's okay if you want to beat him up. We are about to reach the Ridge. Fix him good,' the driver said.

'Can you please just drive?' Neeraj said. 'I am not a criminal.'

'Everyone says the same,' the driver said as we entered the forested area.

'Driver bhaiya, can you give us some privacy?' I said. 'Pull over to the side for ten minutes?'

The driver seemed a bit disappointed to not be a part of the action as he stepped out of the car.

'Show me your phone again,' I said to Neeraj, after the driver had moved away.

'Why?' Neeraj said.

'I want to see your location history,' I said.

'What's that?' Neeraj said.

'Google Maps knows where you were, I want to confirm it.'

Neeraj passed his iPhone to me. Fortunately, like most people, he hadn't switched off his location tracking services. If one doesn't, Google literally tracks every step you take, wherever you have been with your phone.

The 'Your Timeline' feature on the Google Maps app showed in blue lines wherever Neeraj had visited that day.

'Okay, I see you in office at 5.30 p.m. on 17 October. The map shows you went to New Friends Colony. A Block. You reached at 6.05 p.m.'

'I already told you. I reached the A Block park. I sat on the bench. I called Prerna. She didn't talk to me. I sent messages, she replied saying she can't meet. Then she stopped replying completely. I waited for an hour or so and then left.'

'Wait,' I said and checked the phone. The Google Maps history showed that he left A Block at 7.47 p.m.

'You stayed for an hour and forty minutes,' I said.

'Obviously I don't remember the exact duration,' Neeraj said.

'Bhai, that means he was there when Prerna fell down. From the park he would have seen a crowd gather around the house. He saw her dead.'

'Did you?' I said.

Neeraj remained silent.

'Answer us, you idiot. And don't you dare lie,' Saurabh said.

'I did,' Neeraj said softly.

'What did you see, asshole? And why the fuck didn't you tell us that day?' Saurabh said, his face crimson with anger.

'I saw a light come on in the terrace. From a distance, I could make out her silhouette up there.'

'You saw her alive on the terrace. Probably the only person who did,' I said.

'Apart from the killer,' Neeraj said.

'What do you mean?' I said.

Neeraj took a deep breath. 'I couldn't see clearly from that far. I saw Prerna on the terrace, arranging something on the ledge. I tried to call her. She cut my calls.'

'Go on,' I said.

'She went out of sight as she walked away from the terrace edge,' Neeraj said. 'After a few minutes, she became visible again. This time I saw her back against the ledge. She moved away and returned, her back to the ledge, two more times. Then she fell, backwards. Then I heard a loud thud as she hit the ground.'

'What did you do then?' I said.

'I panicked. Something felt wrong. I didn't want to be seen there. My father is a senior IAS officer. He wouldn't want me to get involved in this. I ran away from there. You can check Google Maps. I went straight to my home in Bapa Nagar.'

'Coward,' Saurabh said.

Neeraj didn't respond.

'Did you see anyone else on the terrace?' I said.

'No. It was too far and high. But nobody presses their back against the ledge like that. Someone had to be there, pushing.'

'And it wasn't you?' Saurabh said.

'No,' Neeraj said. 'Not at all, I swear.'

Saurabh slapped Neeraj hard.

'Why? It wasn't me,' Neeraj said, almost in tears.

'Just,' Saurabh said. 'And you could be lying.'

I looked at Neeraj.

Something struck me. If Neeraj had gone to kill Prerna, how would he have planned to get into the house? How would he know Prerna was observing the fast for Karva Chauth? How would he presume Prerna had left the back door open? The killer knew Prerna was on the terrace and had access to the back entrance.

'Leave him, Golu,' I said.

'What?' Saurabh said, surprised.

'It's not him. Go, Neeraj. Do you want us to drop you somewhere?' I said.

'I would rather walk. Thanks,' Neeraj said.

He got out of the car, took fast steps and vanished round the corner.

I told Saurabh my reasoning after Neeraj left.

Saurabh sighed.

'Agree?' I said.

Saurabh nodded.

The Ola driver came back.

'You let him go?' he said.

'Yes, he's innocent,' I said. I changed the destination to Malviya Nagar.

'I like you guys, I will give you five stars as well,' the driver said as the car sped towards our house.

Chapter 26

'Damn, that back door lock. How come it didn't strike us?' Saurabh said, crossing Neeraj's name out from our shortlist.

'Sometimes facts reveal themselves slowly,' I said. 'And what is this drink? Sugar syrup and whiskey?'

'My special cocktail. Honey with whiskey. So satisfying, isn't it?'

'For sugar addicts, yes,' I said.

We were in our Malviya Nagar house, which we had not vacated yet.

'It isn't likely to be Namrata either,' Saurabh said.

'Oh,' I said.

Yes, the back door access logic applied to her too.

Saurabh nodded. He stood up from the sofa, lost in thought, and walked to the kitchen. He came back with an extra-large one-kilo pack of Haldiram's bhujia. How is it legal to sell these unhealthy things? Or why don't they at least come with a warning? Like those cigarette packets have pictures of people with cancer, maybe these can have pictures of super-fat uncles facing cardiac arrest or bedridden, obese Punjabi aunties. I raised an eyebrow.

'C'mon, don't snack-shame me. What are drinks without munchies?' Saurabh said.

'When are you going to go on your diet?' I said.

'Please don't start again. I am sad, no? My fiancée died. Cut me some slack.'

'Seriously? You are going to use that?'

'Sorry, I'll have a salad after this,' Saurabh said. 'Can we come back to the case?'

I wanted to tell him eating healthy meant eating salad *instead* of bhujia, not *after* it. I decided to stick to the case instead.

'Aditya is the only one remaining on our shortlist.'

'Chachu?' Saurabh said.

'He lives right below the terrace. He is strong enough to push her. He hates his brother. Doesn't have money. Sees so much being spent on Prerna's wedding. Gets jealous.'

'Maaji kept saying "O aaya si", remember?' Saurabh said.

'Yes ... "he had come",' I said.

'Exactly. She said "he", a guy. She saw a guy lurking around her room.'

'Maaji is a bit off. Not fully there,' I said.

'I realise that. But sometimes even mentally unstable people say something truthful.'

I finished my drink. Saurabh began to make another one with honey for me. I stopped him.

'Plain water and whiskey for me, please.'

'Bhai, I am hurt you don't like my cocktail,' Saurabh said, with a morose face.

'Focus, Golu.'

Saurabh handed me my drink sans sugar.

'You think it is Chachu?' he said.

'He is definitely prime suspect. To confirm, we have to find more evidence.'

'How?'

'What are we in the Malhotra house for, Mr Almost-son-in-law?'

❖

'Malhotra ji, no need for all this formality,' Singh said.

Saurabh, Ramesh, Singh and I were on the ground floor of the Malhotra house. Gopika placed samosas, pakoras, dhokla, barfi, laddoos and gajar halwa on the huge coffee table in front of us.

'I have some updates. The DNA forensic report came. We also have the cell phone tower location report,' Singh said.

He opened his leather briefcase and took out two files.

'This is the cell phone tower location report,' Singh said, opening the first brown file. 'Everyone was at home apart from Anjali, who seemed to be on the move. We have her cell phone tower locations as the airport, Aerocity, Dhaula Kuan, AIIMS, Ashram Chowk and here.'

'Yes,' Ramesh said. 'She'd been out of town.'

'Yes, we saw her Uber ride too in the testimony. She came after the incident. However, all other family members were at home.'

'I was out,' Ramesh said. 'I told you before, I went to get paan.'

'Possible, sir,' Singh said. 'This is just a cell phone tower location. The paan shop is close, your phone would still be connected to the same tower.'

'Okay,' Ramesh said.

'I have something more interesting, sir.'

'What is it?' Ramesh said, biting his lower lip.

'Ms Namrata Taneja's phone also shows A Block, New Friends Colony cell phone tower location at that time.'

Saurabh and I looked at each other. Namrata lived and worked in Noida.

'You tracked her phone too?' Ramesh said.

'Of course, sir. We don't do a half-job,' Singh said. He clearly expected praise. Instead, Ramesh replied with a grunt. Inspector Singh took a bite of his samosa and continued.

'That's not all. We checked Neeraj Arora. The ex-boyfriend you mentioned in the testimony. Same cell tower location—New Friends Colony.'

'What?' Ramesh said, so loud that even Gopika peeked from the kitchen, wondering what was going on. Singh smiled with pride.

'Told you, sir, we do a thorough job.'

'What was that bastard doing here? Did he do it?' Ramesh said.

Singh shrugged. He smiled and kept the file on the table. He filled his plate with a samosa, a laddoo and a mound of gajar halwa. It's hard for Delhi Police to remain fit. Wherever they go, they are fed.

'Yes, Neeraj was in the park. We know. But it's not him,' Saurabh said.

'What?' Singh said, irritated that we were stealing his thunder.

Saurabh related our meetings with Neeraj and how we had reached our conclusion.

'Damn,' Singh said. 'You guys should have told me this before.'

The inspector put his plate back on the table. We had taken away his primary suspect. Hard to enjoy gajar halwa after that, I guess.

'Forget it, Ramesh ji. There's no point. I will leave,' Singh said and stood up.

'What is this, Singh sir?' Ramesh said, looking up at Singh's upset face.

'Ramesh ji, I need to be valued,' Singh said.

'You are. Sit down. Eat the samosas. They are fresh,' Ramesh said and turned to Saurabh and me. 'And both of you—don't insult the police. Keep them in the loop.'

'But Uncle—'

Ramesh interrupted him.

'Apologise,' he said.

'Sorry, Singh sir,' Saurabh and I said in unison.

After a pause, Singh sat down.

'Singh sir, the second file?' Ramesh said.

'Yes,' Singh said. 'It is the forensic report. Unless these boys already know what's in this too.'

'Of course not, sir. Please share the findings,' Ramesh said.

'Fingerprints and DNA assessments. From two different labs. We don't do all this for every case, Ramesh ji. For you I am doing my level best,' Singh said.

'You are like family to us, Singh sir,' Ramesh said.

Singh opened the second file.

'We did a fingerprint analysis. We took prints from the body, several places on the terrace, the Karva Chauth thali, sieve and dupatta,' Singh said.

'And?' Ramesh said.

'Nothing. On the body or anywhere. Nothing at all,' Singh said, and turned to us. 'Figure that out, Mr Detectives.'

'No fingerprints at all?' Saurabh said.

'Her own, of course. No other fingerprints,' Singh said.

'I just told you, sir. Neeraj saw her struggle on the terrace. There was someone,' Saurabh said.

The inspector rubbed his chin.

'Ever heard of gloves, Mr Saurabh?' Singh said, as if he were the first person in the world to crack that theory.

'What about the terrace? And the thali?' Ramesh said.

'Nothing. Just near the ledge in one place ...' Singh said, and paused mid-sentence.

'One place what?' Saurabh said.

'One place we found your fingerprints, detective sir,' Singh said, his eyes shining with glee.

'Oh,' Saurabh said. 'Of course. I went there and leaned over the ledge. Are you suspecting me again?'

'I had my eyes on Neeraj. But you say no. Who else then?' Singh said.

'Sir, c'mon,' Saurabh said.

'Don't start again, you guys. What else, Singh sir?' Ramesh said.

'We also did a full DNA analysis from two different labs again. Used the latest American machines,' Singh said.

'What is that?' Ramesh said. 'This DNA?'

'All of us have a unique biological DNA, which can be found in any of our body cells. If there was a scuffle, some DNA of the killer is bound to be on the victim's body. Right, Singh sir?' I said.

'Why don't you only do the talking?' Singh said.

'Sorry, sir,' I said. 'I didn't mean to interrupt.'

The inspector gave me a dirty look and continued.

'Skin cells or something from the nails or hair. Something from the killer will usually end up on the dead body in the case of a struggle. That will have the killer's DNA,' Singh said. He flipped to the last page of the report.

'Did we find something?' Ramesh said, drawing out his words.

'Nothing. The team couldn't find any foreign DNA on the body at all. Not even your future son-in-law's.'

'I didn't meet her that day,' Saurabh said.

'Why do you keep explaining yourself?' Singh said.

Ramesh took both the files from Singh. He put on his reading glasses and flipped through the pages.

'I am telling you, sir. Either the killer got lucky and no DNA or fingerprints came on your daughter. Or the killer is too clever. Thought beyond just gloves,' Singh said.

Ramesh spent the next ten minutes reading the files. Singh finished the snacks on his plate and took another helping of the gajar halwa.

'This is a lot of work, Singh sir, thank you so much. We still don't have all the answers, but this is progress. What do you say, boys?'

'Of course, Uncle. Inspector Singh is the best,' Saurabh said.

Now I know Saurabh had the itch to suck up to Singh after we had upset him, but he didn't need to be so fake and overdo it.

'Well,' Singh said and patted Saurabh's back. 'Glad you realise that.'

Wow, he bought it, I thought. Praise can blind even seasoned interrogators, I guess.

Chapter 27

'I want to sleep,' I said. I fumbled for Saurabh's phone in the dark, to shut the annoying, super-loud 5 a.m. alarm. Saurabh was up and had already taken a shower. He was wearing a black hoodie for Operation Adi Search. I shut the alarm and my eyes. Saurabh pulled my arm.

'Get up, our window is limited,' Saurabh said.

I dragged myself out of bed. Half-asleep, I went to the bathroom and splashed ice-cold tap water on my face.

'Okay, so your plan is we get in before Gopika? And hide?'

'There's no other way. Only he has the keys to his apartment.'

I put on a thick black woollen sweater over my T-shirt.

'So, how does this work again?' I said.

'Every morning, around 6 o'clock, Gopika goes to Adi chachu's place to clean it. He wakes up earlier, around 5.30, and leaves the door open for her. She comes, cleans and leaves.'

'While Adi chachu sleeps?'

'No. Most mornings he goes for a jog while she's in the apartment. After he opens the door for her, he goes back to his room to change into running wear. That's when we need to get inside and hide. And we can do the search after Gopika has cleaned the house and left.'

'But Gopika could see us in the apartment. Or Adi chachu himself could, before he leaves for his jog.'

'I told you. We have to hide until both leave.'

'Idiotic plan. We are vulnerable.'

'You have a better one?'

I shook my head.

'Thought so. Follow me to the staircase. Be quiet. Like a nimble cat,' Saurabh said, as the ninety-six kilo feline walked out of the room.

❖

'Saurabh, this is insane,' I whispered. 'Waiting on the steps like this. What if someone wakes up?'

'Shush … Nobody will. It is still so early, and it's cold and dark.'

We sat on the steps going up to the terrace, right above Adi's apartment. I checked the time. It was 5.40 a.m.

'Shh …' Saurabh had his finger on his lips.

Five anxious minutes later, we heard a latch open. The soft creak of a door being opened, followed by absolute silence. Two minutes later, Saurabh gestured for me to stand up.

'You sure?' I mouthed.

Saurabh nodded. We tiptoed our way down the few steps to Adi's apartment. With his frame, Saurabh is no ballerina. Despite all his attempts, his footsteps sounded like small thuds.

Creeeak … Adi's unlocked door made an eerie sound as Saurabh pushed it open. My heart beat super-fast. What would we say if we got caught? What the fuck were we doing trying to get into Adi's residence? Maybe we could say we had been sleepwalking? But both of us?

I told my overactive mind to shut up.

Saurabh and I stepped inside the house, into Aditya's drawing room. It was dark inside. I bumped my right knee into a dining chair. The screeching sound it made sent shivers down my spine. Despite the excruciating pain, I couldn't scream. I breathed hard, deep and long.

'Shh!' Saurabh said. He pointed to the bedroom on the left. We had to avoid that room. We turned towards the room on the right, Adi's studio.

We tiptoed into the room, which had a thick, soundproof door. Total darkness and silence surrounded us as padded noise-reduction walls covered all sides.

'This is scary, Golu,' I said, checking my pulse.

Saurabh walked to the bathroom door inside the studio. He opened it. Both of us moved into our designated hiding place and shut the door from within.

We stood in the bathroom, one ear glued to the door. The soundproofing meant we couldn't hear anything from the outside world. It was sometime before I spoke.

'Let's open the studio door a bit. Otherwise we can't hear anything or figure out what's going on.'

Both of us walked back into the studio. I opened the studio door about ten degrees. Through the tiny gap, I peeped out. I couldn't see anyone. However, I heard the clanking of utensils in the kitchen.

'Gopika is already here,' I whispered.

'What about Chachu? Is his bedroom door open?' Saurabh said.

I opened the studio door some more. The sounds from the kitchen continued. I looked at the bedroom door—it was still shut. I checked the dining table. I saw a packet of Kellogg's Special K cereal, a bowl, a coffee mug and a yellow carton of Amul skimmed milk.

I shut the studio door again.

'Is his room door open? Is he around?' Saurabh said.

'Can't say,' I said, 'but there is breakfast cereal on the table.'

'Oh, which cereal?'

'Special K. Can you focus, Saurabh?' I said. 'When we came in earlier, the cereal wasn't there. Adi must have just eaten.'

'Yeah, maybe he had some right before he went for his jog.'

'Okay, so he's not likely to be around. We can go to his room now.'

Saurabh nodded. I opened the studio door slightly again. I looked across the hall at Adi's room. It would take twenty seconds to dart across, and we would have to do it without making any noise.

I froze as Gopika stepped out of the kitchen into the hall. Why had she suddenly come out? I shut the studio door, only leaving it slightly ajar to get a view. She collected the cereal bowl and mug from the table and took them back to the kitchen. I heard the sound of water splashing. The time was now.

I tugged at Saurabh's hoodie, signalling for him to move. I opened the studio door. We stepped into the hall. A phone rang in the kitchen, making us freeze. Gopika picked it up.

'Arrey, every day good morning, wah, wah,' she said and laughed in a flirtatious manner. I guess, in her circles, she had her own set of fans. She continued to chat with her admirer. I heard her bangles jingle as she continued to scrub in the kitchen.

Saurabh and I took long but silent strides across the room.

I reached Adi's bedroom. I turned the doorknob to open it.

'One minute, Gopika. Changing,' Adi screamed from inside. Chills far greater than driving a bike in the Delhi winter went through me from head to toe. I saw Saurabh's distraught expression. He looked like one of those pigs about to burst open in the Angry Birds game. We didn't breathe, lest we made a sound. Gopika remained busy with her phone call in the kitchen.

I pointed to the studio. Saurabh and I quickly retraced our steps. I kept the door ajar to hear and see what was happening outside.

Adi came into the hall in a little while.

'I'm leaving. Shut the door behind you when you go.'

Gopika cut her call. She came out of the kitchen and into the hall.

'Ji, Aditya saab,' Gopika said. 'Should I clean the studio today?'

Please say no, please say no, I said to myself.

Adi paused before he spoke again.

'Sure. Clean it. Don't touch anything though. But fix my bedroom first. It's very messy.'

'Ji, haan. You're going out in this cold weather? Very brave of you.'

'Have to look good on stage. Need to stay fit. Every day, a six-kilometre run. Then an hour at the gym,' Adi said.

I heard the main door open.

'Also, Gopika, make me scrambled eggs. I'll have them when I come back.'

'Okay, same as before? Six eggs. Whites only?'

'Yeah, thanks,' Aditya said. His apartment door finally slammed shut.

'He's gone,' I said, gently closing the studio door.

Saurabh let out a sigh of relief.

'What the hell?' Saurabh said. 'He was still here. We would've been so screwed.'

'Your plan, mister,' I said.

Saurabh wiped his forehead.

'Close shave,' he said. 'We need some light. This dark studio is killing me.'

'Switch on the bathroom light. The main studio light will be too much. Gopika might notice it.'

Saurabh flicked the bathroom light switch on. The studio became more visible. I looked around. There was a long desk with an iMac computer on it, a digital piano keyboard, a mike and several speakers. A guitar, a saxophone and a violin hung on a wall. The opposite side had wall-to-wall wooden closets. I sat on one of the swivel chairs in the studio.

'What are you sitting so relaxed for? We have a job to do.'

'You heard him. He said clean my room first. We can't go there now.'

Saurabh stood in front of me as I swivelled on my chair.

'He told her to clean the studio too,' Saurabh said.

'Yeah.'

'Aren't you worried? What do we do when she comes here?'

'When she comes here, we will be in Adi's room.'

'How will we cross over?'

'That's what I am thinking too. I suggest you sit down as well, rather than orbiting me.'

Saurabh plonked himself down on another chair. As he adjusted himself, his elbow hit the piano's keys. The loud musical sound filled the room.

'Fuck, Saurabh, what are you doing?' I said.

'Don't worry, soundproof room,' Saurabh said, pointing at the padded walls.

He sat in silence for a minute.

'Thinking about the crossover?' I said.

'Yeah, but I need food to think, bhai. Why didn't we plan for breakfast?'

'Anyone in the family could catch us sneaking around, and you are worried about jam and toast?'

'No, not like that. Although jam and toast sounds good.'

'We are going to be toast.'

'Okay, okay, thinking,' Saurabh said, pressing his temples with his fingers. I stood up and opened the studio door again. I heard the loud whirring sound of a vacuum cleaner. It came from Adi's room.

I checked the time: 6.30. Adi had left ten minutes back. A six-kilometre jog and an hour at the gym meant he'd be gone for about one and a half to two hours. To be safe, we had until 8 to search the place and leave.

I shut the door.

'We have to wait at a third place. Neither the studio, nor Chachu's bedroom. Somewhere else—a holding area,' Saurabh said.

'But where?' I said.

Saurabh shrugged.

'This is a two-bedroom apartment,' Saurabh said. 'There is no safe place.'

I pointed to the wooden closets on one side of the studio.

'No,' Saurabh said. 'No, bhai, no.'

'Open them,' I said.

Saurabh shook his head as he walked up to the closet. He opened the two wooden doors. Inside were four long shelves. On the first were books and magazines related to music. The second one had a collection of CDs, all outdated now in the world of streaming audio. It also had several boxes filled with cables. The third shelf had blankets, towels and bedsheets. The bottom shelf had empty guitar cases and old, discarded packaging material for musical instruments and computer equipment.

'Slide in,' I said.

'Seriously?' Saurabh said.

'No other way. Adi told Gopika not to touch anything. So she won't open this closet, hopefully.'

The shelves were at least four feet wide, three feet deep and twelve inches high. If we scrunched up, we could squeeze in there and wait until Gopika left. I suggested to Saurabh that he take the bottom shelf, given his weight. I preferred the shelf with the soft blankets anyway.

The wood protested as Saurabh climbed in like a bear in a tight cave. I moved a few blankets aside and slid onto mine as well. We kept the closet door slightly open, to feel less claustrophobic and have access to oxygen. Both of us lay facing the closet door, like chickens in compact cages.

'Bhai,' Saurabh groaned.

'Yeah?'

'Too tight. Hard to breathe.'

'She will leave in thirty minutes or so. She has to go down to make breakfast.'

'I hope so. I want to pee.'

'Hold it in.'

'I didn't even use the bathroom in the morning.'

'Shut up, Golu. Too much information.'

Saurabh became silent. For a while, all we could hear was our own breaths. And then something else—a fart. Yes, my best friend farted, in the worst place at the worst time.

'Golu, what the hell?' I said, trying to cover my nose in the cramped space.

'Sorry. Not in my control.'

'Really?'

'Well, I tried my best.'

'Shut up now.'

I opened the closet door a few inches more, to re-circulate the air faster. Every minute seemed like an hour. The studio door opened after ten minutes.

'Sweety? I am your Sweety?' Gopika said and giggled. She was on her phone again.

She entered the studio and plugged in the vacuum cleaner. Loud noise from the appliance filled the room.

'What? Sweety? Can't hear,' she shouted and cut the call.

She vacuumed for another five minutes, after which she disconnected the device and took it out of the room. She returned with a cleaning cloth and was wiping the tables when her phone rang again.

'What Sweety-Sweety you keep doing? Why no gift for Sweety?' Gopika said. Saurabh and I maintained pin-drop silence. She continued to flirt and clean the room at the same time.

'Why should I send photo? Sweety is working, bye now,' she said and cut the call again. She opened the bathroom door. She went in for a few minutes. We heard water being splashed in the bathroom. She came back to the studio and stood outside the closet. My heart was in my mouth. Would she open it? Fortunately, her admirer saved the day.

Her phone rang again.

'What?' she said, now somewhat annoyed. 'What did you send? Let me see.'

She was silent as she browsed her phone. Saurabh shifted a little in the cupboard, making a sound. I froze.

'What is this Amazon voucher? What should I do with this?' she was saying.

She left the room without shutting the studio door. I checked my wristwatch: 7.05. I heard the creaky main door open and then shut again with a loud, hard thud. Total silence followed. I gave it two minutes and then spoke.

'She has left. Get out, time to work,' I said.

❖

'How many clothes does this guy have?' Saurabh said. He rifled through Adi's closet, which covered the entire wall opposite his bed. The six-door closet had at least fifty shirts on hangers. Below them were several drawers filled with T-shirts, pants, gym clothes, socks and underwear. 'And so much underwear,' Saurabh said, holding a stack of Calvin Kleins. 'Who is he? An underwear smuggler?'

'Stop wasting time. We have forty more minutes. Search the entire room. There must be something.'

'Wait,' Saurabh said, as he extended his hand deeper into the underwear drawer. He removed something from the bottom of the drawer.

'Look,' he said, holding out a strip of condoms.

'Wow. Condoms. Horrors. Makes him guilty all right,' I said, sarcasm in my voice.

'Bhai, just showing you what I found.'

'Keep looking,' I said. I fished through Adi's T-shirts and gymwear drawer. Under the stack of gym shorts, I found a polythene-wrapped packet the size of a table-tennis ball.

Carefully, I unwrapped it. After two layers of plastic, I found a lump of a sticky brown substance.

'What's this?' I said.

'Looks like Bournvita. You know when Bournvita absorbs water and coagulates again?' Saurabh said.

I nodded.

'I used to love to eat it when I was a child.'

'Is there anything you don't love to eat, Saurabh?'

'Bhai, don't be mean. As it is I haven't eaten anything.'

'Focus, Golu. We don't have time.'

'Sorry,' Saurabh said. He took the lump from my hand. He sniffed it and made a disgusted face.

'It's not Bournvita. It smells bad. Like vinegar.'

'What is it?'

'Let me Google it,' Saurabh said.

Saurabh pulled out his phone and typed 'brown sticky substance smells like vinegar' in the search engine. He read out the search results.

'It's heroin. Black tar heroin,' Saurabh said.

'Chachu is quite the party man, isn't he?' I said. I broke a tiny piece of the lump for our records. I repacked the rest like before and placed it where I had found it.

'All this means nothing. We need more,' I said. 'Chachu likes to have sex and does drugs. Fine. It's not evidence.'

'Well, it is not in the closets,' Saurabh said. We had checked every nook and cranny of all the cupboards. I pointed to the bed. We lifted up the mattress. The bed had storage space underneath. Saurabh and I lifted the plywood bed surface to reveal the contents inside. Old guitars, a gramophone player and vinyl records gathered dust under the bed.

I took out the contents one by one.

'Why? It will take forever to put it all back,' Saurabh said.

'Just want to be thorough,' I said. 'Come on, help me empty it.'

I took out the gramophone player and placed it on the floor.

'I am checking the bedside tables first. Wait,' Saurabh said.

He opened the two drawers of the table on one side of the bed.

'What's in those drawers?' I said, pulling out the stack of vinyl records.

'Chargers. Sunglasses. Combiflam tablets. Some cash,' Saurabh said, sifting through the contents. Then he moved to the right side of the bed and opened the drawers there. He listed the contents out loud.

'Magazines. Multivitamin capsules. Protein bars. More protein bars. Nothing useful, bhai. Actually, is it okay if I steal a protein bar? I'm hungry. There are a dozen of them.'

'No, it's not okay. Are you sure there's nothing?' I said, as I removed an old and dusty guitar.

'Yes, bhai. Are you sure he's our prime suspect?'

'Yes, I am. Okay, all the big items are out of the storage. Let's check if there is anything else inside.'

'This room looks like a disaster zone.'

I checked the time. We had twenty-eight minutes until 8 o'clock.

I looked inside the storage space again. There didn't seem to be anything apart from a few pieces of paper and some plastic wrappers. The corners of the space were dark.

'Switch on the lights. I can't see clearly,' I said.

Saurabh switched on the lights.

'What is there to see, anyway?' Saurabh said.

'Switch on your phone torch as well,' I said. I did the same on my mobile phone.

The two beams of light fell into the storage space. As we moved the light around, it lit up the contents. I saw tiny bits of paper, plastic sheets, spider webs, a couple of plastic syringes and a strip of unopened needles.

'What are these for?' Saurabh said.

'For his drugs,' I said. I picked up one syringe. It was empty. I tossed the syringe back in the bed storage. It rolled to one of the corners, stopping as it hit a small white plastic pouch. I pointed the light at the pouch.

'Just a plastic bag,' Saurabh said. He lowered his hand in the storage and felt it. 'It's not plastic. It's rubber. Oh wait. Fuck.'

'What?' I said.

'It's gloves.'

He lifted up a pair of thin white rubber gloves. He held them with his nails, pinching them at one end, so as to not destroy any fingerprints. The two gloves swung eerily from Saurabh's hand as my phone's light shone through them.

'Remember the forensic report? No fingerprints,' Saurabh said.

'Damn,' I said.

I looked closer at one of the gloves. There was something inside it.

'What's that?' I said, as I pointed the light at that glove finger.

Saurabh turned the glove upside down. Something metallic fell out of it. I picked it up from the floor. It was a solitaire diamond ring, set in white gold.

'It's a ring,' I said and showed it to Saurabh.

'What the ...' His open mouth froze mid-sentence.

'You recognise this?'

'This is Prerna's engagement ring.'

'What?' I said and jumped back a step in shock. 'Are you sure?'

'Of course. I bought it,' Saurabh said. He took the ring from my hand.

'See, oblong pink diamond, 1.2 carats. Exactly what she selected.'

Before I could respond, a loud ring from my phone made us jump.

'What the hell, bhai? You said phones on silent.'

'Yes, it is on silent,' I said. I pulled out my phone and switched off the alarm. 'I had set a reminder alarm. It is 7.45 now. We need to stop the search and pack up. Restore the place to what it was. Come on, let's go. Help me with this stupid guitar.'

I lifted the instrument.

Saurabh stood like a statue, staring at the ring. 'This was our ring. Our future,' he said, and began to cry. 'How could he do this?' Saurabh rested his head on my shoulder. 'She just wanted to see me and break her fast.'

'Golu, I understand your pain. But we have a more urgent pain now. We only have eleven minutes to get our asses out of here.'

Chapter 28

'Police? Shouldn't we tell someone in the family first?' Saurabh said, leaning over his cubicle wall.

We were in office, and frankly caring very little about cybersecurity in the world. We had only one thing on our mind: the engagement ring we had found in the Malhotras' house.

'We promised the police we would keep them in the loop,' I said. 'And this is big.'

'What was the police doing all this time? They could have searched the bedroom too, right?'

'Leave all that. The point is, we said we are working together.'

My office phone rang. It was big boss Jacob calling.

'That new pitch. For the auto brand.'

'Yeah, sorry, sir. It is a little late.'

'A month late.'

'Sorry, sir. I'll do it right away.'

Jacob ended the call. I stared at my computer.

'Bhai, you have to finish this presentation. We will get fired if we don't do it.'

My body was turned to the computer to work on the pitch, but my mind remained on the case.

'Police first. Then family,' I said.

'You're not going to work on it?' Saurabh said.

'Your fiancée's killer is roaming free—you really think I give a fuck about this pitch?'

'We are useless in corporates. Misfits. Not meant for work. Only a matter of time before they find out and fire us.'

'I don't care,' I said.

'Ramesh uncle hates Adi chachu,' Saurabh said. 'Why not family first?'

'He is still his brother. Hating him is different from tossing him into jail.'

'Even if he killed his daughter?'

I shrugged. 'Can't take that chance. With Punjabi families, blood is thicker than water. Or lassi or whatever.'

❖

'Oh my God,' Singh said. He looked at the pictures of the gloves and the ring on Saurabh's phone.

We were in his office, sitting across from him.

'Where have you kept the ring and gloves?'

'In our Malviya Nagar house,' I said. 'We were careful not to touch the gloves. To preserve fingerprints.'

'Good,' Singh said. 'And gutsy of you to go in like that. Our teams looked around the whole bungalow. They didn't find this.'

I wanted to tell him maybe his team had been too busy eating samosas and kaju katlis served at the Malhotras instead of doing a proper search, but controlled myself.

'We promised to keep you in the loop,' I said.

'You want tea? Something to eat?' Singh said.

Before Saurabh could respond, I shook my head.

'What next, sir?' I said.

Singh returned the phone to Saurabh. He cupped his chin in his right hand and took a deep breath.

'I wanted to speak to Namrata Taneja next. But this is quite something.'

'Is this evidence?' Saurabh said.

'Gloves, ring of deceased. It's evidence for sure,' Singh said.

'Evidence enough?' I said.

Singh sat up straight.

'Enough for what? To get him arrested? Yes. To prove that he is a murderer? Probably yes. But we do that in court. For now, he's prime suspect and accused,' Singh said.

'Are you going to arrest him?' Saurabh said.

'Let me speak to Rana sir,' Singh said. He stood up from his chair and dialled a number on his phone. 'Rana sir? Good evening,' he said and walked out of his office, to make sure we didn't hear the conversation. Saurabh and I looked at each other, wondering if we had done the right thing by coming here first. Singh returned after a few minutes.

'We might arrest him. I need the actual evidence though. You have it, right?'

'Of course,' Saurabh said.

'I'll send someone to collect it,' Singh said.

I wondered if it would be a good idea to give the evidence to the police. If the police cut a deal with Adi, Singh could use this evidence to extract more money. However, what choice did we have?

'Sure, sir,' I said.

'I have to get a warrant executed first. Otherwise, media will say I didn't follow procedure. Is Adi famous? He is a musician, right?'

'He sings at a hotel,' I said. 'Not famous.'

'Good. Give me two days, I'll handcuff him,' Singh said. We stood up to leave. 'And listen, boys,' Singh said.

'Yes, sir?' I said.

'Good work. Just don't tell anyone anything until I get the warrant.'

Saurabh looked at me and rolled his eyes.

'Okay, sir,' I said. 'Whatever you say.'

Chapter 29

When Saurabh is confused, stressed or tense, he turns to one solution. He decides to cook. Somehow, all his remedies to life's problems are linked to food. The more difficult the situation he is in, the more elaborate the dish he chooses to cook.

'Do we have to make butter chicken at home? Let's order in or go out,' I said.

'Don't mess with me now, bhai. I told you I need to de-stress,' he said. He was chopping onions in a fury, like they had a family feud with him.

'Calm down, you're scaring me,' I said.

'Just give me the tomatoes. And the butter too.'

I took out six tomatoes and a newly bought half-kilo pack of butter from the fridge and gave it to him.

He cut the butter into half. He placed one of the halves into a kadhai that was on the lit stove.

'Are you inviting the entire office over?' I said.

'No, I don't want to meet anyone. This is just for us.'

'Shouldn't we use less butter then?' I said.

Saurabh looked at me like I had asked him to change his religion.

'What is the dish called?'

'Butter chicken,' I said.

'Exactly. So it needs butter. Now leave me alone. Let me cook,' Saurabh said. The butter melted and began to bubble in a few seconds. He tossed all the onions into the kadhai, stirring till they turned golden brown. If I were writing an Indian literary novel, the ones white guys in Britain judge and give prizes to, I would write two more paragraphs on the aroma of red onions fried in butter; basically how we Indians are so exotic that we spray cinnamon in the air. However, I had bigger problems on hand. A ninety-six-kilo stress ball, for instance.

I held his arm, the one that was stirring violently, asking him to stop. I turned down the gas flame, wishing he had a similar knob as well.

'What's the problem, Golu? Tell me?' I said.

Saurabh didn't meet my eye.

'I didn't get a good feeling from Singh,' he said. 'I told you, let's inform the family first about Adi.'

'Why?'

'Picture this. Singh goes to Adi chachu. Asks him for ten lakh rupees to throw that evidence away ... By the way, two constables came by an hour ago. They took the ring and gloves.'

'If we can't trust the police of the country, we can't solve any case, Golu,' I said.

'Do you trust them?'

I looked at Saurabh.

'Not a hundred per cent. But neither can we trust the family. Think about this. We tell the family Adi did it. Ramesh uncle says fine but don't go to the police. Can't bring the family more disrepute. Then?'

Saurabh shook his head. He turned up the gas burner again.

'Let's not talk to Ramesh uncle alone, then. We'll talk to everyone in the family. Everyone apart from Adi chachu,' Saurabh said. He began to chop the tomatoes, its red juice spurting all over the place.

'Ramesh uncle dominates that house,' I said.

'But the others may want justice for Prerna. Someone might. I say let's do it soon. Before the police and Adi chachu strike a deal and ... Owww,' Saurabh screamed. He had nicked his thumb while cutting the tomatoes. Blood dripped from it and mixed with the tomato pieces.

'Tonight's dish is going to be special. If not sweat, at least you have put your blood into it,' I said.

'Damn,' he said and lifted his hand. He got the first-aid box, fumbled and found a band-aid.

'Fine,' I said.

'Not fine. Hurts like hell,' Saurabh said.

'I meant, fine, let's talk to the Malhotras. Time for another family meeting.'

Chapter 30

'You're taking us all out? Why?' Anjali said.

'Uncle gave us a place to stay. Least we can do,' I said.

Saurabh and I had organised a dinner at Lotus Pond, a Chinese restaurant in K Block of New Friends Colony. Anjali was the first person to reach the venue.

Saurabh scanned the menu. Announcing the killer would always come second to deciding which hakka noodles to order.

'Private room. Fancy,' Anjali said.

'Here we can all have a conversation,' I said. 'Where are the others?'

'Coming soon. I guess everyone had important things to do. I am the only lazy, jobless kind.' Anjali chuckled. She had cut her hair even shorter. It barely covered her ears. She had her trademark nose ring and silver rings on. She wore a white kurti with a self-design along with a pair of torn jeans that clung to her skinny legs.

I tried not to notice her too much. Even though a part of me found it hard to resist her. School principal Saurabh wouldn't like it.

'You look good today,' Anjali said. 'Have you been working out?'

No, please don't do this, I wanted to say. Don't flirt with me. You are off-limits, and my friend might just explode.

'Same as before,' I said. 'How are things with you?'

Anjali smiled ruefully.

'Turns out there's not much work for a freelance journalist interested in social causes.'

'You write on issues like pollution. It's a huge problem,' I said.

'Apparently not as huge as where to buy the best make-up in Delhi,' Anjali said and laughed. Her white teeth perfectly matched her kurti.

'Make-up?' I said.

'That's the only freelance writing gig I got in the last two weeks. So much for my degree in public policy. Maybe one day I can use my education to recommend laws subsidising make-up products.'

She continued to laugh. Her high cheekbones, angular face and the Malhotra girls' trademark big eyes made it difficult for me to look away. I think she caught me staring at her.

I coughed hard twice to get Saurabh's attention. He looked up from the menu with the air of an academician.

'What?' Saurabh said. I signalled to him with my eyes to talk to Anjali as well.

'How's Parag?' Saurabh said, referring to her boyfriend.

'Must be okay. Heard he found a job selling editorial ads in *Delhi Times*. Pays well. Delhi changes you. Makes you comply, eventually.'

'You are not in touch?' Saurabh said.

Anjali shook her head. My crooked mind churned into action. This means she is single. Maybe she likes me too. How long are relatives of dead ex-fiancées out of bounds, anyway?

I scolded myself for longing for her. Apart from Saurabh's disapproval, I didn't really want a relationship. I didn't want to go down this road of liking someone too much and burdening myself with a million complications and disappointments later.

'Good evening, Ramesh uncle,' Anjali said, breaking my line of thought.

Ramesh arrived with Maaji, Neelam and Bindu. Ajay had a coaching class, and couldn't come. Everyone took a seat around the circular table. Saurabh called for the waiter.

'It's Tuesday, we are all veg today.' Ramesh smiled apologetically.

A bit disappointed, Saurabh ordered a selection of vegetarian dishes. Then he addressed everyone.

'So happy you all could make it. We wanted to say thank you for letting us stay in your home and treating us like family.'

'You are welcome, beta. Don't be formal,' Neelam said.

'We also thought we would brief you on some updates in Prerna's case,' I said.

Everyone stopped smiling.

'Wait, shouldn't we wait for Adi?' Ramesh said.

Saurabh shook his head.

'No, Uncle, Adi chachu is not invited,' Saurabh said.

Ramesh looked shocked.

'What's going on?' Neelam said.

'Is Adi—' Bindu began, but Ramesh cut her short.

'Let them talk.'

'We found a few things in Adi chachu's flat,' Saurabh said.

'Actually, we searched his flat,' I said. Saurabh and I recounted our search operation.

'Strange way to do things. Anyway, what did you find?' Ramesh said.

Saurabh opened his backpack. He took out a set of printouts of photographs of the evidence.

'I am sure you recognise the ring, Uncle,' Saurabh said.

Ramesh took out his reading glasses from his shirt pocket. He wore them and examined the page up close. Neelam looked up from the page she was holding, her face white. Bindu's hands shivered as she held a printout.

Maaji moved the pages up and down.

'What is this? A bangle?'

'It's Prerna's ring,' Ramesh said.

Bindu started crying first. Neelam followed. The waiter arrived with soup. Ramesh signalled to him to go away.

'No, Neelam, no. We told each other, no more tears. No, Bindu, no,' Ramesh said, holding his sister's and wife's hands. Maaji continued to fumble with the printouts. Maybe her hearing and sight were not sharp enough to figure out what was going on, I thought. Ramesh didn't explain anything to her. He asked a waiter to get her soup instead. She looked at him, smiled and began to have the hot liquid with a spoon.

'It's good,' Maaji said. Ramesh smiled at his mother and turned to me.

'So, Adi killed my girl?' Ramesh said, his volume low but with obvious anger. The women at the table heard the word 'killed' and looked up at him.

'This is pretty solid evidence,' I said. 'Of course, must be shocking for you. He is your family.'

'What does this snake know about family?' Ramesh said, his voice soft to ensure Maaji couldn't hear. 'Bloody ungrateful drug addict. Hated me and Prerna for becoming something in life.'

'You think that is the likely motive, Uncle?' I said.

'What?' Ramesh said.

'The police said the evidence is good. Eventually they just need to confirm the motive.'

Ramesh sat up straight.

'How does the police know all this?'

Saurabh told Ramesh about our meeting with Singh.

'Have you lost your mind? Why did you go to the police?' Ramesh said. This time Maaji heard him; she looked up from her soup.

'Ki hoya?' Maaji said in Punjabi, wondering what was going on.

'Nothing, Maaji, let's eat,' Ramesh said. He signalled to the waiter to get the rest of the food. As the waiter hurried to do this, Ramesh clenched his fists.

'Ramesh ji, shaant,' Neelam said in a soft voice.

'What shaant? They stay in my house, snoop around like robbers, find something and go give it to the police? All this without informing me?'

'We are informing you, Uncle. You only told us to work together with the police,' Saurabh said.

'Together, my foot. This is a family matter. I will decide what is right here,' Ramesh said.

Neelam and Bindu froze like scared rabbits, unable to utter a word. Saurabh looked at Bindu, hoping to get support.

'These boys are just trying to—' Bindu said.

'Shut up and eat, Bindu,' Ramesh said. By now food had been served.

Bindu lowered her eyes to her plate of vegetable fried rice. I turned towards Anjali, begging her silently to say something.

'What else could they have done, Uncle? They are obligated to hand over any evidence to the police,' Anjali said.

Ramesh looked at Anjali, shocked at her audacity. He took a spoon and banged it hard on the table.

'What if this idiot Singh goes to the media? What if news gets out? Malhotra Motors family members murder each other. What reputation will we have left?' Ramesh said.

I tried to hand him a glass of water; he ignored me.

'Sorry, Uncle, but if Adi chachu is the murderer, news will eventually come out,' Saurabh said.

'Not if you had kept quiet,' Ramesh said. 'Now I have to handle Singh.'

'What do you mean, Uncle? You don't want Prerna's killer punished?' Saurabh said.

'I do. But I also want to protect our family name and business reputation,' Ramesh said.

'You can let the killer of your daughter go free for that?' Anjali said.

Ramesh glared at Anjali.

'Life doesn't always give you easy choices,' Ramesh said. Everyone fell silent. Ramesh finally served himself some noodles.

Everyone ate without a word. I could tell people wanted to say more and ask more questions. However, with Ramesh around, they preferred to be quiet.

'Enough is enough,' Anjali said. 'I know why you want to keep it quiet. You don't want the family secrets out. Right, Neelam aunty?'

'I don't know what you're talking about,' Neelam said, not looking up from her plate.

'It's about time we tell Saurabh and Keshav. They must be wondering, how can a father not care about his daughter's killer?'

Ramesh stood up, towering over all of us. He pointed a trembling finger at Anjali.

'Anjali. Shut up right now.'

'Why—' Anjali began.

'Bindu? Neelam? You control her, otherwise …' He flexed his hand, as if to slap Anjali.

'Quiet, Anjali beta, quiet,' Bindu said.

'Ki?' Maaji's high-pitched voice startled everyone.

Anjali looked at Maaji.

'Why is Ramesh upset?' Maaji said, fumbling with the hearing device in her ear. 'You better get my hearing aid fixed. Even this new one isn't working.'

'Nothing, Maaji,' Ramesh said, sitting back down.

'O aaya si,' Maaji said.

'Yes, Maaji, please eat,' Ramesh said. He let out a deep breath.

Anjali bit her lower lip. Neelam squeezed Anjali's arm, urging her to stay calm. Ramesh turned to her.

'Anjali beta, it's not like I am going to spare Adi,' Ramesh said in a soft voice, so as to not alarm his mother again. 'Prerna meant the world to me. I will talk to Adi tonight itself.'

When Anjali didn't answer, Ramesh continued.

'But we can't spoil our family image or discuss internal matters in public.'

'What internal matters?' I said, as my curiosity became too much to control.

Ramesh gave me a stern glance.

'Internal means internal. Anyway, it has no relevance to this case,' Ramesh said.

'But, Uncle—' Saurabh said.

'Enough. We are done here,' Ramesh said.

Saurabh sighed and called out to the waiter.

'Get the bill,' Saurabh said.

'Dessert first, sir? Our honey noodle ice cream is famous,' the waiter said.

Chapter 31

'Fuck, he is really yelling,' Saurabh said. We sat on the bed in Prerna's room. We had reached home after dinner at the Lotus Pond. Ramesh had barged straight into Adi's apartment. Bindu was with Neelam in the living room. None of us could make out what was being said on the floor above. However, we could tell Ramesh was livid.

Clang! I heard a loud sound as a hard object fell in the apartment above us.

Saurabh and I sprang up at the same time.

'We need to listen to what they're saying,' I said.

'Fine, let's step out.'

We went out of the bedroom.

'What's happening?' Neelam said in a concerned voice.

'We will go check,' Saurabh said.

'No,' Neelam screamed. 'Ramesh ji said nobody should go there.'

'We will stand at the steps,' Saurabh said. 'Come, Keshav.'

❖

I noticed the outline of her thin figure in the darkness of the stairwell.

'Anjali?' I whispered.

'Shh,' she said, finger on her lips. Saurabh and I tiptoed up the steps.

'What are you doing here?' I said softly.

'Figuring out what is going on. And hoping it doesn't end badly,' Anjali said. 'I heard something break.'

We were right at the entrance of Adi's apartment and were able to eavesdrop a bit.

'I stopped taking drugs,' Aditya was yelling. 'I don't do them anymore.'

'Liar,' Ramesh said.

'Where will I get money for drugs? I have none. My gigs don't pay much. You don't give me any. Where will I get money?' Aditya cried.

Anjali pressed her ear to the door to hear better. As she did that, her shoulder pressed against mine. Her perfume made my head swim a little.

'... killed that little girl. You couldn't stand it. Someone in this house doing well,' Ramesh said.

'I didn't do anything!'

'The ring appeared like magic in your apartment?' Ramesh said. 'Today I won't leave you.'

I heard slaps and punches. 'Don't beat me, Bhaiya. We are grown-ups,' Aditya said.

'You think I like doing this?' Ramesh said. 'I never laid a finger on anyone in this house. I should have. My love spoilt you.'

I heard a few more slaps.

'I didn't kill Prerna. She was to me what she was to you.'

'Nonsense,' Ramesh said. 'The police knows, by the way. And soon the world will. First you bring sorrow to us. Now you will bring us shame.'

'What? How? What is even happening?' Adi said.

'If that's the acting you will do for the police, you will fail miserably.'

'I didn't kill her, Ramesh bhaiya, I swear upon Maaji.'

'You will kill Maaji too. Stop doing drama. Shut up.'

I couldn't hear anything after that. Maybe they were sitting in silence or had moved to another room. I pressed my ear to the door as well; no sound. My cheek touched Anjali's cheek for a second when I leaned forward against the wood of the door. I moved away instantly. She looked at me, clearly worried about the proceedings inside, unaware of the electric spark the accidental touch had caused.

A few minutes later, we heard Ramesh's footsteps in Adi's living room.

'Remember what I told you. Act dignified in front of the police. And for God's sake, stay sober and shave.'

His voice moved closer to the main door. The three of us scampered up the stairs. We waited at the terrace door. We heard Ramesh come out of Adi's apartment, slam the door shut and climb down the steps.

Saurabh and Anjali heaved a sigh of relief.

'Let's go to the terrace. Get some air,' I said.

Chapter 32

The three of us stood on the same terrace Prerna had fallen from.

'I always knew my family was not perfect, but I didn't know it would be so fucked up,' Anjali said. She lit a cigarette and offered it to me. Saurabh's head swung to me. I declined.

'Anything can happen in this world,' I said.

Anjali exhaled smoke and said, 'To think I came down from the US for this. To get a family.'

My phone buzzed in my pocket.

I showed the screen to Saurabh—the call was from Singh.

'Now? It's eleven o'clock,' he said.

'Shall I take it?' I said.

'Of course,' Saurabh said.

I stepped away from Saurabh and Anjali so they couldn't hear me.

Singh gushed on the other side, 'Mr Detective, how are you? I'm not disturbing you, I hope?'

'No, sir,' I said. 'How are you? All good?'

'Yes. I have good news for you,' Singh said.

'Good news?'

'We have a warrant,' Singh said. 'For Aditya Malhotra.'

'Wow.'

'Don't ever doubt the police. I have not sold my soul, detective sahib.'

'We never doubted, sir,' I said.

'We will act on this tomorrow. Let him sleep in his kothi nicely tonight.'

'Right, sir.'

'Don't tell him anything about this. Okay?'

'Yes, sir,' I said.

I walked back to Saurabh and Anjali. Saurabh looked at me curiously.

'What did he say?' Anjali said, lighting another cigarette.

'Nothing. Routine stuff. Anyway, let's go down now. I'm tired.'

❖

'What? Arrest warrant? Why didn't you say that on the terrace?' Saurabh said. He sprang up on the bed. I had taken the mattress on the floor. We had just turned off the lights in Prerna's room.

'Because Anjali was there,' I said. 'Now lie back down, please.'

'So what?'

'She is family, after all.'

'What do you mean?' Saurabh said, scratching his head.

'Maybe she will feel obligated to tell Ramesh uncle. He could try to manage the situation or ask Adi to go underground.'

Saurabh gulped some air.

'Hmm, you may be right,' he said.

Saurabh lay down again.

'So what now?'

'Sleep. We need the rest before tomorrow's drama. Goodnight,' I said and shut my eyes.

Chapter 33

'Wake up, Keshav,' Saurabh said, shaking my shoulder.

I opened one eye. It still seemed dark outside.

'What time is it?'

'6.30. How can you sleep through all this? Can't you hear the siren?'

I rubbed my eyes and stretched out my arms. Yes, I could hear a siren.

'Let's see from the balcony,' Saurabh said.

I opened the door in the room that led to the wrap-around balcony. Winter hit me in the face, full blast.

In the fog, we could make out three police Gypsies parked outside. One of them had revolving lights flashing on its roof and a siren blaring from it. Several men in khaki uniform stood outside the house. I looked to my right. At the other end of our floor, Ramesh stood on his balcony. He walked towards us.

'What's going on?' Ramesh said.

I shrugged. Saurabh didn't respond either.

'Singh ji just called me. He's downstairs. Let's go,' Ramesh said.

❖

Gopika served Ramesh tea as soon as we reached the ground floor. Inspector Singh, Saurabh and I sat on the opposite sofa.

'Get tea for everyone here,' Ramesh said. 'And give the constables outside some naashta.'

Singh explained the entire situation and his reason for being there.

'It's not easy for you, I'm sure,' Singh said. 'That's why we came early. We didn't want the colony to know.'

'So why is your Gypsy still making this horrible sound?' Ramesh said.

'Sorry,' Singh said. He pulled out a walkie-talkie attached to his belt and gave some instructions. The siren stopped.

'There is solid evidence against him. It is difficult not to act now. We just got the warrant last night. These detective boys know. I called them.'

Ramesh gave Saurabh and me a look.

'You knew they'd be coming?' Ramesh said. Saurabh and I remained quiet.

'They helped a lot,' Singh said.

'Yeah, I know. Raiding my own house while I treated them like guests. Then going to the police behind my back.'

Saurabh and I squirmed in our seats. Gopika returned with a cup of tea for Singh. He took a few big slurpy sips of his beverage. He spoke again after Gopika left.

'Sometimes, when news of the warrant leaks, the accused absconds. Out of regard for you, I didn't come last night for the arrest.'

'Arrest?' Ramesh said.

'It's an arrest warrant, Ramesh ji. Not a search warrant.'

'What?' Ramesh said. He turned to us. 'And nobody told me this?'

Saurabh and I continued to squirm.

'He is your brother. But he killed your daughter, Ramesh ji. We found the killer. The man who ruined your family's peace and happiness,' Singh said.

'And you arresting him will bring that happiness back?' Ramesh said, his voice loud.

'It's my duty, sir. To get justice for your daughter.'

Singh seemed baffled by Ramesh's response. He kept his cup down.

Normally, now was the time Singh would be congratulated for catching the criminal. He would get pats on his back, boxes of mithai and be hailed as a hero. Clearly Ramesh had other ideas.

'What about me? What about my family?' Ramesh said. He looked at all of us. Nobody said a word. Ramesh continued.

'Why can't we accept this as an accident? Why bring more shame to our family?'

Singh shrugged. Ramesh turned to Saurabh.

'Tell me, Saurabh. You are almost a part of this family. How would you like it if your family name was dragged through the mud?' Ramesh said.

'It doesn't work like that, Uncle,' Saurabh said in a calm voice.

'What do you mean?' Ramesh said.

'I loved Prerna. I don't care about family name or anything. I want the person who took her away from me to rot in jail.'

'Good. That's the right way to think. And don't worry, he will rot in jail,' Singh said and stood up. 'Let us proceed upstairs. Mr Aditya is at home?'

'Are you sure nothing can be done?' Ramesh said.

Ramesh and Singh exchanged an all-knowing glance. They didn't say a word. As it often happens in India, it seemed clear Ramesh had offered a bribe.

Singh didn't like being propositioned like this, right in front of us. He shook his head.

'Nothing I can do, Malhotra ji. Thanks for the tea,' Singh said. He pulled out his walkie-talkie to instruct his team. Within seconds, half a dozen cops rushed up the steps to Adi's apartment.

❖

'He is not opening the door,' said a constable. He continued to ring the doorbell for a minute. Another cop knocked periodically on the door. Ramesh, Saurabh and I stood outside Adi's apartment.

'Call him,' Singh said.

Ramesh called Adi several times. Nobody answered.

'Is he even there?' Singh said, narrowing his eyes.

'I spoke to him last night—he was there,' Ramesh said.

'Not right, Ramesh ji. You can't help the accused run away like this,' Singh said, disappointment in his voice.

'I didn't do anything,' Ramesh shouted. 'He must be inside. I don't care, break the lock.'

Singh nodded at one of the cops, who ran downstairs and returned with a toolbox from his Gypsy.

Chapter 34

For a few minutes, the only sound that one could hear was the hammering at Adi's door.

'Done,' the constable announced. He pushed the door, which swung wide open as the lock came loose.

All of us entered Adi's apartment. On the dining table was the same Special K cereal box, a milk carton and an empty bowl and spoon. The police moved towards Adi's bedroom.

They knocked on the door many times. No response. A cop turned the knob.

'It's locked,' he said.

'I told you he is inside. Sleeping away after taking all those drugs,' Ramesh said, shaking his head in disapproval.

Singh signalled to the constable with the toolbox. Within minutes, the constable had broken this lock as well.

Singh entered Adi's bedroom. The rest of us waited in the living room.

'Aditya ji? Are you here, Aditya ji? Inspector Singh here,' Singh said in a soft voice. I heard Singh draw open the curtains to let sunlight into the room.

He emerged from the bedroom after a minute. He had his hands on his waist.

'Is he inside?' Ramesh said.

Singh pursed his lips.

'Come with me,' Singh said. All of us entered the bedroom.

Adi lay still, a sliver of sunshine lighting the stubble on his face. He did not seem to have any clothes on, though a white quilt covered his body waist-down. His trackpants, T-shirt and underwear lay on the floor. His neck and shoulders had dark red hickeys and tiny bitemarks, similar to the ones I had seen when we met him at the Leela. They seemed to be from a recent lovemaking session—a usual feature in his life, I guessed. He had trimmed the hair on his flat stomach and chest, and had a tattoo of a lightning rod on his chest. He looked like an Italian hero from a raunchy rom-com movie. On the bedside table, I saw a syringe with a strip of needles.

'Look at him. Drugged-out junkie, sleeping away,' Ramesh said. 'Shame of our family.'

Singh held Adi's wrist to check his pulse.

'He's not sleeping, Ramesh ji. He is dead,' Singh said, dropping Adi's arm.

❖

A tsunami hit the Malhotra household as news of Adi's death broke out. Anjali came running up. She retched on seeing her uncle's corpse. The cops quickly took the body downstairs. Neelam and Bindu sat crying in a corner, obviously in shock. Maaji, looking dazed, stumbled over to the body and started to wail.

'My chota Adi. Ki hoya tennu? What happened to you?' she said over and over again.

Singh went over to Neelam.

'What is even going on in your house, Neelam ji?' he said.

'Someone has cursed us,' Neelam said. Ramesh glared at his wife for talking to the police without his permission. She noticed and turned away from Singh.

Ramesh wanted the body cremated as soon as possible.

'Let us do a quick post-mortem and then you can do the funeral,' Singh said.

'No funeral. Please cremate the body after the post-mortem quietly,' Ramesh said. 'And can you not tell the media, please?'

'I will try my best that they don't find out, Ramesh ji,' Singh said.

Maaji's howls filled the house. She sat next to Adi, holding him tight.

'God, why don't you take me? Why are you coming after the children in my family?' Maaji said. Someone made her let go of Adi and she started beating her chest. Ramesh teared up too, watching his mother in such misery.

'Neelam, take her upstairs, please,' Ramesh said, wiping his tears. He folded his hands and turned to Singh. 'Can you please close this case, Singh ji? I beg you.'

Chapter 35

The womenfolk of Malhotra House huddled together on the sofa, their eyes swollen from weeping. Anjali held Bindu's hand, wiping her aunt's tears intermittently. Neelam stared at the floor. Maaji was not to be seen. Ramesh stood in one corner, arms crossed, face dark as a thundercloud.

Saurabh and I sat on the dining table chairs. We had come back from work. The scene in the house reminded me of the day Prerna died. Gopika came in and broke the silence.

'Neelam madam, what do I make for dinner?' Gopika said.

Ramesh glared at Gopika so hard she could have vaporised.

'Wait in the kitchen. I will come, Gopika,' Neelam said hastily, and Gopika scampered away.

It was Bindu who next broke the silence.

'Veerji, did the inspector confirm? What happened to Adi?' she said.

Ramesh shook his head.

'They are awaiting the post-mortem results. But preliminary examination suggests drug overdose.'

'A drug overdose can kill you?' Bindu said.

'Heroin can. It's too powerful,' Ramesh said and sighed.

'We still haven't told the neighbours anything,' Neelam said.

'Tell them drug overdose. Some friends gave him, he tried, and it proved fatal,' Ramesh said.

'Uncle, are you sure?' Saurabh said.

'What do you mean?' Ramesh said, his voice irritated. 'Accidental overdose. What else?'

'Yes, Uncle, he overdosed. But are we sure about the accidental part?' Saurabh said.

Ramesh's eyes went wide.

'Meaning?' he said.

'He's saying it may not be an accident,' I said. 'There are other possibilities.'

'Like?' Ramesh said in an ominous tone.

'He could have intentionally overdosed himself, a suicide. Maybe unhappy after being yelled at last night,' Saurabh said.

'What nonsense,' Ramesh mumbled.

Saurabh continued to talk. 'Or someone could have given him the overdose, making it a murder.'

Ramesh did not respond. He came to the dining table. He towered over us.

'Get up.'

Saurabh and I stood up from our respective chairs.

'Get out of my house. Now,' he said in a low voice.

'But, Uncle ...' Saurabh was confused.

'I said, get the hell out. Neelam?' he shouted. 'Who the hell are they, Neelam? My daughter never married this idiot, and who is this friend anyway? What are they doing in my house?'

Neelam could have reminded Ramesh he himself had offered us Prerna's room for a few weeks, but she didn't.

'Ramesh ji, shaant. We have been through a lot today,' Neelam said.

'Tell them to leave my house. Right now,' Ramesh said to Neelam, even though we could hear him loud and clear.

Saurabh and I looked at each other. What had we done wrong? Saurabh had simply raised some basic questions.

'You have fifteen minutes. Get out,' Ramesh said.

I nodded. Saurabh and I walked towards the stairs.

'Wait,' Anjali's voice came from behind us.

We turned around. Anjali walked up to Ramesh.

'They are only trying to help us. Why are you are throwing them out, Uncle?' Anjali said.

Ramesh turned to face Anjali.

'I will tell you why. They have fried my brain. We lost Prerna. It was bad enough. Everyone believed it was an accident. But no, these idiots had to do their detective business, so they come up with these random theories and suspects.'

'Not just theories, Uncle. They did find evidence in Adi's room,' Anjali said.

'And I believed them,' Ramesh shouted. His voice softened as he added, '... like a fool.'

His body began to quiver. Finally, he couldn't hold back. For the first time that day, he began to cry. He spoke between sobs.

'I lashed out at my own brother. Didn't realise how weak he was. I don't know if he overdosed by mistake. Or because I hit him. But he's gone. Yeah, he was my good-for-nothing brother. But he was *my* brother. My *only* brother.'

Ramesh began to cry uncontrollably. Neelam placed an arm around him.

He composed himself soon. Saurabh and I remained by the dining table.

'What are they still doing here? Get out,' Ramesh screamed, doing an instant switch from melodrama to angry mode.

'Uncle, stop,' Anjali said, her voice firm.

'Do you young people have no respect for elders? Get out means out. Get out,' Ramesh said.

'No, Uncle. You are kicking out the two people who are trying to find out the truth. Why?' Anjali said.

'I will throw you out too,' Ramesh said to Anjali. Both of them exchanged angry glares until Bindu came between them.

'Ramesh bhaiya, Anjali, please sit down.'

'Tell her to behave. I mean it, or I will throw her out too,' Ramesh said. He sat down on the sofa. Anjali continued to stand.

'I know, Ramesh uncle. It won't be the first time I'm thrown out.'

'Shut up, Anjali,' Bindu said.

I looked at Saurabh. He tilted his head towards the stairs, signalling that we should exit.

'Saurabh and Keshav, wait. You need to know something about our family,' Anjali said.

'Anjali, stop,' Bindu said.

Anjali ignored her.

'Prerna and I were sisters. Twin sisters,' Anjali said.

The entire room fell silent. Saurabh and I looked at Anjali, puzzled. Had I heard her right?

'Yeah,' Anjali said. 'We are not cousins. We are real twin sisters.'

Ramesh raised his hand to slap Anjali. Anjali stared back at him.

'Yeah, slap me, Uncle, for speaking the truth. Slap me, because I think Saurabh and Keshav should know our well-kept family secret. Prerna and I are twins. And she is our mother.'

Anjali pointed a finger at Bindu.

'Anjali, stop,' Bindu said again, faintly.

Okay, I needed a minute to process this. Bindu is Anjali's and Prerna's mother and not their aunt. So that made Bindu's brother, Ramesh, not Prerna's father, but her uncle, her mama. What is this family? A fucking brain-teaser? I looked at Saurabh, who seemed equally perplexed.

While I figured out the real relationships in the Malhotra house, I had another question—why? Why did they keep all this a secret?

Ramesh threw both his hands in the air.

'Fine, so everyone knows now. I sacrificed my whole life for this family and kept it all to myself. To protect you. Now you don't care. Fine.'

'Please sit, Ramesh ji,' Neelam said.

'No, Neelam ji, I am actually glad it is out. You sacrificed so much for these people and kept this secret too. Remember that time?'

Neelam cried softly.

'I did what you told me, Ramesh ji. I have always supported not just you, but your entire family. I accepted your decision. Heavens above know I never complained. Or even said a word about it to anyone.'

'But who cares? Nobody cares about this family and its reputation. We are the villains,' Ramesh said.

'No, Veerji, no, please,' Bindu said. Hands folded and with tears in her eyes, she said, 'You can never be a villain. You are like a god to me.'

She fell at Ramesh's feet. Saurabh and I looked at each other, bewildered. We were two rookie detectives. What were we doing in the middle of this family soap? Had we entered the wrong teleserial?

Bindu turned to us.

'Sit, boys,' Bindu said. 'Before you go, let me tell you what a great man my Veerji is. He is an angel.'

Saurabh and I obediently sat down. We faced Ramesh, who looked away.

'It was twenty-six years ago. I was sixteen when I met Param,' Bindu began.

'The curse on our family,' Ramesh said.

'Veerji is right. But, at that time, I loved him. He used to play cricket well, so I loved him. I was young and foolish, you see.'

Ramesh shook his head. Bindu lowered her voice.

'And then he ran away. Never to be seen in Amritsar again.'

Neelam held Bindu's hand. Bindu continued.

'He was a coward. And so was I. I hid it till I could. But it became impossible after a while. I had his twins in me, after all.'

Chapter 36

Bindu Speaks

Twenty-six years ago

'I am sorry again, Veerji,' I said. I counted in my head. This was my twentieth apology. The first eight times I received hard slaps in response. After that, Veerji didn't care.

Veerji paced around the jute charpoy in the veranda. The winter sun hit our faces, making us scrunch our eyes. Neelam bhabhi sat on the charpoy with me, clutching my hand. Geetu, my elder sister, leaned against the wall.

'Seven months? You have carried his child for seven months? And nobody in this house knows? Neelam?' Veerji said.

Neelam looked up at her husband, unable to answer. She had no clue. I had worn thick sweaters and wrapped a shawl around myself ever since I began to show.

'Geetu?' Ramesh said.

'I could never imagine such a thing, Veerji. She is sixteen,' Geetu said.

Geetu could have known. I had tried to tell her. However, between a bad US–India telephone line and her excitement of coming home for the first time after marriage, she hadn't taken me seriously. Four months ago, on an expensive and time-rationed call with her from Seattle, I told her. I had missed my period a few times. I told her about Param too, the love of my life. She had laughed it off and said it was probably nothing. I hadn't told her about being with Param in an empty classroom at night and doing certain things. Neither could she believe her little sister would do anything like that. I didn't mention it to anyone else either. My mother would have killed me. In any case, Maaji had left two months ago to be with her ageing parents in Haridwar. They had told her their last wish was to go on a pilgrimage all around India. I thought of telling Neelam bhabhi. However, she would tell Veerji, and he would kill Param. Naturally, I avoided it as long as I could.

I didn't mind being pregnant. I foolishly saw it as destiny. Just like my sister one year ago, I too felt I'd found my soulmate. Param would marry me. I would cook for him and raise his child. Param told me, 'I will resolve everything soon, just don't tell anyone.' I didn't, even when I began to show at five months. The shawls kept everyone fooled, even as Param kept me fooled. I hoped Param's parents would come one day to ask for my hand. Instead, he ran away. I had no way to contact him. However, fool that I was, I waited for him and kept it all concealed. Until the day Neelam bhabhi noticed my stomach when I took an afternoon nap on the veranda charpoy. I broke down and told her everything. She said she had no choice but to tell Veerji.

'I will kill him. Where is Param?' Veerji said.

Oh, Veerji, if only I knew, I wanted to say. Veerji circled the charpoy five times before he could bring himself to speak again.

'Did you go to any doctor?'

I shook my head.

'Good. Don't go to just any doctor. News will spread like wildfire. Let me find someone we can trust.'

I nodded.

'Will you go with Neelam and Geetu? And do what I tell you?'

'Of course, Veerji.'

'Geetu, don't tell anyone. Not even Jogi,' Veerji said, referring to Geetu's husband.

Geetu nodded tensely. Jogi had come down from Seattle with Geetu didi for two months. He had taken a break from driving a taxi there. Right now, he was with his own family in Moga.

'Veerji,' I said.

'Yes?'

'Once again, I am sorry.'

❖

Dr Reshma Ahluwalia made me lie down on a bed in a room attached to her cabin. We had come to the Princess of Wales Zenana Hospital at Dhab Khatikan in Amritsar. She applied a cold gel on my stomach and placed a metal probe on it. On a screen in front appeared a hazy, black and white image.

Geetu didi and Neelam bhabhi sat on stools next to the bed.

The doctor moved the probe around.

'First time you have come for ultrasound?' she said, eyes still on the screen.

I nodded.

'You should have come every month after the first term. Why didn't you?'

I didn't answer. I looked at Neelam bhabhi instead.

'Is everything okay?' Neelam bhabhi said. 'How far is she?'

'You should know that,' the doctor said in the scolding-condescending tone that doctors in India often use. She continued to move the probe and speak to us.

'I can see a lot of development. See this? The head of the baby.'

I saw a round shape and nodded. She moved the probe again.

'And you see this? Another head?' the doctor said.

Neelam bhabhi stood up to have a better look at the screen.

'She is having a two-headed baby?' Neelam bhabhi said.

The doctor looked at Neelam bhabhi.

'Are you uneducated? She's having twins. And they are almost ready to come out.'

My heart sank. I felt the room spin around me.

'Congratulations. This is double good news,' the doctor said, even as I contemplated suicide.

❖

'What nonsense are you talking? Abortion?' Dr Ahluwalia said, looking at Neelam bhabhi like she was a criminal.

We were back in the doctor's cabin after the ultrasound.

'Doctor, my husband Ramesh Malhotra arranged this visit. He has repaired your family cars for years ...' Neelam bhabhi said.

'So? It is because of that I've not thrown you out. You are talking about abortion? At seven-and-a-half months, with twins? I was going to tell you to fix a date for the caesarean.'

'We never said abortion as such, Doctor,' Geetu didi said. 'My brother felt we should ask you to just handle the situation.'

'What else does "handle the situation" mean? How can you people do this? There are two living people in her. Even if I operate today, they will be alive,' Reshma said.

I broke down. The doctor's harsh words, the disappointment on Veerji's face, the humiliation of Neelam bhabhi—it all became too much for me. If I couldn't abort, maybe the doctor could give me something to kill myself with. I explained to Dr Ahluwalia my entire situation, and how I couldn't have these children.

'You should have come earlier. Much earlier. We could have terminated the pregnancy. Now, I am sorry. Your kids are due,' she said.

'What do we do, Doctor?' Neelam bhabhi said, bringing her palms together.

'My brother won't let her in the house,' Geetu didi said.

The doctor stood up. She pointed to the exit.

'You should have thought of all that before. Now leave. Come to me only if you want me to deliver the babies. I understand they are not within a marriage. The maximum I can do is deliver them in secrecy, so people don't find out. Please, go now. I have other patients.'

❖

'When is Maaji coming back?' Veerji said to Neelam bhabhi at the small dining table of our Amritsar house.

'They are in Tirupati now and then they proceed to Tamil Nadu before some other places. Two more months at least.'

Veerji nodded.

Geetu didi, Veerji, Neelam bhabhi and I had sat down for dinner. Veerji told my ten-year-old brother Adi to watch TV in Veerji's room. One week after the doctor's visit, we had run out of options. Veerji told me to give the newborns to an orphanage. I couldn't sleep for three nights after that. Somehow, seeing that ultrasound and the two little heads had changed me. I realised I was about to be a mother. A mother who was going to throw her babies away to some random orphanage. My twins would be with dozens of abandoned kids, never to be cuddled or loved.

'I'll raise them,' I said to Veerji at the dining table.

'Are you stupid? As illegitimate children? And how will you pay for them?'

'I will work day and night. Please don't make me give them to an orphanage, Veerji. You have seen how horrible these places are. I will die seeing them go.'

'Then die,' he said.

Tears rolled down my cheeks. I used to be Veerji's favourite, growing up. He would save his pocket money to buy me dolls. Now he didn't care about my kids, feelings or life.

I turned to his wife.

'Please, Neelam bhabhi. Please let me keep my children. I will become a maid if I have to.'

'Yes. Please continue to make the family name shine. Become a maid and raise bastards. Why can't you just go die somewhere?' Veerji said.

'Ramesh ji, please,' Neelam bhabhi said. 'She is a child.'

'Clearly not,' Veerji said, taking deep breaths to control his anger.

'Bhaiya,' Geetu didi said. 'You have always taken care of all of us. This is not you.'

'And what have I got in return? I spend my life covered in grease. And look, Geetu, look. You get to live there in Seattle. I have to deal with all this.'

'She made a mistake,' Geetu didi said. 'She is ready to take responsibility. Let her raise her children.'

'Have you lost your mind, Geetu? This is not the US. This is Amritsar. What will we tell people? Where did the kids come from?'

Dinner remained uneaten on the table. Rajma chawal was Veerji's favourite. Today, he hadn't touched it. He continued to speak.

'Orphanage is not a bad idea. Whatever is the destiny of these kids, they have to live with it.'

One of my babies kicked inside my stomach. I thought of my little newborns, alone and scared in some rat-and-cockroach-infested orphanage. The idea seemed worse than me setting myself on fire. I began to cry loudly. I shouldn't have, but I couldn't control it.

'Stop crying now, gudiya,' Veerji said. 'You know I can't see all this.'

My Veerji is hard on the outside, but I know on the inside he is as soft as a ball of butter. There is no one in the world who cares for his family as much as him, even though all I ever do is disappoint him. Geetu didi and Neelam bhabhi took turns to wipe my tears. It didn't work. Instead, they began to cry as well. Adi peeked outside the bedroom once to see what was happening. Veerji gave him a stern look, making him scurry back into the room.

Veerji spoke after a pause. His tone was serious.

'There is one way, but it is not easy.'

'What?' I said, clinging to any ray of hope.

'Geetu, you love your sister?'

'Of course, Veerji. Bindu is our gudiya.'

'Neelam, will you do something for my family?' Veerji said.

'When have I not? It's my family too.'

'Good. If both of you are ready to make a sacrifice and keep a secret, there is a way.'

'What, Veerji?' I said, getting impatient.

'Geetu, you take one child. Call it yours and Jogi's child. Neelam, you take the other. And we call it our child.'

'What?' Geetu didi and Neelam bhabhi spoke in unison.

'Think about it. There's really no other way. It's either that or the orphanage, which nobody seems to want. I can't have Bindu raise two children on her own. Neither will she be able to afford it, nor will it keep the family's honour.'

Veerji stood up and walked to the centre of the room, leaving us three women at the dining table.

'I will have to talk to Jogi,' Geetu didi said. 'I mean, this is big. I love you, Bindu, but this is so big.'

'I told you, it's not easy. Neelam?' Veerji said.

'It's not like I have a choice. I always do what you say, Ramesh ji,' Neelam bhabhi said, a tinge of disappointment in her voice.

'What about Maaji? Do we tell her?' Geetu didi said.

'Of course not. She should never find out. I can't hurt my mother. Neelam, encourage her to stay with her parents in Haridwar for some more time. Tell her you may be pregnant. When she comes back, she will see the baby,' Veerji said.

'And me?' Geetu didi said.

'You and Jogi leave for the US anyway. Just go after the babies are born, taking one with you. Go there and inform Maaji you are pregnant. You won't come to India for another year or two anyway. When you come next time, everyone will see it as your child.'

'Jogi has to agree, Veerji,' Geetu didi said.

'I know. Tell him it was my idea.'

'I will, Veerji.'

'Remind him that I paid half the money for his taxi medallion. And married you off to him despite him not having a job at that time.'

Geetu didi nodded. Veerji came back to the dining table and sat on one of the chairs.

Still in tears, I went up to him and hugged him from behind. He picked up a plate in response.

'I'm hungry. What's for dinner? Is that rajma chawal?'

Chapter 37

Ramesh sat on the sofa, fighting back tears. Neelam aunty hugged Bindu as the latter finished telling her story. Anjali stood against the wall, arms crossed. Saurabh broke the silence.

'So wait, Prerna is not your daughter, Ramesh uncle?'

'God knows I've never treated her less than my own. Bindu, swear upon Maaji, did I ever discriminate between Prerna and Ajay?'

'Never,' Bindu said, wiping her eyes.

'That's not the point. Uncle, I was marrying Prerna unaware of this. Don't you think someone should have told me?' Saurabh said.

Ramesh threw Saurabh a brief look.

'This is not something we shared with anyone else apart from the family. How did it matter?'

Saurabh looked unconvinced. He tilted his head my way, as if expecting me to say something. I was still processing all I'd heard.

'Unbelievable,' Saurabh said. 'Sick.'

'Prerna was going to tell you. In fact, she was quite excited about having a twin,' Anjali said.

'Really?' Saurabh said, rolling his eyes.

'She only found out a few days before she died,' Anjali said.

'How?' Ramesh said.

'I told her,' Anjali said.

'Why? And how did you find out?' Ramesh said.

He looked at Neelam and Bindu. Neelam shook her head. Bindu made an apologetic face.

'Bindu?' Ramesh said.

'She already knew. She confronted me, Veerji. I couldn't lie after that. I'm sorry.' Before Ramesh could respond, Anjali spoke again.

'My mother told me. Several years ago. I have known for a while, but she swore me to secrecy.'

'Geetu? Why?' Ramesh said.

'It came out by mistake. But she never concealed it after that. She is American now. Maybe she doesn't care about putting on a façade anyway. Or maybe she thought I was mature enough to handle it. And I did. This is why I came to India. To connect with everyone here. Frankly, what is the big deal about hiding all this now, anyway?'

Ramesh looked at Bindu and Neelam.

'This can't go to Maaji, is that clear?' Ramesh said and turned to Anjali. 'I hope you didn't tell her, Anjali?'

'That's all you care about, Ramesh uncle?'

'You have no manners. Answer me, did you tell my old mother?' Ramesh said, his face almost red with anger.

'I didn't,' Anjali said.

'Good. Who else did you tell all this to before today?'

'I only spoke about it to my real mother, Bindu, and my real sister, Prerna. Do I have the right to do that, Ramesh uncle?' Anjali said, her tone sarcastic.

'Bindu, tell this girl to behave,' Ramesh said, and banged his fist on the table. 'I will not be spoken to like this.'

'Veerji, please be calm. Anjali, please don't be like this. Apologise to your uncle,' Bindu said.

'For what? For daring to live a life that's not a lie? Or for acknowledging my own mother and sister?' Anjali said, her thin body stiffening.

'Stop it, Anjali,' Neelam said.

'What about these idiots? They know now. What are they still doing here anyway?' Ramesh said.

'We won't tell anyone, Uncle,' I said, clearing my throat.

'Oh, big favour you are doing me,' Ramesh said in a sarcastic tone.

'I didn't mean it like that, Uncle,' I said.

He got up from the sofa.

'Shall I call the colony security?' Ramesh said.

'What are you saying, Uncle?' Saurabh said. 'It's me, Saurabh.'

'Who are you? What is our relationship?'

'Uncle, I am trying to help. You have had such tragedies ...' Saurabh said.

'So help me. Do me a favour.'

'Sure Uncle, what?' Saurabh said.

'Get the hell out of my house. Now.'

Chapter 38

'You were right, bhai, I got carried away. Prerna, her family, everything was too good to be true. Nothing is perfect in this world.'

Kicked out of the Malhotra residence, we had come back to our flat in Malviya Nagar. We had a few more weeks left on the lease. We still had not found new apartments for ourselves.

'It's not Prerna's fault, Golu,' I said.

'Still, she should have told me the moment she found out,' Saurabh said. He fished out his phone from his trouser pocket and began tapping the screen.

'What are you doing?' I said.

'Ordering pav bhaji on UberEats. This is all too stressful for me,' Saurabh said.

No better stress buster than a thousand calories, I guess.

'You said she had something to tell you?' I said.

Saurabh finished the online payment of his order and looked up.

'What?'

'Her chats on the last day. She had something to share with you,' I said.

Saurabh scrolled through his last few chats with Prerna.

'Yes. She said, "I also have something special to share with you". But how do I know it was about her and Anjali being twins?'

'That's all she said?'

'Yeah. I asked her again. She said it was something unbelievable but special she just found out.'

'Definitely sounds like the same news.'

Saurabh let out a huge sigh. He checked his phone.

'Eleven minutes.'

'What?'

'For the food to get here.'

'Don't change the topic, Golu. I don't want you to blame Prerna. She was going to tell you.'

'But she knew before. Why hide it? The family hid it from me. Prerna hid it from me. And I was to marry her.'

'Maybe she wanted to tell you in person. She would have told you before the marriage.'

Saurabh tossed his phone on the coffee table.

'Leave it. Doesn't matter. I was the fool.'

'No, you weren't. And we still have to solve her case, and now even Adi's case.'

'Fuck the case. Adi wasn't Prerna's chachu, he was her mamu. However fucked up that is.'

'True,' I said.

'Drop the case. I don't want anything to do with that family. Liars, concealers, rude people. See how he kicked us out?'

'That's only Ramesh uncle.'

'Why are you defending the family suddenly? You always told me I was going "gaga" over them. Now you are defending them.'

'I'm just curious about the case. We can't just drop it. In fact, things have become more complex and interesting.'

'Is that all this is to you? An interesting puzzle?' Saurabh was louder than usual. 'You realise there are real people with real emotions here?'

I did realise it. I also realised I had a really hungry person in front of me. Until the food arrived, his lordship's mood wouldn't improve.

I kept silent till the delivery boy found his way to our house. The bell rang. The aroma of melted butter filled our tiny flat. Saurabh brought the food to the dining table. Without bothering with cutlery or plates, he ate straight from the packet. As the carbs and fats hit his bloodstream, I spoke again.

'Saurabh, I know you are hurt.'

'Uh-huh,' Saurabh said, mouth filled with food.

'But it is even more important that we find out the truth now. There are two deaths.'

'Uh-huh,' Saurabh said again.

Was that a yes? Was that even a response? Or was he just enjoying the food? I slid the pav bhaji away from him to get his attention.

'What are you doing?'

'We should keep pursuing this case, right?'

'I don't think so. We have so many other things to do. We have to find an apartment each. We have to move out. CyberSafe work is suffering.'

'I know all that.'

'Plus, the reason I was doing all this was for Prerna and her family. Now that I know I was being hoodwinked ...'

'You don't know that. Let's find out everything first,' I said.

'I don't care.'

'Okay, aren't you curious? If Anjali and Prerna were twins, they should resemble each other a lot, isn't it? How did we miss that? Because Prerna was so fa—?'

Saurabh stared at me. Calling Prerna fat was an eternal no-no.

'Sorry, I didn't mean it like that. I meant because she was ...' I searched for the right word, 'Bigger?'

Anjali was probably forty-five kilos tops. Prerna was around seventy. A twenty-five kilo difference can change facial features.

'Give me back my food. Now.'

I ignored him.

'Totally different hairstyles. Tattoos and a nose ring on Anjali. Maybe that's why they didn't look so similar.'

'Pav bhaji is no good when cold. I said, give me my food.'

I slid the food back to him.

I sat in silence. He spoke after he finished his meal.

'Anyway,' Saurabh said, wiping his mouth with a tissue. 'We neither have access to the house, nor cooperation from the family. We are screwed. What will we do now, anyway?'

Saurabh stood up. He took the packaging and dumped it in the kitchen dustbin. I followed him to the kitchen.

'There will be Adi's post-mortem report,' I said.

'It will get you nowhere. He overdosed. Big fucking deal. The police don't care. Ramesh will silence them with some cash and they will close the case. Prerna, accidental fall. Adi, accidental overdose.'

Saurabh turned on the tap to wash his hands.

'You believe that?' I said.

'No, but my beliefs are irrelevant. I have realised the world is all lies anyway. Spouses, in-laws, best friends. You can't trust anyone.'

'Ouch, that hurt, Saurabh,' I said, hand on chest.

'Good,' Saurabh said, wiping his hands. 'Was meant to. Now let's start looking for our individual apartments soon.'

Chapter 39

'For the record, I didn't want to come here,' Saurabh said, after ordering over half the menu at Bikanervala in Saket.

Two days after we were kicked out from their house, Bindu had called me. She wanted to meet. Saurabh had flat-out refused. He did not want to engage with anyone related to Prerna anymore. I dragged him to the meeting anyway, by ensuring a venue that had enough culinary appeal for him.

'I know. Thank you for coming,' Bindu said. 'I really wanted to meet you both. Anjali did too.'

Anjali wore her usual ripped jeans, a plain black top and a leather jacket. I looked at her face; she did have the same eyes and complexion as Prerna. She also had the same puckered nose and small ears. If you looked for it, Prerna and Anjali had a lot in common.

Bikanervala serves quick. Within minutes, our table was filled with plates of chole bhature, dhokla and paneer pakoras.

'Does Ramesh uncle know you are here?' Saurabh said as he put a dhokla on his plate.

'Of course not,' Anjali said.

Saurabh rolled his eyes.

'Saurabh beta,' Bindu said. 'We need your help. I need to know what happened to my daughter and Anjali's sister.'

'You kept your beta in the dark. Spare me the endearments,' Saurabh said.

'I am indebted to Veerji. I cannot go against his wishes. But my love and affection for you is real.'

Saurabh continued to decorate his plate with an array of chutneys, avoiding eye contact.

'And this secret is not something we ever discuss, even in the family,' Bindu said. 'These two girls were raised as Ramesh's and Geetu's daughters. It's just how it's always been.'

'Leave it, Bindu aunty,' Saurabh said. 'Fact is, I was not told.'

'Prerna planned to tell you, Saurabh,' Anjali said quietly.

'When?' Saurabh said.

'Soon,' Anjali said. 'Before the marriage for sure.'

'Anjali,' Saurabh said, 'you told Prerna about her being your sister. When did you do that?'

'A few weeks before she died. She was opening up about her feelings for you, how much she loved you. We felt close, and I told her.'

'And?' Saurabh said.

'She was overwhelmed. Wanted to tell you first thing. But then said she would save it for a special moment.'

I glanced at Saurabh.

'I told you, she would have told you on Karva Chauth,' I said.

Saurabh played with his food.

'She loved you. A lot,' Bindu said in a soft voice.

Saurabh's eyes welled up. He stood up to leave.

'Don't go, beta,' Bindu said. I pulled Saurabh by his hand, making him sit down again. Bindu opened her handbag and took out a heavy keychain with around a dozen keys. She kept the bunch on the table and slid it towards us.

'What's that?' I said.

'House keys.'

'So many?' I said.

'I copied Veerji's entire set. Whatever he keeps in his briefcase,' Bindu said.

'What do we do with this?' I said.

'Help us find answers,' Bindu said.

'Ramesh uncle doesn't want answers,' Saurabh said.

'You know Veerji. Family name is everything to him,' Bindu said. 'That is why he just wants the case closed.'

Saurabh slid the keys back to Bindu.

'You and Anjali have been good to us. However, I am done with your family,' he said.

I looked at Anjali's disappointed face.

'Saurabh, at least listen to them,' I said.

'I'm done with everyone actually, including you,' Saurabh said. He kept his eyes on the dhokla.

I touched the keys. The answer to what happened to Prerna probably lay in them. You don't just let a murder go unsolved like that, I wanted to tell Saurabh. I also couldn't bear to see Anjali's disappointment.

'Please,' Bindu said and held Saurabh's hand, 'for my sake.'

Saurabh removed his hand from hers and continued to rearrange the food on his plate.

'Prerna did tell me Saurabh was the best thing that happened to her,' Anjali said.

Saurabh kept the dhokla down on his plate. Anjali continued.

'She did love you a lot. More than Eato, any previous relationships and even her family. She valued you above everything and everyone.'

Saurabh looked intensely at her.

'She told you that?'

'Yes,' Anjali said, 'several times. In fact, she said, you wait and see, Saurabh will be so excited to know I have a twin sister. He won't care about anything else. He loves me and just wants to be with me.'

'It's true,' Saurabh said in a soft voice.

'So how does it matter what Veerji says? You wanted to find out the truth for Prerna. Even if Veerji has kicked you out, will you abandon what you started for her?' Bindu said.

'She didn't tell me immediately,' Saurabh said.

'It was I who told her to share this with you on Karva Chauth. I felt it would be a special moment,' Bindu said.

'What?' I said.

'She came to me the day she found out I'm her mother. We hugged and cried. We spoke for hours. Since that day, she started sharing more things with me. She talked a lot about you,

Saurabh. She wanted to fast on Karva Chauth. I told her to tell you everything that day,' said Bindu, with tears in her eyes.

Saurabh placed a hand on the bunch of keys and kept it there. After a few seconds, he dragged the keys towards himself.

'Beta, does this mean you are going to help us?' Bindu said.

Saurabh gave a brief nod.

'Thank you,' Bindu said in an excited voice. 'Anything I can do for you? Anything?'

'Eat the food I have ordered. If pakoras go cold, they taste like rubber.'

Chapter 40

I jiggled the heavy set of keys in my hand.

'Twelve keys.'

'No idea why so many,' Saurabh said and turned to the driver. 'Bhaiya, ignore Google Maps here and take a right. I know a better way.'

We were on our way to meet a broker who would show us rental apartments in Gurgaon. I held up the biggest key, which was double the size of the rest.

'This looks like the main gate key,' I said.

Saurabh took a closer look.

'No. The main gate has a standard lock. This key looks like that of a shutter of a shop,' Saurabh said. 'Maybe Ramesh uncle's showroom?'

'Probably,' I said as I handed the keys back to Saurabh. 'What next?'

Saurabh rolled down his window and waved at a man wearing sunglasses at seven in the evening.

'We have reached. Let's look at some apartments first and talk later,' Saurabh said.

We had come to Hamilton Heights, a gated apartment complex in Gurgaon Phase III. We entered a large garden. Kids played and maids chatted on their phones. If I wanted to start a family I would move here.

'Best building in Gurgaon,' the broker said, sunglasses still on.

He showed us two one-bedroom apartments, one in Tower 2 and the other in Tower 9. The buildings were a short walk apart. I presumed this would be enough 'space' for Saurabh, which he claimed he needed. What's with people who keep saying 'I need space' all the time? What am I supposed to do? Help him join ISRO?

'Separate towers, but the same society. Won't work,' Saurabh said to the broker.

'Sir, don't you want to be near each other?' the broker said, trying to hold three mobile phones in one hand.

'We want to be far away from each other,' Saurabh said.

He wanted to be far away; I didn't.

'Oh,' the broker said. 'Why, sir?'

'Is that any of your business?' Saurabh said.

'No, sir. My business is to get you a good flat. I will line up other apartments,' he said.

❖

'Maybe it is simple. Adi killed Prerna. He felt he would get caught. Instead of jail, he preferred suicide,' Saurabh said.

It was midnight and we were back in our Malviya Nagar house.

When I didn't respond, he said, 'Possible, isn't it? Any other theories?'

I clicked my tongue to indicate 'no'.

'Maggi?'

'What?'

'It's midnight. I will make Maggi. It will help us think.'

'Sit, Golu. No more distractions and, frankly, no more eating. You are on a diet, aren't you?'

'I was, earlier. To look good in the wedding pictures. Now, no wedding, so ...'

'It's good to be fit otherwise too. Now concentrate on the case.'

'Adi kept saying to Ramesh uncle that he didn't do it,' Saurabh said.

'Come on. He wasn't going to admit it. Are you forgetting the ring and gloves?'

'Yeah, wow. This is complex. I do need to eat something,' Saurabh said and stood up. He walked into the kitchen.

'Golu, don't start cooking now,' I said.

'I'm not. I'm just looking for something ready to eat,' he shouted from the kitchen.

He came back with a box of Kellogg's Frosties cornflakes.

'Found something healthy, see?' Saurabh said. He held up the packet of cereal that contained thirty-five grams of sugar per hundred grams.

I shook my head in disapproval.

'C'mon, it's healthy—' Saurabh began, but I interrupted him.

'Oh God, the cereal box,' I said, pointing at the packet.

'Yeah, what about it? Okay, it has a little sugar, so—' Saurabh said before I interrupted him again.

'Saurabh, we saw cereal in Adi's house. Remember?'

'Huh?' Saurabh said, examining the packet in his hand and wondering why I had changed the topic.

'The Special K packet, remember?'

'Yes,' Saurabh said, 'on his dining table. When we went to search his house.'

'No, even on the day we went with the police and found his body. The cereal and bowl were there on the table.'

Saurabh bit his lip as he tried to recollect what he'd seen.

'Fuck, yes, it was there. With the milk and the bowl, yes. The day he died.'

'So he planned to have it, right?'

'Yeah. And then go jogging. Like that earlier day.'

Saurabh took a fistful of crunchy cornflakes and popped it in his mouth.

'Who wakes up, brings out his cereal and milk, then doesn't eat it, goes back to bed and overdoses on drugs to commit suicide?' I said.

'Fuck. It's not suicide. Or an accidental overdose.'

I clapped my hands.

'It's murder. And we have to solve not one, but two of them now,' I said.

❖

'Oh, there you are. India's finest detectives,' Singh said in his usual sarcasm-laced voice.

Saurabh and I stood up to greet him.

'Fancy place you chose to meet,' Singh said.

We had come to the garden café of the Manor Hotel in Friends Colony, a five-minute drive from the New Friends Colony Police Station. The five-star property felt more like an elegant old-money home rather than a hotel. The fourteen-room hotel also used to have the famous restaurant, Indian Accent, where posh Delhiites would spend a week's salary to drink paani puri water in test tubes.

'We felt it's close for you,' Saurabh said, after ordering masala tea.

'You could have just come to the station. It's your home,' Singh said and laughed.

'We can't. Ramesh uncle told us to stay away from the case,' Saurabh said, 'and his family.'

'Really?' Singh smirked. 'Why is that?'

Saurabh sighed.

'Felt we are interfering too much,' I said.

'Maybe you are,' Singh said.

'We just want to help find the truth,' Saurabh said.

'They lost two family members. Be sensitive to that,' Singh said.

The waiter arrived with a tray holding fancy teacups and a kettle. He prepared tea for all of us.

'Two sugars,' Singh said. 'Tea is hot, right?'

The tea was scalding temperature, its heat welcome in the winter evening.

'No point now. I will be closing the case.'

'Really?' I said, surprised.

'Yes, the family visited me three days ago. Ramesh, his wife, sister and that girl with the American accent, Anjali.'

'Oh,' I said. Bindu and Anjali had met us two days ago. Which meant they had gone to the police station before meeting us.

'What did they say?' Saurabh said.

The inspector took a sip of his tea and spoke again.

'They said the investigation has brought a lot of distress to their family. Everyone became a suspect. Adi, being a delicate kind of person, overdosed from stress.'

'What about the ring I found in Adi's room? He didn't become a suspect without reason,' I said, my pitch rising.

'Shh, calm down, Keshav. You guys get too excited. Maybe it is simple. Prerna had an accidental fall. Adi overdosed. These things happen.'

'They do. However, in this case, they were both murdered,' Saurabh said.

'How? How could they have been killed in a house full of people, amidst their own family?'

'Unless someone from the family killed them,' I said.

The inspector shook his head and smiled.

'I like your never-give-up spirit. I had it in my younger days,' Singh said. 'But over time, life teaches you that sometimes you just have to let things go.'

Saurabh and I looked at each other, unconvinced. 'Sometimes a fall is just a fall, and an overdose is just an overdose. A death doesn't have to be exciting just because you are investigating it,' Singh said.

'Sir, we are not looking for excitement. We are looking for the truth. Don't you find it fishy? Adi dying just like that?' I said.

'No, I don't. The family doesn't either. They have no suspects and no inclination to pursue an investigation. In fact, Ramesh ji wants the case closure report as soon as possible.'

'Why?' Saurabh said.

'Who knows? Maybe for some policy.'

'Insurance policy? Prerna's insurance?' I said.

'Yeah. Insurance companies need an all-clear to establish that it was an accident before releasing the claim.'

Saurabh looked at me, shocked. I raised an eyebrow.

'Again, this is normal, my friends. I have investigated cases for two decades. Everything is not a sign or a clue.'

The three of us drank our tea without saying a word. I looked at the elegant outdoor furniture laid out in the hotel. The loud ring on Singh's phone interrupted the awkward silence.

'Sorry,' Singh said to us. 'My wife.'

He took the call.

'Yes, you keep the documents ready,' Singh said. 'The visa guy will come ... No, we are not going to Schengen. That's not a country ... That's what the visa for Europe is called. Yes, for Paris also.' He ended the call and smiled at us.

'Anything else? If not, I'll take your leave,' Singh said.

'What will you do next?' I said.

'Nothing. I have to prepare the case closure report. My senior has to sign it. Will take me around two weeks,' Singh said. 'Have so much to finish before I take some time off.'

We walked him out of the hotel to his Gypsy.

'Adi's post-mortem revealed anything, sir?' I said as we reached his vehicle.

Singh patted my back.

'Let it go, detective sahib. But to answer your question, no. It only said death due to excess heroin in blood.'

'Anything else?' I said.

The inspector sat in the Gypsy and shook his head.

'Fit body. Needle marks showing regular drug use. No sign of force or assault. We thought there were some bruises but ...' Singh laughed.

'But?' I said.

'Nothing. Love bites. People in the family said he always had them. Quite a ladies' man it seems,' Singh said and drove off.

Chapter 41

'Scotch?' Rana said. Right after our meeting with Singh, we had called ACP Rana. Rana, in turn, invited us to the Hyatt Regency hotel in Bhikaji Cama Place. He was on duty there as part of a politician's security detail. The politician made a speech about the slowing economy and left. Post-conference, Rana sat with us at one of the tables in the banquet hall.

'Have a drink—I am not paying for it. The conference sponsors are,' Rana said. 'And this friend of yours. He likes to eat, I know. Kebabs?'

Rana snapped his fingers. Two waiters rushed to our table with several glasses of whiskey and plates of appetisers. Rana clinked his glass with ours and took a sip.

'I'm hungry too,' Rana said. He lifted a tandoori chicken leg and tore it with his teeth. 'Anyway, what brings you boys here? As you can see, I am serving the nation.'

Saurabh and I told him about Singh closing the case.

'Oh yes, Ramesh's junkie brother died too, right? That singer at the Leela?' Rana said.

I nodded.

'Exactly, sir,' Saurabh said. 'But Inspector Singh is filing a closure report.'

'Welcome to the real world, boys. First time you are seeing something like this? This happens all the time.'

'What happens?' I said.

'Let's just say Singh must be a happy man.' Rana winked at me.

'You think Inspector Singh took a bribe, sir?' Saurabh said, eyes wide.

Rana looked to his left and right.

'Shh, never mention that word in my presence.'

'He did get a call from his wife. They are planning a holiday in Europe.'

Rana laughed and shook his head.

'Singh's so obvious. Europe. Too funny. No wonder he has a reputation.'

'What do we do, sir?' Saurabh said.

'Have another drink?' Rana said.

'Seriously, sir,' I said.

Rana let out a sigh.

'Let it go. Or find the killer with solid evidence. Take it to Singh.'

'Take it to him? But you said he may have ...' I stopped mid-sentence.

'He has to reopen the case if there's new watertight evidence. Otherwise, he knows you can go to the media or his seniors.'

'Can he reopen a closed case though?'

'Of course he can reopen. He will have to say something along the lines of "in light of the new evidence XYZ". Find out that XYZ.'

'What about the money he might have taken?' Saurabh said.

'You don't know for sure that he did. So, never ever mention to him that you think he took money. Clear?'

'Of course, sir.'

'Good. And if he did take the money, settling it is his problem. He will return it, or if the evidence is overwhelming, tell Ramesh to stuff it.'

'Fine,' I said.

'Do you even have any new suspects right now?' Rana said.

I shook my head. We had nothing but a bunch of keys.

Rana laughed.

'Fine, best of luck, then. You may not have another suspect, how about another drink?'

❖

'It's time to use these,' I said, spinning the heavy bunch of keys around my index finger.

Four whiskeys and an entire tandoori chicken each inside us, we sat in a cab to go home.

'It's scary to go into that house again,' Saurabh said.

Our car passed South Extension on the Ring Road. The metro line ran above us. From a distance, the bright Porsche showroom sign became visible.

'I don't want to use these keys to go to their house again. I want to check what's in there,' I said, pointing to the Malhotra Motors showroom.

'There are cars there, lots of expensive cars, bhai,' Saurabh slurred. 'Oh, and guards all around. Why there, bhai?'

'Isn't Ramesh uncle's office there too?' I said.

'Yeah, on the first floor. Why?'

'I want to know all about the man who wants to close Prerna's case the most,' I said.

Saurabh did not respond. His eyes had shut. Whiskey and chicken can give you temporary bliss, I guess.

Chapter 42

'That's the main showroom on the ground floor,' Saurabh said.

Saurabh and I were standing across the road from Malhotra Motors in South Extension.

It was 6.30 p.m. We had come to do a recce of the showroom after work.

The lights of the first-floor offices were on.

'See that left corner office? That belongs to Ramesh uncle,' Saurabh said. 'He doesn't seem to be in. Can't see his car in the parking area either.'

'What are the other offices on the first floor?' I said.

'Accounts and general administration. Anyone apart from those directly selling cars sits there.'

'Anything else upstairs?'

'A pantry to make tea and coffee. They also have staff toilets. If customers want to use them, they send them there,' Saurabh said.

'CCTVs all over?' I said.

'Yes, in all common spaces and the main showroom. Not in Ramesh uncle's office though.'

'Problem is, how do we get to his cabin,' I said, 'if there are cameras outside.'

'Yes, and there are guards downstairs. Too risky, bhai. Drop it.'

Before I could respond, my phone rang. It was Bindu.

'Hello, Bindu aunty,' I said and placed the call on speaker mode.

'How is it going? Any progress?' Bindu said.

'You didn't tell me all of you went to the police,' I said.

'Veerji took us. We had no choice. It is after that we came to you. I realised Veerji and the police won't do much.'

'You could have told us,' I said.

'I'm sorry. I felt scared to talk about the police ... Did you guys find anything?'

Saurabh entered the conversation. 'Your great Veerji might have bribed the police, by the way,' he said.

'What?' Bindu said.

'Nothing, Bindu aunty,' I said. 'We're trying to work on it. Where's Ramesh uncle?'

'He is in Amritsar. Had some work in the factory.'

'What factory is it?'

'They make auto parts there.'

'Which auto parts, Bindu aunty?' Saurabh said.

'I don't know, beta. It used to be our old car repair workshop. Now Veerji has a factory there. He went yesterday, for three days.'

'How did he go?' I said.

'With Anwar. He always goes in his Cayenne. He's passionate about his cars.'

I looked at Saurabh. Both Ramesh and Anwar, the two people who could recognise us at the showroom, were not in town. If we had to act, we had to do it in the next two days.

'Okay, we need to search his office in the showroom. We'll need your help,' I said.

Saurabh put the call on mute.

'Why are you asking her?' Saurabh whispered, even though the call was on mute.

'We can't do it any other way. Guards? CCTV cameras? Seriously, James Bond?'

'So what do you want her help for?'

'I have a plan. Don't worry,' I said and unmuted the call.

'Hello? You there?' Bindu was saying on the other side.

'Yes, sorry. Bad line,' I said.

'What help do you need from me? I already gave you the keys. Showroom keys are also in there.'

'I need you and Anjali to both be in the showroom when we go there.'

'What?' Saurabh mouthed the word. I gestured for him to be quiet.

'I don't want to be involved, beta. If Veerji finds out ...' Bindu said.

'You won't get into trouble, I promise.'

❖

'Good evening, I'm Jayesh Varma, head of sales here at Malhotra Motors,' a thirty-ish, somewhat overweight sales agent said as he came up to us. He had an extra-white and extra-fake smile, the ones you see on models in toothpaste ads.

Two days after our recce, we had come to Malhotra Motors again. It was four in the afternoon on a Sunday, and we had dressed in suits. We combed our hair straight and wore zero power glasses. Saurabh flinched a little when he saw the salesperson. The salesperson, however, began his pitch.

'Which of these fine cars interests you, sir?'

'We were thinking of a 911,' I said. 'Although in these potholed Delhi roads I wonder ...'

'Sir, one buys a Porsche to fulfil a lifelong dream. And dreams can't be put on hold because of some potholes.'

The salesperson directed us towards a car on display. A shiny red Porsche 911 Carrera was parked on a circular disc.

'Acceleration zero to hundred in 4.2 seconds,' Jayesh said. 'And if you take the Sport Chrono package, zero to hundred in 4.0 seconds.'

'How much is the Sport Chrono package?' Saurabh said, making conversation.

'Just twenty lakh rupees more,' Jayesh said.

I wondered what kind of people found twenty lakh bucks worth the extra 0.2 seconds of acceleration.

'How much is the car for?' I said.

'1.42 crores ex-showroom for our starting model. On road, around 1.70 crores,' Jayesh said.

Saurabh and I kept a straight face. We had to act cool.

'Only?' Saurabh said, probably overdoing the coolness.

'Yeah, isn't it a beauty for that price?' said an excited Jayesh. I kept my eyes on the entrance door.

In two minutes, Bindu and Anjali entered the showroom.

We did not acknowledge each other. As planned, they went to the Cayenne section, which is the Porsche SUV. The staff recognised them and greeted them with folded hands.

'Malhotra sir's sister,' I heard a salesperson say behind me.

'Can you tell me all the variations and upgrades possible?' Saurabh said. Jayesh looked at Saurabh and smiled.

'Let me get the brochures and explain everything to you. Please come to the meeting table.'

Saurabh and I moved to the meeting area. I could still see and hear Bindu from where we were sitting.

'My niece from the US wanted to check out the SUV. She's a journalist doing a story on luxury cars. That's all,' Bindu was saying.

'No problem, madam,' the salesperson said, opening the door of the vehicle. Anjali stepped inside.

'I am troubling you so much,' Bindu said and smiled.

'This is your showroom, madam. What are you saying? Do you want some coffee?'

Anjali sat inside the cream-coloured Cayenne. She fiddled with the controls. She turned on the wipers, tested the indicators and switched the internal lights on and off a couple of times. The huge car made her look thinner than ever. She wore a baby pink salwar kameez and a bindi, probably to look the part of a journalist. I wanted to place my hand over hers on the steering wheel. I turned to school principal Saurabh instead, who had rendered Anjali off-limits. He shook his leg as we waited for Jayesh.

'Why did you flinch when you saw Jayesh?' I whispered.

'He came for my engagement,' Saurabh whispered back. 'I don't think he recognised me. I must have lost weight.'

'No you haven't,' I said. 'It's the glasses.'

'Fuck off.'

Jayesh and his beaming smile returned in a few minutes.

'Sir, so here are your options. Please fill in this form with all your contact details. Or give me your business card.'

Saurabh took out a card from his pocket and handed it to Jayesh.

'Jacob D'Souza, co-founder and vice president, CyberSafe,' Jayesh read out loud. 'Superb, sir.'

'It's okay,' Saurabh said. 'Long way to go still.'

'Well, wherever you have to go, your 911 will get you there faster,' Jayesh said and grinned at his own cleverness.

We collected all the brochures.

'These are very helpful, thanks. We have to go somewhere now but we'll be in touch,' I said.

Saurabh and I stood up.

'Sure, sir, I will be waiting for your call,' Jayesh said.

'Do you have a washroom in here?' Saurabh said.

'Sure, sir, up the stairs behind you. Shall I walk you there?'

Saurabh turned around to look at the steps.

'No, I'll find my way,' Saurabh said. 'You have other customers waiting.'

'Yes, sir, Sunday. Busy day for us.' Jayesh was all teeth.

'Long drive ahead so ... I will also use it,' I said. 'Nice to meet you, Jayesh. We'll use the washroom and make our way out. You attend to others.'

Saurabh and I shook hands with Jayesh and waved him goodbye. We went up the steps and reached the first floor. We entered the toilet. Nobody else was inside.

'I saw CCTV on the steps,' I said.

'Yeah, but the guards don't care. We are two normal customers,' Saurabh said.

Three more men came to use the toilet and left. Saurabh and I pretended to wash our hands at the sink.

Tweeeeeeet! The sound of a loud alarm filled the entire showroom building. Bindu and Anjali had done what I had told them—to trigger the Cayenne's burglar alarm. First, Bindu locked the car from the outside using the automatic key. Anjali continued to sit inside and fiddle with the controls. In this scenario, the car detects unusual activity and triggers the alarm. The alarm rang for thirty seconds each time, with a ten-second pause in-between.

'Let's go,' I said. We came out of the toilet and made for the corner office.

The alarm distracted the entire staff downstairs, including the security guard at the CCTV monitors. Those few seconds gave us a window to walk from the toilet to Ramesh's office without anyone noticing us on CCTV.

I tried all the keys at Ramesh's office door. Six didn't work. The alarm stopped as the staff downstairs disabled it.

'Hurry,' Saurabh said.

'Fuck,' I said as I tried the seventh. This time the lock turned. 'Welcome,' I said, and opened the door.

❖

Ramesh's cabin had floor-to-ceiling glass walls. The bottom three-fourths of the glass were frosted. From the top one-quarter section, you could see what was going on in the showroom below. I moved up to see what was happening downstairs, bending a little so I would not be seen. Anjali and Bindu were apologising profusely to the showroom staff.

'Bhai, let's start?' Saurabh said.

'Yeah,' I said and turned around. Ramesh's desk was covered with a black leather lining with the Porsche logo. A Dell computer, a filing tray and a few model cars lay on it. Open shelves ran along the wall of the office. A five-foot high and three-foot wide cabinet stood beside the desk.

Saurabh sat down on Ramesh's plush leather chair as he fiddled with the three desk drawers.

'Wow, you do look like the son-in-law. The ones in the movies who take over everything. Like in *Baazigar*,' I said.

'Not funny,' Saurabh said.

'Sorry,' I said, remembering that, in *Baazigar,* the protagonist throws his girlfriend from the roof. 'Where do we begin?'

'If I could hack this computer, we would be all set,' Saurabh said.

He fiddled with the computer's mouse. He typed a few letters when asked for a password.

'Do you know the password?' I said.

'No. Took a guess. "Prerna". Didn't work,' Saurabh said.

Not exactly hi-tech hacking, I wanted to say, but kept quiet.

I went up to the shelves. I picked up a file with utility bills.

'Did you know the electricity bill for this showroom is five lakhs a month?' I said.

Saurabh continued to try various passwords as he spoke to me.

'Didn't the CM of Delhi make electricity free or something?' Saurabh said.

'Not for Porsche showrooms, Golu.'

Saurabh threw up his hands after several failed attempts at the password.

'Leave the computer. Check the rest of the office. Look, sales register for the last three months,' I said, opening another file. 'There are names of every customer.'

'What do I do with this? Call them and ask if they need new seat covers?' Saurabh said.

'Point is to keep looking,' I said.

Saurabh pulled at the drawers of the table, which were locked. I slid the bunch of keys to him.

I flipped through the sales file I had in my hand. 'They sold twenty-six cars in the last three months. That's it. Only twenty-six, Golu.'

'You heard the price of the cars? They're not exactly selling potatoes,' Saurabh said. He tried to open the drawers with the smaller keys in the bunch.

'Did you know Volkswagen owns Porsche?' I said. 'Ramesh uncle has a Volkswagen showroom too?'

'They do, in Amritsar. His partner Taneja manages it, remember?' Saurabh said, eyes still on the drawers.

'Oh yes.'

'Fuck, what is this stupid lock? Help, bhai, a key is stuck in the keyhole,' Saurabh said, wriggling the key to get it out.

I kneeled on the floor to come at eye level with the drawers. I shook the key stuck inside the keyhole.

'If it breaks, we're screwed,' Saurabh said.

'Relax,' I said, and pulled out the key. 'You put it in upside down. Let me take care of this. Check the closet, please.'

Saurabh opened the wooden doors of the unlocked closet.

'There are trophies. "Best dealer north region". How many Porsche showrooms could there be in the north, anyway?' Saurabh said.

'Anything else?' I said as I tried another key in the drawer.

'More trophies, caps, pen stands. A room freshener. I don't think we're going to find anything here.'

Click, the drawers opened.

'Leave all that, come here,' I said. 'Let's check the drawers.'

The first drawer had pens, paper clips, post-it notes, paan masala, a lighter and an open packet of Classic Milds cigarettes.

'Ramesh uncle smokes here? It says "no smoking" all over the showroom,' I said and pointed to the ceiling. 'See, smoke alarms all over.'

'I guess he steps out to get his fix,' Saurabh said.

I opened the second drawer. It had two transparent folders with printed sheets inside.

'Quarterly accounts for Malhotra Motors—Porsche Showroom Delhi', said the first folder.

'Quarterly accounts for Taneja Motors—Volkswagen Amritsar', said the second.

I opened the third drawer. It had a few letters, most of them from Kotak Bank. The third drawer also had envelopes from a life insurance company, a car financing company and a credit card issuer. I took out all the documents and kept them on the desk.

'Let's go through everything,' I said.

Saurabh checked the time. It was 3.30 p.m. We had asked Anjali and Bindu to do the car alarm trick again with another showroom car at 4 p.m. sharp to enable our exit.

'We have exactly half an hour,' Saurabh said.

I opened the quarterly accounts. It had several pages, each with tables full of numbers.

'So much information. Impossible to go through it so fast,' I said.

'Let's just take scanned pictures of these papers. Read them all later?' Saurabh said.

'Really?' I said.

'Yeah. I have a scan app,' Saurabh said.

Over the next twenty minutes, we scanned every document in the folders onto our phones.

'Almost done. Everything okay downstairs?' Saurabh said, scanning in a letter from the bank. I walked over to the frosted glass wall.

I saw Ramesh downstairs, chatting with Bindu and Anjali.

'Golu, f–fuck!' I whispered.

'Did you just say fuck?' Saurabh said, scanning another document onto his phone.

I signalled to him to come closer to the glass. Saurabh looked down and saw Ramesh.

'How on earth ...' he said loudly. I put my hand on his mouth.

'Shh,' I said. I dragged him back to the centre of the room.

He pulled my hand down and whispered, 'How, bhai? Bindu aunty said he was in Amritsar today. Coming back tomorrow.'

'Fuck do I know? He's downstairs. We're trapped.'

'He's going to come up, isn't he?' Saurabh said. 'Damn, we're going to get caught. He's going to kill us.'

'Okay, don't panic. Think.'

'What think? It's five minutes to four o'clock. Bindu and Anjali are supposed to set off the alarm again and distract everyone at that time.'

'That won't happen now, Saurabh. Ramesh is with them. We need to get out some other way. Did we get all the documents?'

'Yes.'

'Fine, put everything back first.'

We kept all the documents back in the drawers.

Saurabh looked at me, worried.

'My heart is exploding. Think of something. All this stress is not good for me, bhai.'

'Shut up and clean up, Golu,' I said.

We restored the place to its original avatar in the next three minutes. I peeked downstairs again. Anjali was standing next to the 911 Carrera, talking animatedly with Ramesh. Did she understand the situation? Was she trying to distract him? Or was she trying to get into the car and set off the alarm? It wouldn't work. We couldn't just walk downstairs and exit now with Ramesh in the middle of the showroom. Anjali continued to talk as Ramesh nodded his head. Mid-conversation, he placed his hand in his jacket pocket and took out a bunch of keys. The same bunch we had duplicates of.

'He's planning to come up,' I whispered.

'Now?' said Saurabh, sweatdrops on his forehead.

'I can try something. Not sure if it will work.'

'I don't care. Do something. I am dying.'

'I need Anjali and Bindu to cooperate. Wait, will send them a message.'

I typed a message to Anjali and Bindu, hoping they'd read it before Ramesh made his way up to the cabin.

'Give me the cigarettes and the lighter, Golu,' I said.

'What? Bhai, this is no time to chill. *Do* something.'

'Just give it to me, please,' I said.

Saurabh passed me the cigarette packet and lighter. I took out five Classic Milds, placed them in my mouth, and lit them all at once.

'Suicide? Your best option?' Saurabh said.

'Um-hun,' I said and shook my head, my mouth full.

I took a huge drag. Five orange tips smouldered and I coughed.

'What is wrong with you, bhai?' Saurabh said, perplexed. I took the cigarettes out of my mouth.

'See that smoke alarm on the ceiling?' I said.

I went to the centre of the room. Above my head, there was a white cylindrical block with a tiny red light. I stood under it and lifted the lit cigarettes up high.

'If we are lucky, this will work,' I said, holding the cigarettes up like an Olympic torch. Nothing happened for a full minute. I stretched my hand higher.

Saurabh went to the window to check the situation.

'Ramesh uncle is walking towards the stairs. Anjali is with him, trying to slow him down,' Saurabh said.

I took a deep puff of all five cigarettes together and blew out the smoke towards the smoke alarm. I repeated the process three times, killing my lungs in the process.

I heard Ramesh and Anjali's voices approaching the cabin as they reached the first floor corridor.

Panic gripped Saurabh. I placed a finger on my lips to signal him to remain quiet. I took a long, deep puff again and let out the smoke.

Vooooootttttt! The smoke alarm went off so loud, I almost lost my balance. The blaring alarm was much louder than that from the SUV. The centralised alarm's sound filled the entire showroom. I checked downstairs. The guards instructed everyone, as per Porsche's strict procedures, to immediately step out of the building while they checked what had happened. My heart pounded. I tiptoed to the office door. I could hear Ramesh and Anjali right outside.

'Let's go out, uncle,' Anjali said, a thin door separating us.

'It's probably nothing. Maybe someone smoked in the parking area. Oversensitive alarms,' Ramesh said.

'Still, let's go, uncle. Better to be safe,' Anjali said.

Ramesh's phone rang. He picked up.

'Yes, Bindu, it's nothing,' Ramesh said. 'Yes, Anjali is with me. Okay, okay, fine, we are coming. Yes, right now, my little sister. How worried you get for me.'

I heard their footsteps move away from us.

I gave Saurabh a thumbs-up from across the room, extinguished the cigarettes on the floor and bundled them in a tissue to be thrown outside later. Saurabh took out the room freshener from the closet and sprayed it liberally across the room to mask the smell.

I peeked downstairs.

Ramesh, Bindu and Anjali stepped outside the showroom and took a right. We would therefore take a left when we exited.

'Let's go,' I said to Saurabh.

We locked the office shut and hurried down the steps.

A guard saw us as we reached the ground level. He gave us a puzzled look.

'We were in the toilet,' I said. 'What happened? We were just in a meeting with Jayesh Varma.'

'Please leave, sir. We have a fire alarm, everyone is supposed to be out,' the guard said.

Chapter 43

'Wait, let's download it all on our laptops. Hard to read on the phone,' Saurabh said.

We were in his cubicle at our CyberSafe office. Jacob was in a particularly bad mood that day. A luxury car salesperson had been calling and pestering him all afternoon.

Saurabh moved all the images from the phone to his laptop.

'There are over eighty images. Let's sort them in folders,' Saurabh said.

We were so absorbed in the task, we didn't notice Jacob had come up behind us.

'Keshav, what am I doing wrong as a manager?' Jacob said.

I wondered if this was some kind of a trick question. Would he hate me forever if I dared to find a flaw in him?

'You are perfect, sir, what are you even saying?' I said.

'Then why isn't the pitch ready? Do I have to beg you, Mr Keshav Rajpurohit?'

'Oh,' I said and stood up, 'actually ...'

Before I could complete my answer, Jacob's phone rang.

'No, Jayesh, or whoever the hell you are, I do not want to buy a Porsche ... And what the hell is a Sports Chrono package? You have to stop calling me,' Jacob said as he walked away.

❖

'Wow. Malhotra Motors is losing fifty lakh rupees a month,' I said.

We sat on my bed in our Malviya Nagar apartment, wrapped in a quilt. We had our laptops in front of us.

I had the profit and loss statement of Malhotra Motors open on my computer.

Saurabh leaned over to get a better look.

'Thirty-seven lakh rupees monthly interest? They must have a huge loan,' Saurabh said. 'Open the balance sheet.'

I moved to the next document in the financials. Saurabh touched the screen with his fingertip.

'Forty-five crore rupees loan from Kotak payable at the end of the financial year. The interest is for that,' Saurabh said.

'Wow, Golu. How do you know all this accounting?' I said.

'Prerna taught me.'

'You guys used to talk about balance sheets? Romantic.'

'Not always. She ran Eato. So she discussed it sometimes. You have a problem?'

'Not at all, sorry,' I said. 'Let's come back to Malhotra Motors' losses.'

'There is a terrible recession in the auto sector. Should we also check Taneja Motors' accounts?' Saurabh said.

We flipped through the downloaded images. Taneja Motors showed losses of twenty lakh rupees a month. It also had another loan of twenty crore rupees from Kotak.

'Why has Ramesh uncle borrowed so much?' I said.

'To fund their losses,' Saurabh said. 'To pay the bills and keep things running in bad times.'

He flipped to the next image.

'This is a letter from Kotak Bank,' I said.

'Prerna used to work at Kotak Bank. That's how they must have started a relationship there,' Saurabh said.

The letter had been sent three months ago. It read as follows.

Dear Mr Malhotra,

We would like to bring to your attention that your current loan of face value:

Rs 45,00,00,000 (Rupees forty-five crores)

is due to us on:

31 March 2020

We would like to inform you that given the downturn in the auto industry, we have been asked to cut exposure to the sector. Therefore, we are unable to renew this loan next year. Please make arrangements to repay the loan accordingly.

Please also note that we currently have the following items of security collateral from you:

a) Residential Property—bungalow 'Malhotra House' measuring approximately 500 square yards located at A–956 New Friends Colony.

b) Industrial Property—plot no. 593/98 measuring 7 hectares in Amritsar Industrial Area.

These properties will be released from security only after the loan is fully repaid.

Regards,

Mahesh Shukla

Manager, Barakhamba Road Branch

'So, Uncle is losing money. Has a huge loan repayment due,' Saurabh said, 'and his properties including Malhotra House are pledged to the bank.'

'How the hell did he pay for that fancy engagement?' I said.

'Maybe that's what part of the loan was for,' Saurabh said.

'Strange. What is this industrial land in Amritsar?' I said.

'No idea,' Saurabh said. My phone rang. Bindu had finally returned my call.

'Thank you for not calling back. For two days,' I said.

'Sorry, sorry. Someone was always around. So sorry about that day at the showroom too,' Bindu said.

I put the call on speaker mode so Saurabh could participate as well.

'I had no idea Veerji would come back so soon. I swear he told us he would be back on Monday.'

'If he had caught us, he would have tossed us into jail for attempted robbery.'

'No, please don't talk like that. Anjali and I got your message. We did convince him to leave the showroom as you said.'

'Lucky save,' I said.

'Yes ... Was it worth it? Did you find anything in his office?'

'We're going through documents. What is this land in Amritsar Industrial Area?'

'Veerji's autoparts factory. Why?'

'Nothing. Did he ever say he has any money problems?'

'Veerji?' Bindu laughed. 'Impossible. He makes a lot of money in his business.'

'Really?' I said.

'He supports me. Gives me fifty thousand rupees every month. Of course, Neelam bhabhi doesn't know.'

'Why?' I said.

'Classic nanad–bhabhi thing. Which woman will like her husband giving money to his sister?'

'Hmm,' I said, flipping through the scanned documents.

'Didn't you see what a grand engagement party he had for Prerna?' Bindu said.

'He spent a lot of money, yes,' I said.

'His own money, right?'

'Loans aren't exactly your own money.'

'What?'

'Nothing. What about Mr Taneja? Ramesh uncle has a car dealership with him, right?'

'Yes, Volkswagen in Amritsar. They are also partners in the autoparts factory. Saurabh has met Mr Taneja, he came for the engagement.'

'Bindu aunty, this is Saurabh,' Saurabh said.

'How are you, beta?'

'I'm good. But things don't look so good for your Veerji's business.'

'What do you mean?' Bindu said.

'He has a big loan. The dealership is making losses,' I said.

'Really?' Bindu said. 'And the factory?'

'We'll find out,' I said. 'We'll call you if we need anything else.'

I ended the call and went back to the documents. I paused at one from an insurance company.

'Saurabh,' I said, 'see this.'

His mouth fell open.

'A five-crore life insurance policy for Prerna?' Saurabh said.

'Done five months before her death,' I said. The letter asked for a checklist of documents to process a pending claim. The checklist included a police closure report and a post-mortem report stating that the death was an accident.

'You thinking what I'm thinking?' I said.

'Yeah. Also, we now know he is not her real father,' Saurabh said.

'Businesses in loss, huge loans and a recent big insurance policy on his deceased adopted daughter. Doesn't. Look. Good,' I said.

'We don't know about the Amritsar factory though. Dealership is losing money. Maybe the factory is fine?'

'Only one way to find out.'

'How?'

'Time to visit the Golden Temple,' I said.

Chapter 44

Amritsar

We reached the Golden Temple at 5.30 in the morning. The sprawling white temple complex, with the gold-plated gurdwara in the centre, could infuse even the most turbulent of minds with peace. After visiting the Darbar Sahib, we stood near the pond. Saurabh mumbled a few prayers facing the shrine. I wondered what he had prayed for. I folded my hands and closed my eyes. My head raced with multiple thoughts.

Saurabh would leave for his own apartment in a couple of weeks. Why did it bother me? Was I afraid to be alone? I'm not alone, I told myself. I slept with ten women last year. Their faces and bodies flashed through my mind. I didn't want to think of all this at a holy place. I hated myself for the person I had become. Why did I feel so empty and alone? Why did I feel that there was no love in my life? Or that I had no friends. For no reason, my eyes filled with tears. Maybe if I solved the case, Saurabh would forgive me and not move to his own apartment. I realised that this was the main reason I wanted to crack the case. To keep my best friend. I wished I hadn't said all those things to him that day. I wished Prerna hadn't been around to hear them. I allowed myself to remember the day Saurabh and I had had the big fight.

Six months ago

'Twilight, that was amazing,' I said. She lay next to me, scrolling through Instagram on her phone. We'd just had drunken sex, and she had turned over and picked up her phone first thing. That's how Gen-Z operates, I guessed. I wondered if I should send her a DM instead.

'What?' she said, sensing I'd said something.

'I said, Twilight, that was amazing.'

'Twilight is only my Tinder name.' She giggled, eyes still on her phone.

'Oh, what's your real name?'

'Does it even matter?' she said, double-tapping several posts to like them.

I gave up; not my fault if she didn't want to know me better. I tried.

'I'm thirsty,' she said.

'There's vodka. We almost finished the whole bottle though,' I said, and lifted the nearly empty bottle of Absolut from under the bed.

'Can I get some water?' she said.

'Sure, it's in the fridge,' I said.

'Thanks,' she said.

She wore my shirt and her underwear to step out of the bedroom. The girl who called herself Twilight had a short frame, no more than five feet tall, and waist-length hair. She staggered outside to the living room.

'Where is the fridge?' she screamed from outside.

'In the kitchen,' I said, still in bed.

'Where? Can't hear you.'

'Damn, wait, I'm coming,' I said.

I stepped out of bed and put on my underwear. I walked into the living room, my head woozy with all the alcohol.

'It's here only, baby,' I said, pointing to the kitchen.

'Thank you,' she said, depositing a peck on my lips.

Saurabh stepped out of his room. He saw us semi-naked and kissing.

'Who's she?' he said as she went into the kitchen.

'She is, well, Twilight,' I said.

'What?'

'I don't know her real name,' I said and grinned. I thought it was sort of funny. Having sex with someone without knowing their real name. Saurabh wasn't amused, of course.

'What the hell is this behaviour, Keshav?' Saurabh said.

'What behaviour?' I said, a bit surprised at his serious tone. Twilight was opening cabinets to find a glass for herself in the kitchen.

'Why are you roaming around drunk in your underwear? And bringing home any random person?' Saurabh said.

'She's not random. She's cute. And hot in bed,' I said, my words slurring.

'You don't even know her name. You are sinking to new lows.'

'I'm not. I'm still doing my work and trying to run the agency. You, on the other hand, are not bothered. Busy with your fiancée or whatever.'

'Keshav, I'm in a new relationship. Prerna is going to be my wife. I have to give her some time, right?'

'Some time? Fuck. You are either with her or thinking about her. All the fucking time.'

'She is my future. Unlike, well, Tubelight in the kitchen.'

'It's Twilight,' I said.

'Trash.'

'She's not trash. At least she's better than the fat cow and her family you are going gaga over.'

As I finished my sentence, Prerna stepped out of Saurabh's bedroom. She had heard our entire conversation. Twilight came out of the kitchen with a glass of water in her hand. She stood next to me, both of us in a state of undress. Prerna didn't say a word to me or to Twilight.

I tried to unfreeze myself, stammering, 'Prerna ... sorry. I didn't mean t-to ...'

But Prerna had left the house. My alcohol high fizzled out in a jiffy. Twilight went to my bedroom, changed into her clothes and left as well. Saurabh stood in the living room, staring disbelievingly at me.

'I'm sorry, man,' I said. 'Forgive me. Just remember I'm your best friend and flatmate. Said it by mistake. Too much vodka.'

'Enough, Keshav,' Saurabh said, holding up a hand. 'We are no longer best friends. We are no longer even friends. And when this current lease ends, we are not going to be flatmates either.'

❖

'Bhai, you okay?' Saurabh said.

'Yeah,' I said and opened my eyes, returning from my private flashback. The Golden Temple shone bright in front of me.

'You are crying?'

'Just,' I said.

'What did you pray for?'

I shook my head.

'Tell me,' Saurabh said.

'I prayed we find the killer soon, that's all.'

❖

The Model Industrial Park in Amritsar is located on Mehta Road, around ten kilometres from the Golden Temple. The 132-acre industrial zone has plots ranging in size from 250 to 5,000 square yards. Nobody stopped us at the gate, so we took our taxi inside, past several sheds, workshops and factories. We followed the signs indicating the plot numbers to reach Ramesh's factory site.

'This one,' I said, matching the address with the one on the bank's letter.

We stepped out of the taxi.

'Just stay here. We will be back soon,' I said to the driver.

We walked up to the entrance. A broken sign saying 'Autospark', five feet by two, lay on the ground. A watchman sat outside, crushing tobacco in his hand. At ten in the morning, there seemed to be little activity inside the plant.

'Is this Ramesh Malhotra's factory?' I said.

'Who?' the watchman said.

'What do they make here?' Saurabh said.

The watchman dialled a number on his phone and mumbled something. In two minutes, a six-foot muscular man came out.

He resembled a villain in B-grade Punjabi films, complete with a shiny printed shirt and multiple golden lockets. Saurabh took a step back.

'Yes, how can I help you?' Muscleman said.

'We have come with Malhotra ji's reference,' I said.

'What for?' Muscleman said.

'New autopart customers,' Saurabh said, making it up as he spoke. 'Wanted to see the manufacturing process.'

Muscleman and the watchman laughed. I couldn't tell why. Did they now like us? Or had they seen through us?

I walked into the factory with confidence. Saurabh followed me as well. Muscleman and the watchman did not stop us.

We entered a dark shed with a high, sloping tin roof, around the size of a basketball court. Inside, I saw rows of empty tables, with chairs on both sides. No sign of any autopart machines or equipment. Instead, I only saw a few jute bags, several plastic packets and a couple of weighing scales on the tables. We reached the end of the shed. I saw a few pipes connecting several steel drums. Next to this was a giant oven radiating heat. Inside, I saw white powder arranged in soft bricks. I couldn't tell what all this was, but it didn't seem to have anything to do with cars. The entire place had a chemical smell, sort of like petrol mixed with nail polish remover.

Six other factory workers entered the shed and stood behind us.

Saurabh looked at me with a scared expression.

'Seen what you had to?' Muscleman said from behind. I turned around to face him.

'Yes, everything is good. We will make our way out,' I said and fake-smiled. Saurabh and I walked as fast as possible towards the exit.

'Stop,' Muscleman said.

'What?' I said, while still taking long strides towards the door.

'Where are you really from? Tell us.'

'We told you. We know Malhotra sir. Okay, we have to go,' I said.

'Why are you walking so fast?'

'I need to use the toilet,' Saurabh said in reflex. I had no idea why he couldn't come up with a better excuse.

Muscleman shouted at his factory workers to catch us.

The workers were ten metres behind us.

'What do we do, bhai, they are coming after us,' Saurabh whispered, walking right next to me.

'Two options. One, I spin another story and try to fool them,' I said.

'Will never work. Option two?' Saurabh said in panic.

'Run for your life.'

Before I finished my sentence, I sprinted towards the entrance, a panting Saurabh at my heels.

'Stop, behenchod, stop,' Muscleman said with great politeness. He shouted at his workers, 'Catch these behenchods. Malhotra owes me money, that's why I have kept his land. And he has the nerve to send his people.'

The factory workers ran behind us. As I ran, I pulled Saurabh's hand, to give his huge mass extra momentum.

'Oi,' one of the workers screamed behind us. I saw a stone fly past me. Then another. Fuck, we had pelters.

I reached the exit, Saurabh attached to my hand. The driver sat in the car, reading a copy of *Punjab Kesari,* enjoying the morning sun.

'Driver bhaiya, let's go,' I screamed.

Maybe the driver heard the tension in my voice, or maybe he thought Saurabh was in labour or something. He started his car in an instant. We sat inside and the driver sped off, even as a rock slammed against the car.

The workers continued to chase us. However, they were no match for the car's horsepower. Within seconds we had left the industrial park and had come out to the main road.

'Who were they?' the driver said, after he looked back and confirmed we weren't being followed.

'His in-laws,' I said, pointing at Saurabh.

'Shut up, bhai,' Saurabh said, panting hard like he was having a cardiac arrest.

'There's a reason I ask you to lose weight,' I said.

'Sure, because goons from a drug factory chase us regularly, right?' Saurabh said, hand on heaving chest.

Chapter 45

'Why are we going to HDFC Bank?' Saurabh said. 'More importantly, why aren't we getting the fuck out of Amritsar?'

'Five minutes. I've got some work here,' I said.

At the HDFC branch in Hall Bazaar, I walked up to the receptionist.

'Can I speak to someone in the business loans section?' I said.

Saurabh looked at me, trying not to appear surprised.

The receptionist told us to wait in the lounge. I picked up a copy of *The Economic Times.*

'GDP growth slips to six-year low of 4.5 per cent,' I read out a headline.

'Seriously?' Saurabh said. 'You are an economist now?'

Two minutes later, a thirty-five-year-old bespectacled man in a white shirt came up to us.

'Sir, I hear you have some loan enquiry?'

'Yes,' I said and stood up.

The man handed us a business card each. It said, 'Rishabh Arora, vice president – SME Loans'.

'And you would be?' Rishabh said.

'I'm Karan,' I said and put my hand in my pocket. 'Oh, I think I left my wallet in my car. I better get it. Come, Arjun.'

Saurabh looked at me, gobsmacked.

'It's okay if—' Rishabh said, but I interrupted him.

'My car is not parked properly, and the wallet is on the seat. We will be right back.'

Saurabh and I walked out of the bank.

'Okay, what was that?' Saurabh said.

'Nothing,' I said and displayed Rishabh's business card. 'I have what I wanted.'

'Whatever. And you couldn't make up better names? Karan and Arjun?'

'C'mon, that was a good movie,' I said.

❖

'How can I help you, ji? I am Taneja,' a tall Sikh gentleman in his fifties walked up to me in the Volkswagen showroom. He spoke with a heavy Punjabi accent.

'I need a few minutes of your time, sir,' I said. 'I am Rishabh Arora from HDFC Bank.'

I handed him the business card I had collected from the bank. I had come alone, as Taneja would have recognised Saurabh from the engagement party.

'I don't need any banking services, ji,' Taneja said. 'I already have a good relationship with Kotak Bank.'

We stood in the centre of the showroom. Three shiny display cars surrounded me. However, there were no customers in the shop.

'But I have a much better deal for you, sir. I could refinance your existing loans at a lower interest rate and for five years,' I said.

Taneja looked at me, wondering how I knew about his existing loans.

I smiled.

'We do our homework, sir. For important clients, we research about them and their needs,' I said.

'Come upstairs to my office,' Taneja said. I followed him to his cabin on the first floor. 'Tea?' he said, as I sat down in front of him.

'No, thanks, sir.' I shook my head. 'I don't want to take too much of your time.'

'Fine, what do you know about my loans? And how can you help?' Taneja said.

'I know from talk within the banking circles. You and your partner have this showroom here and another one in Delhi.'

'Yes, a Porsche showroom. Finest cars.'

'What's not fine is the cars are not selling.'

'Yeah,' Taneja said, spinning a model car paperweight on his table. 'Bad times for us.'

'You have existing loans at this showroom and in Delhi? Around sixty crore rupees in total.'

'Sixty-five, actually. Your intelligence gathering is good.'

'The loans are due soon. My bank could refinance you.'

'Thanks for the offer. But we don't need that now.'

'Really?'

'Yeah, we arranged funding. We have the cash. We will repay our loans ahead of time.'

'Oh,' I said, 'fine then. Congratulations. I really hope we can do business one day.'

I shook hands with Taneja and stood up. He came around the table and patted my back.

'I like your go-getter approach, Rishabh.'

'Thank you, sir,' I said. 'Coming from you, it means a lot. I admire you.'

'Really?' Taneja said and laughed. 'Arrey, sit down. Have a cup of tea.'

He asked his peon to bring us two cups of machine-made and, therefore, horrible tea.

I pretended to like it. I smiled after taking a sip.

'Are you from Amritsar?' Taneja said.

'No, sir, originally from Delhi,' I said.

'Oh, where do you stay in Amritsar?'

My heart beat fast. We had booked an Oyo Rooms near the railway station. I didn't know Amritsar's residential areas.

'Near the bank only, sir. Five-minute walk,' I said. Taneja examined my business card again.

'Hall Bazaar?' Taneja said. 'That's a crowded area. Where near Hall Bazaar?'

'Near the government school, sir,' I said. There's always a government school near everything in India.

'Oh,' Taneja said. Before he could probe further, I changed the topic.

'Don't mind, sir, but just to tell my seniors why I didn't get the business, where did you raise the money from? Which bank?' I said.

Taneja laughed. He kept his cup aside. A layer of tea foam stuck to his moustache.

'We didn't raise the money from a bank,' Taneja said. 'That is not easy these days for auto players.'

'Oh, from where then?' I said and smiled. 'Just between us.'

Taneja paused and then gave a small shrug.

'Fine, I will tell you. Luckily, our kids are doing quite well. They helped us. Can you believe it? We as parents looked after our children. Now they look after us.'

'Wow, you are so fortunate. Your children must be doing really well. And are quite generous too. It is not a small amount.'

'It's an interest-free loan. Nearly seventy crore rupees. Helps us a lot. We can't afford the interest. More details, I am sorry, are confidential.'

I nodded. I pointed to the picture of a car on the wall.

'Is that the poster of the new Jetta?' I said.

'Yes, we have a red one downstairs too. Want to take it for a test drive?'

Chapter 46

'Bhai, if Taneja uncle calls HDFC Bank, we are screwed.'

'He won't. He doesn't need the money now,' I said.

We had come to Jallianwala Bagh, a walled garden near the Golden Temple. In 1919, a maniacal British general sent troops to shoot at a peaceful gathering of Indian civilians. Soldiers blocked the exits. Hundreds died, thousands were seriously injured. The red brick walls of the park still have bullet marks in several places. Even though it all happened a hundred years ago, walking around those gardens can send a shiver down the spine. How could anyone be so heartless, I thought. And when would I feel real personal emotion again?

'Bhai?' Saurabh said, snapping his fingers in front of my eyes.

'Huh? Yes, Saurabh?' I said.

'How can Namrata, Taneja's only child, give her father seventy crore bucks? Eato doesn't have that kind of money. In fact, it is not even profitable yet.'

'Fishy,' I said.

We came out of the garden.

'We haven't had a proper Amritsari meal,' Saurabh said.

He checked Google Maps.

'Come, there's an excellent kulcha place nearby.'

❖

'One gobi, one aloo, one paneer and one mixed. And two lassis,' Saurabh said at the counter. We had come to Bhai Kulwant Singh Kulchian Wale. The small but buzzing kulcha shop was only a five-minute walk from Jallianwala Bagh. The restaurant had zero ambience, but it was one of the top-rated restaurants in the city, on review sites. The menu consisted only of four kinds of kulchas, or stuffed tandoori paranthas. Saurabh had ordered everything on the menu.

The piping hot kulchas came in minutes. Each golden baked bread was topped off with a rectangular slab of butter. The butter turned into a golden liquid and ran across the plate. The kulchas were perfect—crispy on the outside and soft on the inside. The chole came along with pickle, onions and green chillies as accompaniments.

'This is so good. I should just move to Amritsar,' Saurabh said, his eyes closed in ecstasy.

'For kulchas?' I said.

'Why not?' Saurabh said, not sensing my sarcasm. To him, it was perfectly plausible to relocate for food. There are sadhus who meditate on one leg for years in the Himalayas to attain salvation, and then there is Saurabh who attains nirvana from perfect tandoori kulchas.

'We need to find out how Namrata gave money to her father,' I said.

'We could ask her,' Saurabh said, scooping up the last bits of chole from his plate.

'I prefer not to.'

Saurabh shrugged.

'Did Prerna ever use your laptop?' I said.

'Yes, many times. When she used to come home. Why?'

'I was wondering if we could get into Eato's accounts or mails. Maybe your laptop remembers her login and password?'

Saurabh's eyes lit up. He loves it when he gets a chance to play geek.

'That is actually a good idea. Even if my laptop doesn't remember them automatically, I know how to go back in history and find the IDs and passwords used in the past,' Saurabh said.

'Cool,' I said and stood up. 'Let's go right now.'

'Wait, sit down,' Saurabh said.

'Why?'

'Let me finish my lassi. All that spice in the kulchas. Doesn't agree with my stomach.'

Chapter 47

'Fine, I have managed to get her bank login and password. I also have her login and password for Eato's internal server mails. She accessed them both from my laptop several times.'

Saurabh had worked on his laptop for the last hour, going deep into the recesses of its hard drive like only he could. We were back in our cramped Oyo Rooms near the Amritsar Junction railway station. The typical noise of a busy Indian street—bicycle bells, blaring horns, reversing vehicles, people shouting and a general clamour for no reason—came in through our window.

We decided to have a look at Eato's bank accounts first.

We typed in Prerna's official banking credentials.

It opened the account management page of Eato Private Limited. The summary page showed a balance of around ten crore rupees.

'Open the detailed bank statements, to see the transactions,' I said.

'For detailed statements, the bank will send an OTP to Prerna's phone and email,' Saurabh said.

'We don't have her phone or SIM,' I said.

'I do have access to her email, and it comes there too,' Saurabh said, a twinkle in his eye.

He entered the account transaction details page after entering the one-time password. I ran my finger on the screen across the various entries.

'Salary, commissions, credit card payments, office rent, ad agency payment,' I read out loud. 'Wow, what is this big number? Transfer to Taneja Motors, twenty crores?'

'Bhai, see the next one. Transfer to Malhotra Motors, fifty crores. Taneja didn't lie. They recently raised seventy crores. From Eato,' Saurabh said.

'What the hell? Why is food delivery site Eato transferring so much money to Taneja Motors and Malhotra Motors?' I said.

Saurabh and I looked at each other, puzzled.

'And how did Eato have so much money lying around, anyway?' Saurabh said.

We looked further down the statements. Five months ago, there had been a deposit of ninety crore rupees. It came from 'Indus Partners Fund IV'.

'Oh, I get it. This is the third-round fundraising. That's where Eato got the money. Indus Partners is a venture capital firm,' Saurabh said.

'But they only invested in Eato,' I said.

'Yes.'

'So why is Eato giving the money to Taneja Motors and Malhotra Motors instead?'

'That, my friend, is the seventy-crore-rupee question,' Saurabh said. 'A seventy-crore-rupee fraud.'

'Namrata and Prerna controlled Eato, including its money,' I said.

'Prerna would never have played with investor money like this,' Saurabh said and tapped his nose. 'Maybe that is why they had to get rid of her.'

'Who's "they"?'

'Let's try and find out. I already have the login and password for Prerna's office email. Used it to get the OTP. Want me to check some more mails?'

'Of course.'

Saurabh buried himself in his laptop again. A while later, he turned the screen towards me.

'See this mail. Dated 27 September 2019. Twenty days before her death,' Saurabh said.

I read the mail.

To: Prerna Malhotra

From: Ramesh Malhotra, Malhotra Motors

Beta,

This is my humble request to you again. Taneja uncle and I both really need your help. Namrata bitiya has already agreed. Nobody else will find out. Before you know, everything will be okay, and we will return it all.

In tough times, who else can we count on but our family?

Love and regards,

Papa

'Fuck,' I said. 'Namrata agreed. She is alive. Prerna didn't agree. She's dead.'

Saurabh slammed the laptop shut. He slid off the bed and walked up to the hotel room window.

'What is this world? What is happening to people?' Saurabh said. A tear rolled down his cheek.

I went and stood next to him. Men don't know how to console other men. I just stood there, hoping my silence would somehow help.

'Bastard was showing off, offering me a car at my engagement. What was the need when he was broke?' Saurabh said. I placed my hand on his shoulder. 'What all nonsense he said. "Don't talk to anyone. Don't involve the police. Our family honour is at stake." What fucking honour? You are broke, dude, and you killed the child you raised. That's honour for you?' Saurabh said.

'I am sorry, Saurabh,' I said.

'What are you sorry for? You didn't take insurance policies in her name. You didn't siphon off money from the company she worked hard to create. More than anything, you didn't push her off the terrace like that bastard.'

Saurabh banged the window with a fist. The glass cracked on impact.

Saurabh's hand was covered in blood.

'Golu.'

He didn't respond. He didn't wince in pain either. He stood there, watching blood drip down his forearm. Hero he is.

I brought a towel from the bathroom and wiped the blood from his hand.

'I won't leave him. I don't give a fuck about the police closing the case. He killed my Prerna, he has to go to jail.'

I wrapped the towel around his hand. I looked outside the window to see if I could spot a chemist.

'Let's go to Delhi. Now,' Saurabh said.

'Now? It's night. We can take the first flight tomorrow.'

'I need to meet the police. Rana, Singh, whoever. As soon as possible.'

'Yes,' I said, 'I'll fix a meeting.'

'I need to go right now.'

'Right now you need bandages. I will go down and get some for you. Please don't break any more windows.'

❖

'You fixed a meeting with Singh and Rana?'

'Yes, I did, Saurabh. You already asked me three times.'

The plane landed with a mild thud at Delhi airport. The aircraft taxied its way to the aerobridge. I checked the time – it was ten in the morning.

'Both Singh and Rana together? They agreed?' Saurabh said.

'Yes. At 11.30, in Rana's office.'

'That's in one and a half hours,' Saurabh said in a high-pitched voice.

'That's the only time Rana had today, Golu. He is in charge of some farmers' march or something in Delhi today.'

Saurabh shook his head.

'Don't worry. We have already landed in Delhi,' I said.

Saurabh sniffed.

The plane came to a halt. Passengers unbuckled their seatbelts and leaped off their seats. Everyone seemed to be in an urgent rush to get out as if they all had thousand-crore-rupee deals to conclude outside. Saurabh stood up from his aisle seat as well. I continued to sit on my middle seat and switched on my phone.

'You informed Bindu and Anjali?' Saurabh said.

'Yes, sir. I messaged them before take-off. To come to Rana's office in Hauz Khas at 11.30.'

'Their presence is a must. Otherwise that Singh will again say the family wants the case closed. Rana and Singh need to know that the entire family doesn't think that way. Only the culprit does.'

'I know, Golu. Now why have you stood up? Sit down, there is still time for us to exit.'

Golu checked his watch. The flight attendant made an announcement.

'Ladies and gentlemen, we regret to inform you that we are having some technical difficulties with the aerobridge. Airport authorities estimate it will take us another fifteen minutes to open the gate. Passengers are requested to take their seats. We apologise for the inconvenience.'

A collective sigh of disappointment ran through the plane. I smirked at Saurabh.

'I told you, sit down,' I said.

'Damn,' he swore as he sat back down. He checked his watch again. 'We will get late.'

My phone pinged several times due to fresh notifications after it connected to the network. One came from a news site.

'Traffic woes in Delhi due to massive farmers' march.'

I opened WhatsApp. I had several messages from Anjali.

'Sure, we will be there at 11.30,' she had replied.

'Thank you for doing this.'

It was followed by a heart emoji.

The next message had come a few minutes ago.

'Landed?'

I replied.

'Yes. Still in plane.'

'Anjali confirmed. They are coming,' I said to Saurabh.

Saurabh glanced at my chat messages.

'Why did she send you a heart emoji?'

'What?' I said, surprised.

'She sent you a heart.'

'She just thanked me. I went to Amritsar for her dead sister. That's it.'

'Are you sure?' Saurabh said. 'Anything going on?'

'Seriously, Golu?' I said and shook my head.

My phone pinged. Anjali had messaged again.

'Welcome to Delhi. See you soon.'

She followed it with an emoji that had two tiny hearts instead of eyes.

'Why is she sending you a love-struck emoji?' Saurabh said.

'What?'

'That's the love-struck emoji.'

'Girls chat like this, Saurabh. It's not to be taken seriously.'

'Stay away from this entire family. I hate them.'

First, Saurabh wanted me to stay away from Anjali because he loved this family too much, now he wanted me to stay away because he hated them. Sure, I wasn't in love with Anjali or anything. However, we *had* always sort of flirted. These emojis might not mean much, but I can tell when I have a chance with a girl. I found her attractive and interesting. What was Saurabh's problem if I had something going on with her? I thought of her cute face and smiled.

'Is that clear?' Saurabh said as he saw me lost in thought.

'What?' I said, coming back to the present. 'I don't have any feelings for her, Saurabh.'

'Don't hook up or do anything with Anjali. Clear?'

I locked eyes with Saurabh and felt guilty. That was exactly what I wanted to do.

'No, never,' I said.

'Good. Now when will they let us out of this damn plane?' Saurabh said.

The aerobridge finally opened and we walked out of the Terminal 1 building. I checked the time: it was 10.30.

My phone rang. It was Anjali. I took the call. Saurabh stood close to me.

'Hey, where are you guys?' Anjali said.

'Airport. Just came out. We'll come to Rana's office directly. Wow, I see a huge traffic jam at the pick-up point.'

'There are jams all over Delhi. They're showing it on TV, some farmers' rally,' Anjali said.

'Yes, we will reach as soon as we can,' I said.

Saurabh showed me Google Maps on his phone. All roads to Hauz Khas were dark red. The estimated time to Rana's office showed two hours.

'Doesn't look like we're going to make it,' I said.

Saurabh looked at me, upset.

'What?' Anjali said.

'Too much traffic. We'll try still.'

'Do you have a lot of luggage? If not, take the metro. Faster,' Anjali said.

'Really?' I said.

'Yeah, we better leave soon too. I'll see you.'

'Sure, dear Anjali, see you,' I said and ended the call.

'You didn't have to be so friendly and affectionate to her,' Saurabh said.

'What?' I said, my mouth open.

'You said "dear" to Anjali. Why use "dear"?'

'Oh dear,' I said and shook my head. I walked faster so I could be a few steps ahead of him.

'What?' he said from behind.

'Oh dear, oh dear.'

'Why are you saying that?'

'Nothing. Come, metro station's that way, my dear,' I said.

Chapter 48

The metro ensured we reached our meeting on time. Rana seemed to be in a hurry. He constantly checked his phone for messages.

'I am an ACP and they put me in charge of managing these lunatics. How am I supposed to control five lakh people with a few hundred policemen?' Rana said, typing furiously on his phone.

Anjali, Bindu, Saurabh and I sat in front of him in his office. We waited for Singh, who had messaged he would reach in two minutes, eight minutes ago.

'I have to leave soon,' Rana said. 'There is an army marching towards Delhi, literally.'

'Why are they doing this march?' I said.

'Economy is down. They are not making money. What else? Farmers work hard all year and don't get good prices for what they grow.'

I guess from Porsche dealers to crop sellers, everyone was having a tough time in this economy.

'How are you, madam?' Rana said to Bindu, in an extra-sweet voice some Indian men reserve for women.

'Fine, thank you. How are you, sir?' Bindu said.

'Very well, madam. My wife looks just like you, by the way.'

Singh knocked on ACP Rana's door at that precise moment, saving us from the awkward small talk.

'Sorry, traffic is insane today,' Singh said. 'Let's start please.'

'Sit down, Singh. These boys have a lot to say.'

'Really?' Singh said, taking a seat next to me.

'They say Prerna's case shouldn't be closed,' Rana said.

'I am listening,' Singh said.

Over the next fifteen minutes, Saurabh and I explained to everyone what we had found in Ramesh's office and in Amritsar. We displayed all the relevant documents on our laptop.

'Summing up, Mr Malhotra and Mr Taneja are bankrupt. They asked Eato for money. Namrata said yes. Prerna said no,' I said and paused for breath.

Anjali, Bindu, Rana and Singh sat in silence. I showed them Eato's bank statements.

'After Prerna's death, Namrata became the sole signatory. As expected, weeks after her death, funds moved to Malhotra Motors and Taneja Motors.'

I let the people around the table circulate the laptop to see the documents.

'Also, there is a life insurance policy of five crore rupees in Prerna's name. Beneficiary, Ramesh Malhotra. Who has to show that this case is closed if he wants to get that money.'

'Veerji?' Bindu blurted out.

'Yes, your brother,' Saurabh said. 'Prerna's adoptive father, and my almost father-in-law.'

'Veerji pushed my Prerna?' Bindu said.

The two cops had not said anything. Singh looked disturbed; he was probably worried about any side deals that might come undone now.

'What do you think, Singh?' Rana said.

Singh put the laptop aside. He looked up at Rana.

'My report is nearly finished. This case is almost closed, sir,' Singh said.

'Should it be?' Rana said.

'Accidental fall. Victim lost her balance after fasting all day. The family agreed. Bindu ji, all of you came that day, no?'

'What about Adi, Ramesh's brother?' Rana said.

'Just a junkie who overdosed,' Singh said.

Rana sighed.

'What about all this new evidence?' Rana said. He pointed to the laptop and continued. 'You are going to ignore this? There's already a crime here. He has laundered investor money from his daughter's company to himself.'

'Rana sir, that's a separate financial crime. As far as the case of Prerna Malhotra is concerned, the family wanted it closed.'

'The family is here today, isn't it,' Rana said. 'Can't you see? And they want justice.'

'Where's Ramesh ji?' Singh said.

Rana, Anjali and Saurabh rolled their eyes.

'He's the accused, Singh. Are you serious? Don't you see why the accused may want the case closed?' Rana said.

Singh shifted in his seat.

'If this leaks to the media, Singh,' Rana said, 'they will blame Delhi Police, like always. They will say we are incompetent and corrupt. They will publish your name as the police inspector who closed the case. Now, that will be wrong, no, Singh? You aren't incompetent and corrupt, right?'

Singh looked at Rana.

'Sir, please don't talk like that. You are my senior, I respect you.'

'So respect my advice too. Don't close the case. You have the evidence. Go get him. Become a media hero. Headline will be "high-profile car dealer arrested". I am telling you, it will work wonders for your career,' Rana said.

Singh spoke after a few seconds.

'Isn't this still circumstantial evidence, sir? Sure, this establishes motive,' Singh said.

'Damn strong motive. Seventy crore rupees motive. Survival of business and reputation motive,' Rana said.

'Yes, sir, I agree. This tells me why it happened. But how exactly did he do it?' Rana said.

'Where did he say he was at the time of the crime?' Rana said.

'He said he had gone to buy paan,' Singh said.

'He has an alibi?' Rana said. 'Checked with the paan shop?'

'He said he got a call to come back before he could buy the paan.'

'So no alibi.'

Rana turned to the ladies.

'Bindu ji, Anjali, did either of you see Mr Malhotra leave the house or return at the time of Prerna's death?'

'I was in my room, correcting my students' answer sheets,' Bindu said. 'I didn't really see Veerji.'

'What about you, Anjali?' Rana said.

'I was on my way back from the airport. When I arrived, Prerna's body was in the living room. Everyone was around her.'

'Including Mr Malhotra?'

'Including Ramesh uncle, yes,' Anjali said.

'So this paan trip nonsense is bullshit,' Rana said. 'Strong motive, no alibi. Here is what happened. He goes up to his daughter one last time, begging her to move the money. She declines. Stressed, facing bankruptcy and left with little choice, he pushes her over. Prerna is gone, Namrata is sole signatory, and she moves the money. Agree, Singh?'

Singh looked uncomfortable.

'A father will kill his own daughter?' Singh said. 'Rana sir, come on. Think about it.'

Rana became quiet. Anjali spoke after a few seconds.

'If he was the father, that is,' Anjali said.

'Anjali,' Bindu shouted.

'What, Ma? How can we remain quiet about this? It is hampering the investigation.'

'Quiet about what?' Rana said with a puzzled expression. 'And what did you say, Anjali?'

'I think you need to tell the police everything, Bindu aunty,' Saurabh said.

'Inspector Singh, Rana sir, Prerna is not Ramesh uncle's daughter,' Anjali said.

Rana narrowed his eyes.

'What?' Singh said, gobsmacked. Bindu narrated her entire past. The two inspectors listened with their mouths open.

'And that's our truth, Inspector sir. Waheguru knows,' Bindu said, folding her hands as she ended her story.

'Prerna is your daughter? Anjali too? They are twins? Your twins?' Singh said.

'Yes, Inspector sir. It's been our family secret for decades,' Bindu said, hands still folded.

'Twins? Sorry Bindu ji, but I saw pictures. Prerna was so ...' Rana said and paused, as he searched for a word more polite than 'fat'. 'Sorry, she was on the healthier side, wasn't it?'

'It can happen, especially if they grow far apart in different environments,' Bindu said, as she started to cry. 'Look closely. Ignore the weight and hairstyle. Both are the same.'

Singh looked irritated.

'You didn't think it was necessary to tell the police all this during your testimony? You think we are idiots?' Singh shouted, loud enough for the peons outside Rana's office to hear.

'We never told anyone, Inspector sir.'

Singh stood up. He paced up and down Rana's office.

'Cool down, Singh,' Rana said. 'Have a seat. Shall I order nimbu paani?'

'What nimbu paani, sir? This Ramesh, these women, they all took the police for a ride. They don't tell us basics. And they want us to solve the case?'

'It's all my fault,' Bindu said, sobbing as she spoke. 'I caused the situation. Then Veerji rescued the girls. He had only one request—nobody tells anyone, ever. To protect the family honour. Even my mother doesn't know till date, sir.'

'Honour, I can see,' Rana said and laughed. He looked at Saurabh and me, expecting us to join in the mirth. We remained silent.

'Sit down, Singh. Bindu ji, please calm down,' Rana said. 'And in future, never hide things from the police. You can be booked for shielding a criminal.'

'We weren't—' Anjali began, and Rana shushed her.

'It's okay, I get it. This whole Punjabi thing, save family from shame at all costs business. Happens in my Haryana too. But you can't do this when there's a murder. Understand?'

'Yes sir,' Anjali and Bindu said together.

'Good,' Rana said. 'Now Singh, there you have it. The accused is not even the victim's father. Big difference between uncle raising an illegitimate child versus a father, right?'

Anjali looked up at Rana when she heard the word 'illegitimate'.

'Sorry,' Rana said. 'Just legal language we need to use sometimes. Anyway, Singh?'

'I need a moment,' Singh said.

'Sure,' Rana said.

The room fell silent. Singh closed his eyes. He spoke after a minute.

'There's a lot of new information and evidence that was given to the police today. So, with all these developments, I won't be closing the case. In fact, I am left with little choice but to arrest Ramesh Malhotra.'

'Arrest Veerji?' Bindu said, her eyes wide like discs. 'Don't you just want to talk to Veerji first?'

'He has misled us and lied to us before. If he finds out what we know, he may escape. Custody is essential,' Singh said.

Bindu began to cry again. Anjali placed her arm around her shoulder.

Rana stood up to leave.

'I am going to hang out with the farmers. You catch him, Singh. Before he gets away in one of his fast cars,' Rana said and laughed out loud at his own joke.

'I'm going right now, sir,' Singh said. 'Please help me with the warrant before you leave.'

❖

We walked out of Rana's office. Singh sat in his police Gypsy; Bindu and Anjali got into the backseat.

Saurabh and I walked Rana to the ACP's own vehicle.

'Thank you, sir,' I said.

'Don't mention it,' Rana said and put on his sunglasses. 'Mubarak, you cracked another case.'

'All because of you only, sir,' Saurabh said, somewhat emotional.

After Rana drove off, we walked back to Singh. 'We will take a cab and see you in New Friends Colony,' Saurabh said.

'Nobody gets out of my sight or even makes a phone call. Squeeze into this vehicle somehow,' Singh said. 'We are going now. He is in his showroom.'

Saurabh looked at Singh. Singh registered his size. There was no way he and I could fit in along with the two others.

'Fine. I will call for another Gypsy from the station. I need handcuffs anyway,' Singh said.

Chapter 49

The two police Gypsies reached Malhotra Motors at 1.30 in the afternoon.

'You take care of the ladies. I don't want any drama,' Singh said to Saurabh.

All of us entered the Porsche showroom. Salesman Jayesh immediately recognised Saurabh.

'Jacob sir, so nice to see you again. I called you many times,' Jayesh said, his white teeth gleaming from across the room.

Saurabh smiled back. Singh looked from Saurabh to Jayesh.

'Where's Ramesh Malhotra?' Singh said to Jayesh in a firm voice. Jayesh's smile evaporated.

'Sir, how can I help you?' Jayesh said, as he noticed the men in uniform.

'Where's Ramesh uncle?' Anjali said to Jayesh.

'Up–upstairs,' Jayesh said.

Singh and two cops climbed up the steps to the first floor.

Saurabh and I remained downstairs.

'What's happening?' Bindu said.

'We have to wait here. The police will go talk to him,' Saurabh said.

'We should inform Neelam aunty,' Anjali said.

'How do I tell her? And what about Maaji?' Bindu said.

'Please don't rush. Take a seat, Bindu aunty,' Saurabh said, pointing to the meeting area. 'Jayesh, can you get her some tea?'

'Sure. Green tea or regular tea, madam?' Jayesh said.

We heard arguments in the office above but couldn't hear what was being said.

Soon Singh and Ramesh came down the steps. Singh held the handcuffs in his hand. The two cops followed them.

'I'm coming with you, see?' Ramesh said.

Singh kept quiet as they continued to walk down the steps.

'Why are you waving the handcuffs?' Ramesh said. 'My staff is here.'

Singh remained silent.

'Just a misunderstanding, I am telling you, Inspector Singh.'

'Ramesh ji, let's just leave quietly,' Singh said.

'Bindu? Anjali? What are you doing here?' Ramesh said when he caught sight of them.

Bindu folded her hands in a namaste. Anjali looked away.

'You?' Ramesh said, noticing Saurabh and me.

'Good afternoon, Uncle,' Saurabh said. He greets elders with respect out of reflex, even if they are murderers.

'What are these two doing here?' Ramesh said in a louder voice.

'Ramesh ji, quiet,' Singh said. 'Let's not create a scene.'

'Arrey? What scene? Enough, Singh. It's my showroom. You barge in here in the middle of my workday. When I said I would come talk to you later, you display handcuffs. Who do you think you are?' Ramesh said. He sat on one of the chairs at the meeting table.

Singh's face turned red.

'Stand up,' he yelled. Ramesh looked stunned by this sudden aggression, but he stood up.

'Singh? What is wrong with you? You forgot?' Ramesh said in a meek voice.

'Behave, Ramesh ji. Don't make me take you out like a common criminal in front of your family and staff.'

'One minute, Singh, if you are getting to that level. Bindu, can you call Khanna?' Ramesh said.

'Who's Khanna?' Singh said, still stern.

'My lawyer. I have the right to speak to him, no? Now, calm down, Singh sir.' Ramesh sat down again. 'Jayesh, arrange some coffee for Singh sir. That nice Starbucks one.'

'I don't want any coffee,' Singh said.

'Okay sir, but sit, please. I'm not running away.'

A Volkswagen Jetta arrived outside the showroom. Neelam and Maaji stepped out and walked in.

'Why is everyone here?' Ramesh said, throwing his hands up in the air.

Neelam saw the cops.

'What's going on, Singh ji?' Neelam said.

'What are you doing here, Neelam?' Ramesh said.

'Inspector Singh called me to ask where you are. It seemed urgent. I felt worried, so I came here to talk to you,' Neelam said.

'And you had to bring Maaji?' Ramesh said, irritated.

'Nobody is at home, that's why.'

'Maaji, please sit,' Jayesh said. He escorted her to a chair. The matriarch of the Malhotra family took a seat and smiled, unaware of the situation around her.

'Maaji, will you have a cappuccino too?' Jayesh said.

'Kappu ki?' Maaji said loudly. 'Aur ay kaun hege? Police?

'Koi gal nahi, Maaji. Casual meeting,' Ramesh said to his mother. 'Have a latte, it is good. Made with pure milk.'

Singh folded his hands in a namaste to Maaji and she raised a hand to bless him.

'Bindu, what happened to Khanna?' said Ramesh, back in control.

'Veerji, his line was busy. Wait, he is calling back now,' Bindu said. She passed her phone to Ramesh.

'Khanna ji,' Ramesh said in a jovial voice. 'Where are you? Come, your friend needs you. My showroom ... Okay, just finished your hearing? Come fast, please.'

Ramesh ended the call.

'I can't wait. I have to take you with me now,' Singh said.

'Come on, Singh ji, we are family friends. How can you talk like this? Ten minutes is all I'm asking for,' Ramesh said.

Singh sighed.

'Fine. Send Maaji upstairs. I want to talk to the rest of your family anyway.' Jayesh took Maaji upstairs to Ramesh's office. Singh settled down at the table with the rest of us.

'Neelam ji, my call sounded urgent for a reason. I am here to arrest Ramesh ji. For the murder of Prerna Malhotra, who I now understand was your niece.'

'Stop this nonsense, Singh,' Ramesh said.

'What?' Neelam said at the same time, eyes wide.

Bindu clutched Neelam's arm.

'What is he saying, Bindu?' Neelam said, her voice hysterical.

'Bindu ji knows. She will explain it to you. Instead of doing drama, listen to what I am saying,' Singh said in an irritated voice.

Neelam looked around the table with wide eyes. Bindu and Anjali turned their gaze down. Neelam broke down.

Ramesh was staring at Saurabh and me. Somehow, he knew we were behind this.

'You are a traitor,' Ramesh said to Saurabh. 'We were family.'

'You ruined my family,' Saurabh said.

'So you confess to your crime, Ramesh ji? Did you kill Prerna Malhotra? And move seventy crore rupees from her startup to pay your loans?' Singh said.

'Shut up, Singh. I'm not confessing to anything. Khanna told me not to say anything.'

Singh's face froze. In one swoop he stood up, took the handcuffs and snapped it around Malhotra's right wrist.

'Khanna can come to your new home—jail. Mr Ramesh Malhotra, you are under arrest for the murder of Prerna Malhotra.'

Ramesh stood up. Neelam's cry was louder than the Cayenne burglar alarm we set off on our last visit. The rest of us stood up as well.

Singh tugged at the handcuff and began to walk towards the exit.

'I am coming, Singh. This heroism is not necessary,' Ramesh said.

'Where are you taking my husband?' Neelam said. 'Bindu, Anjali, what is happening? Ramesh ji hasn't done anything. He only looked after his family his entire life.'

'You wait and watch, Singh, I will get bail in no time. Then I will make sure you fucking pay for this mistake,' Ramesh said.

Singh didn't answer. He pushed him out of the showroom. Saurabh and I followed them out as well.

Two photographers clicked a picture as Singh and Ramesh stepped out.

'Who the fuck are they?' Ramesh shouted. 'Why are they taking my picture outside my showroom? I am a respectable man.'

The two cops forced Ramesh into the police Gypsy.

'This media stuff is new to me. But I like it. It was Rana sir's idea to call them,' Singh said, winking at me as he drove off.

Chapter 50

Several newspapers carried the story of Ramesh's arrest the next day.

'Luxury car dealer arrested for murder of adopted niece', said one newspaper.

'Feather in cap for Delhi Police: Karva Chauth killer nabbed', read another headline.

'Nice coverage. They don't mention us though, or our detective agency,' Saurabh said, keeping the papers aside.

We were having our morning tea. We had our apartment for one more week. Several packed cardboard boxes were strewn around the house as we prepared to move out.

'We didn't stand there and give media interviews, right?' I smiled.

'Still, Singh could have mentioned us. We literally solved the entire case for him.'

'Not important,' I said.

I could tell he had something bottled up. Ever since Ramesh's arrest, he hadn't shown any emotion at all. It worried me a little. He hadn't even cursed Ramesh, the man who killed his lady-love. Instead, he spoke of getting credit and media mentions as if that was all the case was to him.

'Golu, are you okay, like really okay?'

'What do you mean? I am great.'

'You haven't reacted much.'

'Ramesh uncle did it. We got him. Another murder case solved. Good.'

'You didn't say anything to him.'

'He is in jail. What is there to say?'

'The man who murdered the love of your life. You didn't feel anything when you met him? Rage? Anger?'

'I felt revulsion. I felt sick. Mostly, I felt relieved we had him. That's the thing about working on a case. After a while, the emotion goes away. It's just a problem to solve. We solved it. Done, move on.'

Saurabh stood up restlessly. I noticed he had not touched the Bourbon biscuits in front of him, which was highly unusual. He picked up some books from a shelf and put them in a cardboard box.

'You spoke to the movers?' Saurabh said.

'Yes. Next Wednesday,' I said.

Saurabh filled the box with books. Then he sat on the sofa and stared blankly out the window.

'Look at how much the family lost. Prerna. Adi. And now Ramesh uncle,' Saurabh said.

'Yes, tragic,' I said.

'I used to imagine all of us, the Malhotras and I, having dinner together in their dining room. Lots of laughter, food and Punjabi fun. Nobody will laugh in that house anymore.'

I nodded.

'I thought I would punch Ramesh uncle in the face. But I saw his wife and mother. I just felt sad for the family instead. Why?'

'It's natural. You are attached to them. I feel bad too.'

'That's why I didn't lash out at him. Or feel like celebrating after solving the case.'

'I understand.'

'I almost feel like meeting the rest of the family. To console them.'

'Then you should.'

'I don't know what Neelam aunty thinks of me now. How do I face Maaji?'

'Just pay them a visit. If your heart says so, do it. I will come with you if you want.'

Saurabh looked at me, surprised.

'Heart? You are talking about heart, bhai?'

'Yes. I realise there's no point living life like a machine. Humans have emotions. You do. I do. One can't deny them forever.'

Chapter 51

They didn't kick us out or even scream at us. A subdued Bindu answered the door and let us in. Saurabh and I sipped coffee while she went upstairs and came back with Anjali and Neelam.

All of us now sat like statues. Nobody said a word. Saurabh broke the silence.

'We just came by to check if you guys were okay.'

'Everything is ruined, and you ask if we are okay?' Neelam said.

'I am sorry, Neelam aunty.'

'What did you get out of this, tell me that? This is justice? My husband is in jail. I don't know what to tell his mother. She has already lost her other son.'

Saurabh and I hung our heads.

'Go on, Bindu, congratulate them. They solved your daughter's murder. They are heroes. Make butter chicken for them. Why aren't you celebrating?' Neelam said.

Bindu and Anjali gazed at the floor as well.

'I raised that girl,' Neelam said. 'I cleaned her, fed her, taught her and loved her. Your Veerji paid for everything, gave her an education and made her do something worthy in life. No matter what anyone says, he was her father. So what if he asked her for a loan? Which father in trouble will not ask his own child?' Neelam said.

'He didn't have to kill her,' Saurabh said in a soft voice.

'You saw him kill her? Tell me. Did you see him kill her?' Neelam turned to him aggressively.

Saurabh did not respond.

'You went up to the terrace that night. You could have killed her. Why didn't the police take you?'

'The police have the evidence, Neelam aunty,' Saurabh said.

'Is this why you came here to our house? To humiliate us?' Neelam said. Saurabh didn't answer. Neelam stood up and came to me with folded hands.

'Please, leave us alone now. You have destroyed everything,' she said.

'Didn't we all want justice?' Saurabh said. 'Bindu aunty? Anjali?'

Bindu went up to Neelam and held her hands.

'How would I have known it is Veerji? You know what he means to me.'

'Get lost, bitch. This is all because of you. Ramesh ji did everything for you. You and your bastard daughters.'

'Neelam aunty!' Anjali screamed. Her eyes were scrunched as she glared at Neelam.

'What are you looking at me like that for? Both of you went to these detectives and the police. Ramesh ji had sorted out everything. You destroyed it.'

'I had to make sure the person who killed my sister was punished.'

'You want to know who is being punished? Me. Did I kill her? No. So why am I getting punished?'

I suppose she had the right to vent. Her life had been turned upside down.

'I am sorry, Neelam aunty. I understand how you feel,' Saurabh said.

'Nothing you understand,' Neelam said. In a huff, she left the living room and went upstairs.

'Please don't mind Neelam bhabhi. She is really distressed,' Bindu said after a pause.

'I can imagine,' Saurabh said.

I nodded as well.

'Our family was everything to us. It is all destroyed,' Bindu said.

'Ramesh uncle killed Prerna, Ma. Please blame him for this destruction rather than making these two feel guilty,' Anjali said.

'When did I do that?' Bindu said.

'By going on and on. Ramesh uncle is in jail. He killed my sister. Your daughter. And if these two weren't there, he would have gotten away with it.'

'Yes, I know,' Bindu said, 'and I owe you both for that. Thank you, Keshav and Saurabh.'

'You don't have to thank us,' I said.

'Why not?' Anjali said. 'Enough is enough. We are a dysfunctional family trying to keep up appearances. Inside, we are ready to kill each other. Doesn't take away from what you did for us.'

'Thank you,' I said.

'We should be thanking you,' Anjali said. 'If there's any way we can ever repay you, please let me know.'

'No, it's fine,' I said. 'We are just happy it's over. Hope Prerna's soul is in peace.'

Saurabh bit his lower lip, perhaps trying to fight back tears.

'You have a detective agency, right? This is work for you. Ma, we should give them something for this,' Anjali said.

'No,' Saurabh said and waved his hands vigorously. He stood up. 'We just came to check on you guys. Nothing else. I don't want anything. Like Keshav said, if my Prerna is in peace, it is more than enough.'

'True,' I said, and stood up as well. Although, if they had given me a cheque at that moment, I would have taken it.

'I have some savings. Ma might have something too. We could—' Anjali said, but Saurabh interrupted her.

'Please, don't embarrass us. We don't want anything. In fact, we better leave. We have to move out of our place in five days. A lot of packing to be done.'

Saurabh had found an apartment in Gurgaon and signed the lease. I still hadn't finalised anything and planned to stay in an Oyo Rooms near the office for a while. My family was being destroyed as well.

❖

Anjali walked Saurabh and me out of the house. Even at 8 in the evening, the lane outside was desolate, pitch dark and chilly. Saurabh booked us a cab, which ended up arriving in the parallel lane.

'I will just go find him. Drivers always get confused here,' Saurabh said.

Anjali and I watched Saurabh walk away to locate the cab.

'Thank you once again, Keshav,' Anjali said, her eyes meeting mine.

'You're welcome,' I said. I kept eye contact for a few seconds longer than I should have. 'I'll miss you,' I said.

I had said something emotional like this to someone after years. I did feel something for her. I would miss this girl with the scrawny figure and messy hair the most from Malhotra House. Of course, my best friend would flip if I gave in to those feelings, and I couldn't afford to annoy him any more.

'I'll miss you too, Keshav,' Anjali said. I could tell this was rare for her. Like me, she didn't like to express her emotions much either. She wore a white flannel shirt with blue pinstripes. It fluttered in the winter breeze. She shivered a little.

'You're not wearing anything warm, you should go back inside,' I said.

'It's okay. I'll wait here with you until your cab arrives,' Anjali said and smiled. She fastened the top button of her shirt.

I removed my hoodie and handed it to her.

'What about you?' she said.

'It's okay. I have this,' I said, and pulled at the half-sleeve grey sweater I wore to work.

'Thanks,' she said, draping the hoodie over her shoulders. 'Since I'm part of such a fucked-up family, you must think I'm pretty fucked-up too.'

'Not at all,' I said.

'I noticed how you always avoid me,' Anjali said without a smile.

'That's not true,' I said.

'Oh, really? Tell me honestly, aren't you always in a hurry to cut the call or end a chat?'

I squared my shoulders.

'Well … you're not wrong. But it's not because your family is fucked-up or whatever.'

'Then?'

'Nothing,' I said. I looked to the left and to the right, stalling by pretending to be checking whether Saurabh had found the cab.

'Come on, you can tell me.'

'Leave it, Anjali.'

'Why? Why can't you tell me? I don't even know if we will ever meet again.'

I looked at her. Her eyes, filled with earnestness, were trained on me.

'Two reasons. One, because Saurabh has banned contact with you.'

'What? Why?'

'Because you are family or whatever. And he thinks I only hook up with women for casual sex. He is not wrong, actually; I only meet women on Tinder.'

'Okay, that's something I did not know.'

'Now you do. "Anjali is off-limits" is what he told me,' I said. I didn't tell her he had also told me 'find someone else to fuck' in one of his angry moods.

'I'm off-limits? That's ridiculous. I don't get to have a say in it?'

I shrugged.

'He was damn upset when he saw us sitting like that on that bench at the engagement.'

'Oh, that day,' Anjali said. 'We were just high.'

I smirked.

'What's the second reason?' Anjali said.

'Saurabh should be here soon, you really must go inside. It's cold,' I said.

'Don't avoid the question, Keshav.'

I sighed. I looked into her brown eyes.

'The second reason is, I'm scared. I actually like you. I don't see you like I do those girls on Tinder. I always knew if I spoke to you too much, I would be drawn to you.'

'You're so chicken?' said Anjali, crossing one arm over the other.

'You're off-limits,' I repeated. I pointed at the car headlights in the distance. The cab arrived with Saurabh in it, and I entered the vehicle. Saurabh rolled down his window and waved goodbye to Anjali.

The Uber left A Block behind and came out onto the main road.

'What were you talking to Anjali about?' Saurabh said. The school principal was back.

'What?'

'I saw you guys from the car. You were deep in conversation.'

'Nothing. She wanted to know what happens next.'

'As in?'

'On the case front. I told her the police will frame a chargesheet, while Ramesh and Khanna will try for bail. Is that okay?'

'Okay, as in?'

'Like, is it okay if I spoke to her about that while I waited for you? Do you approve, sir?' I said in a sarcastic tone.

Apart from his attempts to control my interactions with Anjali, I was also irritated with Saurabh's lack of gratitude. I had helped him put his fiancée's killer behind bars. One 'thanks', maybe? No. Sir only wants to know if I have called the movers yet or ask how dare I chat with Anjali for three minutes.

'What approve? I don't care, man. How does it even matter now?' Saurabh said.

'Can you please close your window? I am freezing,' I said.

'You wouldn't be if you hadn't left your jacket behind with her,' Saurabh said.

Chapter 52

I lay in bed, unable to sleep. Anjali's words kept coming back to me. She had accused me of chickening out. Did I hold myself back because of Saurabh? Or because I was afraid to like her? Anyway, I could approach her now, right? Saurabh said he didn't care.

My phone pinged. I lifted it up in the darkness. The screen's glow hit my face.

Anjali had messaged me. I checked the time: 1 a.m. Was she thinking of me as well?

'You left your jacket.'

'I'll collect it later. Or keep it. I have plenty of hoodies,' I replied.

'Thank you.'

'It's okay.'

'Thank you for everything, actually.'

'You are most welcome ☺'

'Not sleeping?'

'Not sleepy.'

'Same here. Going now. Am sure your quota of chat with off-limits Anjali has expired. Goodnight.'

I sat up in bed. With a smile on my face, I typed back:

'No quota. Only self-restraint.'

'You are afraid of liking me?'

'Not just liking you. Afraid of liking you too much and not knowing what to do with it.'

'As in?'

'What am I supposed to do if I like you a lot? Do I tell you? Do I ask you out?'

'Yes and yes.'

'How?'

'Well, how about: I find you interesting, Anjali, want to hang out?'

'That's not what I meant. I know how to ask. But with Saurabh and the family backdrop ... Don't know.'

'No family backdrop now. The wedding, the case, it's all over. So that's no longer an excuse.'

'What about Saurabh's feelings?'

'Isn't he moving out?' Anjali texted.

'How do you know that?'

'Because he keeps mentioning it. And you just sit there with a sullen face. I notice things too, Mr Detective.'

I replied with a smiley emoji. She did not reply immediately. I could see she was still online.

Five minutes later, I gathered the guts to send her a message.

'I find you interesting, Anjali, want to hang out?'

She replied immediately.

'Bold move, mister.'

'You don't have to say yes.'

'Relax, we can hang out. I like you as well.'

'I just said I find you interesting, I didn't say like,' I replied.

'Oh, really. We will see about that. When?'

'After work someday?'

'I freelance. No after-work as such for me. I can meet anytime,' she replied, followed by three laughter emojis.

I opened my office calendar on my phone. I didn't have a busy week. I didn't even feel like going to work that day.

'Do you want to come home for lunch today?' I said. 'We can order from outside.'

'Home?' Anjali replied.

'Yes, Malviya Nagar.'

'You don't have work?'

'I can work from home,' I texted.

I could see the 'typing ...' come on and off a couple of times on my WhatsApp. Would she agree to come home? Or would she refuse? I felt I should give her the choice.

'Or we can meet outside,' I typed.

'No, home is fine. I will bring my laptop. Have to finish an article. We can both work together.'

'Sounds great. 11?' I said.

'Sure. See you. Goodnight, Mr Detective.'

'Goodnight, Ms Activist-journalist,' I replied, adding a few 'zzz' emojis.

❖

'I'm not coming to office. I think I have fever,' I said.

Saurabh stood at the door of my bedroom. He was in a suit, which we wore when we had client meetings.

'You seemed fine last night,' Saurabh said, looking down at his phone as he booked a cab to go to work.

'Yeah, caught a cold,' I said.

'Keep distributing your jackets. What else will happen?' Saurabh said.

'She was shivering. I gave it to her for two minutes. I forgot—'

'Yes, whatever, forget it. Cab is arriving in four minutes. You coming or not?'

I coughed twice and faked a sneeze. 'Can you tell Jacob I will work from home?'

Saurabh shut the door hard behind him.

Chapter 53

The doorbell rang at 11.15. I opened the door.

'Hi,' she said and smiled.

She had a hipster look today. Underneath a leather jacket, she wore a black spaghetti tank top and frayed denim shorts. Her big backpack looked enormous on her. If it weren't for her chunky oxidized silver jewellery and messed-up hair, you'd think she was a high-school student going for tuitions.

She wore a necklace made of leather strands.

'Sorry, am I inappropriately dressed for your gentrified colony?' she said as she caught me staring at her plunging neckline.

'Huh? No. And please come in.'

She looked around the flat; most of our stuff had been packed away.

I said, 'Tea? Coffee?'

'Beer?' she said, removing her jacket. With just the tank top on, I could see a portion of a tattoo on the side of her chest. It seemed to be some letters.

'Oh,' I said. 'Sure.'

I gave her a bottle of Bira from the fridge.

She opened her backpack and pulled out a hand-rolled cigarette.

'Want one?' she said.

'A bit early for me, frankly,' I said and smiled. She walked to the living room window and opened it. She lit her cigarette and took several puffs, pausing to sip her beer in-between.

I tried not to stare at her. Her big eyes and high cheekbones always seemed to have a weird effect on me. Being alone with her at my place, the effect was ten times more. I opened my CyberSafe pitch presentation instead, which was just about as exciting as re-applying for a lost Aadhaar card.

'Busy?' she said, seeing me staring at my laptop screen.

'Not really. This is due today. Thought I would finish it quickly and send it,' I said. 'You have work too, right?'

'Yes, I better finish my article. I've been sitting on it all week,' she said, taking a big sip of beer. She placed her backpack on the dining table and took out her laptop. For the next hour or so, the gentle tap of keys was the only sound in the room.

I finished the pitch and emailed it to Jacob. I stretched my arms.

'Done,' I said.

'Wow, you work a lot,' Anjali said.

'Finished now. Let's order lunch?'

'Sure. Are we allowed to eat it together, though? Or do we eat at our desks, sir?'

I laughed and came to the dining table from where I'd been sitting on the sofa.

'I thought you wanted to meet and work together,' I said and flipped through the UberEats app.

'And I thought you wanted to hang out,' she said.

'Sorry. I'm free to hang out now. Chinese?' I said.

'Noodles always works. Do you have more beer?' she said, and shook her empty bottle in my face.

I ordered food from Chinabox and kept my phone on the dining table. I took out two bottles of Bira from the fridge, one for each of us.

We moved to the sofa. I placed my feet on the coffee table. I was wearing shorts and a workout T-shirt. I took a sip of beer. I could get used to working from home, I thought.

Anjali took a sip of her drink as well.

'Peaceful to be here. Things at home are still rough,' Anjali said.

I nodded.

'Neelam aunty doesn't talk to my mother or me,' Anjali said.

'How's Maaji? You guys have told her everything?'

She shook her head.

'She thinks Ramesh uncle is in Amritsar. That's what Neelam aunty told her. Even my mother won't tell her the truth.'

'It was in the papers,' I said.

'Maaji doesn't read them.'

'Someone will tell her. Maid, neighbour, someone. That will be worse,' I said, raising my bottle to my lips.

'That's exactly what I told them. They didn't agree. Hell, Maaji doesn't even know her daughter Bindu has kids. No, everyone still wants to hide things,' Anjali said. She finished her second beer and plonked the bottle on the table.

'Have more?' she said.

'Beer is over. I do have some vodka.'

'Anything,' she said.

I brought a bottle of Absolut Mandrin from the kitchen, along with two glasses and a carton of orange juice.

'I don't need the juice,' Anjali said.

She poured two large pegs of vodka into the glasses.

'Go slow ... this isn't beer,' I said.

She laughed.

'Relax,' Anjali said and took a sip. 'I won't get drunk.'

I smiled.

'Why do you look at me like that?' she said, catching me staring at her.

'Nothing,' I said.

She removed her leather boots and swung her legs onto the table. Her denim shorts climbed her upper thighs as her slender legs stretched out along mine, our bare feet on the table.

'You always look at me, and then pretend not to have been looking at me. Why does it have to be that way?' she said.

'I told you why.'

'Even now? Your friend is far away in a cubicle in Gurgaon, right?'

'Yes,' I said.

'Why don't you look at me?'

I looked at her. She looked messy and beautiful at the same time. The desire to pull her to me was monstrous. The tension of the past few months, being alone with her in the same room, and the alcohol—a little voice in my head said: 'Kiss her, kiss her ...' I resisted the urge and picked up the vodka instead.

Tears ran down her cheeks. Her slender hands and her glass began to quiver.

'Are you okay, Anjali?' I said.

She nodded and sniffled to fight back her sobs.

'You are not okay,' I said. I wondered what to do next. My mind raced through the options. Move closer to her and hug her? Too much. Hold her hands? Awkward, when she had them in her lap. Give her a tissue? Okay, yes, I could do that. I went up to the dining table and returned with a box of tissues.

'Thanks,' she said. She wiped her eyes. A bit of her mascara came on the tissue, leaving black marks.

I sat down again and placed my legs back on the coffee table. This time, my feet bumped into hers a little. The touch of her toes on mine sent mild electric sparks up my body. I shifted my feet a bit to the right to avoid contact.

'May I ask why you are crying?' I said.

'I am a villain in my own fucking house,' Anjali said. 'For just helping find out who killed my sister.'

'You are not a villain, Anjali,' I said.

She folded her legs and wrapped her arms around her knees.

'They feel I should have remained quiet and supported Ramesh uncle. Kept some fuck-all family honour. Thought about consequences. As if that's all that fucking matters,' Anjali said. She broke down again. I remained silent as she composed herself. She spoke again.

'I came from the US to find a stable family and my roots. Ramesh uncle felt like the patriarch, the father figure who would protect us all. For a while he did, or at least I thought so. And now this. Is everything just a façade?' Anjali said, fighting back tears.

I gave a gentle nod in support. She continued.

'Less than two months. That's it. That's all I had a sister for, officially. That's the length of time Prerna and I both knew we were sisters. She gets murdered, and we should have done nothing about it? Just because someone from the family may have done it?'

'You did the right thing,' I said.

'I didn't even do much. All I said is, we must keep trying. It is you guys who did it. You did it Keshav, you.'

'Thanks. I am happy we could help,' I said.

She wiped her eyes with a fresh tissue and composed herself. She took a big sip of vodka. 'But look at how they treated you guys. Forget thanks, they insulted you. Ramesh uncle did, of course. Even Neelam aunty now.'

'The reaction is understandable, Anjali,' I said. 'But as long as the killer is in jail, we are happy.'

Anjali shook her head.

'He's trying his best to come out. You know that, right?'

'On bail?'

'Yes.'

'With his connections, he could get bail. But bail doesn't mean he is out. The case will be tried in court. He will get punished eventually,' I said.

'I hope so. In this country, anything can happen,' Anjali said. She finished her vodka and poured herself another drink.

'It's not that easy to get away, I hope,' I said. I took a big sip from my glass. The orange-flavoured liquid felt like a fireball was going down my food pipe and into my belly.

Anjali stood up and went to the window. She drew the curtains so that the room became dark. She went to the dining table, rummaged around in her backpack and came back with two hand-rolled cigarettes.

'Try these, they are special.'

'Joint?' I said, taking one from her hand.

She nodded and smiled. She took out a lighter from the pocket of her denim shorts. She lit the joint in her hand and sat next to me again.

'Do you have any music?' she said, taking a puff.

I pulled out a Bluetooth speaker from under the coffee table.

'I can connect this to my phone.'

We stood up and went to the dining table.

I opened the music app on my phone and passed it to her. She selected *I Don't Wanna Live Forever* by Taylor Swift and Zayn Malik. She kept my phone on the table again. We returned to the sofa, to our original seats. The slow, seductive voice of Zayn and marijuana smoke filled the room.

I don't wanna live forever

'Cause I know I will be living in vain…

'I love this song,' she said.

'What was Seattle like?' I said.

'Cold. Boring. Mundane.'

'Really? I thought it would be exciting. Headquarters of Microsoft, Starbucks and Amazon …'

'Maybe for the guys who run those companies. For me, it was mostly just cold, rainy and miserable,' Anjali said and laughed.

She closed her eyes and swayed to the music.

I just wanna keep calling your name

Until you come back home…

'Which album?' I said.

'*Fifty Shades Darker*.'

'The movie? Based on the book?'

'Yes,' she said. 'I read all three books in the series. Seen all the movies too.'

The Fifty Shades series is a trilogy of erotic novels consisting of *Fifty Shades of Grey*, *Fifty Shades Darker* and *Fifty Shades Freed*. The story is about a young and rich businessman, Christian Grey, who introduces his girlfriend to BDSM, or dominant–submissive sexual activities.

With her silver bracelets, tattoos and leather jacket, Anjali could have passed off as a character in Fifty Shades.

'I found it all too ...' I said and paused to find the right word.

'Explicit?' Anjali said.

'Yes, that for sure, but also violent and painful. Made me uncomfortable.'

Anjali laughed.

'Are you squeamish or what? A bit of pain and you are uncomfortable?'

'You liked them? What is the point of this dominance–submission thing?'

'BDSM means different things to different people. The dominant likes the sense of power. It's like a high. The submissive likes the complete surrender—it feels like an escape from all responsibilities and stresses of life. It's obviously more than just the sex.'

I shook my head.

'I still can't relate to it. The books were a fun one-time read though. You seem to be more into it.'

'I am not totally into it. I don't want to be beaten up, for instance,' Anjali said. 'But yes, a drop of pain makes it more exciting, doesn't it?'

'Does it?' I said.

'Yes. Buddha said, "What's better? The mosquito doesn't bite you at all, or that it does and you get to scratch it?" Think about it.'

'Deep,' I said, and took a huge puff. The thing with joints is that every statement becomes deep.

'True, though?'

'Did Buddha actually say that?'

'Internet said he did.'

'Must be true then.'

Both of us laughed. Our eyes met. She let her feet drop to the side on the coffee table. Her toes caressed my soles. I did not move my feet away this time. She caressed her toe up and down on my soles, making me tingly and ticklish at the same time. The vodka began to take effect as well. I shut my eyes. As I relaxed and enjoyed the sensation, she jabbed a toenail hard into my left foot. I opened my eyes, startled.

'Oww,' I said. 'What was that?'

'Pleasure. Pain. Mixed. That was a demo.'

'Some demo that is.'

'Now close your eyes again.'

I did as she told me. She caressed my feet with her toes again. However, this time the anticipation of a jab gave me heightened awareness. Okay, I could see the point of Fifty Shades, although only in mild doses.

The slow and sexy vocals of the song matched the unhurried pace at which she moved her fingers up my legs. Should I open my eyes, I wondered. Will she stop? Should I make her stop? Is this wrong? Will Saurabh approve? At this point, do I even give a fuck?

Sensible and logical questions evaporated as my pleasure levels continued to rise with every passing second. Her fingernails reached above my knees. She brought her mouth close to my legs and blew cool air on my thighs. I shivered with the sensation. She pinched my thigh hard.

'Ouch, that hurt,' I said. My eyes opened in reflex.

'Shh,' she said. 'You want me to stop?'

I didn't answer. I didn't have the brains to, at least at that point. I simply grabbed her shoulders and pulled her close to me. She was lighter than I expected. She sat across my lap, facing me. We kissed long and hard. She bit my lower lip. I winced in pain, and she laughed. Her biting and teasing made me more aggressive. I kissed her hard and peeled off her spaghetti top.

She was wearing a black silk bra. I could see the tattoo on the side of her chest. 'Carpe Diem', it said in a cursive font. The words ran across from under her left breast to below her armpit. I ran my fingers over the tattoo.

'Seize the day, *Dead Poets Society*,' she said, referring to the movie.

'O Captain, my Captain,' I said, quoting one of the famous dialogues from the film.

She smiled and kissed me again. She stood up to remove her shorts and sat on my lap again. I removed my shirt. The music from *Fifty Shades Darker* went from one makeout song to another. She continued to kiss and bite my neck, shoulders, chest and stomach.

I pulled at her hair once.

'Don't be a wuss,' she said. She pushed me back on the couch, making me lie flat on my back. She removed her underwear and lay next to me on the narrow sofa. Almost on cue, the music stopped as the Bluetooth speaker began to ring.

'Golu calling,' a robotic voice screamed in the room.

'What the fuck,' she said.

'Golu calling ... Golu calling,' the speaker continued to yell as I came back to my senses. Relax, it is just a phone call, I told myself.

'What is happening, Keshav?' Anjali sounded rattled.

'Nothing. It's my phone. I'm getting a call. It's connected to this speaker, so ...'

'It's freaking me out.'

'Yes, yes, I am not taking the call,' I said. I realised I had left my phone on the dining table. I decided to cancel the call from the Bluetooth speaker. I stretched out my hand and pressed the cancel button on top of the speaker.

'Hello? Keshav?' Saurabh's voice came on the other side. Fuck, I had pressed the wrong button.

'Wha—' Anjali said out loud as I covered her mouth with my right hand.

'Hey, Saurabh,' I said.

'Where are you? All okay?'

'Home only, why?'

'Nothing, you sound out of breath. Voice also coming from a distance.'

'Ran to my phone from the shower. You are on speaker.'

'Oh, anyway, just wanted you to know that I am coming home early. Had a meeting Delhi side, so no point going back to Gurgaon now.'

'Really? When? Where are you?'

'Civil Lines. Google Maps is showing fifty-four minutes.'

'Okay,' I said. My brain went into overdrive thinking about what I had to finish in the next fifty-four minutes.

'See you then,' Saurabh said and ended the call. Seductive music resumed on the speaker and filled the room, like the call had never happened.

'What the fuck was that?' Anjali said, taking heavy breaths.

I pulled her close to me. Our naked bodies touched. I pointed to the Bluetooth speaker.

'Now that was pain,' I said. 'And now, back to pleasure.'

I entered her.

She moaned loud enough to drown out the music from the speaker. Like her kisses, her lovemaking had a high intensity to it. She moved with speed and passion. Her nails dug hard into my chest as she sat on top of me most of the time. She continued to kiss and bite me. She quivered in climax.

'You can finish now,' she told me, and it didn't take me long. Then we collapsed on each other. As I shut my eyes in exhaustion, the doorbell rang.

'Fuck,' I said. I jumped off the sofa to put my clothes on.

'It's only been what? Twenty minutes?' Anjali said, looking at her watch. She picked up her clothes.

'Yes, the one time in my life I wanted traffic,' I said.

The doorbell rang again.

'What do I do?' she said.

I scanned the house.

'Hide in my room,' I said. 'Take your backpack. Once he goes to his room, I will whisk you out.'

I cleared the vodka bottle and glasses. The doorbell rang again.

'Coming,' I shouted.

My Bluetooth speaker rang again.

'Unknown calling ... unknown calling,' it sang out loud.

'That caller ID sound creeps me out,' Anjali said. She ran into my room and shut the door.

I cut the call on the speaker, this time pressing the correct button. The doorbell rang again. I walked up to the main door and opened it.

'You ordered Chinese food, sir?' the delivery guy said at the entrance.

❖

'Are you sure you don't want to eat now?' I said. 'Relax, we still have twenty-five minutes.'

Anjali didn't answer. She walked around the living room, collecting her belongings. She zipped up her backpack and her jacket. She checked herself in the mirror. I came between her and her reflection.

'It was just the delivery guy, relax. Saurabh will still take a while,' I said.

'No, sir, I'm not taking any more chances. No noodles are worth him walking in and finding me here.'

'He wouldn't care,' I said.

'Yeah, right,' Anjali said and rolled her eyes. She threw the cigarette butts in the dustbin in the kitchen. 'Spray some room freshener here, will you?'

'I will. Take some food with you? You haven't eaten anything.'

I gave her a box of chow mein. She shrugged and took it.

'Wow, you are the caring kinds. I like that. It's rare for me. Thank you,' she said. Even as she spoke to me, she avoided eye contact and looked in the mirror to adjust her hair.

'Are you always this awkward after making love?' I said. Yes, this hadn't felt like hook-up sex. It had felt like making love.

She looked at me and smiled. She came up to me and pecked me on the lips. She checked her watch.

'I would love to give an elaborate speech. On how good it all was. But I should leave. Before your uncle-cum-friend-cum-school principal enters the lane. Save it all for next time, bye,' she said.

Before I could respond, she had opened the door and left. She had said 'next time', though. Good. It meant there would be a next time.

The bell rang again after twenty minutes. I ran and opened the door. Saurabh stood there, fumbling for his house keys inside his pockets.

'Did you break a perfume bottle?' Saurabh said, sniffing as he walked in.

'No, just sprayed some room freshener,' I said.

He came in and dropped his briefcase on the sofa.

'Was someone there in the house when I called?' Saurabh said.

I stiffened.

'No, why?' I said.

'I don't know. Heard someone.'

Damn, does he have to cross-examine me as soon as he enters the house?

'Maybe I was watching a show on my laptop,' I said.

'You weren't working? Jacob wanted the pitch,' Saurabh said, removing his jacket.

'Already sent it.'

Saurabh nodded as he removed his tie.

'He may get bail,' Saurabh said.

'Ramesh?'

'Yes. I called Singh. He said he can keep him inside for now, but Ramesh's lawyers are getting close.'

'I'm not surprised,' I said.

'It doesn't fucking end at finding the killer or arresting

him? One has to deal with all the legal drama as well, to get him punished?'

'We are detectives, we found out who did it. We handed him to the police. Technically, our job is done, Golu.'

'That's what this is? Just a job?'

'Of course not. I'm just saying we are not lawyers.'

'He kills my Prerna and may soon be out drinking Scotch in his house.'

'Not for long.'

'Whatever,' Saurabh said and shook his head. Apart from the room freshener, his keen nose picked up something else.

'Did you order Chinese food? I smell soy sauce.'

'Arrived a few minutes ago,' I said, and pointed to the boxes of Chinese food.

We moved to the dining table. Saurabh tore open the boxes.

'Gobi manchurian? Superb. There's momos and clear soup, good. Where is the chow mein?'

'I don't remember if I ordered it.'

'How can we eat gobi manchurian without noodles? There's a receipt here, it says you ordered chow mein. Where is it?'

While he is always a good investigator, when it comes to food, Saurabh's detecting skills are legendary.

'Looks like they forgot to pack it. Shall I make some rice?' I said.

'No, it will take a long time. Sit. Let's eat.'

'Sure,' I said. We sat down. Saurabh placed two momos in his mouth one after the other. His face too looked like a giant momo.

'Don't give this delivery guy five stars. What is the fun of Chinese food without noodles?'

'Take my momos. I'm not that hungry,' I said.

'If you insist,' Saurabh said.

I had a spoonful of soup.

'Do you have bedbugs in your room?' Saurabh said.

'What?' I said.

'Your neck. Also, your arms. They haven't even spared your legs,' Saurabh said with his mouth full. Anjali's lovemaking had left its presence. The 'bedbugs' had caused considerable damage.

'We need to do pest control. But why pay for it when we are leaving in four days.'

'Exactly,' I said.

'Apply calamine lotion.'

'Absolutely,' I said, hoping I would see my bedbug again soon.

Chapter 54

'Sleeping?' Anjali sent me a message.

It was a little past midnight. I was sitting on my bed, surfing on my laptop for apartments and Oyo Rooms. Saurabh was in his room. I had to figure out where I would stay next week.

'No,' I replied.

'This afternoon was wonderful. Sorry, I got flustered.'

'You are cute when flustered. And yes, it was amazing.'

'Principal sir okay?'

'Mostly.'

'Mostly?'

'He seemed worried about bedbugs biting me.'

'Oops. Many bedbugs?'

'Many.'

'Memories. Of an incredible afternoon.'

'When do you want to work together again?'

'Haha. Whenever you say, sir.'

We fixed to meet again in two days and ended our chat.

I switched off the lamp next to my bed and kept my phone aside. The laptop screen's light still glowed in the room. I got off the bed to change into an old, more comfortable, cotton T-shirt. I removed the workout T-shirt I'd worn since morning. I saw my reflection in the bedroom mirror. I had lost weight. Two more of my ribs had become visible. I could see them even in the limited light. I came closer to the mirror and looked at my face. I touched some of the bedbug bites on my neck. Fortunately, Saurabh had not seen the bigger ones on my chest. I continued to look at myself in the mirror. I put on an old T-shirt and returned to bed. I shut down the laptop as darkness engulfed the room. If only my mind could shut down as fast as my computer, so I could go to sleep soon.

Chapter 55

One month later

'What do you mean he is out of jail?' Saurabh said. 'Unbelievable.'

Saurabh, Inspector Singh and I had met at Chaayos near our office in Gurgaon. Singh had some work at the Gurgaon Police Station and had called Saurabh, saying he wanted to share something face to face.

'The court granted him bail. The police didn't,' Singh said. The three of us sipped hot and spicy ginger tea from earthen cups. Steam from my cup hit my face, helping with the winter chill.

Saurabh cursed under his breath.

'You are disappointed, but he has a right to apply for bail. Don't worry. We will prove the crime in court. That's how it is done, anyway,' Singh said.

Saurabh shook his head.

'Saurabh ji, I didn't take any money. The bail wasn't in my hands. He hired top lawyers.'

Saurabh slurped his tea loudly in response.

'What if he absconds? Runs away and hides somewhere in Punjab. Or even abroad,' Saurabh said.

'He can't. Bail conditions say he can't leave Delhi, forget the country. If he tries any such stunt, courts will come down hard on him.'

'When does the trial start?' I said.

'Soon. Hope to have the first hearing in one month.'

'One month? How is that soon?' Saurabh said.

'One month is jet-speed for our courts,' Singh said.

Saurabh finished his tea in one gulp. He slammed the cup down on the table. The little earthen pot bore his entire frustration with the Indian judicial system. I had to somehow make him feel better.

'Golu, have you tried the moong daal halwa here?' I said.

❖

I had moved to a cheap Oyo Rooms near my office for a month. It saved me money, bought me time until I found an apartment, and I could walk to work. It also meant my trysts with Anjali had to stop, though we continued to grow closer over time. The strict hotel rules didn't allow unmarried members of the opposite gender in the same room.

'What if a boy and girl are just friends?' I said.

'Not allowed,' said the strict-looking, forty-ish man at the reception, who should have been a jail warden instead.

'What about cousins?' I said.

'No.'

'Real brother and sister?'

'Not allowed.'

'Father and daughter? Devar and bhabhi? Jija and saali? Sasur and bahu?'

'No, no, no and no. No females in your room. You want to stay here or not?'

'Fine. Please make sure there are no female mosquitoes in my room as well,' I said.

Given the curfew at my hotel, Anjali and I now met on dates in the outside world: malls, cinemas, cafes, bars.

We had come to Antidote, a health food cafe in Hauz Khas. Ramesh had returned to Malhotra House after obtaining bail. Anjali told me about the situation at home.

'Things are super-weird between his family and us. They neither talk to my mother, nor to me,' she said. She mixed her smoothie with the metal straw she always carried with her to save the planet.

'How's Maaji?' I said, as I took a sip of my green smoothie. It tasted like blended grass.

'She still doesn't know. She shares the floor with us. Ramesh uncle comes and meets her in her room. But he doesn't even acknowledge us.'

'Tough,' I said.

'On top of that, Ma is sucking up to him again. She keeps saying sorry to Neelam aunty and Ramesh uncle over and over again.'

'And?'

'They insult her, what else? I'd love to move out, but we have no choice. Ma and I can't afford another place right now.'

'Why should you guys move? Anyway, the trial will start soon. After that, he will be back inside.'

'They will try to delay. Stretch the trial out as much as they can,' Anjali said.

Unlike her usual bohemian attire, today she wore a light pink salwar kameez with white flowers all over it. Instead of her usual chunky metal earrings, she had dainty silver ones on.

I placed my palm on top of Anjali's.

'It's all going to be okay,' I said.

'Thank you,' she said. 'I needed to hear that.'

'Anjali,' I said.

'Yes?'

'I love you.' I clasped both her hands. 'I do. And I want this to be meaningful. To go somewhere.'

'Keshav,' she said, her voice soft, 'are you serious?'

'I mean it. This is so strange, meeting without telling anyone. Like we are doing something wrong. We need to tell Saurabh. Others too,' I said.

'Really?' said Anjali, cheeks pink enough to match her outfit.

'Why are you so surprised? You thought this was just a fling?' I said.

Her eyes turned damp. She held my hand.

'I love you too, Keshav,' she said, 'and yeah, I needed to hear and say these words too.'

The waiter at Antidote brought the bill, interrupting our moment.

'I have an idea,' Anjali said after I paid the bill.

'What about?'

'Coming to your room. What if I dress up as a boy? I can do it pretty well. Will your Oyo Rooms headmaster let me in then?'

'No, please. They'll kick me out if they find out. And there's nothing else so cheap near the office.'

'They won't find out.'

'They will,' I said.

'How?'

'You are too pretty to be a boy,' I said. 'And in any case, they will know when I can't take my eyes off you.'

She smiled and continued to look at me for a long time.

Chapter 56

'You need to talk about what? You and Anjali?' Saurabh looked aghast.

'Relax, sit down. No need to stand in front of my face.'

I had come to his new apartment. The only decoration so far was a giant fridge. It was three times the size of what we had in Malviya Nagar. It could store enough rations to see him through World War III. He had found a deal and taken a two-bedroom apartment on the seventeenth floor of a fancy condominium. Its key selling point was a pool and a gym. I'd bet both my kidneys Saurabh would never use either for the entire two-year duration of his lease.

I sat on one of the two easy chairs in his small balcony on this Sunday afternoon, enjoying the rare pollution-free winter sun. His large frame in front of me blocked the sunlight.

Saurabh huffed and puffed a little as he sat down on the other easy chair. He bit into the last slice of the pizza we had ordered. 'I always suspected it,' Saurabh said. 'I wasn't wrong on the day of the engagement, was I?'

'That day nothing happened.'

'But later it did? Seriously, Keshav? The one person I tell you to stay away from. Why her? Why can't you leave Prerna's family alone?'

I wanted to pay attention to him, but the strand of cheese hanging from his mouth distracted me. I wanted to point it out to him. However, his red face and upset tone meant he wouldn't want to be ticked off right now.

'It's not what you think, Golu. This is not just a secret fling. I'm telling you because it matters. I don't want to hide it anymore,' I said.

'It matters? Like I haven't seen you with girls.'

Saurabh took the empty pizza box to the kitchen. I looked

at the over-constructed skyline of Gurgaon and waited for him to return. He came back after wiping his face. I spoke again.

'I have done stupid things in the past. But this is different. In fact, I want to make it official.'

'Official?' said Saurabh.

'Why? Isn't that what you wanted? That I don't treat her like some casual Tinder date.'

'I wanted you to stay away from her. Or rather any woman in the Malhotra family.'

'I am not a creep, Saurabh.'

'I didn't say that. But you yourself said you don't believe in relationships anymore.'

'I do now. Anjali is different.'

Saurabh rolled his eyes.

'I knew you wouldn't believe me,' I said. 'That's why I want you to come along as well.'

'Come where?'

'To the Malhotras. I want to get an okay from Bindu aunty.'

'What? Have you gone mad?'

'Maybe. But it's the right thing to do, isn't it?'

'What is? Getting killed by Ramesh uncle?'

'I'm sure he is done with his killing quota for now,' I said and grinned.

'It's not funny, Keshav. First you say you are dating Anjali. Now you want to go to the Malhotras. For what? To ask for her hand in marriage?'

'Sort of,' I said. 'I just want everyone to know that we are together. And that my intentions are serious. The last thing I want is for them to find out from someone else.'

'What do you think will happen? Maaji will get an aarti thali and give you her blessings? Neelam aunty will throw flowers on you? Ramesh uncle will do a roka?'

'I don't know what will happen, but I need you to come with me. As long as Bindu aunty approves, it is okay. She is her mother.'

'We put that man in jail. He is not going to let us enter the house. In fact, if he could, he would throw Anjali and Bindu aunty out of the house too.'

'He can't. Not while Maaji is around. They stay on Maaji's floor.'

'He will never approve of this relationship.'

'I'm not asking for his permission. Anjali and I just want to inform everyone. I want to be able to visit her freely, openly. We want things formalised ...'

'Formalised? You guys are getting married? Wow, you will marry her? My dead ex-fiancée's sister?'

'I thought she was her cousin for the longest time. And so what if she is Prerna's sister?'

'You don't think there's anything wrong? After all that has happened?'

I did not respond. Saurabh looked away from me and towards the playground on the ground floor. Little kids kicked a football around as they jostled and laughed through their game. Why are childhood friendships so easy? What happens when we grow up that we complicate things so much?

'I'll have to convince the family. It may not go down well—that's why I want you to come. Just this once, Saurabh, please. I beg you.'

❖

'You *what*?'

'Coming to meet your family. To formally ask for your hand.'

She covered her face with her hands.

'Is that a proposal?' she said. 'Fuck.'

'The F word is not how people respond normally.'

'Sorry, nobody has ever proposed to me before.'

Her face had turned red. She slid her fingers up to cover her eyes as well. We had come to Andaz hotel at Aerocity. We sat on the bar stools in the lobby. She was in tight black jeans and a black turtleneck. She had her trademark leather jacket on. She was not wearing any accessories today.

'Are you crying?' I said.

She shook her head vigorously, hands covering her entire face.

I smiled.

'Keshav, are you serious?' she said, finally bringing her arms down.

'Yes.'

'And you want to meet Ma?'

'And others.'

'Geetu ma? Greg?' she said.

'Them too, eventually, but they are in the US right now.'

'Who else? Maaji?'

'Yes, everyone. Ramesh uncle and Neelam aunty too. I don't expect support from them, but they should at least know.'

'No, no, Keshav, that's a terrible idea. My mother has just about thawed them a bit. This will make it bad again.'

'Thawed how?'

'Ma apologised a million times. Said she was misled. Kept listening to Neelam aunty's nasty taunts. Things are slightly better now. Like they at least nod and greet us. Trust me, leave them out of it.'

'How do I come see you at home then?'

'You don't have to. You will eventually leave your rented room, right?'

'It's not just about having a place to make out, Anjali. Until how long will we hide? One day they have to know.'

'One day, yes. If we are serious.'

'Are we not?'

Anjali looked at me and smiled.

'You are so damn cute, Keshav,' Anjali said. 'Let's take a room in this hotel. Right now.'

'No, let's do the right thing. Let me meet your entire family and ask for your hand.'

'Ask for my hand, aww ...' Anjali said. 'You realise how old-fashioned yet sweet that sounds? In the country I come from, men propose to the girl directly.'

'In the country we are in now, men propose to the entire family,' I said.

'Ramesh uncle will never agree to meet you.'

'Let me try. I will ask him for some time next week.'

'He is only going to abuse you a lot.'

'If I get you at the end, all the abuse will be worth it.'

She didn't respond, only gave me a shy smile.

❖

'Ramesh uncle agreed to meet you? Really?' Saurabh said, swinging his chair in the office cubicle to face me.

'Ten minutes is all I asked for,' I said, turning my own chair towards him.

'And?'

'I had to hear some gaalis. I had to be polite. Told him it is an important matter.'

'Did he threaten you?'

'No. His lawyers have advised him well. He can't be planning any violence.'

'He obviously has no idea what you are going to talk about.'

'He will soon. Wednesday, 8 p.m.'

Chapter 57

I rang the bell. Bindu answered the door and I saw that the house looked pretty much the same as when we had visited last month.

We said namaste. I thought about touching her feet, but felt it could be too much too soon. Saurabh and I followed her into the hall, and we sat down. Bindu smiled at me and patted me on the head. Had Anjali already told her about our relationship?

'Soft drink, beta?' Bindu said.

I shook my head.

'Fanta would be great, Bindu aunty,' Saurabh said.

Bindu asked Gopika to get us some soft drinks and paneer pakoras.

'Is Anjali around?' I said.

'Yes, she's just coming. Spending extra time on her clothes today. Dresses like a street urchin otherwise.'

We heard Anjali come down the steps. She was wearing a plain mustard colour saree with a thin gold border, but had contrasted it with a bright bottle green, full-sleeved silk blouse. She had a tiny red bindi on her forehead. I had never seen her in a saree. I tried, but couldn't take my eyes off her. She hugged Saurabh and me and sat opposite us.

'Others?' I said.

'Are you sure, beta?' Bindu said.

'Yes. Don't worry, it will all be fine.'

Bindu went upstairs and returned with Maaji. Saurabh and I touched Maaji's feet. All of us sat down again and sipped our drinks.

Soon Ramesh and Neelam joined us; Ramesh in a crisp white kurta pyjama, with neatly combed wet hair, and Neelam in a nondescript salwar kameez with a sweaty forehead from cooking in the kitchen.

'Hello, Uncle,' Saurabh said.

Ramesh grunted.

They too sat down.

'What do you want now?' Ramesh said to me.

'I wanted to share something with you,' I said.

'Haven't you said enough?' Ramesh said.

'Veerji, please hear him out,' Bindu said, pointing at Maaji.

'Why?' Neelam said, her voice agitated. 'You and your Anjali fall into their trap again and again. You know how much trouble Ramesh ji is in? And they have the audacity to ask for another meeting? Poor Ramesh ji—scared what trouble they will create with the police, he had no choice but to comply.'

'I didn't want to meet, he did,' Saurabh said, pointing a finger at me.

'Ki hoya?' Maaji said, sensing some kind of conflict.

'Nothing, Maaji,' Ramesh said. 'Keep the volume low,' he said to us. 'I don't want my mother to hear.'

'I apologised to Veerji and you,' Bindu whispered to Neelam.

'It's not going to help, right? Do you know the tension he is in?' Neelam said.

'Listen to Keshav, Neelam aunty—it is not what you think,' Anjali said, clutching the side of her saree pallu.

'It really isn't,' I said.

Ramesh raised his hand, gesturing everyone to be quiet. He turned to me.

'I am listening.'

'How's your case going?' I said.

'Don't pretend you care. I know you can't wait to see me behind bars again,' he said softly so Maaji wouldn't hear.

'That's not true, Uncle,' I said.

'You don't want to see me behind bars? Really? You want them to hang me then?' Ramesh said.

'No, Uncle, I don't think you should be hanged,' I said.

'Yeah, right,' Ramesh said. Anjali gently moved the plate of pakoras towards him.

'In fact, Uncle, I don't even think you should go to jail,' I said.

Saurabh looked at me, surprised.

'Why don't you say what you came here to say?' Ramesh said.

'I did,' I said.

'What?'

'I told you. I don't think you should go to jail.'

'Is this another trap?' Ramesh said.

'No,' I said.

'What the hell are you talking about then?'

'Three months back, we lost Prerna. Someone in this house killed her. The killer is in this room right now, in fact,' I said, loud enough for Maaji to hear.

Maaji turned towards me.

'You found the killer? Who is it?' she said.

'Don't listen to him Maaji,' Neelam said and turned to me. 'Didn't we tell you to keep Maaji out of it?'

'It's not Ramesh uncle, relax,' I said.

Saurabh looked at me, gobsmacked. All eyes in the room locked on me. I pulled out my phone.

'It took me a while to get the final confirmation. I have it in here. A CCTV video from 17 October 2019.'

'What video?' Ramesh said. 'We don't have any CCTV in this house.'

'It's not from this house. It's a video from the Delhi Metro, Magenta line. Even though ACP Rana helped, it still took a couple of weeks to get it.'

I played a video on my phone. It had black and white footage of a crowd in the metro train compartment. It didn't have any audio. Ramesh, Neelam and Bindu leaned in to have a better look at the screen. They couldn't figure anything out. Anjali shot up from the sofa.

'Fuck you, Keshav,' Anjali screamed. 'Fuck you, asshole.'

'Sit, Anjali,' I said.

'We had something. Didn't we? What are you doing this for? We could have had a life together.'

I remained silent. Everyone else in the room looked at me, puzzled. Anjali began to scream incoherently.

'I believed you. I fucking actually did. What an idiot I am. Wore a saree and shit.' She turned towards the stairs.

'Neelam aunty, if you don't want your husband to go to jail, you better make sure the killer doesn't escape through the back door.'

Neelam and Ramesh seemed paralysed at first, but then Neelam ran towards Anjali and grabbed her wrist.

'Neelam aunty, let me go,' Anjali said in a shaky voice.

Ramesh stood up. He bolted the front door. 'I'm not running away. You know I won't, Keshav. Tell them there is no need for this,' Anjali said, her eyes so full of rage they seemed like flames.

Neelam released Anjali's hand upon my signal. Anjali came back and sat on the sofa. Saurabh sat still like he was playing statue, mouth open, paneer pakora in hand, eyes going left to right and back, wondering what on earth was going on.

'Anjali?' he said as she sat down.

'Yes, Saurabh. Congratulations,' Anjali said. 'Your best friend finally solved the case. Happy now?'

'What? How?' Saurabh said.

'What is going on?' Bindu said to me. 'Anjali said you came here to ask for her hand.'

'I did. But for the police to handcuff it. Bindu aunty, your daughter Anjali murdered your other daughter, Prerna. Maaji, your granddaughter Anjali also murdered your son Adi. I'm so sorry,' I said.

'That's nonsense.' Bindu wore an exasperated expression. She turned to her daughter. 'Isn't it, Anjali?'

'She? She killed them?' Maaji said, pointing at Anjali.

'Yes, yes, yes, Maaji, I killed them,' Anjali said and turned to her mother. 'It is not nonsense. Keshav is right. He's a great detective, even if he is a shitty boyfriend. I'm the killer. Happy, everyone?'

Everybody sat silently, horrified by Anjali's confession. She still looked stunning in her mustard and gold saree, even though her body language had become weak. Her shoulders drooped. She kept her gaze down, avoiding eye contact with everyone.

'Bhai, how? You told me you loved her. You came to tell the family about your relationship,' Saurabh said.

'The relationship helped me confirm something. But yes, Anjali, I do owe you a separate apology for that,' I said. 'And for what it's worth, I did love you.'

Anjali looked at me with menacing eyes and smirked out of disbelief.

'Bhai, but how? She was not in the house,' Saurabh said.

'Yes, she came later. How did she kill Prerna?' Neelam said.

'Anjali, the curiosity here is unbelievable. Why don't you only tell them in your own words?' I said.

Chapter 58

Anjali Speaks

Damn, the one man I ever loved did me in. The one man who I thought actually cared. The man I actually believed.

Yes, you got me, Keshav. I did it. Feeling all accomplished? Worth destroying what we had? Happy? I sure hope so. One of us should be happy, at least.

I killed my twin sister. Biological twin, yes. You see, I never really grew up with her. I didn't even really know her until a few months ago. In that sense, we weren't typical twins. We didn't have the twin bond they keep talking about on Discovery channel or in psychology articles. How could we? We were born bastards. Is there a bastard bond?

I saw her on the terrace, looking so pretty. She was wearing yet another expensive red and gold lehenga. She had her three-lakh-rupee engagement ring on as well. More than my annual salary on her ring finger, which is of course when I had a job.

I waited for her on the terrace. She came up and greeted me, all excited.

Saurabh had not come yet. I had asked her to come to the terrace before, so I could see her all decked up first.

'My beautiful sister,' I said.

'Thank you. I'm so hungry. He better come soon.'

She held a pooja plate in her hand. I walked up to the ledge. She followed me there.

'Such a beautiful evening,' I said.

'The moon will be out soon,' she said, looking up at the sky. In some ways, Karva Chauth is such a romantic festival. The girl waiting for the moon and her lover. At another level, what a regressive, sexist celebration, considering only the girl stays hungry.

Despite eating nothing all day, Prerna was buzzing like a bee, energetic and happy, almost delirious with joy.

'Just imagine, next Karva Chauth, I will be all married,' she said.

'Can't wait to see you as a bride,' I said. 'Let me fix your make-up. Your eyeliner is smudging a bit.'

'Is it?' she said.

We couldn't see each other's faces clearly in the darkness.

'Yeah, give me your phone. I will use the flashlight to see better. I left mine to charge downstairs.'

She gave me her phone—the iPhone 11 Promax. It had released just two weeks ago and cost over one lakh rupees.

I held her phone in my left hand and focused its flashlight on her face.

I took out a tissue from my pocket and dabbed at her eyelashes.

'Shut your eyes,' I said, as I moved from one eye to the next. She complied.

'One second, let me wet the tissue with my water bottle. Keep your eyes closed, okay?' I said.

She nodded, eyes still shut. I moved fast. I kept her phone down. I moved back a few steps from her. I ran towards her with full force, my arms extended out in her direction.

Bam! Both my stretched hands hit her at the same time. I hoped my momentum would be enough to topple her over. But … her upper body fell back on the ledge and her left leg lifted off the ground. Her right leg stubbornly remained on the terrace floor. Her backbone had hit the ledge, causing her to yell in pain.

'Oww,' she screamed. Her eyes opened.

'Anjali?' she said, trembling in fear. 'What are you doing?'

She tried to fight back. I punched her in the face as I saw fear and confusion in her eyes. She tried to stand up straight, and as she tried to find her balance, her footing, I sprinted across the terrace. From a corner, I charged at her again.

This time, my hands hit her right on her shoulders. Her body went over the ledge and she fell. She screamed on her way down the four floors. I didn't do too well in physics in school, but I remember about gravity. Acceleration of around ten metres per second squared. Scream, thud, the roaring silence. It all lasted less than five seconds.

I picked up Prerna's phone, smashed it with a brick, and the screen shattered with a satisfying crunch. I went up to the ledge and looked down. I saw her on the road, face down. Nobody had spotted her yet. I tossed her phone towards her, aiming as close to her as possible.

I checked the time; ten minutes to get back to my meeting point. I couldn't waste a second. I couldn't ponder over what I had done or break down or whatever. No, I had work to do. Every moment mattered.

I left the terrace and ran down the steps. I wanted to go straight down. However, I heard footsteps from a couple of floors below.

In panic, I took out my keys to Adi's apartment. I opened his main door and went inside. I could hear him playing on his guitar and ran to the studio.

'Anjali, you are back? How was your trip?' Adi said. He stood up to hug me. We kissed. He wanted to keep kissing, but I couldn't. I didn't have time.

'Trip was good. Adi, I did it.'

'What?' Adi said, surprised.

'She's there on the road.'

He ran up to his balcony and looked down.

'Anjali, what is this? You mentioned it, but I thought you were just venting in frustration. I didn't actually think you'd go ahead with it.'

'I told you, Adi—I always mean what I say.'

'What will happen now?' he said, panic in his voice.

'I have to leave. You better be the first one to get to the body on the road. Go now, while everyone is in the kitchen.'

'Why?'

'You know she wears a three-lakh-rupee ring, right?'

His eyes met mine. Three lakh rupees can buy a lot of drugs, he knew.

'What about my fingerprints?' he said.

'I've seen gloves in your kitchen,' I said.

'Yes, okay fine,' he said.

'Bye,' I said and gave him a peck on the cheek. 'I'll be back soon.'

I ran out of his apartment. I checked the stairwell, up and down. I couldn't see anyone. I had worn cushioned sneakers and they made little noise as I tiptoed down. As I reached the first floor, I heard movement in the kitchen below, on the mezzanine level. Someone was carrying utensils to the ground floor dining table. I paused at the first floor, worried Gopika might see me. I opened the door to my apartment, which was dark as the lights were off. My mother Bindu's bedroom was shut, even though her room's light was switched on. I stepped inside into the darkness of the living room. Maaji was snoozing on the sofa.

'Kaun,' her voice startled me. I moved and hit the side shelf.

'Kaun hai?' she said again. She tried to find her spectacles in the darkness. Meanwhile, I heard Gopika climb the steps from the ground floor as she re-entered the kitchen on the mezzanine level.

With the stairs quiet, I stepped outside the apartment and tiptoed down the steps again. In seconds I was out of the back door.

I ran towards the end of the back lane. My auto driver waited there, checking messages on his phone.

'I'm done. Back to Sukhdev Vihar Metro Station,' I said.

I reached the station in five minutes, at 7.59 p.m. I couldn't find my Uber driver. I waited at the designated spot outside the parking lot, near the Patanjali banner. Three minutes later, the car arrived. 'Ah, found you. Your work is done, madam?' the driver said.

'Yes.'

'Great. Your luggage is safe. You want me to remove it?'

'Actually, I need to go nearby to A Block. A–956. Can you drop me there?'

'Sure. You already entered the destination, right?' he said.

I nodded and got in. My huge mountain of a backpack still remained on the backseat. I took out my phone and opened the Uber app. It still had my original destination.

'A–956, New Friends Colony.'

'We will be there in five minutes, madam,' the driver said as he checked his navigation screen.

Chapter 59

'What are you saying, Anjali?' Bindu said, her voice trembling just like her body.

'Yes, Ma, I'm your non-achiever, murderer daughter. Sorry,' Anjali said.

Bindu burst into tears.

'You killed my Prerna?' Bindu sank back into the sofa.

'Yes, Ma, "*your* Prerna". The daughter you kept. How did you decide I was the one to be given away? Did you toss a coin?'

'What are you talking about?' Bindu said. She turned to Neelam. 'What is she saying, Bhabhi? She pushed my Prerna?'

Neelam looked at her husband for cues on how to respond.

Ramesh didn't say anything. He simply leaned forward on the sofa, elbows resting on his thighs, hands clasped.

'It wasn't an accident,' Ramesh mumbled to himself. 'She didn't just fall off.'

'No, Uncle. We told you from day one,' I said.

'And sent me to jail for it,' Ramesh said. I hung my head.

'I wanted you inside for a while, Uncle,' I said. 'So sorry for that.'

'You knew?' Ramesh said and looked at me. 'You realised I hadn't done it but still sent me to Tihar?'

'I wasn't sure. The only way of knowing was to gain the killer's trust. It would only happen if you were inside. She had to think the case was solved and she was safe.'

Anjali clapped slowly.

'Wow, Mr Detective,' she said, continuing the applause, 'you not only solve crimes. You also specialise in fake feelings. To pretend to love someone to trap them.'

My eyes met Anjali's. She looked angry, betrayed, cornered and sad. How could I tell her that my feelings for her weren't fake? That I loved her even though I suspected her.

'Love someone?' Ramesh said. 'Who?'

'Nothing, Uncle,' I said. 'It's not important.'

'You are a total asshole, Keshav,' Anjali screamed out loud. 'You realise that?'

Maaji was looking at Anjali closely; she had heard the entire confession, even though she hadn't reacted immediately.

'Put this kameeni in jail,' Maaji said in a rare loud voice. 'I knew she was trouble the day she arrived from abroad.'

'Shh, Maaji, sat naam Waheguru, shaant Maaji shaant,' Neelam said and tapped her palm on Maaji's hand to calm her down.

'Take her upstairs,' Ramesh said.

'No, I want to listen to everything this kameeni has to say,' Maaji said.

Saurabh scratched his head.

'Bhai,' Saurabh said, raising a finger. 'One minute. I'm still confused.'

'What?'

'How did Anjali come before Prerna died? She returned from the trek, took an Uber from Delhi airport. Police checked the ride details and her cell phone tower locations. Everything matched up. She had the best alibi.'

Anjali laughed seeing Saurabh's perplexed face.

'See, I had a good plan, isn't it?' Anjali said to me.

I shrugged.

'My only mistake was that I liked you, Keshav,' she said. 'Love made me stupid.'

I didn't respond as I swallowed hard to keep my own emotions in check.

Ramesh looked at me.

'She came later. Prerna's body was already in the living room when she arrived, I remember that.'

'Yes, Veerji, impossible,' Bindu said, desperate to find a way to exonerate her daughter. 'And Anjali loved Prerna. They were sisters. Why would she do it?'

I shook my head and smiled. I turned to Anjali.

'Anjali, why don't you explain it to everyone?'

Anjali Speaks II

One of the signs that you've planned a murder well is that people find it hard to believe you did it even after you confess. Of course, I had planned it well from the start. Right when Prerna told me about Karva Chauth.

Three weeks before I left for my trek, we stood on the terrace.

'I'm going to keep a fast for him. On Karva Chauth.'

'Oh,' I said, taking a drag from my cigarette.

'It is old-fashioned. I'm not his wife yet. Still, I want to.'

'If that's what you want.' I shrugged and Googled Karva Chauth on my phone. It fell on 17 October.

'All day I stay hungry. At dusk I dress up. I come to the terrace and wait for the moon to rise. I look at the moon and then at my man. After that, I eat,' she said, and gave me a blissful smile.

'Cute,' I said.

'Don't tell anyone at home. It's embarrassing to do this before marriage. I don't want to be teased. It's just between him and me.'

I Googled the moonrise time on 17 October. That would be the time she would be on the terrace. Alone.

'Sure, I won't tell anyone,' I said. I scanned the terrace. I figured it would be hard for anyone in a neighbouring house to see what was going on here at night, since Malhotra House is taller than the adjacent homes.

I checked flights from Kathmandu to Delhi on 17 October. Any routing that made me land early evening would work. Oh, and I had to make sure I landed at the Domestic Terminal 1, which had a metro station with a direct connection to Sukhdev Vihar, the station for New Friends Colony. I found a routing via Kolkata.

'Thank you,' she said.

'If Neelam aunty is keeping the fast, won't she come on the terrace and find out?' I said.

'She doesn't keep it. She is diabetic and has low blood pressure. Doesn't suit her,' she said.

I smiled and pulled her cheek.

'You are too romantic, sister,' I said.

'Thank you. Actually, I also plan to tell him that day about us being twins,' she said.

'Really?' I said.

'Yeah, that's an auspicious day, I feel. He will be the first person I will tell after you told me.'

'How sweet.'

'You will be back from your trek by then?'

'I'll try,' I said. I definitely will, I said to myself.

'Good. Are you applying for jobs?' she said, switching subjects. I hate this topic. It gives me anxiety. Still, she keeps bringing it up again and again. Stop talking to me about this, I wanted to tell her.

'I freelance now, didi,' I said.

'Sure,' she said and rolled her eyes. She does that, her JER, the judgemental eye roll. We have the same eyes. But I don't do the JER. Yeah, I know what she is thinking. Freelance is just a euphemism for being unemployed. I sit around hoping an article, report, or any other writing gig lands in my lap. My lap has been pretty empty the last few months, though.

'I'm going to apply for jobs too,' I said.

'If you want to work for Eato—' she started to say.

'Not again, sis,' I said. 'Stop. I told you, I don't want to work for a stupid app that helps people stuff their faces.'

'Ouch,' she said and looked away.

'Sorry, I didn't mean it that way,' I said. She didn't respond.

'Eato is my baby,' she said after a minute.

'I know.'

'Don't demean anyone's work. I've told you so many times. Writing about social issues doesn't make you superior to others.'

'Fine, sis. Drop it now.'

'I hire fifty people. They run their homes because of Eato. That's real social impact. Not writing for some loss-making, left-wing, elitist English language news portal nobody reads.'

'Nice to know your true feeling about my work.'

'Don't call Eato stupid, that's all.'

'I said sorry.'

'Get a grip on yourself, Anjali. You are smart and bright.'

'I know.'

'You do? You quit your job, roll joints all day, and of course the Adi chachu thing,' she said and made a disgusted face.

'First of all, he is your mamu, not chachu. Second of all, you promised you will never talk about it to anyone.'

'I am only talking about it to you.'

'It was nothing, a one-time thing, sis,' I said.

'I know it is not a one-time thing. I said I would not tell anyone, provided you stop. You haven't.'

'I have,' I said.

'Don't lie to your own sister.'

I kept quiet. I pulled out a joint from my pocket in defiance.

'Great. Smoke ganja when you don't have an answer.'

I wanted to slap her. She never lost an opportunity to pick on me.

It's my fucking life, sister, I wanted to tell her. Go suck up to your capitalist investors and make your money. Sell your unhealthy fast food crap and give out coupon codes for it. Stuff your face, get fat and then cover that fat with sequins. I don't stop you, do I? Then who the hell are you to stop me from doing whatever I want, with whoever I want?

I didn't say or do anything, of course. I kept silent. You could be a twin, but if your sibling is doing much better than you in life, you lose the right to be an equal.

'He's your uncle, Anjali,' she said, 'your mother's brother.'

'People don't exactly follow relationships in this family as they are supposed to.'

'It still doesn't make it okay. What if my dad finds out?'

'Ramesh uncle is not your dad. We don't know our dad.'

She stared at me. I continued.

'How will Ramesh uncle find out? Unless you tell him. You are the only one who knows. You snooped on us.'

'I haven't told him yet, but I swear I will if you don't stop.'

'Is that a threat?'

'Can you please just end it, Anjali? Don't bring shame to the family.'

Fuck this smug, fake family and fuck their all-consuming phenomenal fear of shame, I wanted to say. I turned around to leave the terrace. She continued to sermonise after me even as I left. I ignored her. It's not the first time we had argued about this. I knew her script. I took a drag of my joint to relieve the pain of her words. It didn't help. I walked down the steps to Adi's floor. I took out the duplicate key he had given me.

'Hey,' he said as I walked in. 'What's up.' He had a glass of whiskey in his hand.

'I need harder stuff,' I said, and tossed my joint aside.

'What happened, babe?' he said.

'Can you not ask me any questions and give me a line?'

'Sure,' he said and stood up. He came back from his room with a small packet of white powder. Like a pro, he made a line on the dining table.

'When are you leaving for your trek?'

'In a week,' I said. I bent over to snort the cocaine.

'And when will you be back, babe?'

'17 October—mark that date,' I said, and inhaled deeply as the powder hit my insides.

Three weeks later

My Indigo flight from Kathmandu via Kolkata landed fifteen minutes early in Delhi, at 6.15 p.m. at Terminal 1, Indira Gandhi International Airport. I collected my bag and came out of the terminal building.

I messaged Prerna.

'I'm back. Just landed.'

'See you soon, sis.'

'All set for Karva Chauth?'

'Yesss, getting ready,' she replied, along with a selfie of hers wearing a red-gold lehenga.

'You look stunning,' I responded.

'Thank you.'

'When are moon and man coming?'

'Moon should be up in the sky in an hour or so. Accordingly, man would be leaving Malviya Nagar soon.'

I replied with two laughter emojis.

She had her evening plans. I had mine. I ordered an Uber. A Maruti Swift Dzire, driven by Kartar Singh, who had a rating of 4.6 stars, came to pick me up in five minutes.

He asked if I needed help with my huge backpack. I had carried it for weeks in Nepal's mountains.

'It's fine. I'll keep it with me on the backseat itself,' I said.

'Okay, madam. May I start the ride?'

'Sure.'

He swiped the 'ride start' button on his phone. The Uber screen displayed the best route and the estimated time to our destination.

'New Friends Colony, madam? Lot of traffic at this time. One hour and fifteen minutes.'

Great, I said in my head.

'Damn, I have an urgent meeting,' I said.

'I'll go as fast as possible. But office time now so ... ' the driver said.

'Someone is waiting at New Friends Colony for my signature. He has a train afterwards from Nizamuddin.'

I opened Google Maps on my phone. From my location to Malhotra House, it also showed the exact same driving time as the Uber app—one hour and fifteen minutes. However, it also showed the metro option. Using the Magenta line of the Delhi Metro, it was only thirty-seven minutes to my destination. It involved taking a thirty-minute metro ride from Terminal 1 until Sukhdev Vihar station, which was a five-minute drive from Malhotra House. This thirty-seven-minute option gave me a full thirty-eight minutes over the taxi.

'May I ask you for a huge favour, driver bhaiya?'

'Sure, madam, happy to help.'

'There's a metro station at this terminal. I can take that to Sukhdev Vihar metro station. I will call my person there and sign my papers. By that time, you reach with my luggage. Meet me there at the station parking. There's a huge Patanjali banner. Unmissable.'

The driver took a few seconds to absorb my instructions.

'So you will keep my ride also? For the luggage?'

'Yes, my bag is twenty kilos and bulky. It'll be much easier in the metro without it. Don't worry, you will get paid like a regular ride.'

'Okay, madam, as you wish,' the driver said. I checked the time on my phone: 6.52 p.m. An hour and fifteen from now would be 8.07 p.m. I messaged Prerna:

'My phone is dying so may not be reachable. But can you come to the terrace in exactly forty-five minutes? I want to quickly see my pretty sister and leave before he arrives.'

'Oh. Okay, sure,' she replied with a smiley.

'See you soon. Forty-five minutes, okay?'

She replied with a thumbs up emoji.

I put my phone on silent mode and slipped it into one of the pockets of my backpack.

'Patanjali banner, okay? Sukhdev Vihar metro station. See you,' I said and stepped out of the car.

❖

The metro crowd in the evening can crush you even in the ladies compartment. Fortunately, I found a train with enough standing room. The metro departed Terminal 1 at 6.56 p.m. The overbridge train zipped through Delhi. I like how the metro turns class upside down and delivers justice. The middle classes move fast, while the upper classes face traffic jams in their fancy cars below us. Justice, that's what's missing sometimes. To put it mildly, life hasn't been fair to me.

As the train sped, my past rushed at me.

Seattle

Twenty-one years ago

'Ma, why is your American friend living with us now?'

'He's not just my friend, he's Greg, your dad,' Geetu said. She poured a golden liquid from a bottle into her glass. I sat at the dining table of our one-room house. A can of baked beans and two dry slices of toast lay in front of me.

'No. My dad is Jogi. Where is he? You said he went to work on a ship.'

'No, he didn't. He left us. He still drives a cab in Seattle.'

Geetu took a sip of her drink.

'But you said he went to work on a ship. You lied?'

'Eat your dinner, Anjali,' she said.

'I don't like this dinner. You give me this every day. I hate it.'

Geetu glared at me. 'I have to take care of you. Every day. Do I love it?'

I picked up a spoon to eat my food; I had heard this many times.

'Why does Greg have to be my dad?' I said, after a few bites of the ketchup-soaked soggy beans.

'Because he pays for everything.'

'Why did Jogi dad leave us?' I said.

'Eat your food quietly or I will slap you again,' Geetu said, finishing her drink in one gulp.

❖

Seattle

Two-and-a-half years ago

Greg slammed the door shut in disgust and left the house. Geetu and I sat on the couches facing the fireplace. She turned to me, agitated.

'Did you have to annoy him?' she said. 'I told you he likes Trump. He's a die-hard Republican. Did you have to go to that anti-Trump rally?'

'Do you even know what Trump has been saying and doing?' I said.

'No, and I don't care. All I care about is saving my already troubled marriage. And you aren't helping.'

'How am I responsible for your bad marriage, Ma?'

'You know Greg doesn't like you much.'

'Whatever. The feeling is mutual.'

'Why did you even come to live here? You're twenty-three, old enough to be on your own.'

'I thought you would be happy. I was between jobs. I thought I would live with you for a while.'

'Well, I'm not happy. And you were fired from your job. Why? Did you also argue with your seniors there like you did with Greg?'

I stared at Geetu.

'Greg's an ass. He's rude and narrow-minded. He can't stand a woman with her own strong opinions, like me.'

'Neither can I,' Geetu said. She took a sip of her whiskey, her fourth drink for the evening.

'What?'

Geetu's phone pinged. She showed the message to me.

'It's either her or me. Choose,' Greg had sent her.

'What the hell,' I said. 'Tell him to fuck off.'

Geetu kept her phone aside. She poured herself another drink.

'What? Tell him. Tell him he can't ask you to abandon your own daughter.'

Geetu simply sighed and took a sip. Her phone pinged again.

'Choose now. Or you will hear from a divorce lawyer,' Greg had messaged her.

Geetu's hand began to shake. Tears rolled down her cheeks.

'Ma, these are bullshit threats. He's sulking.'

'Enough. Leave, Anjali. I don't care, get a job and a home. We can be in touch. But you can't stay in this house.'

'What are you saying, Ma ...'

'I can't lose one more husband because of you.'

'What?'

'Please. I have raised you. I did my duty. Now figure your life out.'

The whiskey had made her say things she wouldn't have normally.

'What duty? What lose one more husband?'

'Jogi left me because of you,' she said and began to sob. 'And now Greg will too. Don't be a curse on me. Please, please, I beg you.'

When Geetu drinks, she gets emotional. When she drinks extra, she gets extra-emotional. Her tears didn't stop.

'Curse? And what do you mean Jogi left you because of me?'

'Yes, and now Greg will too. And I will be homeless again. You don't remember those days, moving from one homeless shelter to another. Until Greg gave us a home.'

'But why me? What did Jogi have against me? I was three years old.'

'But you were not ours,' Geetu said.

Over the next hour, she told me how I'd come to live with her. It shook my world as I knew it. I remember blacking out, even though I had not had a drop to drink that night.

❖

The jerk as the train stopped at the Vasant Vihar station brought me back to the present. The train continued and passed Munirka and R.K. Puram. The rocking motion and flashing lights of the city cast shadows inside my head. I was the abandoned twin, while Prerna had everything. Why? She was wealthier, happier, more accomplished ... and more than anything, loved. Why did my chosen field—journalism—face one layoff after another, while Prerna's startup received one round of funding after another? Why did I grow up in tiny council houses, at the mercy of Geetu's husbands, while Prerna lived in opulence? Why did Prerna have all the money, while I had to beg people for two-thousand-rupee-an-article jobs? Why did she find love and marriage, while I struggled from one relationship to the next? How dare she lecture me to stop being with Adi while she dressed up to celebrate Karva Chauth before her marriage?

Adi and I weren't what she thought. Adi and I actually connected. We were the Malhotra family misfits, after all.

I remember when I came up with this amazing idea of a professional music video for Adi. I would have produced and directed it. It could have given Adi's career a boost. It could have given me an alternative career as well. It had meant so much to us. Yes, it would have cost twenty lakh rupees. Ramesh uncle, we asked you, and you didn't think it was such a great idea. Not economically viable, is what he said you told him. Really? Only your ideas are great?

'You think twenty lakhs is a joke?' Ramesh uncle had said to Adi's face. No, it is not a joke; the joke is that the next month he spent fifty lakhs on Prerna's engagement. Fifty fucking lakhs for a stupid party.

Everybody cared about Prerna. Prerna, Prerna, Prerna. Who could have been me. If the toss were different. If I got the head and she the tail.

Do you know the hardest emotion to admit to in this world? It's envy. Well, it isn't hard for me. I am envious. Of the life she had as a child, the love she got from this family and then from Saurabh. The normalcy and ease with which everything worked out for her. Her entitlement and smug indifference to it all. I hate it. All this consumes me, in my thoughts, all the fucking time, even though I hate thinking about all this. Well, that was going to end today.

The train reached the Kalkaji Mandir stop. I prayed from the metro coach itself, seeking forgiveness for what I was about to do. I had the conscience to realise what I was about to do was wrong, even though I was still going to do it. After one more stop, Okhla NSIC, the train pulled into Sukhdev Vihar. I checked the time on my wristwatch: 7.26 p.m.

I ran down the steps of the metro station to the autos waiting outside. I found a small queue.

'I'm unwell. Feel like vomiting. I need to get home. Can I please jump the queue, Uncle?' I said to a man at the front. He stepped aside.

'A-956, New Friends Colony,' I told the auto driver.

The three-wheeler drove through the narrow lanes into New Friends Colony. My heart beat fast as each minute felt like an hour.

'Drop me in the back lane,' I said as I reached A Block. He took me ten metres away from the back door entrance of Malhotra House. My watch said 7.33 p.m. The sky outside had turned dark. The moon hadn't come out yet.

'I have work for fifteen minutes. If you wait at the end of the lane, I will go back to the station with you. I'll give you two hundred rupees extra.'

The auto driver's eyes lit up. He nodded in agreement.

I ran out of the auto to the back door. I had a key. However, Prerna had left the back door open for Saurabh. I pushed it open. I checked the stairs above me. I couldn't see anyone. I tiptoed up the stairs, with only my loud heart for company. I passed the kitchen. I heard frying sounds and Neelam aunty and Gopika talking about spices. I climbed up to the terrace. I couldn't see anyone there. I stood at the ledge.

I checked the time—7.37 p.m.

Prerna wasn't there yet. She had promised to meet me in forty-five minutes, when I had messaged her from the airport. That would be around now. If she didn't arrive in the next few minutes, or if Saurabh arrived before her, the entire plan would fall apart.

I stared at my watch. 7.38 p.m. 7.39 p.m.

Creakkk, the sound of the door opening made me look towards it. The girl in the red-gold lehenga was there, with a pooja plate in her hand.

'Anjali, wow, you are already here,' she said. 'You must be tired after your trip.'

'My beautiful sister,' I said.

'Thank you. I'm so hungry. He better come soon,' she said.

Chapter 60

'Hey Bhagwan,' Neelam said, her hands covering her face.

'Didn't I say before? O aaya si. She came. Looks like a boy anyway with her short hair and thin frame,' Maaji said.

Neelam removed her hands from her face.

'What a plan,' Ramesh said.

'Yes, Uncle. She did have the perfect alibi. She arrived after the murder. The police checked her phone. It showed her being en route from the airport to home. She had kept it in her backpack, which was in the car. The Uber ride times and routes also matched. Only, she wasn't in the Uber or near her phone. Clever, Anjali, very clever,' Saurabh said.

'What am I supposed to say? Thanks?' Anjali said.

'Not as clever as my friend though,' Saurabh said and turned to me. 'How did you even find out, bhai?'

'Yeah, I'm curious too. With such a perfect plan, how did you suspect her?' Ramesh said.

I smiled at Ramesh and Saurabh.

'Golu, remember when we landed from Amritsar?'

'Yes,' Saurabh said.

'We had to go to Rana's office. We were late. I called Anjali. You were upset with the whole "why did you say dear" thing.'

'I wasn't—' Saurabh said but I interrupted him.

'You were. Anyway, doesn't matter. Remember?'

'Yes,' Saurabh said. 'Farmers' rally. Google Maps said two hours from the airport.'

'And Anjali suggested we take the metro from Terminal 1. It's much faster.'

'Oh,' Saurabh said, his mouth open. 'Oh yeah. To go to Rana's office.'

'She gave a simple suggestion, but it made me think.'

'Anything else?' Saurabh said.

'Then I remembered Prerna's DNA report.'

'What? They found nothing. No foreign DNA,' Saurabh said.

'Exactly. But neighbours heard noises and Neeraj saw a struggle. Still no one else's DNA? Strange, right?'

'Gloves?' Saurabh said.

'Other body parts come into contact in an intense struggle. Hair, nail residue, dead skin. Gloves can't conceal everything. This is DNA, not fingerprints. But the police found nothing.'

'So? And how is this connected to Anjali?' Ramesh said.

'What were Anjali and Prerna? In reality?' I said.

'Twin sisters,' Ramesh said.

'Exactly. They are identical twins,' I said. 'Identical. Got it?'

Saurabh scratched his head.

'Oh my God. Identical DNA too. Twins have identical DNA.'

'They found *no other* DNA. They found the *same* DNA as Prerna,' I said.

'Wow,' Saurabh said. Everyone took a moment to absorb the new information. I continued.

'Then I thought of the motives. Resentment of a sibling who had got the better end of the deal in life, in almost everything. No emotional attachment as such, because they grew up apart.'

'I did love Prerna,' Anjali said in a soft voice.

I let out a sigh.

'Some love that was, Anjali,' Saurabh said. 'Go on, bhai, anything else?'

'Yes. I had the motive, method and maybe even some corroboration with the no-DNA found on the body point. I needed more. A hundred per cent confirmation. And for that reason, I had to get close to Anjali.'

Anjali looked at me.

I took out my phone. I opened a picture.

I displayed my phone to everyone.

'This is the close-up picture of Adi's dead body. See the marks on the chest—love bites, or hickeys.'

Ramesh adjusted his spectacles to look at the picture.

'These are intense,' Saurabh said.

'Yes, some like to mix pleasure with pain,' I said. Anjali's look turned into a glare. I swiped to the next picture.

'And this is the picture of my chest. Taken at my house, after Anjali and I ...' I said and became quiet. People understood what I meant.

'You and Anjali? Where? When?' Saurabh said.

'Malviya Nagar. Not important. Look at the picture.'

'Oh, the exact same marks,' Saurabh said. 'Similar teeth bites.'

I shrugged.

'Unbelievable. So you also know how my brother died?' Ramesh said.

'You scolded Adi that night. Anjali went to see him later. He was broken. He wanted to come clean to you. He had stolen the ring, but he had not murdered Prerna. He wanted to tell you everything, Uncle. Anjali couldn't let that happen. She came to meet him again early in the morning, right before he went for his jog. They made love. She suggested they do heroin. She overdosed him. And gave him some more when he passed out. Right, Anjali?'

'Yes,' Anjali said. 'So? I did it to protect myself. In my book, it's still better than the asshole who makes love for evidence.'

'You killed Adi too? *Slept* with him?' Ramesh said, mouth open in shock.

'You had an affair with Adi?' Bindu said.

Anjali didn't answer. She just turned her gaze downwards.

'Prerna knew about the affair and did not approve of it. Anjali was always worried she would reveal everything to you, Ramesh uncle. Apart from the resentment, this also became another reason to kill her,' I said.

Anjali did not respond.

'All these,' Bindu said, her voice breaking, 'all these are just theories. You are not going to send my daughter to jail. She is all I have.'

'She has already confessed,' I said.

'Not in front of the police or in court. All your nonsense theories mean nothing. Where is the proof?' Bindu said.

'All this is not proof?' Saurabh said. 'Similar love bites on Adi's body as she gave to Keshav?'

I signalled to Saurabh, asking him to be quiet. I smiled.

'I know, Bindu aunty. What is needed in court is solid, irrefutable evidence. That is why it took me some time. You see, ACP Rana had to use his influence. With someone senior in the Delhi Metro.'

'Why?' Ramesh said.

'To get the entire CCTV footage for the Magenta line from the airport. From 6.45p.m. to 7.45 p.m. On 17 October.'

I played the video of the CCTV metro footage again.

'That's her. Praying at the Kalkaji temple stop. The same trekking jacket she wore that day. Remember?' I said.

Anjali stood up.

'Okay, the game is up. Fine, Keshav, what do you want them to do with me? Kill me? Fine, go ahead.'

I shook my head.

'That's not how the justice system works. ACP Rana and Inspector Singh are on their way.'

Everyone froze.

'One thing, bhai,' Saurabh said, 'the police said Namrata's phone was in the same cell tower location as Malhotra House.'

'That's because of me,' Ramesh said.

Everyone turned to Ramesh.

'I had called her to the New Friends Colony market. To discuss how to convince Prerna to agree to give me the money. I didn't go for paan. I was just on the way to meet Namrata, when all this happened.'

Saurabh let out a sigh and nodded.

'Police?' Maaji said, as sirens became audible in the distance.

'No,' Bindu screamed, as she broke down in tears. She hugged Anjali tight, but Anjali did not reciprocate. She continued to stare at me.

The doorbell rang. Justice had finally arrived at Malhotra House.

Chapter 61

'You guys solved the Karva Chauth murder?' Jacob said.

Two days after Anjali's arrest, I was back in office. I looked up at Jacob from my cubicle, surprised.

'Sir? How did you know?'

'Here, it is in the papers. Congrats.'

Jacob dropped the newspaper on my table and left.

I read the headline on page two.

'How two detectives worked with Delhi Metro to solve the Karva Chauth murder'.

The article mentioned our modus operandi. It even carried our names and tiny pictures.

I turned to Saurabh in the adjacent cubicle.

'Hey, you saw this?' I said.

'Saw it? I made it happen,' Saurabh said and winked at me.

'What?'

'I couldn't let the police take all the credit this time. I called the guy in Delhi Metro who helped you. I asked him if he wanted to be famous. He did, so he helped me circulate some press releases.'

'Wow,' I said.

'What?' Saurabh said.

I shook my head and smiled.

'I could have given them a better picture,' I said.

One week later

I sat in my Oyo Rooms at night, scanning through Anjali's romantic chats with me over the past two months.

'I love you, Keshav. This is the first time I have loved someone like this,' she had said in one of the messages.

'Do you love me too?' she had sent me later. I had only replied with a smiley emoji.

I looked up at the low ceiling of my tiny room and thought of her. Tears filled my eyes.

'I did love you too,' I whispered.

The loud ring of the landline in my room interrupted my thoughts. It was the receptionist. I had a guest called Saurabh. Since he appeared male, he could come upstairs.

'Bhai, this is one tiny room,' Saurabh said as he came inside.

'Now that the case is done, I will look for an apartment.'

Saurabh sat down on the corner of the bed.

'What kind of place are you looking for?'

'Has to be low-cost. I plan to quit CyberSafe,' I said.

'Oh. Why? You will never find a boss easier to fool than Jacob.'

'It's not that. My heart is not in the job. I have one life, I don't want to live it doing something I don't want to.'

'What are you going to do?'

'Run Z Detectives. Try to find and solve good cases. The recent news coverage will help. And in the spare time, prepare for IPS.'

'IPS? Police?'

'Yes, I'm tired of going to the police for everything. Investigating cases with no authority. If I love it so much, might as well go all in.'

'Nice idea,' Saurabh said.

'You could consider it too. You are a great detective.'

'Thank you.'

We kept quiet for a few seconds. Saurabh broke the silence.

'Did you love Anjali?' he said.

I looked at him.

'Okay, don't answer that.'

'I did,' I said.

'I'm sorry, bhai, that it turned out this way.'

'The case is more important. I care for you more than I ever did for her. I had to get you justice.'

Saurabh looked at me.

'Bhai, can you come live in my house?'

'What?'

'Yes, that's why I came to see you. It's lonely living alone. I have a small spare bedroom. Use it to prepare for your IPS exam.'

'Saurabh, that's nice of you, but I thought you wanted to—'

Saurabh interrupted me. 'I was an idiot. Sorry. I don't want to be away from my best friend. Ever.'

Even though I hate doing senti stuff, the moment warranted that we give each other a hug. I embraced him. His eyes were moist.

'Just come back. Please,' he said, 'don't make me beg you.'

'Okay, okay, I will,' I said.

'This room is tiny,' he said.

'I know.'

'Do they have any food though? Room service?'

Two weeks later

I piled up the set of heavy IPS preparation books on my study table.

'Why do they need people in the police to study so much?' Saurabh said and shook his head.

I had moved into his house a week ago. I switched on my table lamp. Light fell on the books, which hopefully would be my obsession for the next year. Saurabh had just showered and was wearing a white kurta pyjama. Saurabh's part-time maid had prepared food and kept it on the table.

'Come, dinner will get cold,' Saurabh said.

'One minute,' I said and opened my phone.

'What are you doing?' Saurabh said.

'Deleting Tinder,' I said.

'What? Why?' Saurabh said.

'I want a real relationship. Or none at all.'

'You sure?'

'Yes, I want to be in love again. And for someone to love me.'

'But hopefully that someone won't be a murderer.'

I looked at him. He seemed worried I would take offence. I burst into laughter instead. He joined in as well. We high-fived at our odd life. Love seemed elusive to us, but we had something else. We had friendship, which in many ways is even more beautiful than love.

'Okay, come, let's eat now. She's made excellent pav bhaji. It's no good when cold.'

***

About the Author

Chetan Bhagat is one of India's most acclaimed contemporary authors, with fourteen bestselling books to his credit. He is the author of ten blockbuster novels—*Five Point Someone, One Night @ the Call Center, The 3 Mistakes of My Life, 2 States, Revolution 2020, Half Girlfriend, One Indian Girl, The Girl in Room 105, One Arranged Murder* and *400 Days*, and most recently, *12 Years: My Messed-Up Love Story*—and four successful non-fiction titles—*What Young India Wants, Making India Awesome, India Positive* and *11 Rules for Life*. Chetan's books have remained bestsellers since their release. Many of his novels have been adapted into successful Bollywood films such as *3 Idiots, 2 States, Kai Po Che* and *Half Girlfriend*.

The New York Times called him the 'the biggest-selling English-language novelist in India's history'. *Time* magazine recognized him amongst the '100 most influential people in the world', while Fast Company, USA, listed him as one of the world's '100 most creative people in business'. Chetan writes columns for leading English and Hindi newspapers, focusing on youth and national development issues. He is also a motivational speaker, screenplay writer, YouTuber and podcaster.

Chetan quit his international investment-banking career in 2009 to dedicate his time entirely to writing and driving positive change in the country.

Chetan studied at IIT Delhi and IIM Ahmedabad. He is married to Anusha, an ex-classmate from IIMA, and they have twin boys, Shyam and Ishaan.

BESTSELLERS BY CHETAN BHAGAT

FICTION

400 Days

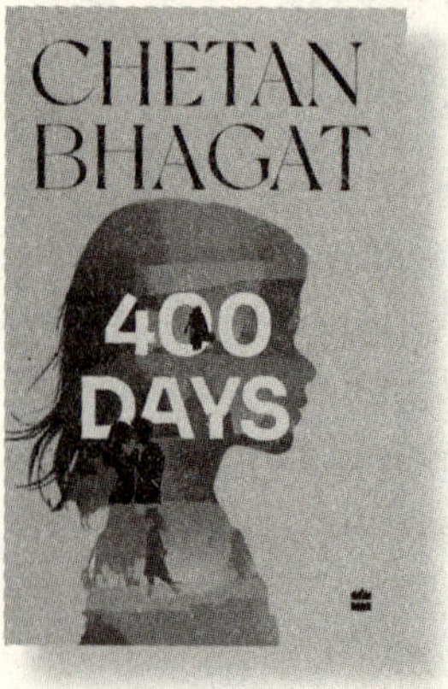

Hi, I am Keshav Raj Purohit and I am a disappointment to everyone around me.

I live with my parents, who keep telling me how I should:

a) get married,

b) focus on my IPS exams,

c) meet more people, and

d) close my detective agency.

But Alia Arora, neighbour and ex-model, wanted my help. And I couldn't take my eyes off her face ... I mean ... her case.

'My daughter Siya was kidnapped. Nine months ago,' Alia said. The police had given up. They called it a cold case. Even the rest of her family had stopped searching. Alia wouldn't stop looking, though. She wanted to know if I could help her.

Welcome to *400 Days*. A mystery and romance story like no other. An unputdownable tale of suspense, human relationships, love, friendship, the crazy world we live in and, above all, a mother's determination to never give up. From India's highest-selling author comes a page-turner that will not only keep you glued to the story but also touch you deeply.

One Arranged Murder

'Ever since you found Prerna, I lost my best friend ...'

Hi, this is Keshav, and Saurabh, my best friend, flatmate, colleague and business partner, won't talk to me. Because I made fun of him and his fiancé.

Saurabh and Prerna will be getting married soon. It is an arranged marriage. However, there is more cheesy romance between them than any love-marriage couple.

On Karva Chauth, she fasted for him. She didn't eat all day. In the evening, she called him and waited on the terrace for the moon and for Saurabh to return to break her fast. Excited, Saurabh ran up the steps of her three-storey house. But when he reached ...

Keshav has set up an investigation agency with his best friend, Saurabh. Can the two amateur detectives successfully solve another murder case that affects them personally? And where will it leave their friendship?

Welcome to *One Arranged Murder*, an unputdownable thriller from India's highest-selling author. A story about love, friendship, family and crime. It will keep you entertained and hooked right till the end.

The Girl in Room 105: An Unlove Story

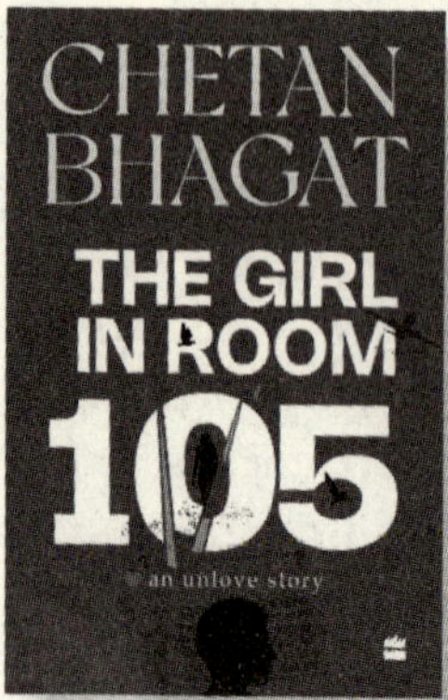

Hi, I'm Keshav, and my life is screwed.

I hate my job and my girlfriend left me. Ah, the beautiful Zara. Zara is from Kashmir. She is Muslim. And did I tell you that my family is a bit, well, traditional? Anyway, leave that aside.

Zara and I broke up four years ago. She moved on in life. I didn't. I drank every night to forget her. I called, messaged, and stalked her on social media. She just ignored me.

However, that night, on the eve of her birthday, Zara messaged me. She called me over, like old times, to her hostel room 105. I shouldn't have gone, but I did ... and my life changed forever.

This is not a love story. It is an unlove story. From the author of *Five Point Someone* and *2 States*, comes a fast-paced, funny and unputdownable thriller about obsessive love and finding purpose in life against the backdrop of contemporary India.

12 Years: My Messed-Up Love Story

He's 33. She's 21.

He's a struggling stand-up comic. She's a rising star in private equity.

He's divorced. She's never had a boyfriend.

He's Punjabi. She's from a conservative Jain family.

They shouldn't be together. But they can't stay apart.

Welcome to *12 Years: My Messed-Up Love Story.*

Saket and Payal couldn't be more different—age, background, beliefs. Yet, they're drawn to each other in ways they can't explain. Is it just chemistry, or something deeper? Is it madness and lust, or is it love?

Unputdownable and thoroughly entertaining, *12 Years* tries to answer the eternal question: How do you know if someone is *the one*—especially when everything says they're not?

From India's top-selling writer Chetan Bhagat comes a powerful new love story that will make you laugh, cry and rethink everything you know about love.

NON-FICTION

India Positive: Simple Takes on India's Burning Issues

Does it make any difference to the ordinary citizen which party is in power? Whether it's a majority or a coalition?

What can we do to better job prospects for India's youth?

How can we create a more equal society?

How do we create more world-class educational institutes?

What can we do about social media warriors and trolls?

In *India Positive*, bestselling author and columnist Chetan Bhagat brings together essays that work as a manifesto for change. Examining a gamut of subjects—from education to employment, from GST to infrastructure, from corruption to casteism—Bhagat reflects on what we can do right in order to move forward and become a truly modern, progressive country. He expresses in these pages his belief that, if we want to see reform, we—as citizens—need to be the solution. If our country is to shine, Bhagat says, we need to stand up and be 'India Positive Citizens'.

In a world ridden with negativity, these simply written, perceptive and solution-driven essays are a must-read for anyone invested in the present and future of India.

11 Rules for Life: Secrets to Level Up

MANDATORY READING FOR ALL INDIANS

One summer afternoon, Viraj, a food delivery guy, brings lunch for an author named Chetan. He is late and appears to be in distress. When Chetan asks him what the matter is, Viraj breaks down.

'I hate my life. My career is going nowhere. My girlfriend left me. I have no future,' he says.

The author offers Viraj a deal. 'I can fix this for you. Come back every day, when I order lunch. Each day, I will tell you one secret I've learnt about life.'

Welcome to *11 Rules for Life*, a no-holds-barred book that will transform your life.

In his most personal book yet, Chetan draws on his failures and triumphs, his many conversations with high achievers from all walks of life and over two decades as a celebrated motivational speaker.

Written in the inimitable style that has made Chetan one of India's top-selling writers, this inspiring, easy-to-read and straight-talking guide will help you rewire your brain for success in today's ultra-competitive and unfair world.

Ready to live your best life? If one book can change your life, this is it.

All these titles are also available in Hindi.

HarperCollins *Publishers* India

At HarperCollins India, we believe in telling the best stories and finding the widest readership for our books in every format possible. We started publishing in 1992; a great deal has changed since then, but what has remained constant is the passion with which our authors write their books, the love with which readers receive them, and the sheer joy and excitement that we as publishers feel in being a part of the publishing process.

Over the years, we've had the pleasure of publishing some of the finest writing from the subcontinent and around the world, including several award-winning titles and some of the biggest bestsellers in India's publishing history. But nothing has meant more to us than the fact that millions of people have read the books we published, and that somewhere, a book of ours might have made a difference.

As we look to the future, we go back to that one word—a word which has been a driving force for us all these years.

Read.

Harper Collins
Harper Sport
HARPER FICTION
HARPER NON-FICTION
हार्पर हिन्दी
HARPER LEARNING
HARPER VANTAGE
HCCB HARPERCOLLINS CHILDREN'S BOOKS
4th
HARPER PERENNIAL
HARPER DESIGN
BOOKTOPUS
HARPER BUSINESS